Shelby's Vacation

For information, contact: henrygraypub2022@gmail.com

Publisher's Cataloging-in-Publication Data:

Names: Beverly, Nancy.
Title: Shelby's vacation / Nancy Beverly.
Description: Granada Hills, CA : Henry Gray Publishing,2023. |Includes 53 b&w photos.|
Identifiers: LCCN 2023903412 | ISBN 9781960415004 (pbk.)| ISBN9781960415011 (ebook)
Subjects: LCSH: Hiking -- Fiction. | Lesbians -- Fiction. | Self-actualization (Psychology) in
     women -- Fiction. | Self-realization-- Fiction. | California -- Fiction. |Sierra Nevada
     (Calif. and Nev.) -- Fiction.| BISAC: FICTION/ Romance / LGBTQ+ / Lesbian.
Classification: LCC PS3602.E94 S54 2023 | DDC 813 B48—dc23
LC record available at https://lccn.loc.gov/2023903412

Library of Congress Control Number: 2023903412

Made in the United States of America.

Published by Henry Gray Publishing, P.O. Box 33832, Granada Hills, California 91394.

For more information or to join our mailing list, visit HenryGrayPublishing.com.

Shelby's Vacation

Nancy Beverly

Northridge, CA
"Select books for selective readers"

Author's Note

Many years ago, I was driving back to Los Angeles from the Grand Canyon and stopped for a break in Kingman, Arizona. My passenger side window was down, and after I parked the car and opened the driver's door, all of my directions and maps flew around like crazed birds. Some years later, I thought this moment would be a great beginning of a story. Granted, when it happened to me it was before the internet, so losing your directions was way scarier. But still, it was a good image to get a tale rolling.

I first wrote *Shelby's Vacation* as a feature-length screenplay, using California for the locations instead of Arizona. And then I let it sit for a number of years, unsure of how to get a lesbian film out into the world back then.

I went on a camping trip with a bunch of lesbians several years later up to Rock Creek Lake in the Sierra Nevada Mountains (or as you will soon learn, just call it the Sierra Nevada). I fell in love with the place and thought, "Hey, this could be a great location to film *Shelby's Vacation!*"

I got the script out, did some rewrites and entered it into Chicago's Pride Films and Plays competition. Lo and behold, I made the semi-finals. Even better, the script was hand-picked by that contest's exec director for a staged reading at a gay pride event in Randolph, Vermont, in the summer of 2011. I flew to Vermont and had such a wonderful experience, I decided to really give things a go to get *Shelby's Vacation* made as a feature film. I learned how to do a film's business plan, how to court investors and production companies, but even with a talented director attached (Vickie Sampson), we still couldn't get the film financed.

I came up with Plan B. I told Vickie we could shoot a short version of *Shelby's Vacation*—and then I would write the whole thing as a novel so I could tell the complete story of the characters.

Vickie and I were very successful in raising the money from friends and loved ones to make our 40-minute film in 2016. We had a great cast and crew and are very proud of how the movie turned out.

We premiered in 2017, were featured in over a dozen film festivals, and won some awards to boot.

The next step was to write the novel and polish it. And, hey, I didn't have to worry about budgets, locations, forest fires, or actors dropping out.

So here we are. And a couple of final notes: While some of the places in this novel are real—the California towns of Bishop and Lone Pine, the hike up to Kearsarge Pass to name a few—the characters and where they work and live—Pacific University, Sierra Glen Cabins and Little Pine—are fictional.

And please do not try hiking in the Sierra Nevada without proper training and equipment.

Enjoy the journey!

Part One

Red Rock Canyon

Chapter One

Marion, Mojave & Mini-Coop

She had freckles on her neck. Shelby had never noticed that before. But then she'd never stood this close to Marion before. Marion was a brunette, not a redhead, so freckles weren't a given. This was bonus material.

She could also see the color of Marion's bra strap. Fuchsia.

Shelby and her boss Marion were standing side by side in Marion's office at L.A.'s Pacific University, bent over Marion's glass-covered wooden conference table in early June. They were laying out the seating chart for the Summer Splash Alumni Dinner.

Even though Marion was only twenty-seven, she'd taken over the school's Alumni Relations like a seasoned pro four months before and had injected rocket fuel into a sluggish department. Shelby was thrilled (in more ways than one...) to be working for someone so dynamic, someone who could pull off wearing leopard print pants while breezing into a staff meeting in "sky-high" high heels with the confidence of a runway model.

It didn't bother Shelby at all to be working for someone who was ten years younger. In fact, being around Marion made her feel ten years younger. She could also feel a tingle in her nether regions as Marion's arm brushed hers while moving a Post-it.

"Am I standing too close?" Marion asked, her voice seductively low.

"No, I like you close," Shelby coyly responded.

"Want me closer?"

"That could work."

Marion unzipped Shelby's gray dress slacks and—

"If we put the Melvilles here...we can put the Wilsons there," Marion said, adjusting the neon yellow Post-it squares with names of Alumni donors on them.

Shelby snapped back to reality and covered by saying, "Bad move, they're feuding." She deftly plucked the Post-its and made a series of quick chess moves to keep the Melvilles, the Wilsons and a few other donor diners at a civil distance from one another.

"Shelby! Life Saver!" Marion grabbed Shelby's arm.

They giggled at one another.

~ ❦ ~

"Ma'am? 'Scuse me? MA'AM? Are you buying those Life Savers?"

And now Shelby snapped back to the present. She'd been fingering a rainbow package of Life Savers at the AM/PM mini-mart gas station in Mojave, California. The teenaged clerk behind the counter pushed up her thick glasses and waited for Shelby's response.

"Uh, no, no. Just the gas, thanks."

The clerk handed Shelby her change and Shelby angled for the door, leaving behind the Life Savers and her thoughts about Marion.

The wind buffeted Shelby as she made her way back to her black Honda Fit. She remembered the winds of Mojave from her childhood vacations. Her dad would announce, "Batten down the hatches, we're stoppin' in Mojave!" The desert town was the last best place to get gas before heading up Highway 395 and on into the Sierra Nevada Mountains, according to him. "Everything's overpriced in those damn foothill towns," he'd announce. "They see us tourists comin' and they jack up the prices!"

About a half hour north of Mojave on the current road trip to escape Los Angeles in late July, Shelby looked out the car window to her left and saw the formations of Red Rock Canyon State Park. When she was eleven and her sister Roxanne was fifteen, they had camped there once with their parents. The formations had names like "The Sultan's Turban" and "Camel's Head." She and Roxanne had a field day naming some of the others: "Dog Poop Pile," "Tilted Cupcake," "Dragon Fangs," "Pointy Boobs."

Shelby glanced in her rearview mirror for one final glimpse of the burnt umber and cream-colored formations and then noted the time on her dashboard clock, 10 a.m. She looked quickly at her typed itinerary on the passenger seat: Official Snack Time. She carefully moved aside her map and trip notes, opened an air-tight Tupperware container, and pulled out a cheese and cracker sandwich she'd made fresh that morning—buffalo mozzarella on Triscuits.

And just when she had a hefty cracker snack in her mouth...a royal blue Mini-Cooper convertible appeared suddenly in the passing lane. Shelby glanced over: a blonde, mid-thirties, hair blowing like crazy, who had rock 'n' roll cranked up so loud that Shelby could hear it inside her own car.

I wish my hair was that shade of blonde, Shelby mused. *I've been cursed with, what's the phrase, dishwater blonde? Who comes up with shit phrases like that? I wish my hair had curvy, wavy natural body like Marion's.*

Shelby quickly chewed the snack and contemplated if she should make eye contact with Miss Mini-Coop. *Wave? Smile? What the hell, I'm on vacation,* Shelby thought. She nodded at the blonde.

The blonde nodded back. And smiled.

Yeah, a vacation. Time for a new start.

"Isn't it time for you to move from manager to <u>director</u>?" Marion said, as they finalized their list of dinner attendees at the wooden table in her office.

"Oh gosh, Marion...."

"You've been here at the university how long?"

"Since I graduated."

"Let's get on it! Tonight we're going to our favorite Santa Monica restaurant—"

"—Lotus Flower," they both said simultaneously in low sexy voices, followed by giggles.

"And over sizzling rice..." Marion said, at which point Shelby did a "sizzle" sound effect, which resulted in more giggles. They had this whole routine down.

"...With a touch of saffron," Marion continued, "we will discuss your future. <u>Our</u> future."

"Our?" Shelby asked. It took every ounce of her being not to envision a white picket fence, the house behind it, and a U-Haul-It truck in the driveway. Okay, she did envision all of that.

"Yes, I need a good director."

"Director. I like it," Shelby said. And she decided to take the leap. After all, they'd been doing the office flirting thing for weeks now.

"Is that the only thing you need?" Shelby asked, with a seductive spin, her cheeks flushing.

Marion playfully answered, "No, I need a dinner reservation."

"I'll go make a dinner reservation," Shelby said, winking.

～ ❦ ～

I wonder where the blonde is heading, Shelby thought. *Wouldn't it be cool if we were both going on the same hiking tour? She looks like a sturdy, capable person, firm jawline, no fancy nail polish. Outdoor equipment is stuffed in the back of the Mini-Cooper, and she's wearing a hiking shirt....*

And then the blonde pulled away, taking the fantasy with her, effortlessly nudging the Mini-Coop up to eighty-plus. Shelby tried giving her ol' Honda Fit a little extra gas, but the engine started to ping. Oh, the joys of driving an eight-year-old sedan. *You know what,* she thought, *BLOW HER AWAY, BLOW THEM ALL AWAY.* With that, she pressed the window button down to get some fresh air.

Except the button she pressed was for the passenger side window. She then pressed the driver's side window button down...and got a huge rush of crosswind, which resulted in every one of her detailed notes, itinerary, map and brochures flying around like crazed birds. Finally, the pièce de resistance: a motorcycle caravan of ten roaring Harley Davidsons ZOOOMMMED by to Shelby's left, adding a little extra oomph.

The papers all flew out the passenger side window.

"SHIT."

Chapter Two

A New Generator, A New Song

"Is it ready?" asked Larry.

Larry and Carol stood hovering as Julio-the-handyman finished repairing the emergency generator. Larry Chang, owner of Sierra Glen Cabins, had been checking in with Julio every fifteen minutes to see how the repairs were coming on this late July morning.

Larry and Julio were contemporaries in age (early sixties) but any similarities ended there. Julio was a chubby, affable fellow and Larry was the focused, lean, Asian boss. And Julio was too polite to push back. That job always fell to Carol, the manager of Sierra Glen Cabins.

"Larry," Carol had said more than a few times that week, "it's the <u>backup</u> generator. We're still under full electrical power."

Larry didn't care; he worried about <u>everything</u>, leaning his angular body into every problem. Not enough trout in the fishing pond, shipment of toilet paper was a day late, the gift shop was low on medium-sized souvenir T-shirts—Larry had it covered. The backup generator had gone out on Tuesday, this was Thursday, and Julio had just gotten the replacement pull-cord a few hours ago.

"Larry, we're not gonna have either a snowstorm or an electrical storm, the power lines aren't falling, we'll be fine," Carol kept pointing out, in her calm, low-key way. As manager, Carol's job was to troubleshoot—and keep Larry's worrying to a minimum.

"You never know!" was Larry's mantra. On the one hand, he drove Carol nuts with the worrying, but on the other, his attitude beat to hell-and-back the previous owner's laissez-faire approach...which had allowed the cabins to fall into disrepair.

"Fire it up!" Larry commanded.

Julio pulled the new cord and the generator roared to life. Smiles all around.

Larry was a retired accountant who had run his own company until his mid-fifties, but he longed for the Great Outdoors. Every weekend he and his wife had hiked in the San Gabriel Mountains near Los Angeles, so once he left behind the corporate world, they hit the road. She passed away from breast cancer a few years into that chapter of their lives...and Larry couldn't stand traveling alone. Or being without work, Carol surmised. Hence, he had taken part of his nest egg and purchased Sierra Glen Cabins four years ago. The best of both worlds, he could be in his beloved outdoors and worry about the bottom line.

Carol, thirty-seven, had been there for fifteen years. By year eleven, when the previous owner had stopped minding the store, the furnishings were showing a lot of wear-and-tear and the attendance numbers were droopy. Carol had started to worry. *Damn, what if the place goes under, where the hell would I go?* This was the only gig she'd had since she graduated college. But then it was Larry to the rescue. Both she and Julio were massively relieved.

She and Larry also made a bit of an odd (non-romantic) couple, and yet it pretty much worked. She wasn't sure he grokked the concept of her being a lesbian, even though she always had her dark-brown hair in a short bob, rarely wore makeup or jewelry and always had a Swiss Army knife in her pocket. Luckily for Carol, the uniform he had the dozen or so staffers wear—hiking boots, jeans or khaki cargo hiking pants and Oxford cloth short-sleeved shirts with his new logo—she would've worn anyway.

Larry went off to worry about the lunch menu ("Are the blueberries still fresh enough to serve with the sorbet?"), and Carol headed toward two male hikers in their mid-forties who looked indecisive. This was her specialty, chatting up the hikers, and she knew Larry did appreciate that because it meant return business.

"Need some help, fellas?"

"We were thinking of going up to Pinyon Pass, how long will it take?" the bearded one in the Rolling Stones T-shirt asked.

"Out and back, about five, six hours. It's ten miles round trip," Carol answered. "It's gonna get up to about eighty-five down here but it'll be a cool seventy up there, so the heat won't drag ya down."

And then as the man yammered on about the rest of their vacation, out of the corner of her eye, Carol could see Darcy getting out of her Coke-can-red vintage Delta 88, guitar case in hand. *Huh. She's here mighty early,* Carol noted. *It's barely lunchtime, not even close to happy hour.*

"DO WE NEED HIKING POLES?"

Carol blinked and realized the bearded hiker had asked that question more than once.

"How are your knees?"

"Not great."

"Rent some from the gift store."

"Thanks!"

But before the guys could head off, they asked if there were any creek crossings. Carol gave them the lowdown on that and wrapped up the conversation with a hearty, "<u>You're all set</u>," practically shoving them toward the trailhead.

Now then, where did Darcy and her guitar head to? Carol casually (i.e., surreptitiously) strolled around the cottonwood-tree-shaded cabin area...the trout pond...and finally the patio area off of the restaurant. No patrons were there, but Darcy was sitting on her usual wooden stool practicing a song.

Carol slipped behind Darcy and then inched a little closer. The tune wasn't familiar to her. *She's taking it slowly, so it must be a new one,*

Carol figured. Darcy was intently bent over the guitar, her maple-syrup-light-brown shoulder-length hair covering most of her face.

Carol knew that posture well.

She was dying to hear the lyrics but couldn't risk getting any closer. *Okay, I <u>could</u> risk it, go talk to her,* Carol reasoned, *but we haven't spoken for six weeks. It's now beyond awkward. Better to let Darcy play in peace,* she thought, *and just...just what?*

Mt. Whitney

Chapter Three
Lotus Flower

"Stop-Stop-Stop! Get-the-papers! Get-the-papers! Get-the-papers," Shelby mantra-ed as she quickly pulled over to the side of the highway and got out of her car. She nearly lost the door to a strong gust. "AHHHHH!" After slamming it shut, she ran several feet south…but all of her papers were, in fact, Gone with the Wind. "DAMN IT! Re-group, re-group, regroup!"

She held her hair out of her face, ran pell-mell to her car, pulled back onto Highway 395 and sped toward Lone Pine. *All I need is a map and to check my emails. I can recreate the directions,* she reasoned. She pulled up the buttons on her car door to "roll up" the windows, and the passenger's side closed just fine…but the driver's side window went up one inch and stopped. "SHIT!" Shelby fiddled and fiddled with the little button to no avail. "DAMN IT!"

Ninety wind-blown minutes later she was in Lone Pine, new map in hand and sunscreen on her left ear and left arm. She made some notes from old emails she read on her cell phone while drinking a cold soda at the Lone Pine Pizza Factory. There would be no cell phone service once she turned off of Highway 395, but she felt confident she'd sketched out the route on paper that would get her to the John Muir Tour on time. The tour was to start up near the eastern entrance of Yosemite and that meant she still had a long drive ahead of her.

As Shelby slowly crept out of town, observing the 25 m.p.h. speed limit, more childhood memories flooded back. To the east was Mt. Whitney, the pinnacle of the Sierra Nevada and the tallest peak in the lower forty-eight states. Her dad often talked of climbing it when he was a young man on leave with a couple of his Air Force buddies. Shelby would hang on his every word—how they saw the eyes of a black bear reflected in their headlamps as they came down from the peak in darkness and her dad had shoo-shooed the bear away by clicking a couple of hiking sticks together. To her right was the local tavern with the bucking white stallion statue outside. She had asked her dad to hold her up on the horse's back so her mom could take their picture. *Why did vacations have to end? Why did we have to go home?*

~ ❀ ~

Shelby made the Santa Monica Lotus Flower dinner reservation for 6:45. She and Marion would need to leave their university office by six to get to the restaurant on time since traffic on the west side of L.A. would be at its molasses slowest. Shelby was grateful she was wearing her teal dolphin earrings and sleek teal blouse today; they made her look sophisticated. She unbuttoned the top button of her shirt for an "evening" look, freshened up her lipstick and put on some lightly scented lavender hand cream that Marion had given her. She was all set. They'd had a few lunches together but never dinner.

Sitting next to each other in-the-booth-in-the-back-in-the-corner-in-the-near-dark, with candlelight adding a soft glow, they leaned in for their own private appetizer.

Shelby got up from her desk and went over to Marion's office door, but before she went in, she noticed that her boss was on the phone. Shelby started to turn around...but there was something in Marion's tone that caught her ear. It was low and husky. This was not a business call.

After the briefest of hesitations, Shelby leaned in...and goddamn it, she still couldn't hear what Marion was saying. She stood very still—and then suddenly Marion's voice got louder as she was wrapping things up.

"Okay, I'll call you about eight. I should be able to make it!"

Shelby shot back to her desk. *Call WHO at eight and make WHAT?*

Marion appeared at her door and if Shelby wasn't mistaken, her cheeks were flushed.

"Ready?" Marion asked.

Shelby didn't know what to say. She knew something was off. "Would-would it be better if we did this as a lunch thing? I-I don't want to take up too much of your time...." *God, that doesn't sound very confident—or romantic.*

"Um, no, we can do dinner. I just can't linger." *CAN'T LINGER? Oh, well, that's a recipe for love,* Shelby thought. *Sorry, it's eight, gotta run!*

"Well, I just don't want to rush you, and I want this to be...a fun meal," Shelby offered.

"An hour is plenty of time to strategize. A friend of mine won tickets to Florence and the Machine at the El Rey and they don't go on 'til nine."

Friend? What kind of friend? Florence and the Machine wasn't a super-romantic date, it was just a concert...although Florence herself was mighty hot and could rock the style end of the clothing spectrum. As Shelby dithered inside her head, Marion jumped in.

"You know what? Once again, you're absolutely right. We don't want to rush, we want to focus and do this right, create the job and then really line you up to land it. Let's do a long lunch Friday."

Shelby put on her brave soldier face. "Sure. Lunch Friday is great."

"Perfect. See ya!" Marion went back to her office.

Shelby grabbed her shoulder bag and quickly hustled down the hall. Once she got outside to her car in the big open-air parking lot, Shelby decided to phone Lotus Flower to cancel the reservation. She didn't want to be one of those L.A. types who flake and don't bother to call.

The hostess who answered the phone was puzzled. "I'm sorry, but there's no reservation for a Shelby. I think it was just changed to Marion."

Chapter Four

Verbal Shrapnel

*"I met a mountain girl
Living in her mountain world
She was dancing with the breeze
And calling to the trees...."*

Darcy carefully made her way through the song, singing quietly to herself on the restaurant patio at Sierra Glen Cabins on this late July afternoon. She'd been trying to find a way to channel her anger and frustration at Carol, so putting thoughts to music was a great outlet. But at the same time, she wasn't ready for Carol to hear these songs.

She was looking forward to debuting this latest song during happy hour tonight, although happy hour could be a dicey proposition. Maybe once a week she'd get a few people who would actually pay attention and listen. Most of the time, though, drinkers would chatter away like lively blue jays, ignoring her. Some nights the drinkers got so loud, she knew no one could hear the music. She specialized in introspective folk songs, so it wasn't like she was going to go electric and crank it up like Joan Jett. (One time, though, she got so fed up with a particularly raucous bunch, she ripped into "I Love Rock & Roll" at full blast and the drinkers ended up singing along. Larry smiled but intimated, "Don't do it again.")

> *"Listening to the bubbling stream*
> *Where do you sail to in your dream?*
> *What new world have you made*
> *As you watch the present fade?"*

Darcy was also figuring out a way to honor Carol, what she meant to her, all she'd done to help her heal when she'd first landed at Sierra Glen a little over a year ago.

~ ❧ ~

Darcy signed the guest register.

"We have horseback riding, trout fishing, hiking," Carol said brightly.

Without making eye contact, Darcy mumbled, "I just need a place to stay for a few days."

"Peace and quiet?"

"Yeah."

"We've got that in spades. How'd you hear about us?"

Darcy pulled out her credit card to pay and ignored the question.

"The owner likes to know. He wants to see what marketing is working."

"Grocery store in Little Pine," Darcy said tersely.

"Great. I'll tell him. Here's your key, Cabin 6. Let me know if you have any questions."

Darcy exited the main building without so much as a thank you. Carol looked after her, perplexed. She was wearing torn jeans, a Runaways band T-shirt with the sleeves ripped off, a messy hairdo and looked to be in her early forties. *Probably just came from a big city,* Carol surmised. *Yeah, that life can be stressful.*

A few days later, Darcy and her guitar found a quiet glen away from the cabins and the hiking trails. Her music carried on the cool May evening air. Carol could hear it when she was checking a trailhead sign some guests had reported as damaged. She ambled over to see where the music was coming from and stood behind a tree for several minutes enjoying Darcy's tunes, even though she couldn't make out the words. She snuck away before Darcy saw her.

A couple of evenings later, Carol couldn't resist and went back to the woods, finding Darcy playing in the same secluded spot. This time, Carol's hiking boot crunched on some dead leaves and Darcy looked over. Carol was caught like a proverbial Bambi in the headlights.

"I heard you the other night by accident," Carol said gently. "I like your music."

Darcy turned away and didn't answer.

"It'd be nice to hear the lyrics some time."

"I don't play for people anymore."

"Oh." Carol took a few breaths and then decided to leave rather than rustle the hornet's nest of anger she could sense behind that comment.

The next morning when Carol was helping Julio fix a set of cabin steps, she could see Darcy hanging around nearby, as if she were waiting for something. Carol put her hammer down and went over.

"Need something?" Carol asked politely.

"I just wanted to apologize. I'm having a rough time."

"I figured. You don't have to play for me, I just wanted to let you know I enjoyed your music. We can leave it at that." Carol turned to go.

Darcy could feel her eyes tingling with tears at Carol's kindness. "Uh...."

Carol stopped and looked back with empathy.

"Thank you," Darcy added.

Carol nodded...and then waited. It felt as if Darcy were going to say something else.

"Um...well...maybe it's okay if you hear the songs. Like if you're walking by."

"If I'm...?"

"Yeah."

Carol wasn't sure what that meant, nor did she want to press the issue. So she said a neutral, "Okay." She gave a little smile and then went back to Julio and the cabin steps.

Around 6:30, after she'd closed up the main building (latecomers had to knock on Larry's personal cabin door), Carol hung out for a bit under a large oak tree. *Trees don't have to make decisions like this, do they,* she thought, looking up. *They just grow.* But Carol finally went back to the glen and found Darcy perched on a flat gray rock...eyes closed...deeply into a song.

> *"Standing in the drizzly rain*
> *Nothing left but bone-tired pain"*

Carol sat on a nearby fallen log and listened for a half hour, saying nothing. It was like peeking into someone's broken core, all crumbs and shards.

Darcy never looked at her. Nor did they talk that evening, except for Carol simply saying when it was nearly dark, "Thank you. Your music is beautiful." She then walked away without looking back.

The next day, Carol headed off to have her usual lunch of tuna fish and a history book at a picnic table. Larry, her boss, would've been happier if she worked through her lunch hour. But since that hour was a refuge and a tradition she'd started many years ago, she'd chosen to fight back on that front. He'd finally stopped bugging her about it.

A few minutes after Carol had settled in at her lunch site, Darcy came over with her guitar plus a turkey sandwich she'd purchased from the restaurant.

"Thanks," Darcy said, referring to last night, as she sat down on the opposite side of the table, but a few feet down.

Doesn't want to get too close, Carol noted. She said aloud, "The pleasure was mine."

After they'd finished their respective lunches, Darcy took out her guitar and started noodling. Carol said nothing, just took in the lilting, introspective notes...and then after a couple of songs (no lyrics, Darcy wasn't about to bare her soul in public just yet), a handful of guests sat at nearby tables. When Carol's lunch hour was over, and Darcy had ended her final song, the listeners applauded. She looked up, startled, but then smiled her appreciation. It was the first time Carol had seen her smile all week.

Back at the main building five minutes later, Larry came up to Carol. "Who was that?"

"A guest. Darcy Pennebaker."

"She's good. Did you notice how people were drawn to her?"

"Yes, I did, Larry. I've heard her a few times now. She's quite the professional."

"How long is she staying?"

"I don't think she knows."

"Do you think she would play for happy hour?"

"Are you paying her, Larry?"

Larry paused a moment. "We could work something out."

"I'll ask her, but don't get your hopes up. She's on the mend from something."

Larry raised his eyebrows as if to say, "So?" His idea of healing was to dive in to work and ignore any pain. Carol had yet to hear the full details of his wife's illness and death. Once in a great while he'd allude to something, like when he painted the interior of the main building yellow "because Helen liked yellow."

Carol had hoped to speak to Darcy after work that day, maybe back at the glen after another little concert in the woods. Instead, Larry jumped the gun in the late afternoon when he spotted Darcy getting something from her car.

"I don't play for anybody," Darcy declared, waving a metal water bottle threateningly, spraying verbal shrapnel in his face. "And I don't work for anybody!" The proclamation was loud enough for Carol to hear from the main building's front porch; she hustled over to the brouhaha.

"You played at lunch today," Larry said.

"That wasn't a concert, that was lunch!" Darcy said fiercely.

"I'm not asking for a concert, I just wanted some, how you say, ambience music!"

"I don't do AMBIENT music!" Darcy yelled. "I'm a professional musician!"

"Then why not play?"

"WHAT THE FUCK DO YOU CARE WHAT I DO?"

Carol stepped in between them. "Larry, back off, Jesus." Larry strode away.

"I'm sorry, he can come across as a hardass," she said. "He's not, he's just blunt and to the point."

"I don't need that in my life right now."

"What DO you need?"

And with that, Darcy burst into tears. Carol put her arm around her.

Chapter Five
S'mores

Independence.

That was the next little town Shelby drove through on Highway 395. By now it was late morning and must've been close to a hundred degrees out. She had to have the air-conditioning on since her window was stuck in the down position, which bummed her to no end. She'd read once that you should do one or the other, either a.c. OR windows down, and the gas mileage would be about the same. But now with both options in play, her gas mileage was going to suck on this trip. Her dad would've foregone the air-conditioning and made her tough it out, like the troops who served under him did.

The John Muir Tour would be way up in the cool mountains, where it probably would get down to the high forties at night. Shelby couldn't wait. She was looking forward to learning more about John Muir, explorer of the Sierra Nevada, champion of Yosemite, founder of the Sierra Club. Her dad would throw a few facts their way about Muir as they camped ("And don't call it the Sierra Nevada Mountains, just say 'the Sierra Nevada' so you'll sound like a local."). This week's vacation was going to take a handful of hikers to Muir's favorite spots and immerse them in his writings and experiences.

Independence.

Her mom must've decided to take the town's name to heart when they were here.

～ ❧ ～

It was a couple of years after the Red Rock Canyon Trip and Dad thought Shelby and Roxanne were ready for something more challenging. They were camping about a half hour above Independence at Onion Valley campground, the gateway to Kearsarge Pass. Dad had raved about the Pass for months leading up to the trip and had promised to take his daughters all the way to the tippy-top at 11,760 feet. Their mom thought he was nuts and kept nattering at him that the girls shouldn't do such a hike.

"Mark, they're not used to hiking at that elevation!"

"Maxine, they'll GET used to it—we're camping for a couple of days at nine thousand feet. They'll be just fine!"

At some point, Shelby realized their arguments weren't really about hiking to the Pass.

"Every summer it's this Death March," her mom huffed as she slammed plastic food containers onto the picnic table at their Onion Valley campsite.

"Don't leave any food out. The ground squirrels will get it," Dad barked.

"Everything is in TUPPERWARE!"

Shelby and Roxanne kept their heads down and worked on setting up the tent.

"Stakes first," Shelby whispered. Roxanne nodded; they had been trained well. Then they snapped the extension pole stakes together and threaded them through the tent sleeves. Finally, they put the tent poles into the grommets at the edges of the tent and the tent lifted as if by magic. It was always Shelby's favorite tent-pitching moment.

"Look, Dad!"

But her mom was on a rage roll. "The girls need stability!"

"They love these vacations!"

"Not the vacations, Mark, the moving every few years from one base to another."

"I have to go where the Air Force needs me! Besides, the girls are learning to be adaptable!"

Adaptable. Shelby hadn't thought about it that way. It sounded good.

"Look, Dad!"

Her mom shot her a look. "Shelby, stop!"

Stop what? Putting up the tent? Talking?

"You knew what the deal was, Maxine."

"It's been going on for twenty years, at some point this nonsense has to stop."

"NONSENSE?"

Roxanne and Shelby exchanged a look. Roxanne threw her sleeping bag inside the tent and then added, marching away, "I'm outta here!"

"Where are you going?" their mom demanded.

But Roxanne was already headed for the creek. In a couple of years she'd make that Outta Here proclamation permanent, moving in with a boyfriend at age eighteen.

Shelby, though, at thirteen, wasn't old enough to proclaim much of anything so she went to work on setting up the evening campfire. They'd brought a bundle of log pieces with them from home; Shelby set about gathering smaller sticks and dried leaves to use as kindling. As her parents got increasingly louder about her father's frequent military moves, she built the perfect teepee of firewood. "Leave room for the oxygen," her dad had always instructed. She personally had packed the marshmallows, graham crackers and chocolate bars to make s'mores later.

Dinner was a tense affair lacking in both civility and oxygen. After one too many Fatherly Edicts about how he had provided a comfortable living for his family and this was the thanks he got, it was Mom's turn to storm off to take refuge creekside.

Shelby was the only family member to make s'mores that night. Roxanne huddled next to the lantern listening to Sinead O'Connor's "Nothing Compares 2 U" on her Discman. (The following year, Roxanne would shave her head; that went over well with the folks. Roxanne, "IT'S OKAY FOR YOUR RECRUITS!" Dad, "THEN MAKE YOUR BEDROOM AS CLEAN AS THEIR BARRACKS!")

Shelby sat on a log and huddled in front of her glorious crackling flames toasting the marshmallows to a medium golden brown. She ate three s'mores sandwiches that night since none of her guests wanted to partake in her exquisite dessert cuisine.

About midnight she threw up. They packed up the tent the next day and drove home to California City, using the excuse that Shelby was too sick to hike.

~ ❧ ~

Adult Shelby looked out her Honda's window toward Kearsarge Pass as she drove through Independence. She could feel tears coming to her eyes. She picked up the Tupperware container next to her and heaved it at the passenger side door.

Jeffrey Pine

Chapter Six
Molten Lava

The same day Julio fixed the emergency generator, Carol ended up entertaining Larry's old pals from his previous accounting firm who were in from L.A. She was used to doing short talks several days a week but for this event, to please Larry, she upped the usual twenty-minute chat to forty and got out her old-timey 1920s and '30s photos and a chart detailing the history of Yosemite (which was just over the pass from Sierra Glen Cabins). Carol managed to stay focused—until Pal showed up to fix Julio's pickup truck.

Pal was a local lesbian who lived on the outskirts of the itty-bitty town of Little Pine, way down the mountain on Highway 395. A smidge younger than Carol, she worked at a garage and was so far at the end of the butch scale, people coming in for auto repair often mistook her for a man.

It wasn't Pal per se that pulled Carol's focus, it was the fact that <u>Darcy</u> ambled over to hang with Pal and Julio. The two women glanced over at Carol.

Great, Carol thought, *I'll bet they're talking about me.*

~ ❦ ~

On their first hike together a year ago, Carol and Darcy stood beneath a two-hundred-year-old Jeffrey Pine that filled the air with a sweet aroma from the afternoon June sun warming its bark. Darcy stuck her nose in the raggedy tree bark and inhaled deeply. "You're right, it smells like butterscotch!" Then she looked straight up. "Man alive, I've never seen trees like this. They must be a hundred feet tall! I gotta write a song about 'em."

"They're named after John Jeffrey, a Scottish botanist," Carol said.

Darcy smiled and stared up at the waving pine needles again.

Carol let her have her moment of taking in the majesty and then asked, "Okay, wanna give this a shot?"

Darcy had been staying at the cabins for ten days, and Carol had noticed that she had anger issues with not just Larry but Julio as well. Julio was so quiet and polite, people barely knew he was around.

"Why do I have to move my car?" Darcy had yelled at Julio. He'd needed to get into the maintenance shed and Darcy had parked her red Delta 88 right in front of it. Carol thought she'd better offer a way for Darcy to let go of her anger. So, this particular day, they weren't in the woods to just sightsee.

"We'll start by getting centered and setting our intention."

"Setting our intention?" Darcy asked.

"To get the process going in the right direction for the anger release."

"This is too weird."

"Yeah, but you're like Vesuvius getting ready to blow. Julio just made a simple request."

Darcy scowled at that observation.

"Then after we set our intention, we'll start the role-play thing. You're gonna yell at me and let all that molten lava shoot out."

Hesitating, Darcy sighed.

"Don't worry," said Carol. "I can take it."

"I don't want to yell at you."

"Not as me. Me as a music company executive."

Darcy was scared. *Fuck, what am I doing? I escaped from L.A. and now I'm tangled up with this resort manager who does crazy things in the woods?*

"PASS." Darcy bolted and left the glen. Carol sighed and looked after her.

~ ❦ ~

In the present, the group of a half dozen of Larry's number crunchers applauded when Carol was done with her Yosemite talk. Then she answered a few questions about the vintage photos, which they really loved. Afterward, she headed over to her usual picnic table for lunch and today's book, *Magic in the Celtic Otherworld.*

Carol saw Pal and Darcy glance her way another time or two. *Sue me, I like to read.* But she could barely concentrate after that, so she slammed her book shut and cut her lunch hour short.

Chapter Seven

Lotus Flower Take Two

Decked out in her gold earrings shaped like Ginko Biloba tree leaves and a black knit top with gold thread woven into it, Shelby was all set for the Friday Lotus Flower lunch. That would be the postponed meal with Marion.

Once food had been ordered, they settled in to making a long list on a legal tablet of the cool things this new Director position could do.

Shelby would be in charge of Special Programs and Events for the college's alumni, adding planning to her role, not just implementing, as she'd been doing. As they filled the page, Marion went into Jubilant Mode.

"You're going to totally rock this job!"

"Oh gosh! Thanks!"

"Let's get this list to the Associate Vice Chancellor today! We're gonna help alumni bring in more money this year than the past three combined!"

Shelby smiled a big smile. That was Marion, dynamic to a fault. But Shelby also felt a niggling worry, as if the paperwork and administrative stuff in the new job might crowd out what she loved about her current one. That is, going on the actual outings with the alumni (Kayaking in the marina! Touring Descanso Gardens! Art walks at the Getty Museum!). Also, it was her personal connection to them that was helping bring in the donations, she felt.

"What's the matter?" Marion sensed the hesitation behind Shelby's smile.

"Oh, nothing, it just looks a little...."

"What?" Marion leaned forward.

Shelby could see today's bra color: light pink.

"The logistics are...."

"You're so great at logistics!"

"Thank you. But I want to be able to use my other strength, connecting one-on-one with them."

"You'll be able to do that! This infrastructure thing: we build it, they come, then you connect!"

"Okay!" said Shelby, smiling, relieved.

In Marion's Audi on the drive back to the office, Shelby decided it was time to get to know her boss a little better.

"Is this your dream job?" Shelby asked.

"I've got a lot of dreams. I want to run my own company someday, be my own boss. But this will do for now, while we launch the Take Charge Campaign. Then when that brings in a gazillion dollars, I'll have the leverage to start a consulting firm or something."

"You seem pretty driven."

"Yeah. Why not?" Marion said, laughing.

Shelby was not driven, but she loved being in Marion's car, feeling as if they were going places together.

"What do you do to relax?" Shelby asked.

"I'm learning how to surf, baby!"

"Oh, something easy," Shelby joked.

Marion laughed. "I'm getting the hang of it."

Now that Marion was warmed up, Shelby steered toward the personal.

"I forget, did you move to L.A. with someone?"

"Nope. Closed that chapter in St. Louis."

"How's the social life here compared to St. Louis?"

"Even more to choose from, in better weather."

They chuckled.

"Been getting out?"

"Yeah, went to the downtown music fest last weekend."

Shelby waited to see if she would offer some details but no.

"Have you found your 'crowd' yet...or made some new friends?"

"Working on it. Joined a couple of Meetup groups online."

Okay, let's go for the big kahuna question, Shelby thought. "Tried any of those dating sites?"

"Mm, no. I like meeting people face-to-face."

"Me too."

Marion seemed all chipper and forthcoming, but she actually held back on the specifics. She was more open about her career thoughts.

Finally, Shelby decided to see if Marion would play one of their favorite games: Two Words. They would say two words and see how much of a sexual spin they could put on them. Shelby noticed a UPS driver heading down the sidewalk on Santa Monica Boulevard toting a big brown box, so she seductively said, "Big Package."

Marion grinned and dove right in.

"Short Shorts."

"Gear Shift."

"Special Delivery."

"Front-Loaded."

It went on like this for several blocks until Marion put her hand on Shelby's knee as they waited at the light just before their parking lot and said in a seductive tone, "Director of...wait for it...*Special Programs.*"

They cracked up laughing. *Yeah, baby, that's the Marion I know and love,* she thought. *We're Going Places. Together.*

~ ❧ ~

On her voyage up Highway 395, Shelby snagged a parking spot at Schat's Bakery (score!) and got out of her car. The August oven air and the heat rising off the blacktop nearly made her knees buckle; she hurried toward the front door and the air-conditioning. Even though it was after two, the lunch line was long. She looked at her watch: the John Muir Tour orientation was at five and she wanted to be there by four to set up her tent. By the time she got her food, she figured she'd be a good forty-five minutes behind schedule. *Well,* she thought, *it's worth it. I needed to take a break from driving in the scorching heat. Besides Schat's will give me something pleasant to talk to Mom about.* Shelby had hinted to her mom that she had met A Special Someone at the office and things were progressing. Now it would be one more romantic fuck-up to add to a long list that she was embarrassed about. The irony was Roxanne, the rebel, had settled down (if that's the phrase) nicely with a guy who ran a pub in Steamboat Springs, Colorado. They'd been together eight years as a couple and as a team to run the place.

Neither her mom nor Roxanne came on the final Family Vacation when Shelby was fifteen. Her dad had proposed camping and hiking out of Big Pine, just a few miles south of Bishop. The draw for that trip was going to be the hike up to Lon Chaney's cabin, THE Lon Chaney, silent film star of *The Hunchback of Notre Dame* and *Phantom of the Opera.* Shelby and her dad had gone to Silent Movie Night when they'd lived in San Antonio.

The folks were barely speaking by the time Shelby was in her mid-teens. She'd felt cheated out of the Kearsarge Pass hike because of the s'mores snafu, but shoot, she didn't want to miss Lon Chaney's cabin. Roxanne was too heavily into her skeevy boyfriend-of-the-month, naturally, to be bothered with anything resembling a family outing.

So, it would be Shelby and her dad.

Chapter Eight

I AM ME!

It's so loud in here, Carol thought, as she clung to the wall of her college dorm's multi-purpose room, terrified to get out into the thick of the eighteen-year-olds laughing. But she was equally terrified of going four years without making any friends…so here she was at the mixer.

The room was furnished (if you could call it that) with light-gray, worn-down carpet, bad fluorescent lighting, white plastic scooped chairs that looked like rejects from *The Jetsons*, some long folding tables and a TV hanging from the wall. Adding a festive (?) touch to the mix: a banner proclaiming "Welcome to Chico State!" on the wall with a *What was that, a panther? A cougar? Some sort of wild cat growling at us freshmen,* Carol wondered. She didn't feel very welcome. It was a miracle she was here.

She was so quiet and withdrawn in high school, some of her teachers thought she had a learning disorder. But she did shine in English class when it came to conjuring fantastical stories. Her favorite teacher, Mrs. Massey, came up to her at the end of her junior year and buttonholed her in the hallway. "Your paper on Celtic heroines was remarkable, Carol. The best essay I've read in years."

Carol was stunned. "Uh, thank you."

Mrs. Massey was Old School: dyed cinnamon-colored hair that she had done at the beauty shop every week, floral print conservative dresses, sensible pumps with barely any heel. And Carol not only liked her, she trusted her.

"I, uh, just like that stuff."

"I can tell. So, what would you like to do with your life when you're done here at Bradford High?"

Carol was dumbstruck. She hadn't thought beyond *GET ME OUT OF HERE.*

"We should talk sometime," Mrs. Massey said in response to the confounded silence.

Carol nodded.

They eventually did talk. Mrs. Massey got Carol on the track to go to college, specifically, Chico State, a school she promised wasn't too big, wasn't too small, a place where Carol could flourish.

And so Carol was here at a "Welcome freshmen" mixer wanting to melt into the walls. A lot of students gain the "freshmen ten" (pounds); Carol had already lost five pounds in the first week. She hated the loud noise of the cafeteria and took a little bit of food outside, wrapped in a napkin, trying to find a quiet, woodsy spot to eat and read a book.

Now she was staring at a room full of intense, overachieving, over-smiling girls and wishing she could run for the hills and be with a real Wild Cat instead of making small talk.

"Why don't they make team mascots something cool like unicorns?"

Carol looked over to her right. Staring at the Wild Cat, and then at her, was a freckled-face, red-haired student wearing bright green pants and a pink shirt festooned with little white polka dots. And she was barefoot. *Man, she doesn't give a flying fart about fashion, Carol mused.*

"Huh?"

"Unicorns," repeated Gillian.

"Oh. Yeah. Unicorns. I second that. Or Gazelles."

"Love gazelles. I'm Gillian."

"I'm Carol."

"Let's blow this pop-stand."

"Huh?"

"Get the hell out of Dodge, go explore someplace that has better acoustics and lighting that doesn't makes us look like zombies."

"I was thinking the same thing."

Gillian put her hand up for a high five, Carol slapped it, and a friendship was born.

They stepped outside and wandered over to a towering grove of campus oak trees.

"I want to stage *The Tempest* out here," Gillian announced as she looked around the massive trees.

"Cool."

"What are you here for?" Gillian then added.

"Armed robbery."

Gillian laughed, "Good one!"

"What are you in for?" asked Carol, smiling.

"Grand larceny."

Now Carol laughed. "Man, I haven't laughed since I got here!"

"Feels good, right?"

"Damn right."

"I'm in the theatre department, directing and set design."

"Cool. I'm a history major, gonna specialize in Celtic Studies," said Carol.

"Way cool!" They did another high five.

They walked around the woodsy area looking at the trees and shrubs.

"I actually talk to trees," Gillian said.

"I used to talk to the animals on our farm." Carol didn't usually admit such a thing to complete strangers, but she felt so comfortable with Gillian that she knew she would be okay.

Gillian nodded, totally getting it. "They can be so much more understanding than humans."

"YES," Carol agreed.

"Whoa, got some half-wit humans at home?"

"YES," Carol said again.

"Who are your favorite animals?"

"All of them. But Susie Q and Buddy Boy, my dogs, were particularly patient. When I'd toss them their treats, we'd have these deep discussions."

"About...?"

Carol hesitated...and then admitted, "Well, about how I really didn't want to go to college."

"NO!"

They laughed.

"Yeah, my mom was all over me to go," Carol added. "'Get out there in the world, make some friends, stop being a hermit!' But I REALLY wanted to be a farmer or a ranger or something where I'm outdoors, not stuck in a classroom, as much as I love books. Then she insisted that my dad sell the farm...so I couldn't even take it over."

"That sucks. But I'm glad you're here. We will have many awesome adventures together, I can feel it."

Carol nodded, having no idea where any of this was going. At the moment, though, they had arrived at the glass doors to the cafeteria, whereupon Gillian asked, "So, you like women?"

Carol was completely caught off guard. *Am I a, a, a...?*

"Sorry. Did I overstep?"

"Uh, no. I like women."

"I mean, do you DATE women?"

"Uh...."

"It's complicated: You date women sometimes, but then the occasional guy, plus a unicorn and a gazelle now and then."

"Yes. All of that."

Gillian smiled. "Cool." But then she added another observation. "You've never dated anyone."

Carol was speechless.

"A lot of people in high school don't date. Not a biggie."

Gillian was holding the door open for her. Carol hesitated, as if going into the cafeteria was sealing her fate. All she could say was, "You're going to go to dinner barefoot?"

"Yeah. I might step on the occasional French Fry and get ketchup in between my toes, but I like things that are squishy and moist." Gillian added with a seductive spin, "How about you?"

Carol was speechless. Again.

"You know what you need?" Gillian proposed.

"What?"

"A ritual."

"What?"

"To put all of your demons behind you. Because you have a shot at an AMAZING new start here at Chico State." Then Gillian growled, like the Wild Cat on the rec room wall, and with that, she went inside the cafeteria and let the door close behind her.

Carol did not follow her in that day. And regretted it. She didn't know which dorm room was Gillian's or have her phone number, so she steered herself toward the Drama Department a couple of times a day in hopes that she would run into her. Finally, Carol saw her four days after their first encounter. Gillian was standing outside of the scene shop's roll-up metal door holding a script and gesticulating wildly with it while talking to a statuesque actress in a tank top that left nothing to the imagination. Carol dithered for a moment and then started to slink away.

"HEY."

Carol whipped around. Gillian was now gesticulating wildly at HER with the script.

"Get back over here!"

Ms. Statuesque went on her merry way and Carol slowly crept over.

"Where'd you learn that slooooow walk?"

"My cat. Mr. Speedy."

"An ironic name, I like it. Wanna do that ritual?" Gillian asked.

"Uh, what's it involve?"

"I'm gonna make it up as we go along."

Carol half-nodded, nervously.

"Kidding. Kinda. I read a book on rituals for women on how to take back their power."

"Oh. Okay," Carol said.

"Meet me over there by the big California Live Oak grove at nine o'clock tonight. Should be good and dark by then."

Carol nodded.

A couple hours later inside the dining hall, Carol looked around to see if Gillian was partaking of the evening's fish sticks and fries. Sure enough, Gillian was yammering away, the life of the party at a table of eight. *Hm. Must be Drama Department students, and I can't keep up with them*, thought Carol. She finished her food quickly, put her dinner tray on the kitchen's conveyer belt and left.

A couple of minutes before nine, Carol was still in her dorm room (her roommate was absent, scoping out sororities) reading *Tales of the Great Northern Bogs*. She kept glancing at the alarm clock...thinking of some excuse she would give Gillian for why she didn't make it to the Oak Grove. At precisely 9 p.m., there came a knock at the door. Carol hesitated…and finally opened it.

"Hi, listen, I think I—"

"—Let's go," said Gillian.

"How did you—?"

"—Got your room number from the R.A. on your floor."

"Resident Assistants are allowed to—?"

"—I said I'd found your wallet in the cafeteria."

"You lied?"

"I think of it as being clever. Let's go."

And so they went. Carol was sweating so much her feet were sliding in her sneakers. "Do you do this ritual thing a lot?" she asked as they headed for the trees.

"Now and then. When I feel the need."

"When have you done it before?"

"When I needed to get rid of my father's voice in my head. He's a glass half-empty kind of guy, sees the worst in every situation, in every humanoid."

"Wow." Carol looked at Gillian with a newfound appreciation. "You sure you want to go into theatre? Maybe you should be a shaman or something."

"I'm gonna do it all. But I go nuts if I'm not creating something. Hence, theatre. Okay, we're here."

Gillian looked up, and so Carol looked up.

"Wow, I hadn't taken in this view yet," Carol whispered.

The huge limbs of the mighty oak trees spread dozens of feet across, like titan protectors of the campus.

"Yeah," said Gillian, inhaling, as if she were breathing in the life force from the trees.

Carol decided to do the same thing.

"Our farm, we had some good trees there, too."

"And you loved them. I knew there was something special about you."

Carol blushed and wondered if Gillian could see the redness of her face in the evening light.

"Okay. A stick, here, take this," Gillian said, picking up a two-foot-long little branch and handing to Carol. "Hold it over your head."

Carol did as she was told.

"You and the stick are facing your nemesis. Give it or her or him a name."

"Uhhh...my mom?"

"Something more descriptive, per chance?"

Carol paused and then quietly said, "Monster Mom." She could hear the catch in her voice, as if she were going to get caught doing something forbidden.

"Monster Mom. Cool. Stand up straight, as it were."

"As it were?"

"It's a joke. For gay people."

"Got it."

"Pretend Monster Mom is right in front of us."

Carol took another deep breath and straightened her back.

"Raise the sword," instructed Gillian.

Carol raised the stick.

"Now tell her what you really think of her."

Tears flooded Carol's eyes and she dropped the stick, then dropped to her knees. Gillian knelt down beside her.

"Plan B. Whisper to me what you think of her."

"...She doesn't get me. At all. She made fun of how much reading I did. I showed her a story of mine about a magic portal where animals and people would go through and trade roles. She thought it was a waste of time. She thought the animals on our farm were a commodity. The crops were a commodity. She has no soul. I hate her."

"Totally get it," Gillian whispered back, rubbing Carol's shoulder.

After the tears subsided and Carol had wiped her nose on her sleeve, Gillian took her by the elbow. She gently helped her to a standing position, as if she were a knight escorting a lady to a fancy castle coronation. Gillian raised her own arm up, and Carol got the hint to do likewise, holding the stick high.

"Tell her who you are."

Carol shakily said, "I am...Carol. Protector of animals, Susie Q, Buddy Boy, Mr. Speedy, Ruff 'n Ready, Chickadee and all of her fellow chickens...."

Gillian nodded encouragingly.

Carol's voice gained some oomph as she added, "I am a conduit between worlds, past and present, animal and human, future and now, seen and unseen, I am a story writer, a maker-upper of fantastical worlds...."

"I love it."

"I am ME. I have always been me. I will always be me. So there!"

"Bravo, bravo, bravo!" Gillian clapped and smiled broadly.

Carol threw the stick as if it were a spear. "I SEND MY ENERGY OFF TO MANY WORLDS AND WELCOME BACK WHAT THE COSMOS HAS TO OFFER!"

"YES!" yelled Gillian.

They looked at each other. And then Carol grabbed Gillian's red-haired head and planted a big kiss right on her lips.

~&~

"So, close your eyes," Carol said quietly to Darcy. They were back in their now-favorite glen where Carol had first heard Darcy play her guitar.

There had been a few more low-key lunchtime chats, during which Carol had shared some of her own journeys, including the freshmen dorm mixer where she and Gillian had met. Carol also had talked about her first ritual with Gillian under the mighty oak trees, and she had convinced Darcy to give this process another shot.

Darcy hesitated, then closed her eyes.

"Take three deep breaths...and feel your feet connected to the earth," Carol instructed.

Darcy complied.

Carol herself took a deep breath and then said, "We bless the song creator Darcy and her magical words and tunes. May today's transformation allow her work to be heard far and wide."

Darcy's eyes popped open. "Excuse me? I'm not asking you to promote my music!"

Carol knew she'd hit a nerve. "What would they say that would tick you off?"

"What you just said. Far and wide, let's get your stuff way, way out there!"

"What's wrong with that?"

"I can't appeal to EVERYONE! I'm not McDonald's! Plus, they want me to tweet and twitter and flitter and I can't do all that social networking shit."

"But don't you want people to—"

"—I FELT LIKE A FUCKING BLAND CHEESEBURGER COMING OFF THE FUCKING GRILL ASSEMBLY LINE!"

"Okay, got it. So who are you?"

Darcy tried to leave, but Carol blocked her and got right in her face. "C'mon, tell me."

"Why do you give a rat's ass about my problems? I don't even fucking know you!"

"Because you're really talented and you're throwing it away."

"That's MY business!"

"You wouldn't have come out here today if you didn't think you had a problem. So what's the problem?"

"YOU CAN'T TELL ME WHAT TO DO!"

"Who do you mean <u>really</u>?"

Darcy took a beat and then admitted, "Music company guys."

"Then do what <u>you</u> want and ignore them!"

"THEY HAVE ALL THE POWER AND THE MONEY!"

"Take it back!"

"They won't give it to me…."

"No, they won't. So stop asking permission, just TAKE IT!"

Then Carol grabbed a hefty stick. "Hold this up, way up, like it's a spear."

Darcy slowly did.

"Now stand on the tree stump there."

Darcy hesitated, then climbed up.

"Feel how tall you are. Take some deep breaths."

Darcy inhaled deeply.

"<u>Now take back your power</u>. <u>Tell them</u>."

Darcy's voice trembled at first. "I'm-I'm a person, a real person, and I'll-I'll connect with people how I want to connect. I'll sell my-my music how I want to. My music…has value, even if it's not for everyone."

And then Darcy really breathed into it and gathered momentum.

"I'm not 'fast food,' I'm not a commodity. I'm…me. And me is just fine out there in the world. I have stories to tell, important stories. They may not appeal to everyone but that's okay. There's an audience for a lesbian singer songwriter who ISN'T LIKE ANYONE ELSE ON THE PLANET AND THAT'S OKAY!"

With that, Darcy heaved the wooden "spear" high into the air. They watched it sail away.

"It is," agreed Carol.

A week later, Darcy perched on a stool with her guitar during happy hour at Sierra Glen. She stayed in her own world, head bent down, but the music added a soulful, yes, ambience.

Chapter Nine

Lon Chaney's Cabin

The first afternoon of the Dynamic Duo Camping Trip (that would be Shelby and Dad, sans Mom and sister Roxanne), Dad let Shelby spearhead the tent-pitching at Big Pine Campground.

But he couldn't resist asking, "Did you sweep the ground to make sure we won't be sleeping on pine cones?"

"Yes, Dad."

"Collect some rocks? We might need them to hold things in place. It could get windy tonight the camp host said."

"Already got 'em, Dad."

She did the levitation moment of the guide poles lifting the tent up.

"I really like this," Shelby said. "Airlift magic!"

He nodded and went to fiddle with his fishing pole at the picnic table. She wished he had said something. She wished he had already noticed she'd swept the ground of rocks, stray sticks, and yes, pine cones.

"What are we having for dinner?" Shelby asked, as she finished staking down the rainfly and putting some softball-sized rocks around the edges.

"Cold cuts or something. I think there's bread to make sandwiches."

Her dad wasn't much of a cook, unlike her mom, who would make sure to pack surprises for their camping trips, like angel food cake with fresh strawberries.

"I'm kinda hungry now...." Shelby hinted.

"You're a big girl, you can fix your own dinner."

"Are you going to join me?"

"Not right now. I'll rustle up something later."

So, Shelby fixed a baloney sandwich and made it special by adding oodles of lettuce, tomato and pickles and topping it all with brown mustard. She pointed out her mile-high creation to her dad and got yet another nod. She sat at the other end of the picnic table from him and read *To Kill a Mockingbird* to get a jump on next fall's sophomore reading list.

She had thought this trip was somehow going to be, well, a bonding experience with her father. She knew if she asked him questions about his camping trips of yore, he could regale her with high adventure tales—crazy creek crossings, lightning storm bivouacs, blizzard whiteouts. But now that she was fifteen, Shelby thought she should be treated more like an adult, an equal, not just a passive listener, a little kid hanging on to Words of Wisdom.

"Time for the campfire?" she asked as the sun began to set.

"Whatever you want, Pumpkin."

She liked it when he called her Pumpkin, although she looked nothing like one and didn't even remotely have orange hair.

"Should we have s'mores tonight or wait 'til tomorrow after our big hike to Lon Chaney's cabin? To kinda celebrate?"

"Either way is fine."

Gosh, wouldn't Atticus Finch be a little more engaged in this enterprise, she wondered. Shelby was starting to miss Roxanne and her mom.

Roxanne always had the funniest under-the-breath comments about the parental units and other vacationers they came upon.

"Warning: Dad's got a corkscrew up his ass."

Shelby built a fire but skipped roasting marshmallows; it just wasn't fun eating them alone. She read more of *Mockingbird* by lantern light... wondering if she could get her dad to read it, too; maybe he would pick up tips on how to be empathetic from Atticus.

"Hey, Dad, ever read this?" She held up the book so he could see the front cover.

He glanced up from his *Field and Stream* magazine. "No."

"Want to borrow it when I'm done? It's really good."

"No thanks. Don't have time to get into something that deep."

Aaaand that was that. Shelby got up from the picnic table and headed for the tent and her sleeping bag.

The wind did, indeed, pick up after the sun went down. The strong breeze buffeted the tent like a giant ogre shaking a little play toy. Her dad could sleep through anything, but Shelby didn't nod off 'til the wee hours.

And then they got up before daybreak. Shelby wasn't sure exactly why. It wasn't as if they needed to beat the heat, it would be cool in the mountains, but she'd learned not to fight her dad on minor details like this. They were on the trail hiking while it was still dark out. Shelby tried to put a positive spin on it.

"Gosh, I'll bet the sunrise will be really pretty. This was a good idea, Dad."

"Uh-huh."

"What's your favorite Lon Chaney movie?"

"*Phantom of the Opera.*"

Shelby waited to see if he'd explain why. Nope. *Maybe I should try not talking to him, maybe that would make him happy.* Her mom wasn't talking to him much these days, just news bulletins that seemed important: "The plumber's coming Friday to fix the utility room pipes for the washer."

Shelby inched along very carefully in the predawn; it was so dark beneath the trees, she was afraid she'd trip on a rock. Plus she was tired from not getting enough sleep. They were walking right next to Big Pine Creek. During the day it was spectacular, but in the darkness the creek seemed like a roaring washing machine. Shelby finally decided she'd better get her headlamp out. Her dad rarely used one, only for emergencies.

"Ruins your night vision," he'd say. She stopped, took off her daypack and rummaged around. *Shoot, where is it?*

"Dad? I can't find my headlamp." Shelby looked up: her dad didn't even stop.

"DAD. I CAN'T FIND MY HEADLAMP."

He yelled back, still without stopping, "You don't need it, it'll be light in ten minutes."

"It's not gonna be light in ten minutes, jeeze."

Dad stopped and wheeled around. "What was that?"

"I don't feel comfortable walking in the dark! I don't think it's a crime against civilization if I put my headlamp on!"

"Suit yourself." He turned on his heel and marched off.

"Dang it!" Shelby dug and dug in her pack and could not find the lamp—and then realized she'd left it in the tent next to her sleeping bag. "DANG IT."

Shelby stuffed everything back in her pack and quickly swung it over her shoulder. As she hurried along the trail, she opened her eyes wide, hoping that would help her see. She looked up to see how far ahead her dad was: she could sort've make out his silhouette...and just as she did, she tripped over a tree root, WHAM, down she went on her face. In spite of not wanting to, she started to cry. She pushed herself to her knees and wiped the dirt off her face. Her nose was skinned and her right hand burned with an abrasion. She squinted up ahead. Just darkness. She seriously considered turning around and going back to the tent...but she'd never hear the end of it.

She slowly picked herself up and trudged on, sniffling for ten minutes, at the end of which, it was not light out, but the sky at least was getting lighter. When she was out of the tree cover, she could see her dad up on a switchback above her.

She hurried to catch him and came to the trail turnoff he must've taken, but there was no sign saying, "LON CHANEY'S CABIN THIS WAY!" *Well, I hope that was him up ahead,* she thought anxiously, as she took the right fork. *Jeeze, why didn't he wait for me?*

Shelby walked as fast as she could, but it was challenging; she wasn't used to hiking at over 9000 feet. Finally, out of breath, she stopped, bent over and concentrated on just breathing. Then she got out her water bottle and took several good swigs and stayed put for a few minutes to let her heart stop pound-pound-pounding. She looked east, the sun was about to crest over the mountains on the other side of Highway 395. One little cloud was getting some orange and pink on its edges.

Twenty minutes later, walking at a steady pace, Shelby came upon her father, finishing up a protein bar, sitting beside Big Pine Creek at a series of waterfalls. The thundering water was churning, foaming white.

"You didn't wait for me!" Shelby yelled over the tumult.

"You found your way, didn't you?"

"I fell. In the dark."

"Turning on a headlamp ruins—"

"—RUINS YOUR NIGHT VISION, yes, I know! What if I'd broken my arm!"

"Did you?"

"No, but—"

"—Then let's move on."

With that, he got up from the rocks and stepped back onto the trail. Shelby wanted to yell to Roxanne all the way back home in California City, "Corkscrew-up-the-butt-alert!"

She stood there fuming for a few moments but didn't want to lose him AGAIN, so she headed up the trail. As much as she wanted to rip Dad a new one (corkscrew or not), the cottonwood trees with their waving heart-shaped leaves were so intoxicating that pretty soon they'd waved her anger away. What she was left with, though, was wanting to share the beauty with someone. It sure as heck wasn't going to be with Mr. Air Force Asshole. She wished her best friend from high school, Delia, were here.

They had played on the volleyball team together, and Shelby loved being behind her and watching that perfect strawberry blond ponytail flip and sway with every jump. Deelie (as Shelby called her) also had the best calf-muscles on the whole team. Michelangelo could've sculpted them. Truth be told, Shelby had snuck a few glances her way when they were changing clothes after a game.

Shelby looked around, no one was in the locker room but them. The steam was rising from the shower...Shelby slipped off her bra and panties and quietly edged over to the big, open communal shower area. Deelie was waiting for her...soap in hand....

She wondered if Deelie had snuck some sideways looks at her. And when you're in your early teens, exactly how do you ask out a person of the same sex? For the time being, Shelby was content with playing volleyball and getting frozen yogurt after practice with Delia—and whatever she could conjure in her overactive imagination.

"How old do you think these pine trees are?" Shelby asked the invisible-but-present Delia.

"At least a hundred years," said Deelie.

"I want to live here," Shelby told her.

"Let's build a cabin together," Deelie answered, grabbing a pine cone and tossing it high in the air and then catching it. Delia was forever tossing and catching things.

"Look, there's grass growing here—it wasn't out on the ridgeline but now that we're tucked into the woods...."

"Looks soft and inviting," Deelie said with a grin.

"We've got all day...." Shelby grinned back.

Deelie dropped her backpack. Shelby did likewise and then unbuttoned her lover's plaid hiking shirt—no bra for the trail trip, hallelujah. She licked Deelie between her breasts, tasting her warmth mingled with a bit of salt. Delia pulled her down to the soft grass and—

Shelby looked up and realized she'd lost her father again by getting lost in her reverie.

The Sierra Nevadas

Chapter Ten
The First Summer Together

After a few weeks, Darcy moved out of her cabin at Sierra Glen to save money and began renting a room down in Little Pine from Pal, the wise-cracking mechanic. Pal had a good-sized (if run-down) three-bedroom home on the fringes of the town (Little Pine was so small, the "heart" of the town was hard to discern from the "fringes"). Car parts in the front yard were part of the Pal homestead charm.

"Need a carburetor?" Pal had joked as Darcy pulled up in her red Delta and got out for her first look-see.

"Not right this second, but I'm making a mental note."

"Love the 88," Pal added.

"Keep your hands off, babe," Darcy joked back.

Pal liked Darcy's snappy comebacks and then to one-up things, she let her fingertips caress the hood sensuously. "Mind if I cop a feel?"

They cracked up laughing and instantly bonded.

Meanwhile, Darcy and Carol had developed a few routines. They would have lunch together, then Darcy would practice her latest songs off in the glen by herself...returning by 4 p.m. to play at happy hour.

Post-happy-hour, Carol and Darcy would get to-go dinners from the restaurant and head out for walks after Carol had closed up the office. Carol showed off some of her other favorite glens, and since the August days were still long, they would hike up into the mountains now and then.

"Have you written that song about the Jeffrey Pine yet?" Carol asked one evening, as they ate their box salads sitting on slabs of stone just off the trail that would lead to Palisades Point.

"Working on it. Trees are starting to talk to me now," Darcy said, looking up at the gnarled trunks and branches reaching to the sky.

"Good."

A few bites of arugula and goat cheese later, Darcy asked, "You don't think that's weird? Trees talking to me?"

"Not at all." Carol wondered if she should share her previous foray into that world...

"What? Your eyebrows are doing a thing," Darcy said.

O-kay, here we go, thought Carol. "I know someone else who talked to trees. My first girlfriend."

"Do tell."

"College. She was a theatre major."

Carol took a bite of salad and Darcy bit the bait of what she sensed was a good story.

"And?"

Why did I open myself up to this? Carol thought.

"Hey. I bared my soul on the music front. Tell me about your college crush."

"She wasn't a crush. She's the most important person in my life. Ever," Carol said firmly.

"Uh, got it," Darcy said, leaning back so the intense howitzer energy wouldn't singe her eyebrows.

"I'm sorry," Carol said, reeling in the fire power. "It's just that before I met Gillian, I hadn't dated anyone. But with Gillian, I came alive."

Darcy nodded. "We all need those people."

"We started out playing *Dungeons & Dragons* with some other kids at college, and before long, we went off on our own and made up other worlds, other lives. We'd be out at midnight in the woods on campus conjuring and wandering."

One chilly Saturday night in February their freshman year, Gillian and Carol showed up at Vinnie Butoryak's home a few blocks from campus, a ramshackle affair the lively directing major shared with three other drama geeks. Vinnie himself answered the door.

"GREETINGS! GREETINGS!"

Vinnie bowed at the waist with great ceremony. "ENTER! ENTER!" He hugged and kissed Gillian and nodded at Carol. "Your first D&D, my dear?"

"Uh, yeah."

"You'll love it. Booze in the kitchen, game's in the dining room, the quest will begin shortly."

The girls went to the kitchen and not only was there booze, there was booze of every stripe and color on every free countertop and table space.

"If the world is ending," Gillian said, "I'm coming here—plenty of ways to get wasted and not mind the apocalypse."

Gillian proceeded to make herself a rum and Coke like a pro (*how long has she been doing this*, Carol wondered), but Carol decided to stick to just Coke since she: (a) had never had liquor before and (b) didn't want to come off like an idiot playing her first D&D game.

"Let us gather, let us gather!" Vinnie called as he gestured for the group of a dozen to sit at the dining room table. And what a table it was—a massive wooden slab with hefty elephant-sized legs that ended in curls.

Gillian called over to him. "I've been meaning to ask, can we use this table for the spring production of *You Can't Take It with You?*"

"It was my grandmother's and no you may not, you sneaky scene designer, you!"

"Can't fault me for trying!" Gillian responded smartly.

"Man, she's only a freshman and she's trying to cadge my heirlooms!"

Everyone laughed, and Carol felt a twinge of jealousy. Even as a freshman, Gillian fit in and was treated like an equal. Carol also noted nearly every Drama Department kid here was over-the-top, as if, truly, all the world was a stage. *I can't keep up*, she thought.

Vinnie continued, "I am your Dungeon Master, affectionately known as DM for short, and today's quest, dear players, is to the mysterious town of GrungeCork."

Everyone laughed again as Carol looked at Gillian for an explanation. "There's a running joke about grungy rotting wine corks people have found here at Vinnie's."

"But first you must travel through the Woods of WoodCock," Vinnie said in a low, ominous tone.

"Named after something of YOURS?" asked Gillian.

The gang laughed as Vinnie wiggled his eyebrows, "Want to find out?"

More laughter ensued.

"When do we actually start the game?" whispered Carol.

"Right now," Gillian whispered back. Then she added loudly, "How about the character sheets, oh wise and honorable DM?"

Vinnie handed out the character sheets.

"What are you?" Carol asked Gillian.

"I'm Morgan, a half-elf Druid, and I can turn into a tiger."

Vinnie did a tiger purr / meow / growl. By now Carol's teeth were on edge which Gillian didn't seem to notice at all.

After staring at the character sheet for an eternity, Carol decided she would go for a half-elf as well but added in SwordMaid. She figured that might give her a fighting chance going through the damn woods of WoodCock.

"You find yourselves face-to-face with two hulking ogres," Vinnie announced. Then in a croaky ogre voice he added, "WHAT ARE YOU DOING IN MY WOODS?"

"I draw my quarter staff!" yelled a player.

Gillian shot Carol a look.

"I draw my broadsword," Carol piped up.

Dice were rolled, ogres were defeated, and seemingly random items were revealed behind locked doors: mulled wine, tattered armor and a walking stick.

No one seemed too impressed with the items, but Carol said, "Well, I like walking sticks, 'cause I like hiking in the woods."

"Perfect!" proclaimed Vinnie. "If you place that stick into this crevice on the floor of the Aye Matey Ale House, the bar will pivot and reveal a magical kingdom below the building."

Gillian was thrilled her girlfriend had found the right "key" to the untold treasures. "Way to go, Babe!"

But then Vinnie revealed the treasures—scantily-clad siren women wearing pearls. Carol rolled her eyes at Gillian, who just shrugged

~ ❧ ~

When they were back home in Carol's dorm room later that night (her roommate was out on the town on HER version of a treasure hunt, trolling for cute boys), they snuggled naked under the covers.

"Well, what did you think of it?" Gillian asked, stroking Carol's pubic hair.

"It was fun."

"But?"

"...There was a lot of guy energy and guy jokes."

"True. But Vinnie is sooo creative."

"He is. But still. Wouldn't it be more fun if it was all women?"

"Hey, great idea. We should get on that," Gillian purred, poking a finger in a Treasure Spot Down Below.

"Yeah," continued Carol, "beyond the woods of WoodCock. Let's create our own game."

"Yes!" Gillian said gleefully.

~ ❧ ~

"Cool. So why did you hesitate to tell me about Gillian?" Darcy asked, taking another bite of salad as she and Carol ate dinner on their stone perch.

"The breakup was kind've messy."

"Ha! They always are."

Carol pondered that for a bit...yeah, it was pretty much true for her. "And you, train wrecks left and right?"

"Hell yeah," snorted Darcy.

Carol didn't do a follow-up question. Because if she had, that would've given Darcy the right to follow up about Gillian and Carol didn't want to go there. Instead, she said, "You seem to be...on more of an even-keel. Not so many volcanic explosions."

"Maybe," Darcy said, letting a sly grin appear.

"Oh?" Carol asked playfully. "Still need to do some releasing?"

Then Darcy took a radish from her salad and threw a fastball pitch with it. "Take that, Music Mongers!"

Carol laughed and joined in. "I hereby vanquish you to the tenth circle of Muzak Hell!" She heaved a radish of her own into a thicket of trees.

"Listening to Kenny G for an eterni-t-y!" Darcy yelled with another airborne radish.

When they'd finished their salads (and all of the radishes had been flung), Carol proposed, "Wanna go above the tree line tonight? We'll have a full moon to guide our way back down."

"Sounds luminous."

Carol smiled. She liked how Darcy played with words.

So, the gals headed up the trail another half mile until they were out in the open, with a clear view of the razor-sharp granite peaks above and the lush valley below.

"Those are some serious mountain tip-tops," Darcy said, marveling at the jagged ridge.

"Fourteeners they're called. They're all above fourteen thousand feet."

"You've hiked up that high?"

"A few times. I prefer the forests and the glens. That's where the magic is for me," Carol said.

"So, do you still do wanderings and conjurings? I love that phrase, by the way."

Carol paused and weighed how much to reveal. They'd known each other less than two months, but Darcy had trusted her with the anger release process. And besides, she was darn cute with her straight brown hair that moved with the slightest breeze. Carol also was taken with the tie-dyed T-shirts Darcy favored and her embroidered jeans.

"Yes. I kept going, even after Gillian and I parted ways. I create worlds and stories, the way you create songs."

"Do you publish them?"

"Not exactly...it was more for fun."

"But you wrote them down?"

"Yes. Most definitely."

"'Most definitely,'" Darcy repeated, with a faux British accent.

They cracked up laughing.

Then Darcy asked, "What kind of stories?"

"Sometimes off in the future...sometimes back in the past. There's usually magic involved."

"Poof!" Darcy said as she waved an imaginary wand.

"Yes. Okay, your turn. So, what's the Jeffrey Pine saying?"

Darcy took a full breath and then said, "...All the ridges and twists and turns in the bark are character, it's building layer by layer."

Carol nodded and added, "Our twists and turns in life."

"To answer your earlier question, mostly I feel great. Like I'm healing, but sometimes I'm back in Volcanic Mode."

"It can take a while," observed Carol. "How long have you worked in the music industry?"

"Industry, yeah that's the word for it," Darcy said cynically.

Carol waited to see if Darcy would actually answer the question. After a few moments, she did.

"Officially, about eighteen years. I've been playing guitar and writing songs since college, though. Like you with your stories."

"Nice. So, you've recorded some albums?"

"Yep. Four of 'em. With a big L.A. recording company and everything. I've toured almost all fifty states, too."

"Wow. I'm sorry I haven't heard of you. I never listen to current music."

"Well, I don't know how current I am," Darcy said wistfully.

Carol decided to take another angle. "Maybe the more you do other things, like write music, connect with new people, then the more that anger and hurt will fade."

Darcy nodded but sighed.

Carol decided she felt safe enough to propose another bold step.

"Sometimes my made-up stories are just for fun but sometimes I use them to heal. Create a new world that rights some wrongs, that fills a void."

"Nature abhors a vacuum?"

Carol laughed. "Something like that. Want to give it a try sometime?"

"Well...this can't be any weirder than standing on a tree stump yelling with a stick in my hand, right?"

"Right."

They both chuckled.

"How about giving it a shot?"

"Now?" Darcy said.

"Yeah. As we hike. We trade lines back and forth and build and build... then we'll write it down."

Darcy looked confused.

"I'll get us started," Carol said. "We call upon the great and wise muses of the universe...to guide us as we create a world of OUR OWN." She let Darcy absorb that, and after a nod of approval, she started hiking up the trail again and asked her, "Backward or forward in time?"

"I get to pick?" Darcy asked.

"Most certainly," Carol said in a faux British accent.

"Uh...forward," Darcy tentatively proposed.

"How far into the future?"

"Mm...three hundred years?"

"Nice. Planet Earth?" Carol asked.

"Sure."

"And what's the action of the story, what are we trying to do?" Carol asked.

Darcy gave this some serious thought for a few moments...and then said, "We gotta track down the Music Mongers and make them pay for what they've done. They've ruined music for hundreds of years."

"Excellent. Okay. I'll start the story, and you repeat a little of what I said and then add on to it."

Darcy still looked lost but was game. Carol peered up ahead as the sun was dipping behind the western peaks.

"I see two women walking along a brook in a green meadow filled with birdsongs that inspire the SongMaker...."

"...Filled with birdsongs that inspire the SongMaker...." Darcy trailed off but after a moment added, "to write tunes that...."

"...To write tunes that cause them to shapeshift."

Darcy stopped in the middle of the trail. "Shippidy Dippity Shapeshift, I like it." She thought for a moment and then added with glee, "To write tunes that cause the women to shapeshift into hawks who can travel at the speed of light...."

"Travel at the speed of light and hunt down the Music Mongers!"

"Yes!" Darcy cried and pumped her fist in the air. "They swooped down into the canyons of Lost Angeles—"

"Love it!"

"And crashed into the boardroom of the biggest recording conglomerate...."

"And pecked out the cold, black hearts of the Music Mongers!"

Darcy went running up the trail, waving her arms as if they were hawk wings. "Caaaa! Caaaa!"

By the time dusk settled in and the first stars began to twinkle, the hawks had shapeshifted back into SongMakers, taken over the board room, and sang whatever tunes they damn well pleased.

Darcy looked content and the most relaxed that Carol had seen her.

They walked to the edge of a rock outcropping and pulled jackets out of their daypacks for the evening chill.

"Which star is that?" Darcy asked, pointing to the southwest.

"I think that's Venus, not a star," Carol answered. "It's always so bright."

They sat down, with feet dangling over the edge of the cliff, to watch the light evaporate and the stars come out. When the Milky Way was in full view, its delicate white mist strewn across the center of their panorama, Carol leaned into Darcy sideways...who leaned right back. Simultaneously they turned to each other and kissed.

Lon Chaney's Cabin

Chapter Eleven
Left Turn

Teenaged Shelby hustled along, her heart pounding, both from the altitude and from losing her dad on the way up to Lon Chaney's cabin in the mountains. Fortunately, the trail was well-trod, so there was no other path he could've taken. Up ahead, through the red lodgepole pines, Shelby could make out a structure. *Was that even a cabin?*

She cut through the trees to get a closer look. This was not some tiny, wooden, godforsaken thing but a granite stone structure the size of a three-bedroom house with a green tin roof to boot. *How in the world did they get all of these building supplies up here?* Shelby wondered. She slowly circled the cabin in amazement and then ran into another hiker, a woman in her fifties.

"Gosh, is this—?"

"Lon Chaney's cabin, it sure is!" the woman answered and then went on her way.

The windows and doors were boarded up and locked, but still, it was worth the hike up. And then Shelby turned the corner and came to the long front porch. There sat her dad on the stone steps, getting his fishing pole ready to do a little catch and release. He looked up and saw her appreciation.

"Quite a building, huh?" he observed.

"Yeah. It's all boarded up, though."

"Forest Service has had it for many years, but they don't have the money to do upkeep."

Shelby looked at the building in awe. "I wish I could live here."

"I read where Lon got to enjoy it only a few months before he died of lung cancer."

Shelby blinked and whispered, "That sucks."

"Yep. No time like the present to enjoy life."

He stood and walked across a patch of tall, soft, wild grass to the quiet stream.

"This is the Cienega Mirth section of Big Pine Creek. Gonna try my luck with the local trout. Hope the ones down at camp haven't told them I was coming."

Shelby smiled and joined him, plopping down at the stream's edge to take off her hiking boots and heavy wool socks so she could stick her feet in the water.

"AHHH!" Shelby immediately yanked her feet out of the water.

"Snowmelt," her dad said, chuckling.

Shelby laughed as they shared the icy water moment. Life was back to being good.

~ ❀ ~

Adult Shelby headed out of Bishop, wolfing down her Schat's egg salad sandwich and apple strudel in the car. Both the egg salad and the apple drippings made guest appearances on her casual-but-nice turquoise shirt. She figured, *Hell, I'm on vacation* (although she did get out the Handi Wipes and vigorously attempted to get the stains out). She wanted to make a good first impression at the John Muir Tour. *Never know who might be there,* she thought. *Perhaps the blonde in the Mini-Cooper.* After that, Shelby knew she wouldn't be able to clean off stains because she'd be backpacking for a week and bathing in alpine lakes and creeks.

The next leg of the road trip was the tricky part. According to her jottings, she needed to make a left turn just north of a town called Little Pine and go west from Highway 395 to start climbing into the Sierra Nevada.

The speed limit dropped to forty-five, then thirty-five, then twenty-five and Shelby figured this community was Little Pine. It was even smaller than Lone Pine, which at least had one stoplight. The main drag consisted of a bar, a gas station, a steakhouse, a tiny grocery store and a few random buildings.

Shelby squinted and tried to see the decrepit street signs under the gnarled trees on the street corners. She finally found what she thought was Hilltop Avenue, made a left and began the long, slow climb into the mountains, leaving Little Pine behind.

$$\sim \text{\$a} \sim$$

In the days following that lunch at Lotus Flower and the sex-tinged Two Words game on the drive back to the office, Shelby had thought that things were fine between her and Marion. Even so, she was still cautious about asking her out on a real date. If things didn't work out, then things at the office would be majorly awkward.

To cover her bets (and/or her ass), she decided to enlist her office pals Randall and Howie for some help.

"I need a little input here," Shelby said when they were at the Nifty Café for lunch one day.

"What's her name?" asked Howie. He always knew where she was coming from, being the thirty-year-old hormone nutball that he was.

"Lucy," Shelby lied.

"Have you slept with her?"

"No, in fact, we haven't officially gone on a Date Date yet."

"Do you want to?" asked Randall. He was the logical one of the two, which counterbalanced Howie's libido. Randall had been in a relationship with a guy named Ron for ten years, and at forty, he was the older brother Shelby wished she'd had.

"Yes, in a big way."

"What's stopping you?" Randall asked.

"Oh, gosh, well, there's an age difference...."

"If she's hot, who cares?" Howie grinned.

"Oh, she's hot. But, um, what if, um, okay, this isn't it, but what if she's a donor for our school?"

"Good customer service!" Howie said.

"It's a conflict of interest and could get messy," Randall pointed out. "Be careful." Although Randall had a calm poker face, Shelby suspected he was on to her.

"So keep it a casual date," Howie advised. "Go to lunch, have drinks."

"We've done that. I want to do the romantic candlelight evening thing."

"The worst that can happen is she says no. I hear 'no' all the time. Well, not all the time," Howie said, laughing.

"And you'll lose your job because she could tell Marion that an employee was hitting on her," Randall warned.

Shelby met Randall's eyes. He knew SOMETHING.

"But we have such a great time together."

"Then do what you like, kiddo, just make sure it's consensual." Randall had been down a few of these roads with her before.

Shelby nodded. "Thank you, Randall."

"And fuck her brains out," Howie added.

"Thank you, Howie," Shelby and Randall said in unison.

And then back at the office, as if the gods were sending a sign, Shelby found out Marion's birthday was the following week. Shelby decided to throw a birthday party at work.

~ ❦ ~

Shelby climbed Hilltop Avenue out of Little Pine a good two miles, and yes, the mountains were getting closer. But she was supposed to be looking for an <u>unmarked</u> (the key word) turnoff to the left. *Where the hell is it?* There were absolutely no other cars around so she couldn't flag someone down for directions.

~ ❦ ~

Are you checking traffic on Wilshire Boulevard?" Shelby was on the phone with Lotus Flower for the second time on Marion's Birthday Party Day. The manager assured her they would get the food to her office by four.

"But are you checking traffic, it can be a nightmare!"

"Not to worry," he said. "We'll have the food to you on time." And then he hung up.

Shelby rubbed her temples. She so wanted this birthday party to go smoothly and thought her entire professional and personal next steps hinged on Lotus Flower coming through for her. Which was ridiculous, she admitted to herself, but still.

She had Marion's favorite roses for decoration, French Perfume they were called (light yellow in the center, delicate pink on the outer edges). Right now, the roses were stored in Randall's office and when she dropped them off earlier that morning, he gave her a knowing look that said, "Mmmhmm." Shelby had shrugged an "Oh, well, sue me!"

She'd hinted to Marion about the party because her boss hated surprises. Shelby asked if she had anywhere to go after her three o'clock meeting with the Associate Vice Chancellor, and Marion replied merrily, "Only back here to be with you!"

Yeah, baby!

Shelby had wanted to strike the right tone on the birthday card but not bleed into Gushy Land, so she went with something simple and elegant: "I love working with you and look forward to seeing where our exciting journey <u>together</u> takes us." Shelby also thought she had plausible deniability: she could always say it was their <u>professional</u> journey. But she did underline "together" hoping Marion caught the emphasis.

The 20-something Lotus Flower delivery guy showed up at four, as promised. Shelby tipped him big and thanked him profusely. He grinned at the twenty-dollar bill in his hand and looked as if he might ask <u>her</u> out on a date, but she hustled him out the door. She laid out the lettuce chicken wraps and the saffron sizzling rice on Marion's glasstopped wooden table, along with the chocolate birthday cake from the nearby bakery. She artfully set vases of roses here and there and made sure to leave room for presents and cards. She placed her card right at the head of the table along with a bottle of Marion's favorite truffle oil.

Then, as staffers started to drift into Marion's office, she had a sudden realization. People here didn't usually go this hog wild when it came to birthdays at work. A cake was the extent of it. No card, no hors d'oeuvres. *Yikes.* Shelby looked at the truffle oil in its pretty party bag with the oodles of curly red ribbons on it and the maroon envelope that had a smattering of silver glitter on it and realized it was all screaming, "TRYING TOO HARD!"

Before Shelby could come up with Plan B, Marion was at her office door, back from her meeting. Other staffers crowded in and there manifested a palpable giddiness in the air.

Marion absolutely beamed. "Thank you SO much! My first birthday at my new job!"

Then Howie announced, "Ready for our off-key rendition of Happy Birthday?"

"Bring it on!" Marion shouted.

The room sang at top volume, followed it up with applause and then Marion looked to her left and smiled at someone Shelby had only vaguely been aware of—a red-headed woman in tight black pants and a black leather dinner jacket, sort've a Roy Orbison look without the sunglasses. Shelby had assumed it was just a staffer she hadn't met...until Marion kissed her.

"Everyone, meet Jane. Jane, meet everyone!"

Everyone laughed. Well, not everyone. Guess who didn't?

"And look what she got me for my birthday!" Marion then proudly held up her left hand and showed off a ring on her ring finger.

WHAT? IS THAT A DIAMOND? Shelby felt her stomach drop fourteen stories down to Wilshire Boulevard.

"We're celebrating six months of dating and we hope to set an official you-know-what date soon!"

Shelby's eyes met Randall's. Given the circumstances, he could've signaled "I told you so," but instead he gave her an "Oh, well" look.

"Wooo, look at that spread!" Marion's attention was now on the yummy treats before her.

THE CARD. Get the card! Shelby thought suddenly.

Shelby lurched to the table, accidentally hit Velma, the office manager, in the back, stepped on a few toes—literally—and snagged the card just before Marion got her paws on it.

"I'll explain later," Shelby said to her.

Then she stumbled back toward the door, where Randall and Howie were hanging out.

"Whatsamatter?" Howie asked.

Shelby was so stunned she couldn't even answer.

"Marion was the one," Randall whispered to him.

"Ohhhh. She's hot!"

"And she's engaged to Jane!" Shelby hissed.

"Well, just don't let her make you plan the wedding, ha ha," Howie offered.

Shelby was hyperventilating.

"Shelby, get down off the ledge," said Randall. "A month of office flirting does not a relationship make."

"We had a THING, a synergy. We were a well-oiled, truffle-oiled machine!"

Just then, Marion held up a glass of bubbly water.

"I recently read this great quote from Dr. Seuss—of all people!" Marion announced.

The crowd laughed as they saw Marion about to make a toast.

"'You know you're in love when you can't fall asleep because reality is finally better than your dreams.'"

"LOVE? How well do they even KNOW each other?" Shelby hissed as she huddled with her friends.

"Hello? Pot, kettle, black," said Randall.

"Randall, back me up here!"

"How many crushes have you had that you thought were true love?"

"I'll bet Jane doesn't even know Marion's shoe size!" Shelby fumed.

"And you do?" asked Howie, fairly amazed.

Randall rattled off a list of Shelby's past endeavors: "Keelie, Barbara, Megan, Amy—"

"—Stop!"

"If the shoe size fits," added Randall.

In that moment, Shelby knew deep down that Randall was on to something, but she was imploding on all levels and couldn't take in the observation. Instead, she pivoted out of Marion's office, grabbed her shoulder bag from her desk and hightailed it out of there.

~ ❧ ~

Driving along the two-lane mountain road, Shelby could feel her eyes and nose burning as she tried to hold back tears while remembering the birthday blunder. She blinked furiously, but it was a losing battle. She finally stopped the car in the middle of the two-laner. *Why pull over? There's not another living soul on this road in middle of fucking nowhere,* she thought.

And then she cried.

Half Dome

Chapter Twelve
Lost

Shelby and Deelie's high school volleyball team, the Desert High Scorpions, won their district tournament in the late spring of their sophomore year. The two of them were a superhero spiking machine. They led the gals to a twelve-game winning streak in the back end of the regular season before capturing their district's championship.

The celebration party was at Shakey's Pizza Parlor in California City, and Shelby's favorite part of the event was sitting right next to Delia on a wooden bench. They had on their matching purple Scorpion sweatpants with the white stripe down the outside of each leg...and most importantly, their thighs were touching. The two would lean in and giggle as they gossiped a little about the other players, nothing mean, just jokes about what idiotic choices they had made for their boyfriends. Since Delia didn't seem to EVER mention dating a guy, Shelby thought it was getting time to say something. She wasn't quite sure what, but the momentum was building.

Shelby had hatched a bit of a plan the night before. It involved going to see a movie, after which she could declare her undying love for Delia, or at the very least, how much she liked her.

"So, hey, school's gonna be out soon," Shelby said, pausing before another bite of pizza and trying to sound casual.

"Can't wait."

"Me, too. Whatcha got planned for the summer?"

"Ohhh, stuff." Delia also took a bite of pizza.

Shelby decided to keep going and said, "I'll probably work parttime helping at a nursery—trees, not little kids!"

Delia laughed.

Okay, here we go, Shelby thought. *She's laughing, make a move.*

"In a couple of weeks this movie is gonna open, *Sleepless in Seattle.* Have you heard of it?"

"Not really," said Delia.

"Tom Hanks? Meg Ryan?"

"Oh, yeah, right."

"I think they're a really cute couple, movie-wise."

"Uh-huh."

Hmmm...not much of a reaction there.

"Anyway, it's about this woman, Meg Ryan, who is convinced it's her destiny to date this guy, Tom Hanks."

"Oh, uh-huh."

"I thought we could go, it's supposed to be really good. And romantic." That was Shelby's attempt at tipping her hand.

"Um, I'm not sure I can go. See, we're moving the end of June."

Shelby was so thunderstruck all she could say was, "<u>We</u>?"

"My family. My dad got a job in Nashville, he's being transferred."

Shelby felt every ounce of blood drain and pool at her feet.

"You're...?"

"I was gonna tell ya, we just found out last week. I didn't want to ruin our concentration for today's game."

Shelby had stopped chewing the piece of pepperoni pizza in her mouth. She had absolutely no idea what to do with it and had completely forgotten how to swallow. After an eternity of silence between them, she fumbled her way through a reply. "…Uh, we've moved a lot. My mom said we're done moving." The tears were starting to come. "I finally get to stay…at the same…school…."

And with that Shelby got up from the table without saying good-bye, stumbled toward the door, flung herself out into the parking lot and heaved up the pepperoni victory pizza into some bushes.

Shelby sleepwalked through the last days of her sophomore year, avoiding Deelie as best she could. When they were in the same classes together, Shelby just kept staring at the teacher, pretending to be super engaged by things like sentence structure diagrams on the board so eye contact with Deelie wouldn't accidentally happen.

After the final class on the last day of school, she hurried home, made straight for her bedroom, slammed the door and dove onto her bed.

Bad move. Her mom knocked and didn't wait to be invited in.

"What is WRONG with you? Did you fail algebra?"

"No." Shelby put a book quickly up in front of her face.

"Have you learned to read upside down?"

Shelby realized she was holding *Lord of the Flies* wrong. She threw the book overboard.

Her mom waited. Finally:

"Deelie's moving to Nashville. Her family is. And she's going with them."

"I'm so sorry." Then her mom added, "Do you want to give her a going away party?"

"No. The volleyball championship party was hard enough."

"I'm so sorry."

As her mom was about to leave, Shelby asked, "Should I *do* something?"

"When you've left towns and schools behind, did you appreciate it when your friends did something for you?"

Shelby thought about it. Almost no one had. And it sucked.

So, she walked over to Delia's house on that Saturday morning in June when they were set to leave. Snails have crossed the sidewalk faster than Shelby on her voyage there. The moving truck was parked in the driveway and already half full. She found Delia in her bedroom packing up the last of her boxes. Shelby looked at the walls: the posters of Steffi Graf and Jodie Foster were gone. The homemade banner commemorating their court victories against all the schools up and down Highway 395—Trona,

Boron, Mojave, Rosemund, Bishop and Mammoth—was gone. The torn jersey from freshman year (Shelby had ripped it as Deelie jumped up in the air celebrating a hard-won game), the photos from summer-conditioning camp, their birthday parties, all gone.

"Got room in the moving truck for all your stuff?"

"Barely. If the company wasn't paying for it, my dad would've asked my mom to chuck half of her antiques."

They laughed, kinda like old times. Kinda.

"Well, here." Shelby handed Deelie a going-away card and a stuffed bear wearing, yes, purple sweatpants.

Deelie looked sad, fingered the bear's ears.

"Stay in touch," Shelby said.

"Will do."

"You guys got a new home already?"

"Sort've. A house to rent 'til we buy one."

"Cool." Shelby waited to see if Deelie would give her the address...but no such luck.

"Well, stay in touch," Shelby said again.

"Will do."

"Bye."

"Bye."

They did an awkward hug. Deelie didn't make eye contact at that moment. Or when Shelby walked out the bedroom door. Shelby held back tears until she got outside and down the damn block.

Shelby spent her junior year with an empty crater in the center of her heart. She quit the volleyball team, it just wasn't the same. She did keep talking to Deelie, but it was only in her mind. She built an elaborate fantasy of them reuniting as freshmen at the same college and having a glorious time playing volleyball again...and taking their relationship All The Way. But in reality, there was no way to contact her, email didn't exist yet and Delia never sent Shelby her street address.

～ ❦ ～

After the Marion Birthday Misfire, Shelby crawled under the covers at home and stayed in bed for two solid days. Randall kept calling and leaving phone messages.

"Marion's beside herself, she has no idea what's going on. CALL ME."

After listening to Randall's pleading, she threw her cell phone across the room. That simple effort made her realize how hungry she was.

As she slowly swung her legs over the edge of the bed and lethargically sat up, she looked just above her bedside table and lamp and saw a poster of Yosemite. She'd asked her dad to buy it during their trip to the park when she was eight, her first taste of the Sierra Nevada.

It was a classic shot of Yosemite Valley with Half Dome and a quote from John Muir across the bottom: "Nature...all scars she heals, whether in rocks or water or sky or hearts."

That's what I need, Shelby thought, *time in nature.*

~ ❦ ~

And so here she was on Day 1 of her Restorative Vacation in a puddle of tears in her car in the middle of Fucking Nowhere.

She looked at her odometer; she'd now driven a good three miles up alleged "Hilltop" Avenue. She turned on her cell phone to see if she could get a map to come up. But no, of course not. There was no service here in the middle of Fucking Nowhere. She got out her brand-new printed map and studied it. Of course, there was no Hilltop Avenue on it, or ANY named streets in Little Pine. She looked at her watch: Just past 3:30. *Grrrrr.*

Delia, Keelie, Barbara, Megan, Amy, Marion. Fuck, fuck, fuck.

Okay, I will drive one more mile, she decided. *And then that's it. Either the left turn is there or it's not.*

Chapter Thirteen
Right Turn

Pal wiped her hands on a mechanic's cloth and lowered the hood of Julio's pickup truck. "All systems go!"

Darcy started it up; she liked pretending she was Pal's assistant mechanic.

"We're good, new water pump is in place," announced Pal, calling over to Julio who'd been replacing a patio railing.

Darcy cut the engine.

"What do I owe you, Miss Pal?" asked Julio. He was so darned polite, he called everyone miss or mister.

"Forty even ought to do it."

"My kind of price," Julio said, as he reached for a couple of twenties in his wallet. And then he saw one of the waiters from the restaurant walking by with a metal basket of Coronas on ice to put out for happy hour. Julio grabbed a couple and handed them to Pal and Darcy.

"My kind of tip!" Pal said.

Darcy laughed.

"What?" Pal retorted. "It's not like I'm out on the highway with a sign: 'Will Work for Booze.'"

They all laughed some more, and Julio went back to his railing job.

After he was out of earshot, Pal turned to Darcy.

"Carol come out and say boo to ya today?"

"Na," said Darcy, trying to sound as if she didn't give two hoots.

"Man."

"It's okay."

"No, it's not. How long has it been?"

"Six weeks. Stop asking," said Darcy.

"Want me to give her what for?"

"No. Stop offering."

"I fix things for a living. It's my calling."

"Stick to car engines, Pal."

Pal swatted her with the mechanic's rag playfully.

"Hey, that's got grease on it," Darcy said, fake jumping away. "I gotta look good for my public."

Pal snorted a laugh, and Darcy laughed, too. It felt good to kid around with Pal and that had done as much for Darcy's healing as her time spent with Carol.

~ ⁖ ~

Shelby continued to head up the two-laner; there were trees on both sides of her now, shade at last. Her mind flitted around while she wondered what to do if she missed the orientation to the tour. *Well, I'm sure they could give me the CliffsNotes Version. All I need to do is get there by dark, right?*

And just then she saw a road to the right and a sign that read: "Sierra Glen Cabins, 1/2 mile ahead."

Maybe they will have heard of the John Muir Tour, Shelby thought.

She turned right.

Part Two

Foxtail Pine

Chapter Fourteen

Cabin 8

Shelby slowly inched her way down a gravel road and found herself in a clearing filled with a dozen or so rustic cabins. At one end of the property, she saw at least that many campsites as well, reminiscent of Ye Old Family Campouts. She smiled.

She got out of her Honda, grabbed her backpack and looked around: cottonwood trees fluttered their heart-shaped leaves in the late afternoon breeze. It was as if they were waving hello. She gave them a little wave back...and then angled over to the main building, with its deep red clapboard siding and wooden white awning. She stepped onto the front porch and noted a carved wooden bear just a little shorter than she was, standing beside the main door with its arms raised in the air as if to signal "Touchdown!" (Actually, the sign on its belly warned, "Don't feed me or any of my live cousins!")

Off to the side hung a ladybug flag that said "Welcome," and on the front door a little hummingbird sign said "Open." Shelby was already feeling a little better. She opened the wooden-framed screen door and the first thing she heard was Carol saying, "Wiggle your toes."

"What?" said a fifteen-year-old boy with a buzz cut.

"Wiggle your toes. Works every time."

Shelby stepped inside and saw the boy had a fishhook in the top of his ear that Carol was trying to remove.

The boy wiggled his toes, which distracted him enough so that Carol could pull the fishhook all the way through. The boy gasped (as did Shelby), but he didn't scream.

Carol put a couple of gauze squares already coated with Betadine on the boy's ear. "Hold this." He gingerly held the gauze pad.

"And ask your mom if you've had a tetanus shot. Okay, you're good to go. Try to hook a trout next time."

He barely nodded and then hustled out by way of the screen door, letting it slam behind him.

"So how can I help you?" Carol asked, as she dropped the used fishhook into the garbage can behind the counter.

"No fishhooks, but, gosh, am I lost. Have you ever heard of John Muir Historical Tours?"

"Yes, I have," said Carol, noting that Shelby was wearing a turquoise striped top, turquoise shorts and turquoise earrings. For someone so aware of clothing details, how could she be so lost?

"<u>Great, oh, thank God!</u>"

"I'm not God but I am the manager. Hi, I'm Carol."

"Hi! So where's the tour group? Near here?"

"Well, it depends on where they're starting the tour from. It varies."

Shelby unzipped her backpack and pulled out the chicken scratches she'd jotted down.

"I'm normally more organized than this, but my directions all flew out the car window when—never mind, it's a long story."

"No worries. Let's see what ya got there...."

Carol squinted at the directions, pursed her lips, and after a few moments said, "Hillstop Avenue?"

"Hilltop."

"Sorry, yes, I'm pretty sure Hilltop is out of Lee Vining not Little Pine."

"But I thought from my original directions it was Little Pine. Can you check on your computer?"

"Sure." Carol typed John Muir Historical Tour into a search engine. "Yeah, Lee Vining—this is your tour, isn't it?" Carol swung the computer monitor around so Shelby could check it out.

"Yes! That's it!"

"See, it says to go through Little Pine...."

"Shit! I'm normally better than this! I'm normally really organized! It's been...a long day...."

"No worries at all."

"So how far is Lee Vining from here?"

"Well, you'd head all the way back out to 395, then north another ninety minutes. They're having you start near the eastern entrance to Yosemite, and you'd have to climb another hour to get into the mountains. That last stretch is on a gravel road...."

Shelby visibly paled.

Carol tried to put a good spin on it. "If you left now, what is it..." she said, checking her watch. "Four o'clock—you could make it for dinner. Well, a late dinner."

"God, I'm driven out, my left ear and left arm hurt from the wind and the sun because my window's stuck...." For what seemed like the millionth time today, Shelby could feel her eyes tearing up.

"Tell you what. I've got a cancellation. Would you like a cabin for the night, leave early tomorrow when you're feeling a lot fresher?"

"That's the best idea I've heard all day."

"Okay then." Carol swung the guest register around so Shelby could sign in. "And how would you like to pay for that?"

Shelby reached for her travel wallet and pulled out a charge card.

"If you ever come back, we've got some great hiking trails, nature talks, bird-watching, and of course, fishing, but you knew that."

They both smiled and connected. Carol rang up the charge card and handed it back.

"Welcome to Sierra Glen Cabins," she said, flipping the register back around so she could read it. "Shelby Kincaid. Let me know if you need anything."

"Thank you so much. You have no idea how much I appreciate...."

Carol handed her a room key. "No worries. Cabin 8's down thataways and happy hour on the restaurant's patio is going on right now."

"Second best idea all day."

They exchanged smiles again, and Shelby hoisted her backpack over her shoulder, feeling relieved. Carol reminded her of one of her favorite volleyball camp counselors, a confident woman who knew all the answers and was on an even keel no matter what life threw at her. Carol's cute brown-bob haircut and dimples that appeared every time she grinned added to the scenery. Shelby pushed the screen door open and went outside to look for Cabin 8.

Meanwhile, happy hour with Darcy and her guitar was underway. Pal was hanging out on the periphery of the restaurant's deck, finishing up the Corona that Julio had handed her.

"Hey," Pal said, when Darcy ended a tune to sparse applause, "you joining us for the annual full moon picnic tonight?"

"Na."

"C'mon. It's a tradition. You've got to."

"It'll be soooooo awfully awkward, Pal. You'll be able to cut the tension with a buzz saw."

"You're dodging and avoiding. If you want the tension with Carol to go away, you've gotta do something."

"Y'know, this whole thing is not MY problem, it's Carol's," Darcy said firmly. And before she could launch into chapter and verse about what Carol had done wrong in her eyes, she saw Larry giving her the eye. She quickly launched into her next song.

"Takes two, takes two!" Pal said as she tossed her beer bottle into the recycling bin and stepped away. Darcy jumped a little when she heard the bottle crash-land and played a "hiccup" chord. Pal laughed.

Over at Cabin 8, Shelby stepped inside, opened the curtains and looked around. It was nothing fancy, but she loved the inviting fluffy forest-green comforter on the bed as well as the handcrafted wooden desk. She noted the desk even came with some free postcards on it for sending chipper messages back home to city slickers ("Having miserable time! Wish you were here, Marion, and in love with me!"). The artwork on the walls was what really caught her eye, though, a delicate watercolor painting of a sun-dappled creek with pink shooting star flowers lining its banks. On the wall above the bed hung a photo of Yosemite. Not Half Dome this time, but Vernal Falls...with a quote from John Muir she'd never seen before: "Everybody needs beauty as well as bread, places to play in and pray in, where nature may heal and give strength to body and soul alike."

Shelby took it as a sign. *Tomorrow morning, I'll join the John Muir Tour and begin my healing. For now, a shower, a change of clothes and a goddamn margarita.*

Cast and crew of the film Shelby's Vacation

Chapter Fifteen

Happy Hour

"I met a mountain girl
Living in her mountain world
She was dancing with the breeze
And calling to the trees...
She's listening to the bubbling stream
Where do you sail to in your dream?
What new world have you made
As you watch the present fade?"

Darcy had her eyes closed, her head down, not looking at the happy hour patrons.

> *"I thought I could sail there with you*
> *I thought this was a world for two*
> *But I was wrong...."*

Darcy stopped as she tried to remember the new lyrics she'd been adding. Suddenly she heard applause and opened her eyes. Shelby was standing nearby, totally captivated—and applauding. Darcy blushed.

"Wow, that was great. How does it end?"

"Hell if I know."

They both laughed.

"Well, keep at it. I'll bet you could have quite a career in music."

Darcy answered that with a speedy guitar lick. Shelby immediately realized her faux pas.

"Which I'm sure you already have."

Darcy answered with another spiffy run on the strings. "Darcy."

"Shelby. Nice to meet you."

"And thank you. It's been weeks since someone's bothered to compliment me here."

"What? Are they deaf?"

"Na. They're just excited about the hoo-ha hike they're gonna do or the tasty trout they're gonna land."

"Well, I think you're great—and I like your shirt, too."

Darcy was wearing one of her cream-colored linen tops that a friend of hers in L.A. had hand-embroidered; multi-colored spirals danced on her shoulders and around her neck. She nodded her thanks and then began another song, an instrumental.

Just then, a few feet away, Shelby could hear a big guffaw from a vivacious tourist. The 40-something woman was talking to a handful of others.

"Okay, so I hear you saying it heightens the pleasure, but goddamn, I don't know if I could stand the initial pain!"

Once again, Shelby wondered what she'd stumbled into. The woman happened to catch Shelby looking at her and added, "Nipple piercing."

"Oh. Got it. Pass."

"Not right this second. In general."

"Still passing."

They both laughed, and the woman's boyfriend, a blue-collar sort, holding a beer, shook his head in disbelief that their happy hour conversation had taken this turn.

"Bunny, I'm sure everyone isn't interested in—"

"—Sure they are, Mikey. Anywho, I like my pleasure without pain," Bunny added with a grin. "In fact, we're on our way to Grizzly Hot Springs. They have these mineral baths...."

"Oh really?" asked Shelby, as Mike rolled his eyes.

"Mike thinks it's too touchy-feely. I think it's gonna be a BLAST! I can't wait to feel all those tingly bubbles."

Bunny leaned into Mike and gave him a big smooch, while her non-drink hand squeezed his ass. Shelby wasn't sure if it was the woman's energy field or her own margarita, but either way she was feeling A LOT better now.

"Tingly wingly," Bunny added, raising her drink in a toast and shaking her blond curls that matched the sunny yellow daisies on her powder-blue spaghetti strap dress.

Shelby lifted her glass in solidarity. "Yeah, this is what I've been needing!" She took a huge swig of her drink. She and Bunny connected...and then out of the corner of her eye, Shelby saw someone else, a man grinning at her.

"We had a friend recommend this place," Bunny said. "How did you hear about it?"

"Uh, by accident. I took a wrong turn. I was actually on my way to the John Muir Historical Tour."

"Ohhh, cool! What's that all about?"

"You hike around to places John Muir visited and hear bits of his writing...it's almost a meditative kind of thing...."

"Nice!" said Bunny.

And then Shelby noticed the man was right next to her, although now she could see it wasn't a man. It was a butch woman in car mechanic clothes with a name patch that said "Pal."

"How'd you end up pickin' the John Muir Tour?" asked the butch dyke.

"I needed a change of pace."

"Trapped in an office all day?"

"Something like that," said Shelby.

"Boss drivin' ya nuts?"

"Something like that." Shelby focused on Bunny again. "How about you, what do you do?"

"I hate office work," Bunny said. "That's why I got into massage therapy."

"Oh, gosh, I'll bet you're great at that!" Shelby said…and then realized maybe she put a little too much enthusiasm into that statement.

Pal grinned at her, totally picking up that Shelby was smitten with Bunny.

"Why thank you, I am, right, Mikey?" Bunny said to her boyfriend.

Mike raised his drink in a toast and the crowd laughed. Then he and Bunny kissed again, and she playacted massaging his chest, replete with "Mmmmm" sensuous sound effects.

Shelby watched them but became so aware of Pal watching her that she ducked off to the side and went to find another margarita.

A couple of hours later, the full moon picnic group was gathering in the Sierra Glen parking area. Carol locked up the main building for the day and headed over to join Pal and Felicia-and-Veronica from Little Pine. They were a madly-in-lust couple in their late twenties who always managed to dress alike (T-shirts, baggy shorts and basketball shoes) whether by design or not.

"Great to see you guys!" Carol called over to them. "Harvest some fresh basil for tonight?"

"You betcha," answered Felicia.

"Where's Darcy?" asked Veronica. "Isn't happy hour about over with?"

Carol's eyes met Pal's. Neither had explained to the women the latest lowdown on the Relationship Front. In fact, they hadn't seen Felicia-and-Veronica since the summer solstice picnic, which was about the time things were going south for Carol and Darcy.

"I'm not sure if she's coming," Carol said casually.

Felicia-and-Veronica immediately looked at Pal for an explanation. Pal held her hands up as if to say, "No answers here, folks!"

"Oh, c'mon, one of you, what's going on?" asked Veronica.

"We're dragging the truth out of you guys, one way or another," Felicia added.

Meanwhile, over at the restaurant's patio, Darcy was packing up her guitar. Shelby had found a lounge chair several minutes prior and was in Cocktail Comatose Mode. She'd been surreptitiously watching Bunny and Mike slow dance to Darcy's romantic tunes. She wondered what it would be like to nuzzle her nose in Bunny's curls. They looked soft, not as if she'd put on a ton of hair product to hold them in place. Just as Shelby was imagining snuggling up to Bunny's ample cleavage, she heard a voice:

"You gonna be okay?"

It was Darcy.

"Uh, yeah, sure. Gosh, what time is it?"

"Dinner time."

"Oh, right."

Shelby rolled over to get out of the lounge chair and rolled right onto the deck. She stayed there for a few moments.

"You okay?"

"Yeah, yeah."

Shelby slowly picked herself up (thanking God that her glass was already empty) and carefully walked to the patio steps.

"Know where you're headed?"

"Yeah. Cabin 8."

"Gonna skip dinner?"

"Oh, right, dinner."

Shelby stopped and stared at the restaurant door. She might as well have been peering to the North Pole, it seemed so far away. She then looked toward Cabin 8, basically Siberia...then back to the restaurant. Tough decision. Then she looked at Darcy.

"Do you know 'Crazy'?" Shelby asked the musician.

"Patsy Cline?"

"Yeah."

"I do. You want me to play it for you right now?"

Shelby pondered the question in her drunken haze.

"Maybe that would be pathetic...."

"Totally up to you," Darcy offered.

"Well...."

"I think you need to eat something," said Darcy.

"I do. But first I have to pee."

"Sounds like a plan."

Shelby tipsily staggered off toward Cabin 8 while digging in her jeans pocket to get her room key. That was the easy part. Getting it in the door lock...a lot more challenging. As she jiggled and wiggled the key...she heard passionate noises coming from Cabin 9. She finally stopped fumbling and slowly moved toward the cabin next door. She carefully peeked in the front window from a distance: Bunny and Mike were going at it hot and heavy. Shelby was curious and embarrassed all at the same time. She started to walk away...and then Bunny's cries of ecstasy pulled her back in for another look.

Darcy had followed Shelby partway to make sure she didn't fall down and now was halfway between Shelby and the picnic group in the parking lot. *Oh Lord, what to do,* wondered Darcy. *Can I sneak away without the picnic crowd seeing me and pushing me to join them?* She could hear they were in the middle of some silly discussion.

"You can't say attic items as things you throw away," Pal said.

"Okay, okay, we know, we know," Felicia yelled.

"And a jukebox is not an appliance," Pal yelled back, laughing.

"Well, what the hell is it? A vegetable?" Felicia retorted.

Veronica threw in her two cents. "We still kicked your butt!"

"Game Night Scattergories rematch!" Pal proclaimed.

"We will stomp you," Felicia declared.

They all laughed...and then looked across the way. There was Darcy and her guitar trying to tiptoe out of view and there was Shelby a few yards beyond her staring in Bunny and Mike's window.

"What the...?" Pal asked

Pal, Carol, Felicia and Veronica all took a few steps closer.

"Am I hearing...?" Carol whispered.

Pal did a loud stage whisper to Darcy, as she pointed to Cabin 9, "What's going on?"

"How open is that curtain?" Veronica said at full volume.

They all started to giggle as Darcy was waving for them to pipe down.

And just then Bunny climaxed, full-on operatic shrieks followed by sensuous moans. The gang all laughed...which caused Shelby to spin around and see them. *Shit. Caught.*

Everyone turned away and tried to stop laughing while pretending to talk amongst themselves. Darcy fake-casual sauntered down to them as if she'd been nowhere near The Action. Carol realized she needed to cover for the gang, so she brightly called, "Hey, Shelby!"

Shelby waved tentatively. *What had they seen?*

"Hey," she answered.

"How was happy hour?" Carol asked.

"I'll bet she's happy now," Pal said under her breath.

"Shhh!" Carol shushed.

"Good. It was good." Shelby inched cautiously toward the gang, not sure if this was a good idea.

Carol added, "So, heading to dinner?"

"Yes. Yes, I am," Shelby said with fake confidence. "Then I'm gonna... crash in my cabin so I can head to my tour. Tomorrow."

"Wonder if Bunny was giving head to Mikey?" Pal mused.

Carol swatted at her.

"That's right. Your tour," said Carol.

"'John Muir Tour,'" Pal added in a sing-song voice. "I just like saying it."

"You're on a tour?" asked Felicia.

"Not yet. Soon. I hope," answered Shelby.

"Hell, we can give you a tour," Pal offered. "We're on our way to Porcupine Ridge. Summer tradition. Full moon, fresh basil, buffalo mozzarella, pasta with pine nuts...."

"Ohhh, gosh, thanks," answered Shelby. "That sounds delicious. But really. I was just gonna get takeout and curl up with a good book."

"You're in God's country and you're gonna read a damn book?" Pal said.

Carol swatted at her yet again.

"Hey, I'm filing for workman's comp!" Pal protested.

"And I'm filing for assault with a deadly weapon, your mouth," Carol retorted.

Everyone laughed, even Shelby. Then Carol said, "Bookworms unite."

Shelby raised a fist in solidarity, Carol did the same.

"When I was a kid," Carol added, "I had a book glued to my hand, even at dinner."

"Me, too," said Shelby.

"What are you reading right now?" Carol asked.

"*Wild* by Cheryl Strayed."

"I LOVED IT! The hiking boot—"

"—the hiking boot over the edge!"

And then the two women went on and on as they overlapped each other's sentences.

Pal remarked, "You two gonna start a book club here in the parking lot?"

"Is she always like this?" Shelby asked.

"Pretty much," said Carol. "Look, we have plenty of food and it is stunning up on the ridge. You'll be able to see the Milky Way."

"Wow, gosh, mozzarella and the Milky Way...okay, sure, it sounds like fun," Shelby said.

Pal rolled her eyes, bookworm Carol had convinced the newcomer.

"You drivin'?" Pal asked Carol.

"How come you never drive?"

"I can drive, if you guys don't mind cuddling up to carburetors."

"I'll drive," Carol said, doing some eye-rolling of her own. "Hop in everyone."

Pal and Felicia-and-Veronica angled for the truck bed of Carol's pickup. Darcy and Shelby simultaneously took a step toward the passenger side door....

"Shotgun?" Darcy offered.

"Uh, no, that's okay, I can ride in back, if you're used to, ah...."

Darcy nodded a little nod, but it wasn't exactly a nod of thanks. Shelby couldn't figure out what the story was...but thought she'd let Darcy make the big decision about Where to Sit.

"Could you tell Carol I'm gonna hit the bathroom and grab a jacket before we head out?"

"Will do," Darcy answered, as she reluctantly climbed in the passenger side, putting her guitar in the space behind her seat.

Chapter Sixteen

Porcupine Ridge

Yes, if there had been a buzz saw available, it could've been used to cut the tension in the cab of Carol's truck. Once they were off the gravel and onto the blacktop, Carol took a stab at small talk with Darcy. "We finally got the backup generator operating again."

"Great. Larry must be thrilled."

Carol nodded. Several more seconds of tense silence dragged by. Carol reached for the fan knob and said, "Need some air?"

"No, I'm good," Darcy answered, nodding to her partially open window. She looked at the striped hawk feathers hanging from the rear-view mirror dancing a twirly dance in the wind. Darcy missed those feathers; she hadn't ridden in Carol's truck since her birthday dinner in Little Pine back in June.

~ ♫ ~

For Darcy's birthday in mid-June, Carol took her out to eat at Steve's Steakhouse, the one decent restaurant in Little Pine. From its generic name, you'd never know the food was actually good.

Carol was particularly excited because they were also approaching their one-year anniversary.

Darcy was particularly nervous because they were also approaching their one-year anniversary.

Carol raised her glass of Zinfandel in a toast. "It's been a wonderful year."

Darcy raised her mug of Stella Artois. "It has."

They clinked their drinks. Darcy gathered her thoughts for a few moments. During the long winter months, the only people who came to Sierra Glen were a handful of cross-country skiers and snowshoe enthusiasts which meant no happy hour music. So Darcy had been playing at local Little Pine and Bishop taverns to make a few bucks. Her living expenses were minimal but, still, money was tight.

"I'm a different person," she finally said, "thanks to you."

Carol blushed. "I'm just a conduit."

"A mighty fine one. I wasn't sure I'd ever write another song or sing in public again."

"If you could call our patio 'in public,'" Carol said, chuckling.

Darcy grinned. *Okay, the gratitude part went well, now how to segue into the future...a future with Carol but <u>beyond</u> the patio.*

"I've written a boatload of songs...."

"How many do you think?"

"Oh, a couple dozen at least. Not all of them are worthy of being recorded, but I've definitely got enough for a new album."

"I'll bet they're all worthy."

Now it was Darcy's turn to blush. *Okay, new album. That was the stepping stone. Would Carol step on it?*

"I'm starting to narrow my choices down...."

"How many songs do you put on an album?"

"Oh, ten, twelve...."

"Very nice."

"Here's the deal: I need to test the songs in public. A bigger audience than happy hour."

"Mmm." But Carol didn't venture any further. Instead, she took another sip of wine...and went for mindless chitchat, like how little snow they'd had last winter.

When the artichoke-heart appetizer arrived, Darcy tried again. "It's hard for me to tell how good the songs are. There's something that happens when I sing them in concert. I can tell if an audience is getting them."

"That makes sense."

"At the patio, people don't really hear the lyrics."

"Right. 'Ambient music,' as Larry would say."

"Yeah."

"I like all the ones I've heard."

"Thanks, Carol. I really appreciate that."

"I'm sure you'll figure out which ones are the best."

"Not without doing them in front of people."

"Of course."

Do I just flat out say I've gotta leave here and go tour? Then the shrimp scampi and eggplant lasagna arrived, and Darcy decided to leave Future Plans to the Future. For now.

They went back to Carol's home after dinner (Darcy was sleeping there at least half the week by now), a small cabin surrounded by trees on some property halfway between Little Pine and Sierra Glen. Carol was no Suzy Homemaker; there was clutter everywhere—books, magazines, CDs, hiking equipment, tools...and in the spare bedroom, an homage to Carol's love of all things Celtic. Darcy tried not to go in there.

"Close your eyes," said Carol, as Darcy plopped down on the sagging couch.

"Closing them."

"Don't kill me. I know how sentimental you are...." Darcy could hear Carol's voice from the bedroom.

"Not as much as YOU are!"

"Yeah, yeah," Carol said, coming back into the room. "Okay, if you don't like it, I can return it."

Darcy opened her eyes and saw Carol standing there with a new brown guitar case decorated with a big purple bow. Darcy lit up.

"I did good?" Carol asked.

"Good? It's purple-licious!"

Carol exhaled, relieved. "I know how much you love your beloved Boomer." That's what Darcy had named her guitar case, which she got when she was sixteen; it was now barely held together with duct tape. During a late March snowstorm, she'd dropped it in the slush by accident and it had come completely unhinged, literally. Darcy had added more duct tape, but even she conceded it looked pathetic and not professional. The old case was covered with stickers from places where Darcy had played: Provincetown, Boston, Chicago, Louisville, Orlando, Denver…. Whenever she felt blue, Darcy would look at those stickers and remember all the fun she'd had on the road.

"Thank you. Thank you for everything."

"You're most welcome," said Carol. "I didn't put any stickers on it 'cause it's leather and hand-crafted…."

"That's fine. Thank you."

They both leaned in for a long kiss, and that one lingering kiss led to Carol's hands unbuttoning Darcy's shirt. Of course, Darcy reciprocated and soon enough they were in Carol's bed minus all clothes. Darcy loved Carol's body. It was just perfect, not model-thin, but still lean and muscular from hiking and doing repair work. Her breasts were perfect, as well, not too large and not too small. Darcy could entertain herself for endless stretches licking and sucking them—Carol seemed to endlessly enjoy that as well. Once the nipples were good and hard, Darcy would move her clit over one of them and allow the nipple to tickle her and send her over the ecstasy edge. Which was where she was headed right now, her birthday treat.

An hour or so later, when they were both sprawled on the bed, as relaxed as lazy cats, Carol decided to go get her big homemade storybook out of the Celtic room. She brought it back into the bed and began to write.

"Whatcha writin'?" asked Darcy, pretending she was okay with Carol's creative scribblings.

"Ancient Shapeshifters."

"Ah."

Darcy had loved the Shapeshifter concept when they first came up with it last summer, and she had even written in Carol's homemade hand-crafted storybook to commemorate the Shapeshifter vs. Music Mongers Battle they had concocted.

But it had become a rabbit hole.

Every time she came over to Carol's cabin, Carol would get the book out. After a hike, after dinner, after sex.

Darcy tried the positive approach at first ("Babe, you have an amazingly awesome imagination...but what's shakin' in the present?"). And Carol always bristled.

So now, on the birthday evening...Darcy was ready to move on. And she certainly didn't want to get pulled into the ancient version of Shapeshifters.

"It's a lost heritage...to be rediscovered in the present when explorers find artifacts in a cave," Carol explained.

"Uh, cool." *This is it. Go for it,* thought Darcy. "Lost heritage. Interesting, 'cause I don't feel too lost anymore."

Carol nodded and kept on writing. "The Goddess Shapeshifter was the last to survive of her tribe, but she made sure she left behind clues. And the women explorers have become so disconnected from their souls they NEED to find this civilization to heal."

"I don't feel disconnected anymore. I feel I'm ready...for…a new future."

"Mmmhmm." Carol kept writing.

"Our new future," Darcy added.

Carol didn't respond <u>at all</u>.

She's deliberately avoiding me, Darcy thought. So, she gently took the storybook away from Carol, who looked a little irritated.

"I feel a thousand times better than when I got here. And now it's time to do something else. I'm not sure what it is. Can we talk about it?"

"It's your life."

Darcy felt as if she'd been stabbed in the chest with one of Carol's swords from the Celtic room.

"I thought it was <u>our</u> life."

"Your music, your life."

"Excuse me?"

"I can't tell you how to do your next album or make your next career move."

"Whatever decision I make will affect BOTH of us!" *Okay, that came out too sharp and loud,* Darcy realized, *but damn it, Carol was doing the passive thing.*

"You don't need to yell, you always yell when you get going on a point."

"I'm yelling because you're not hearing me!" Darcy yelled.

"Yelling won't make me hear better!"

"Then acknowledge that if I go away and record an album and go on tour to support it, those circumstances will change our life together."

"Do what you need to do."

"CAROL!" Darcy screamed as she grabbed the storybook and threw it across the room. "You've lived here for over fifteen years! Away from everything! Are you living your life or are you hiding in your damn stories?"

And now it was Carol's turn to feel as if she'd been stabbed. Darcy knew she'd gone too far. But rather than apologize, she grabbed her shirt and jeans, put them on, slipped her feet into her boots and stormed out. She left the new guitar case behind.

~ ⸎ ~

"Welcome and thank you for coming, adventuresome ladies!" proclaimed Gillian as she and Carol were about to begin a new Quest Adventure at Chico State. Yes, they had stepped away from Vinnie's *Dungeon & Dragons* game. Now they stood before a baker's dozen of college women under their favorite oak tree on a chilly Saturday night in March. The tree was just beginning to bud, and that felt appropriate for this budding adventure.

"I've collected props and costume pieces from *Romeo and Juliet, Threepenny Opera,* and other shows from the Drama Department," Gillian told the eager adventurers.

The gals immediately were entranced and started to pull feather caps, bodices, monocles, and empty magic potion bottles out of a cardboard box. Gillian immediately turned to Carol to hand over the reins.

"Yes," Carol added, "or we could make props and clothes. It's totally up to us. I wanted to create our own thing, not someone telling us what to do."

The group cheered. Carol flushed with her first taste of success in this new venture.

"I made up a thing, a-a preamble I guess you could call it, to get us going. Uh, here goes. 'We call upon the great and wise muses of the universe to guide us as we create a world of our own.' How's that sound?"

Everyone whooped and clapped.

Carol continued, "Okay, past, present or future, it's YOUR vote."

The gang exchanged looks and the word FUTURE became their buzzword. Gillian was grinning from ear to ear as she watched Carol come into her own, asking the next set of questions: How far into the future? What are we called? What's the name of our planet? What is our special mission?

At one point, bubbly and eager freshman actress MaryAnne said, "What about conflict? You need conflict, that's what makes a good story, right?"

Carol looked a little hesitant and Gillian sensed the problem: the holdover male energy from the D&D group.

"Conflict is great, yeah," Gillian said. "But how about we resolve it in clever ways, without men or guns or bombs?!"

Carol looked at her with gratitude and the group was on its way.

"We are Goddess Questers from Planet StarMist!" Carol announced as they marched across the lawn.

As the Questers encountered Bad-Ass Barracudas and other assorted miscreants, they were chattering all at once and Carol and Gillian exchanged glances. Gillian grabbed a stick from the ground. "A talking stick—we'll speak one at a time! Pass it when you're done talking!"

"Great solution," whispered Carol.

A complication arose: Questers were about to go toe-to-toe with the Tree Topplers.

"How do we take them down?" asked MaryAnne.

The other participants chimed in. "Do we have special powers?" and "Do the Tree Topplers have a fatal flaw?" they asked.

As the group debated, Carol realized why Vinnie had made some unilateral decisions—this was taking forever. And then Carol had a Light Bulb Moment. "Hey, you guys, most of us are motivated by fear, right? What are the Tree Topplers afraid of?"

"Running out of booze."

Carol and the gang looked to their collective left to see who had chimed in: <u>Vinnie</u>.

"Um, h-hi," stammered Carol.

"You're toppling who?"

"The Tree Topplers. They're ruining the habitat of the Cottontops," said Carol.

"Cottontop? Is that like Peter Cottontail?" Vinnie asked with a smirk.

Carol felt her nostrils flare and her ears ring. "Fuck off." She rarely used the F-word as a teenager but now seemed the perfect moment for it.

"Rent a sense of humor, why dontcha?" he retorted. Then he added to Gillian, "Missed you last week at D&D. Happy to have you back. Any time."

And with that, Vinnie slid into the night.

Silence enveloped the Questers. Gillian had some ideas of how to proceed but wanted to let Carol speak up. Carol decided to throw in the towel, though. "Uh, let's call it a night. We'll pick back up in a week or two. We'll get those Tree Topplers."

"We will," said MaryAnne, and everyone else raised fists in solidarity, did some high-fives and agreed it had been an awesome night.

Back at Gillian's dorm room a few minutes later, Carol and Gillian changed into sweats.

"So, are you going to join Vinnie again?"

"I don't *have* to," Gillian said.

"The Theatre Department is small," observed Carol. "Will it be awkward if you don't go back to D&D?"

"A bunch of people in our department don't play D&D and they survive."

"...But you really love it."

"It's a game, that's all." Gillian looked away. It was more than a game. It was her future career at stake, she felt, in that heightened way young drama majors think. She was bonding with people who probably would be vital for her professional growth. And she hoped to stay on Vinnie's good side because she wanted to design his senior directing project next fall: *The Importance of Being Earnest.* She was salivating at the thought.

So, Gillian tried to think of a compromise with Carol, as they crawled into bed.

"Let's schedule our questing on Friday nights, that way there's no conflict."

"Okay," said Carol, looking at the ceiling, wondering how this would unfold. "But if you go to Vinnie's on Saturday nights...what if we want to, like, go to a movie or a party or something? That's a Saturday night thing to do."

"It is and we'll go. No worries." Gillian rolled over and put her full body on top of Carol's and began to kiss her.

But a couple of weeks later when they tried Questing again, only four women showed up. Rumors had been flying around that Vinnie and Carol had nearly come to blows over her start-up adventure and was "stealing" players from his game night. Gillian kept dismissing the gossip snippets but it seemed an uphill battle. So she came with up Plan B.

One Friday night in April, Gillian escorted Carol back to their favorite campus oak tree. She'd brought her sketchbook, in which she'd started scribbles of set designs (not for public consumption), along with some fancy drawing pens and her watercolors.

"What's all this?" Carol asked as Gillian took out the art supplies from a rucksack.

"Tools for conjuring magic. Of our own. We won't need a group to do this."

Carol looked at the front of the sketchbook; Gillian had already painted the title *Conjurings and Wanderings* on it.

"What do you think, my love?" asked Gillian.

"I like it. A lot!"

They smiled at each other...and then plopped down under the oak tree.

"The best of both worlds," proclaimed Gillian. "I can be social now and then at Vinnie's so I stay connected to the gang. But you and I can create our own quests—and I'll get to practice my artwork at the same time!"

"Brilliant. Thank you."

They kissed.

"I think I shall start with Barton the Bellicose," said Gillian as she sketched a creature who was mostly mouth.

"Any relation to Vinnie Butoryak?"

"My goodness, how in the world did you guess?"

Carol giggled and dove in. "We call upon the great and wise muses of the universe to guide us as we create a world of OUR OWN."

Gillian announced, "Barton was tired of working under the thumb of Mayor Mnooken."

And with that, Gillian sketched a tall lady mayor with a giant thumb.

Carol smiled grandly, then told her, "I love you."

Gillian looked up and put a dab of red paint on Carol's forehead.

"What did you just do?"

"I gave you my heart."

"Awwww...And you have mine. Forever and ever."

~ ❧ ~

"I'd like to apologize," Darcy said, as Carol took the turnoff from Highway 395 to Porcupine Ridge to head for the full moon picnic spot.

"Mmhm."

What kind of noncommittal sound was that? She pretends she's being centered but is just avoiding the obvious, Darcy fumed in the passenger seat of Carol's truck.

But she let go of the fumes and angled for humble pie instead. "For criticizing your life. Back on my birthday."

Carol nodded but didn't say anything.

"I was just...frustrated. I really wanted to talk about how to navigate a future together, but I can't do it without your active participation." *God, I sound like a fucking therapist,* Darcy thought. *Well, so does Carol sometimes, so there.*

"Okay."

"Okay...you'll talk about it...?"

"Not right now."

"But sometime?" Darcy asked.

"Tell me what you're thinking, so I know where you're coming from," Carol told her.

Therapist talk, Darcy thought, *but okay, here goes:*

"I want to record again. I want to go the indie route. I think that's better than trying to deal with the Music Mongers in the Big City. I might get a booking agent for tours but that could be it."

"What about the business end of things? You can't keep avoiding that part. Isn't there business stuff to deal with in the indie route?"

"Don't worry about the business stuff, I'll handle that. But how will YOU handle me being gone several weeks, or even months, to tour and promote the album?"

"I'm fine with that."

"So you'll just stay up at Sierra Glen forever?"

"What's wrong with that?"

"I think YOU'RE the one avoiding things. Your *Conjurings and Wanderings* storybook isn't just an outlet, I think you're hiding in your stories," Darcy said with strained civility.

Carol's mouth became a thin line and her dimples all but disappeared.

"More importantly," Darcy said, quickly shifting things back to her own self, "I need to make money again. The salary from happy hour is enough for just getting by, but come winter, I've got to get some serious moolah comin' in. And I still want you as a part of my life. Can we please talk about it sometime soon, so I can lay the groundwork this summer?"

Carol checked the rearview mirror and quietly said, "Okay. Sure."

Darcy exhaled.

Meanwhile, in the truck bed, Shelby was enjoying letting her hair blow like crazy as the air was finally cooling off, a welcome relief.

"So your name's Pal?" Shelby asked, pulling her hair out of her mouth.

"Yeah. Short for Palomino. My dad was a horse rancher not too far from here."

"You're lucky they didn't name you Appaloosa."

That tickled Pal, who let out a big laughing snort.

Meanwhile, mere inches from them, Felicia-and-Veronica were making out. Shelby tried not to stare but it was hard not to since they were so close. Pal seemed to be taking the Lip-Lock-Twins in stride as if they were just chewing bubblegum. But she noticed Shelby's eyes were bugging out at the action.

"Basically," Pal said with a sly grin, "Felicia saved Veronica's life by moving here, she's just expressing her gratitude."

"Got it," replied Shelby. Then she asked Pal, "Do you have a girlfriend?"

"Hell, no," scoffed Pal. "Right here in the truck, you're looking at the entire lesbian population of Greater Little Pine. Except for maybe Maude, who runs the second-hand shop. She's seventy-five and has books by May Sarton and Eileen Myles on her tables, so it's not verified but we're pretty sure."

"I'd call that verified. Does it drive you nuts to have no one to choose from?"

"Newp. I go to San Fran a few times a year to hook up."

"You...?

"Hook up. Get Down."

"I'm familiar with the term, thanks. You don't want a longterm...?"

"No muss, no fuss this way. I have fun and come home without baggage."

"Well, that's one way of doing it."

Carol turned the truck onto a bumpy gravel road, calling out her window as she did, "Hang on!"

Shelby was flung toward Pal, her face landing right between Pal's boobs. They both laughed, and Shelby grabbed the tailgate to hold on to.

"Oh, c'mon, don't you want to hold on to these babies," Pal said, lifting her ample cleavage hidden below her work shirt.

"Maybe for dessert tonight," Shelby joked back.

Pal laughed.

Shelby smiled, glad to finally be having some fun on this trip.

Meanwhile, Felicia-and-Veronica went into fits of giggling as they tried to maintain lip contact with all of the bumps. Then Shelby saw Carol protectively reach over to Darcy when they made another sharp turn... and Darcy brushed her hand away.

"Is there something going on between Carol and Darcy?" Shelby half-whispered to the group. When both of the Lip-Lock-Twins rolled their eyes simultaneously, she knew the answer was yes.

"Unfinished business," said Pal. "And what about you? Single?"

"<u>Yes</u>."

"Whoa, got some spin on that ansah, sistah."

"Yeah, things didn't work out."

"So you blew her away with a bazooka?"

"Maybe I should've tried that."

"Never too late."

"Well, she's my boss. So besides facing murder charges, I'd probably lose my job."

"The boss! I didn't peg you for that type."

"Oh?"

"You're so polite and well-mannered."

"Uh, thank you?"

"Any time. What didn't she like about you?" asked Pal.

"I have no idea. All I know is she fell for Jane and she's got wedding bells going off in her head."

"Her loss."

"Thank you."

In spite of Pal's blunt and in-your-face pronouncements, Shelby appreciated her full engagement of life and not being afraid to say what she thought.

"You're really fine without a partner?" Shelby asked.

"'Partner.' I hate that term. It sounds so corporate. Yes, I'm fine. Love my job, love the small-town feeling here. I watch the heartache Carol goes through every few years and <u>No Thank You</u>."

"Got some spin on that ansah, sistah." Pal chuckled at how Shelby threw her own comeback back at her. "It doesn't always have to end in heartache," Shelby added.

"'And they lived happily ever after,'" Pal said, fluttering her eyes. "You been watching too many Disney cartoons."

"I didn't say there wouldn't be challenges."

"Then have at it and bon voyage!"

"I'm sure Felicia-and-Veronica would back me up, that it's worth it. Right?" Shelby said, looking at them for support.

The gals nodded.

"What do they know, they've got so many hormones running through them right now they'd hook up with a three-legged dog."

Felicia threw a roll of paper towels from Carol's emergency provisions box at Pal, who batted it away like a volleyball, and then Shelby got in on the act and knocked it to Veronica.

"Score!" yelled Pal

"You should see me with a real volleyball."

"I'd love to," Pal said with a wink. "I'll bet you can set up and spike like a pro."

"I can," Shelby answered. And she knew darn well Pal was putting some sexual spin on that courtside talk, shades of her and Marion playing Two Words. Shelby didn't care, though. Hell, she was on vacation.

Chapter Seventeen

The Milky Way

"Hand me the firewood," Pal said to Felicia-and-Veronica.

From the bed of the truck, they handed her a bundle of small logs that Carol had precut and wrapped together with bungie cords. Then they hopped down to join Pal and Shelby and pulled their cooler over the tailgate to take with them to the picnic spot.

"Want me to collect small bits for kindling?" Shelby asked Pal.

"You know about kindling?"

"I was the Number One Campfire Maker in my family."

"You go, girl!"

Shelby smiled and began to look around for twigs and dead leaves to contribute. Once she had a couple big fistfuls of them, she headed to the clearing where a circle of stones was already in place with burnt bits from previous full moon fireside chats. There were also a couple of giant logs for sitting upon. Shelby artfully constructed a tinder teepee in the fire circle and Pal lit a match to it. Soon flames were leaping at the wood.

Carol helped set out the picnic food on a tarp that she'd placed on a hefty flat rock slab, while Darcy stood a few feet away and stared at the moon. *Carol and Darcy seemed to be steering clear of one another,* Shelby noticed.

"Nice job on the fire, Ace," said Pal, grinning at Shelby.

"Thank you."

"Camp a lot growing up?"

"Yeah."

"I didn't peg you for that, either."

"Is it the lipstick?"

"Yeah, and you know, the well-ironed blouse, the fancy earrings."

"That'll teach ya to judge a book by its cover. I can also fillet a trout."

"Holy smokes. Carol, hire this woman! She can fillet a trout!"

Carol smiled and brought over a plate of sliced mozzarella, tomato, basil and crisp crackers. "Your reward for building our fire, madam. Plus, we've got pesto pasta salad."

The booze had worn off and Shelby suddenly realized she was starving. "Thank you. Mind if I load up?"

"Please do."

Once everyone had filled their plates and sat down by the roaring fire (well, Darcy chose to sit on a different log a few feet away), there was some light chitchat. Shelby learned Felicia worked at the Bureau of Land Management putting together environmental education programs and Veronica taught science and physical education at the local high school.

"I'm a walking cliché, a dyke who teaches gym," she told Shelby, who laughed.

Darcy said next-to-nothing, and Carol played amiable host while the others waited for some sort of news bulletin about what was going on between them.

"The Pacific Crest Trail, what Cheryl was hiking in her *Wild* book, overlaps with the J.M.T., the John Muir Trail," Carol said to Shelby. Then, pointing to a high ridge they could make out in the moonlight, she added, "And right up there is where both trails cut across, so you've got a two-fer by being up here tonight."

"Very nice," Shelby said, admiring the craggy line of rocks.

"Are you a Sierra Nevada history buff?" Carol asked.

"Not exactly."

"A John Muir Tour seems so...specific."

"I have fond memories of vacationing up here with my family. It was the one time of year we all got along...well, sort've." They both laughed a knowing laugh. "Anyway, I thought I'd feel better by coming on vacation to a place I love so much."

"So you need to do some mending?"

"Yeah. A broken heart."

Carol nodded sympathetically. "This is a good place for healing."

Then Carol glanced over at her truck and saw Darcy getting her guitar. That had also become part of the full moon picnic tradition; Darcy would serenade them a bit. Carol was glad she felt up to the task tonight.

Darcy pulled her battered guitar case out of the jump-seat behind the driver's area and approached the campfire. Even though she tried to be careful with the case as she opened it, the top half of Boomer came right off in her hand.

"Holy smokes, get a new case," Pal said.

Carol and Darcy looked at each other. Everyone instantly knew something was up.

"I'll get it to you, I'll bring it to happy hour this week," Carol said.

"So there already IS a new one?" Pal asked.

"For my birthday," Darcy answered politely.

"And let me guess, it's still at Carol's, since I haven't seen it at my place," Pal said.

Felicia dove in. "So what's up with you two?"

Carol and Darcy simultaneously said, "Nothing."

Everyone laughed and knew that was a flat-out lie.

Then they both said in unison, "Things are fine."

More laughs followed and Carol tap-danced a little. "We're working out a few things."

Darcy added, "Figuring out the future." She tried to downplay it since she'd been so intense previously with Carol on the subject.

Felicia-and-Veronica seemed moderately appeased. Pal (who knew more of the Behind-the-Scenes Story) less so, but she wasn't going to hold a gun to either of their heads and demand transparency.

"I'll take another brownie, if that's okay," Shelby said, to change the subject.

Veronica held out the Tupperware container for her. Shelby snagged one, and then Veronica plucked another one as well to feed to Felicia, who then got into licking Veronica's fingers.

"Bet that's not the only thing you want to lick," Pal said, grinning.

Everyone laughed, and then the Lip-Lock Twins went for a big chocolaty smooch. Shelby was again mesmerized by their total lack of inhibition. She also felt a wave of melancholy...if only she'd actually gotten to do that kind of kissing with Marion. Pal once again noticed Shelby watching the women making out.

"You into the voyeur thing?"

"No!"

"Hey, no worries. You were groovin' on the Bunny and Mike action earlier, so I thought...."

"No, no. No. I just...."

"...Wish someone was kissing you like that?"

"Yeah," said Shelby wistfully.

"What can we do to help?" Pal stepped closer to Shelby, who tried valiantly to smile, but the corners of her mouth were trembling and her eyes couldn't meet Pal's. So Pal cupped Shelby's head between her hands and then laid a massively moist kiss on Shelby's lips. Shelby's knees buckled and Pal caught her around the waist.

"How was that?"

Shelby just nodded, she was otherwise speechless.

"Want to go a little further?" Pal asked in a sultry voice that completely defied her mechanic's jacket.

"A-hem." That was Carol piping up.

"Did someone die and appoint you hall monitor?" Pal asked.

"No, but she's a guest at my place of employment."

"And she's on vacation. This is what vacations are for. I'm sure Bunny and Mike would agree." Pal looked at Shelby, who gave the tiniest of nods.

"Hang on while I get the blanket out of the emergency bin in Carol's truck. I'm sure this would classify as an emergency, your heart's broken. Meet me under the pine tree over there in two shakes of a lamb's tail." Pal merrily went off to the truck, adding, "Gonna be a helluva lot more fun than inching your way up El Capitan."

108

Felicia-and-Veronica had stopped making out and Darcy had stopped tuning her guitar as all of this was unfolding.

Carol looked at Shelby. "Listen, if you really want to, it's fine by me, but if you feel she's crossed a line, just say so."

Shelby stared at the evening sky, looking for inspiration. "I need...I'm feeling...It's just...I had a thing with my boss, not a full-blown thing, but we had this great synergy...but I was an idiot...and she's the latest in a series of...."

"And taking a walk on the wild side with Pal would help in what way?" Carol asked.

"All set!"

Shelby and Carol looked over to the pine tree where Pal had laid out the blanket and turned on a little battery-operated lantern with a bandana over it to create a romantic glow. She'd thought of everything. Well, except how important it was for Shelby to carefully navigate her next heart move.

"Uhhh...." said Shelby.

Pal squinted, not able to read what was happening, so she came back toward the campfire. Once she could see Shelby's face, she picked up on the indecision and turned to Carol.

"I was gone eight seconds and you threw cold water on the fire?"

"No, it was me," said Shelby, "and I'd love to, you have no idea how much I'd love to, but I have this history of short-term things that don't pan out, so—"

"—You're overthinking it, Shel." With that, Pal kissed her one more time.

Shelby thought she would melt right into the fire. It was all she could do not to rub her clit against Pal's thigh.

"Mmmm, see, what could be better?" asked Pal.

And then Shelby flashed back to Randall nailing her at Marion's birthday party: "Keelie, Barbara, Megan, Amy...." The humiliation came back full-force. Fucking Pal would feel great for a few minutes but tomorrow morning Shelby'd want to cling to her but she'd need to move on but she'd fantasize about her for months but-but-but oh, shit, déjà vu all over again.

"A real long-term girlfriend," Shelby said, as she pulled away from Pal. "Huh?"

"That's what could be better. Instead of a short-term thing or a fantasy."

"I'm not a fantasy," Pal said, grinning.

"But when I get back to L.A., you'll seem like a fantasy. I want a real girlfriend."

"No worries. I'm not looking to be anybody's girlfriend."

"Oh, good grief!"

"All right, all right. I try to accommodate guests as much as Carol does, but okey-dokey."

"Thank you anyway. Really," Shelby said.

Pal went to put away the blanket and lantern, and Shelby turned to Carol, "You must think I'm...."

"No worries. And Pal can be pretty forthright."

"Well, I give her points for knowing what she wants."

Carol laughed. "That's one way of putting it."

With the distraction of Pal gone, Shelby shivered and realized how cold she was in the nighttime mountain air. "Better put on my jacket...."

Shelby grabbed her gray fluffy fleece number from the rock where she'd set it. After she zipped up, she and Carol both angled toward the fire. Carol poked the burning wood with a long stick and an outlier log fell into the thick of things causing a shower of embers to rise up, filling the air with popping and crackling.

The intense flames inspired Shelby. She asked Carol, "Do you have some paper and a pen?"

"Um, I think so...." Carol reached in a small pocket at the top of her daypack and pulled out a three-by-five spiral notepad and a pen.

"Here ya go."

"Thanks."

Then Shelby wrote on one of the pages, "Keelie, Barbara, Megan, Amy, Marion." She closed her eyes, took several deep breaths, said a prayer to whatever gods were listening at this high altitude, at this late hour...and then ripped the page out. She crumpled it into a little ball and tossed it into the fire. There was no popping, crackling or hosannas; the page turned to anti-climactic ash in seconds. Shelby pursed her lips and blew the smoke away from her. And thought, *Done.*

She handed the small notepad and pen back to Carol, who nodded encouragement and said, "I love rituals."

A few minutes later Shelby stepped away from the fire to let her night vision take over (her dad would've been proud) so she could get a better look at the heavens. What she'd thought were wispy clouds overhead were in fact the stars of the Milky Way, as promised by Carol.

Chapter Eighteen

The Morning After

"I have some new ideas: a massage therapist and an acupuncturist."

Carol was unlocking the main building a little after 7:30 a.m. and Larry had come striding up with his latest ideas.

"Excuse me?" Carol was a little tired and hung over from the full moon party the night before, but that still didn't account for Larry's lack of logic.

"We turn the back storage structure into a massage center, maybe put in a hot tub. Or a spa, a full-blown spa. Go more upscale and luxury."

"Okay, I'll admit our better menu worked, and the plusher bedding and original artwork in the cabins is great. But honestly, Larry, people come here for fishing and hiking. This isn't the Hilton."

"Picture it. Acupuncture under the pine trees, opens up the meridians and the chi flows even better. Add singing bowls and whooo!"

"Larry, who needs singing bowls when we have meadowlarks? And they sing for free."

"You're too set in your ways!" Larry huffed and went on through the front door that Carol had just unlocked. He strode into his office off the main reception area and said nothing else.

Am I too set in my ways, Carol wondered. *Haven't I adapted to all of his OTHER ideas?*

"What's the matter, Miss Carol?"

She looked up. Julio had just arrived, unwrapping his breakfast burrito that his wife prepared for him every morning.

"Oh, nothing," she whispered on the front porch. "Larry has another idea: massage therapy and acupuncture under the pine trees."

Julio blinked and nodded as if he were seriously considering these options. He was too diplomatic to contradict Larry's schemes.

Well, whatever, Carol thought. *We'll figure it out.*

"Do you have time to get to the gutters today?" Carol asked.

"Yes. That's my big project, cleaning the gutters," Julio answered.

"Great. Thanks." Carol looked across the way...and suddenly realized something. Julio followed her gaze.

"Something wrong, Miss Carol?"

"Maybe. Let me check something."

Carol stepped inside the main building and opened the guest register, which listed car types and license plate numbers. Once she'd done that, she came back out and looked inside the "drop box" next to the wooden bear on the porch to see who had turned in their keys already.

"Cabin 8, the key isn't in here."

"Should it be?" asked Julio.

"Yes. She was trying to make a tour this morning. Maybe she left it in her room."

Carol went over to the parking area, Julio and his burrito following, to see if Shelby's car was still there. It was.

"Oh, dear."

"What?"

"She overslept and didn't ask for a wake-up call."

"Should you wake her up now?"

"I don't know. To make her tour up north, I'm guessing she should've left by five at the latest."

"Uh oh."

"Yeah," sighed Carol.

"Maybe she needed the rest."

"She did. But she really wanted to go on that tour. Oh, dear."

"What would you want, if you were in her shoes?"

Carol pondered that one. Shelby needed to heal her heart apparently, so would the John Muir Tour provide that? Who's to say? She'd probably spent some bucks on the tour; maybe she'd be pissed about being out that money.

"I'd better go wake her up."

"Okay." Julio took a big bite of his burrito.

"You never get tired of those?" Carol asked with polite curiosity.

"No," he mumbled with his mouth full.

"You don't feel you're in a rut eating the same thing every day?"

"No. Too tasty."

Carol nodded.

"Why? Should I eat something else?"

"No, not at all, if it makes you happy."

"It makes me happy. Makes my wife happy."

"Wonderful." Carol smiled and then headed to Cabin 8.

Julio went to get his ladder out of the maintenance shed.

The curtains at Cabin 8 were drawn, of course, so Carol was flying blind. She assumed Shelby was asleep. *Here goes,* she thought, as she knocked gently on the door. No response. She knocked again, a little louder. Nothing. On the third knock, she added, "Shelby?" Nothing.

Jeeze, what if she's in the restaurant and then I yell her name so loud that I wake up Bunny and Mike next door?

Just then, the door suddenly flung open. Shelby stood there in her rumpled "Volleyball Champs" T-shirt and cyclone hair, stunned.

"SHIT! I set my alarm for five p.m. instead of five a.m.!"

"I'm so sorry."

"Fuck! Shit! Damn!"

Carol took a small step into the room as Shelby whirled around, wondering what to do next. Carol noted that for someone about to go camping in the wilderness, Shelby certainly was mighty neat 'n tidy—all of her clothes were laid out perfectly, along with her mini-cosmetic bottles, which were lined up like little soldiers.

"What if...." Carol offered.

Shelby stared at Carol, as if a lifeline were about to be thrown.

Great, no pressure, Carol thought. "What if...you took the broad view? What is it you wanted to do on this vacation?"

"Uhhhhhhh, hike, listen to birds, enjoy amazing scenery...forget about Marion...."

"Okay, well, we have all of that here in abundance, although I can't promise you'll forget about Marion."

Shelby blinked, considered the offer.

"It's just a thought."

Shelby ruminated some more, hands on hips, brow furrowed.

Carol then added, "And Cabin 8 is available for a few more days, 'til the next wave of weekend warriors arrives. I could give it to you at a discount, and Larry would be thrilled to have it occupied."

Shelby looked into Carol's welcoming eyes, just above that dimpled smile.

"Okay. Yeah. That's a good idea."

"Great. Let me know when you want some hike recommendations."

"Thank you. And thanks...for not judging me last night."

"No problem at all." And with that, Carol nodded goodbye and closed the cabin door.

Chapter Nineteen

The First Dinner

Shelby had a late morning hearty breakfast at the Sierra Glen restaurant, a spinach and mushroom omelet that was as savory as any back in L.A. She then took Carol's first hiking suggestion and picked up the Quiet Creek Trail right out of the back end of the property.

It was just what the doctor ordered. Quiet Creek itself lived up to its name, a soothing bubbler, no roaring washing machine. Following the creek, the trail went up gradually, with not much elevation gain, so no Death March with Dad. Shelby sometimes stayed on the trail and sometimes hopped from rock to rock in the water. At one point she sat on the creek's bank and placed spent oak leaves one by one in the current to watch them float merrily, merrily, merrily downstream.

A couple of miles up, the creek left the tree canopy and cut through an open area with shorter chaparral vegetation like yellow Western Wallflowers and Red Heather. Shelby stopped several times just to close her eyes and feel the warm sun on her face. A little further up the mountain, she came upon a rocky section of stones strewn from the trail down to the creek, white in color with pink and orange streaks. Alabaster? Quartz? Granite? Shelby wasn't sure...but Keelie would've known.

Ah, Keelie. Up-and-coming real estate agent and appreciator of The Finer Things in Life. She made every culture trip a sensuous experience. Artists loved her because of how she gushed over their work. Shelby would beam, taking in the gratitude coming toward her girlfriend.

Shelby rubbed her hand on the rocks in the present, also warm from sunning themselves and smooth as if an artisan had sanded them for hours.

~ &a ~

Keelie slowly rubbed her hand on the robin's-egg-blue bowl, feeling the dark blue speckles one by one. "I'd love to have this in my kitchen," she said.

"I'd love to have your hand doing that to me," Shelby whispered in her ear.

Keelie put her hand down the back of Shelby's jeans, then inside her blouse, then up to the middle of her back and surreptitiously undid her bra.

Okay, she didn't actually do that last part. They were at the Pasadena Convention Center for a pottery show ten years or so ago. Shelby's private parts were throbbing every time Keelie massaged a glazed bowl. When Shelby mentioned being on the receiving end of the hand action, Keelie laughed and Shelby felt connected to her.

Here in the Sierra Nevada, Shelby had to remind herself how it really played out: when they were walking to the convention center parking lot, Keelie said, "Babe, those jeans—they almost look like bell-bottoms." Shelby looked down. *Okay, yeah, they're retro, but jeans are jeans. Aren't they?*

To please Keelie, though, Shelby went out the next day and got new jeans, forking over WAY more than she'd ever paid for jeans before. They were skin-tight and tapered at the ankle, she could barely get into them, but she thought she looked totally fab.

She wore them on their next date to a concert at the Troubadour to see Melissa Etheridge. As she and Keelie stood on the West Hollywood sidewalk waiting for the doors to open, Shelby noticed Keelie was checking her emails and texts every few minutes.

"Can't you put that away?" Shelby asked. "We're about to go inside."

"I'm waiting for a big offer to come in. You'll thank me later. We'll be able to take that long trip to New York. And stay at a swanky hotel, not some dive in the East Village."

New York. Shelby had always wanted to go to there. Broadway shows. The Metropolitan Museum of Art. A carriage ride in Central Park. Her dad had never been stationed near there nor was it the type of vacation her family ever took. But Keelie, who had been there multiple times, could show her the sights, the best restaurants, how to get good seats at those restaurants. *I wonder if I'll need some new clothes, so I look chic when we go? Speaking of which:*

Shelby said in a low tone, "What do you think of my new jeans?"

Keelie glanced down at Shelby's feet on the sidewalk. "Boots with higher heels would make them even sexier."

And then she DID kiss Shelby, whose private parts did a happy dance...but after the concert, the private parts didn't get their full due...

Keelie had to finish that business deal.

Shelby went shopping for boots the next day and found what she thought were the perfect ones: black with a stiletto heel. She'd never worn heels like that before. So when she brought them home, she practiced walking in them, giving it her sexy runway model best.

When she went into the bedroom to take them off, she looked at the bed and realized she'd already gotten a new comforter, new sheets, and come to think of it, new wine glasses to please Keelie.

When Keelie came over for dinner a couple of nights later, Shelby decided to try a science experiment and not say anything about the new boots she was wearing. And neither did Keelie.

I'm paying way too much for these fancy items and she's not paying enough attention to me, Shelby realized. She returned the boots and the jeans...and broke it off with Keelie shortly thereafter.

~ ❀ ~

Midafternoon in the Sierra Nevada, Shelby found a shady spot right next to the creek and using her backpack as a pillow, took a nap. She dreamed she was creating artwork out of oak leaves and wildflowers, circles alternating between the two with a fist-sized alabaster rock as the centerpiece. She felt mighty proud of her creation and could hear the audience murmuring its approval (which was actually the noise from the nearby creek). And then Keelie came along. She took one look at the nature collection and simply turned away and walked off.

Shelby woke with a start. So much for a relaxing afternoon snooze.

She hoisted her pack onto her back and set off for the cabins. By the time she returned, it was late afternoon. She went to see what time the restaurant started serving dinner. *Hmm, I never eat this early,* Shelby thought. *Oh, what else should I do? Read a book? But that's so solitary, I already spent the whole day alone, and it'd be nice to share the beauty of the day, the craziness of the dream, with someone.*

And just then, she saw Carol chatting with some vacationers. *Hmm, maybe she could join me. Oh, gosh, that's too much to ask. Carol's job isn't to entertain me...well, maybe just drinks...or dessert...oh, heck, go for it.*

Shelby slowly ambled over to Carol, trying to figure out what to say.

"Yeah, Eddie's Auto Repair on Elm, north side of town, off Main Street, which is Highway 395. Just ask for Pal," Carol said to one of the vacationers.

Shelby remembered that she needed to get her car window fixed. As she was making a mental note of those directions to Pal's, the vacationers moved on.

Carol turned and smiled brightly at her. "How was the hike?"

"Huh? Oh—excellent. Thanks, you picked a good one."

"You're welcome. I have more suggestions when you're ready."

"Great. I'll probably be up for a higher altitude tomorrow. No pun intended."

Carol laughed. "Wonderful, I have some ideas."

Carol almost stepped away but could sense Shelby had something else to say. Shelby froze, so Carol offered, "Would you like the ideas right now, so you can get an early start tomorrow?"

"Uh, maybe. I think I'll get my car window fixed first thing but then I could hike."

"Sounds like a plan."

"But right now...." Shelby's voice trailed off.

Carol waited, smiling.

Oh, those dimples.

"Ah, gosh, I was wondering…since I don't have my tour group…would you…I know this isn't your job…but would you like to have dinner with me tonight? I could even buy."

"Oh. Uh—"

"—Unless it's against company policy. Dinner. Or me buying. Either one. I could just read a book. Honest. I read during dinner all the time."

"So do I. Why don't we have dinner? Sounds as if it'd be a break in the routine for both of us."

"Great!" Shelby realized that once again she probably sounded too enthusiastic. "Sorry, I just haven't talked to anyone all day."

"I understand completely. Why don't we eat here?" said Carol, looking over at the restaurant. "Otherwise, it's a long drive to town."

"Sure. What time…?"

"I get off between six-thirty and seven. Feel free to have an appetizer if you're starving."

"Okay, will do."

They exchanged smiles and Shelby headed to Cabin 8 to get cleaned up.

Carol went back to her office with a little bounce in her step, looking forward to a pleasant dinner with no drama on the side. She also thought it would keep Darcy from scheduling the Big Life Plans Meeting tonight.

An hour later, Shelby grabbed a table on the outside patio where she enjoyed some guacamole and chips while watching the nervy ground squirrels jockey for a handout. Carol joined her after closing up shop and once they ordered their main courses, they launched into some getting-to-know-you chitchat.

"So you played volleyball?" Carol asked.

Shelby looked puzzled.

"Your nightshirt."

"OH! Right. Yes. Back in high school."

"You must've been good, the shirt said 'champs,' didn't it?"

"Yeah, we were. We were a spiking machine." Shelby looked up at the oak tree overhead for advice. *Should I bring up Delia?*

"We?" asked Carol, noticing Shelby's slightly puzzled look.

"Uh…my first real crush was on that team."

"Sweet."

"When was your first crush?" ventured Shelby.

"Uhhhh, I got a slightly later start. She was at my college." *I'm not bringing up Gillian,* Carol thought.

"Cool."

That exchange was followed by polite silence since neither of them wanted to get into the details. So Shelby went for a less personal angle. "Where did you go to school?"

"Chico State, Northern California. Smallish but a solid education," said Carol.

"What'd you major in?" asked Shelby.

"History, Celtic Studies."

"Really? Sorry. I just...well...figured you majored in forestry or something."

"I understand, I get that every time I bring it up."

"Did you used to teach?"

"No. I didn't get my masters, I would've needed it to teach. I found a good home here, though, so it all worked out."

Hmm, that sounded like a perfunctory canned answer, Shelby mused. Out loud she said, "Yeah. This seems like such a magical spot. No papers to grade, no pressure to publish to get tenure. I hear about that stress from professors at my school."

Carol nodded politely and looked away. Shelby could tell that, yep, this wasn't a topic Carol wanted to pursue.

Sure enough, Carol changed the subject. "About last night, Pal can be too forward. I'm sorry if she overstepped."

"No, no, it's all right, really. She helped me turn a corner."

"And that corner is...?"

Shit, do we really have to get into this? I'm on VACATION, Shelby thought.

"Or you don't have to talk about it."

"Uh, well...let's just say...I've, uh, dated a variety of women...some short-term stuff, some that were just crushes—did I say 'just'? They were crushes, but they took up a lot of space in my head."

"So, you're trying to get beyond the crush and short-term into the long-term real-deal?"

"Yeah." *MAN, I FEEL ON THE SPOT,* Shelby yelled inside her head. *How the hell did we get onto this fucking topic?*

"I hope this vacation helps you heal and gets you going on a better path," Carol said.

Shelby nodded…looked at the floor, contemplated all that she been through the past few days. And then she did something she'd never done before, she admitted, "My imagination…gets carried away."

Carol nodded again, and this time, she glanced at the floor, which Shelby noticed. Then Carol asked quietly, "When did your fantasies start?"

Whoa, she said the word "fantasies" and I said "imagination," Shelby noted. *Okay, I have fantasies. And is Carol psychic?* From Carol's tone, Shelby could tell this wasn't just an idle question, either. So she took a moment to pinpoint the scene from her childhood that would provide the answer: "The day my mom threw a crystal vase at the wall when she told my dad she wasn't moving to any more military bases. I was in my early teens. I holed up in my room with books and made up different lives."

"What kind of lives?"

"Ohhh, I was flying with Amelia Earhart, solving mysteries with Nancy Drew, hiking the mountains with Sir Edmund Hillary. And then when I met Delia, she was in those lives with me."

Carol grinned, charmed.

"Sounds like fun."

"It was. Up to a point. But when you're well into your thirties…."

Carol nodded. And glanced at the floor. Again.

There is <u>something</u> going on here, Shelby suspected, but she wasn't sure how to wade in. *Hmm, maybe I'd better stick with the kid stuff.*

"So, Carol, when you were a kid, besides having a book glued to your hand, what else did you do for fun?"

"I played with our farm animals," Carol said. "We had cows and chickens and horses. Well, I talked to them, it's not like we all played dodgeball together."

They both chuckled.

"Nice. I talked to our cocker spaniel, Freckles," Shelby told her. "He was my main confidante."

"Excellent. Dogs are the best listeners."

Okay, I'm going for it, Shelby decided. "So, did you create imaginary lives, like I did?"

Gulp. Okay, pretend this is a positive thing. "Uh, sure. I was a Celtic Warrior creating my own kingdom even then."

"Even then?"

Shit, thought Carol. *I slipped up.*

"So you're still creating your kingdoms?" Shelby asked, only half-kidding.

Carol blushed and Shelby realized that was a piece of the puzzle. "Yeah."

A sizeable pause ensued as Carol reached for another chip.

"Did you go into Celtic studies because of that childhood interest?"

"Sort've. I've always been a history buff."

Carol took a sip of her Zinfandel and didn't offer any more personal tidbits, having been judged and burned by Darcy, among others. Instead, she asked, "So where all did you live as a kid?"

Okay, that's the end of THAT discussion, Shelby realized, so she moved on.

"Hawaii, San Antonio, Anchorage, and finally California City so my dad could be at Edwards Air Force Base."

"You're quite the traveler. What was your favorite?"

"Hawaii. But by being at Edwards, my dad got to introduce us to the Sierra Nevada range. How about you? Any favorite travel destinations?"

Carol simply gestured to their current surroundings.

"Of course. It's beautiful here," Shelby said, looking around and smiling. "But growing up on a farm, did you yearn for big cities or to travel abroad to get a taste of other cultures?"

"It didn't even occur to me."

"And when you got older?"

Carol shook her head. "I love it here." And then she conveniently dropped that topic by looking toward the waiter who was carrying their trout and salmon main courses.

"Here we go," Carol said.

Shelby inhaled the aroma of the grilled herbs, but the mystery of Carol was what was really reeling her in. Perhaps there would be another dinner.

Meanwhile, Darcy had packed up her guitar after playing at the outdoor happy hour around the side of the restaurant from Shelby and Carol. This time, the guitar went into its brand spanking new case, which Carol had brought to work that day for her. Darcy had to admit she loved the feel of it, a luscious leather with intricate flower and leaf carvings. It reminded her of some of the leather belts she'd worn over the years.

Then, as she walked by the outdoor seating area of the restaurant, she saw Carol. Dining with Shelby, the new guest.

Darcy felt a twinge in her stomach. She knew firsthand and from Pal that Carol had a history of taking guests under her wing, getting intimate with them...and then locking horns over how to proceed.

This time, Darcy decided, she was going to co-create with Carol a different storyline with a different ending.

Chapter Twenty

Pinyon Pass

"Yeah, we can fix that, right, Eddie?" Pal turned to her co-mechanic and co-owner of the auto repair shop, who'd been nearby as she looked at Shelby's stuck car window.

"Oh, yeah," said Eddie, "just gotta take the door off." Forty-five and as skinny as a fishing pole, he was a man of few words who let his skills do the talking. He nodded at Shelby; the conversation was done as far as he was concerned.

When Pal started working here several years ago, she'd lobbied him for changing the name of the place. He was up for that, but both of them were too cheap to spring for new signage, so the name stayed "Eddie's Auto Repair." Pal loved pretending to be Eddie when new customers came in and he wasn't around. She could tell they couldn't figure out if she was a man or a woman, since her work shirt was so loose and her boobs didn't pull focus.

"Do you guys give a written estimate or...?" Shelby asked.

"Na," said Pal. "It'll be less than a hundred bucks."

Eddie nodded in agreement and went back to the oil change he was in the middle of.

"Thanks. Sooooo, should I hang around, or wander Little Pine, or...?"

"Whatever floats yer flippers," said Pal.

Shelby smiled at Pal's goofy phrase.

"Okay, I think I saw a grocery store? I need to pick up some hiking food for the rest of the week."

"Back out on Main, north two blocks."

"Thanks."

"When do you hook up with John Muir?" asked Pal.

"Oh, ah, well, I threw in the towel on that. I'm going to stay at Sierra Glen instead."

"Ah."

What did she mean by that, Shelby wondered. "I really liked Quiet Creek yesterday and today I'm hoping to get up to Pinyon Pass."

"Well, be careful, you're gonna get a late start, probably early afternoon."

"I'll be fine," said Shelby. "It's light out 'til after eight."

"If you get into trouble, you can always fillet a trout to hold ya."

"That's right!" Shelby smiled and headed off.

At the local Little Pine grocery store, Shelby stocked up on protein bars, apples, peanut butter, crackers, cheese and nuts to tide her over for lunches this week. Then she wandered around Little Pine, swinging by Maude's secondhand shop, since Pal had mentioned her during their truck ride the other night.

Maude herself was out on the porch stacking used books and looking spry in spite of her gray hair and weathered face. She was decked out in a vintage T-shirt: "A Woman's Place is in The House...and The Senate." She gave Shelby a friendly wave, the flesh under her arm doing a jiggle dance.

"'Lo! Welcome to Maude's!"

"Thanks!" Shelby stepped onto the weathered porch and glanced around; this seemed more like a permanent yard sale than a real store. Peering past Maude, she could see the entire front room was packed to the rafters with junk. Perhaps somewhere buried in it was a bargain or two, but Shelby really didn't have the energy to find out. Garage sales, flea markets, secondhand stores, not her speed.

"How about DOROTHY ALLISON, I've got a Dorothy Allison over here!" Maude spun around and grabbed a copy of *Two or Three Things I Know for Sure.*

"Oh, gosh, thanks, but I've read that. It's wonderful."

"Ohhhhhh, you're dialed in, GOOD!" And Maude gave her a wink. *Was that a "I know you're a lesbian" wink or a "You've got good taste in writers" wink,* Shelby wondered. Probably both, but Shelby wasn't going to stick around to find out; she was feeling anxious about the clutter. She moved on, giving a little wave.

"Come again!" Maude called.

Back at the garage, Eddie and Pal were making quick work of the stuck window. Shelby approached and Pal gave her a thumbs-up. "Be done in two shakes, Shel."

"Thanks."

Pal was already calling her Shel, as if they'd been friends for years. Shelby wandered around the garage and over to the "office" area, basically a desk with a computer and a lot of paperwork on it. Up above the desk was a poster: a photo of Earth taken from a rocket in space with a bit of the rocket framing the bottom of the view. The caption up top said, "Go Places!" Shelby wondered whose poster it was, Eddie's or Pal's, and then how they ended up being a mechanic in a bump of a town instead of an astronaut on top of the world.

A half hour later, she was on her way back up to the cabins and as Pal had predicted, she started her hike to Pinyon Pass in the early afternoon.

Darcy came to work early that afternoon. Come holy hell or high water she was going to talk to Carol—and she had a plan. She didn't even need some big honkin' discussion for this first leg of the journey.

She watched the picnic table area as Carol ate her lunch. Once Carol had finished eating and was focused only on her book, Darcy approached.

"Hey."

"Hey."

"Got a couple minutes?" Darcy asked in a friendly tone.

"Just a couple. Larry has another group of friends he wants me to give a special talk to."

Yeah, yeah, another excuse, thought Darcy, but she continued. "That's okay, I won't take too long. So. I have a Big Cool Idea: Do an ACTUAL CONCERT here at THE CABINS. Not a happy hour thing, but have people sit down in chairs while I sing for an hour or so."

Carol blinked, absorbing the info.

What the hell did she think I proposed, Darcy wondered. *LET'S FLY TO MARS ON BUTTERFLY WINGS?*

"Do you want me to repeat that?" Darcy asked, trying to stay centered.

"No. Uh, I'm—could you give me some details?"

"Remember I said I need to hear how the songs work in front of an audience? Well, this is the first step. Let's invite people to a show, the vacationers, other friends, have them come on up. I'll bet Larry would love the business. Charge a little something for the concert, plus sell drinks. It's a win-win for everybody."

Carol nodded. "Ah, okay. That could be wonderful for you."

Darcy ventured further with "Do you feel like it could be a win for you?"

"I have no idea. They're your songs."

"Yes, they are. But this could impact you, your future."

Carol said nothing, she just listened politely. As the ground began to shift beneath her.

Darcy gave up on having a deeper discussion and angled for the practical instead. "I could use your help with one thing: could you ask Larry when is a good Saturday night to do it? I'm ready as soon as he is."

Carol deliberately closed her *Magic in the Celtic Otherworld* book and after some careful consideration said, "Well, I could. But maybe you need to practice dealing with the real world. If you're going to organize your own concerts and such, you'll have a lot of Larry-types to deal with."

Darcy could feel the bile rising up from her stomach. *THANKS, CAROL.* But a teeny, tiny voice way, way, way in the back of her head was saying, *Um, yeah, you know, she's right....*

"Okay, I'll talk to Larry. It's gonna be awesomingly awesome. Hope you can make it."

And with that Darcy sharply turned on her heel and went to find Larry.

Carol felt stung with that Hope You Can Make It sign-off, which sounded more like FUCK YOU. And then there were the bigger issues running like crazy hamsters on a wheel through Carol's mind: *Is this a win for me? What does it mean for me? What does the future look like?*

She opened her book and of course couldn't concentrate. After a few moments, she slammed it shut and went back to the main building to work on her tourist talk.

Darcy found Larry standing next to his out-of-town friends who were seated at their table inside the restaurant. He was at his convivial best, generating lots of smiles and laughter. *This is a PERFECT time, go for it,* Darcy said to herself. *And make Carol WRONG. Show her you can deal with the Larry-types of the world.*

"Hey, Larry!" Darcy waved at him.

Larry looked over at her and grinned.

Still smiling, excellent, noted Darcy. "Got a sec?"

He nodded and came over.

"I have an idea, it could be a win for both of us. I have a lot of new songs to try out, and I wanted to put together an informal concert here. We could do it after dinner, say 8:30 to 9:30. Have a small cover fee for people coming up from town, sell drinks. You make a little money and I get to see if my songs work."

"Sounds great. Love it."

And that was it. *Easy-peasy,* thought Darcy.

"Okay then!" she said. "When works for you? Maybe ten days or so out, Saturday night? I'll see if I can get some friends to come up from L.A."

"That could work. And put up some flyers around Little Pine and Bishop."

"Absolutely. Thanks!"

Larry nodded and went back to his friends.

Darcy trotted over to the main building, pumping her arms up and down. *Yeah, I'm turning a corner, boom-de-boom, here we go.* She opened the door and jumped over the threshold. Carol was typing something on the computer and looked up to see Darcy's mega-watt smile.

"Larry said yes. I'm gonna do it a week from Saturday."

Carol was stunned that Darcy had already set it up. She smiled and said with genuine affection, "That's great, I'm proud of you."

"I have another favor to ask. Okay if I use your computer to design a flyer and print it to put up around town?"

"Uh, sure, just give me a couple of minutes."

"Thanks."

This was all happening quickly, Carol realized. She started to finish her email and looked at the computer screen; she'd accidentally locked the caps button: CHECK-OUT TIME IS…as if a voice were screaming that.

$$\sim \text{\textit{ex}} \sim$$

"OMIGOD, THIS IS AWESOME!" Gillian shrieked as she thumbed through the *Conjurings and Wanderings* book. She and Carol had just arrived at their dorm room for sophomore year at Chico State. Now, of course, they were roommates as well as lovers. Before any luggage or bedding had been unpacked, Carol had pulled out the book.

"You pasted in everything I sent you!" Gillian noted. "Oh, this is rich and glorious!"

"Since we couldn't be together over the summer, this was the next best thing, passing the talking stick back and forth via mail!" Carol said, grinning.

"Planet StarMist is ALIVE, I can FEEL it," exclaimed Gillian as she ran her fingers over the words that they both had written plus the artwork she had painted and sent to Carol the past three months.

"It is, isn't it?"

Carol kissed Gillian on the cheek, and Gillian replied with a frisky tongue that was ready to lick every inch of Carol's suntanned body. The book got tossed onto one bed as the women fell onto each other and got to work doing some cosmic StarMist humping.

When they were spent from orgasmic climaxing, Carol murmured, "And I have ideas for further StarMist stories…."

"Do tell," whispered Gillian, playing with Carol's right nipple.

"Creatures called FlameTongues."

"Oh, that would be you going after my pussy, right?"

Carol threw back her head and laughed. "Well, yes, but not in our book. A FlameTongue is like a Komodo dragon lizard but one that breathes fire. It represents the male hatred and judgment energy that's been on the planet for so long."

"Ah. Very good, very good," Gillian said as she continued to massage Carol's breast.

"Do you want to hear the storyline?"

"Uh, sure."

Carol paused, she could tell Gillian had checked out a little. *Maybe this is a bad time, just go with the sex afterglow and leave the FlameTongues 'til later.*

"I'll tell ya when we're under the oak tree. Bring your paints and we'll do it up right."

"Sounds great," said Gillian.

And with that, Gillian scooched down to Carol's nether regions to go for some more FlameTongue fun.

~ ❦ ~

Shelby crossed rushing Pinyon Creek a dozen times in the early going of today's outing and luckily, she had her hiking poles. Then, as with yesterday's hike, a few miles in, she left the tree cover and was out in the bright sun. She put her baseball hat on ("Life is Good" with a stick-figure hiker on it) and tried to see Pinyon Pass off in the far distance, but there were too many twists and turns in the trail between here and there. Carol had said the pass was at 11,000 feet; Shelby could feel her hands sweating from nerves. She hadn't hiked up to that elevation in many years.

Her second girlfriend, Barbara, a high-school science teacher, was the one partner she'd been with who'd loved hiking. Together they'd conquered Angels Landing in Zion, one of the scariest things Shelby had ever done. Barb would've made sure they got to the top of the pass today.

~ ❦ ~

Eight years ago, as they pitched their tent beside the Virgin River, Barb had insisted on tackling Angels Landing the very afternoon they'd arrived at Zion National Park. Shelby wanted to please Barb. So as soon as they'd set up camp, they went to find the trailhead.

After climbing up "Walter's Wiggles," a series of twenty-one paved switchbacks (Shelby counted them to keep her mind off how hard she was panting), they reached a flat spot which Shelby thought was the end of the line. But no. Barb pointed at their ultimate destination.

"YES, HOT DAMN, YES!" Barb yelled.

Shelby gulped: looking across the way, she could see a red tower of stacked rock as tall as three football fields, towering over the valley. It had <u>chains</u> to hold on to, the trail was so precarious.

"I have a better idea. Let's go back for cocktails at the lodge!" Shelby joked, hoping to entice Barb to turn around.

"No way, this is gonna be AWESOME!"

Barb took off and Shelby had no recourse but to follow.

Shelby never looked down the whole way over. She moved at a geriatric pace, holding on tightly to the chains. When they made it to the pinnacle, ground squirrels ran around greeting them with the frivolity and abandon of cartoon characters. Shelby sat perfectly still, afraid to move from the top slab that was no bigger than her living room. And then they had to make the return trip (*Where's a helicopter when you need it,* Shelby wondered, *and could a helicopter EVEN LAND on this tiny mountain top?*). Barb wasn't fazed in the least. She headed back with as much energy as the ground squirrels.

The return descent for Shelby was a solid hour of heart-pounding fear. It was now unavoidable to look down. Cars below were the size of ants. When she and Barb finally got back to Walter's Wiggles, her knees were doing their own wiggle-wobble.

"Ya made it," crowed Barb.

All Shelby could do was collapse on a red rock in disbelief.

Later that evening, after Barb's homemade beef and potato stew (being a control freak, she did all of the cooking on their trips), it was time for some well-deserved vacation sex with the moonglow coming through their tent walls.

"Lean back, relax and I'm going to take you on the trip of a lifetime," said Barb. "Hard, soft, fast, slow, top, bottom? It's your vacation!"

Okay, that's not exactly what happened. Barb never talked during sex nor asked Shelby what she wanted. Shelby enjoyed the ride, but it was kind've like when Barb was making the stew...a one-person show and Shelby had to go with that.

～ ⚮ ～

Stopping for a brief moment on the Pinyon Pass trail in the present, Shelby wondered if she had earned the sex with Barb, as if it had been a reward for having conquered Angels Landing. Earlier in their relationship, Shelby had fantasized traveling the world with Barb—Borneo, New Zealand, Costa Rica. And Barb was the one girlfriend she'd introduced to her dad because they both had a left-brain GET IT DONE attitude.

But Shelby never made it to those exotic places with Barb. They got to a few more national parks together, but during those trips there were some hikes that Shelby had to bail on, they were too grueling. At least she'd developed a little backbone after Angels Landing, but Barb would end up in a snippy mood at not achieving her mountain goal. No peak, no sex.

As Shelby started up her current trail, she realized that's not unconditional love. She broke it off with Barb after a couple of years. At the time, she thought it was because she couldn't keep up. But hell, now she was realizing who wants to keep up with conditionals? Kinda like with Keelie who'd wanted her to ditch the bell-bottom jeans....

Would Carol care if I didn't make it to the pass today? And why am I even thinking about Carol?

She shifted to worrying about something else: the new job she and Marion had crafted. *How in the world will I be able to work even closer with Marion without dying from heartache every day?* And then there was this: *Do I even WANT the job? Wouldn't it be more fun to have a cool outdoor job like Carol's, being in nature, plus chatting with people. Okay, Carol has her hands full solving problems, but still.*

Carol. Stop it, Shelby, she said to herself. *You're doing it again.*

At four in the afternoon, Shelby sat on a rock to eat cashews and almonds while having a pleasant chat with a couple of fifty-ish women who had made it all the way to the pass—and they raved about it. "The view at the top goes on for MILES," one of them said. "And HELL, you're younger than we are. You could be up there by five and back down by seven, since coming down will be a breeze in comparison!"

Actually, this would give me something cool to talk to <u>Dad</u> about, Shelby realized. Since her parents had divorced, communication with her dad had been sporadic, just a few times a year. *Pinyon Pass, here I come.*

Meanwhile, Darcy finished up the concert flyer and emailed it to friends back in L.A., and then she grabbed some hot pink color paper Carol had lying around and loaded up the printer. "I'll put these up around here tonight and hit Little Pine and Bishop tomorrow!" she told Carol.

And with that, she was out of there.

Carol watched her go; she'd never seen Darcy so upbeat and positive. *Why can't I get behind her on this? Why am I dragging my feet?* Carol mused. *How would all of this work? Do I ultimately leave here to be with her? But if she's on the road, I can't follow her around from town to town unless she wants me to be a roadie. I have to be stationed somewhere, and it might as well be here.* Carol resolved that when she and Darcy had The Big Talk, she would point this out.

Before heading home that day, Carol wandered over to the outdoor dining area to see if Shelby had returned yet. No sign of her. Carol went ahead and poked her head inside the restaurant. Didn't see her there, either. *Hmm…she should be back by now.* Shelby's car was in the lot (*With the window rolled up,* Carol noted. *Pal must've fixed it*), so Carol knocked on Shelby's cabin door. No answer.

She's an experienced hiker, Carol reasoned, *and my job is not to hover over the vacationers like a mama hen. She's probably just enjoying the views up top.*

But Carol couldn't shake the feeling that something was amiss. *I'll wait 'til 7:30,* she decided. So she got her book, a water bottle, some granola, and went over to the Pinyon Pass trailhead and read for a few minutes. At 7:30 exactly, Carol put her stuff in her daypack and started up the trail.

Well, the older women hikers were wrong. Shelby didn't get up to the pass until nearly six; her lungs were burning and her heart was beating so loudly she thought her eardrums would explode.

The view did not disappoint—huge lakes reduced to the size of nickels off in the distance, jagged fourteeners surrounded her ("Look, dragon fangs, Roxanne!"). She longed to lounge up there but knew she needed to hustle back. After fifteen minutes and a mint chocolate CLIF bar at the top, she headed down.

Then, even worse, the women were wrong about the descent. It was not a breeze, there were a lot of rocks on the trail, so Shelby had to pick her way carefully over them. The other thing she didn't count on was the sun going behind the mountains. Even though it would still be light out for a quite bit longer, it was instantly chilly without the direct sun. Shelby took out her lightweight jacket but didn't have any other layers with her. Once she was back under the tree cover, it was even chillier. Barb and her dad yelled at her in her head, *"You should've brought layers! You should've started earlier! You should've done an easier hike!"*

Shelby was hurrying as quickly as she could but navigating the creek rocks in deep dusk shade made it challenging. She prided herself on being sure-footed. *See, look how I'm hopping from rock to rock! Don't I get points for that?*

And just as she was screaming internally at Barb and Dad, she slipped and SPLASH, down she went into Pinyon Creek.

"Damn it!"

"You should've brought dry socks!" the dynamic duo yelled.

She quickly got up and shakily sloshed through the rushing water toward the riverbank, the current tugging at her legs, making her unsteady. Just as she thought the white water would topple her, she looked up to see…Carol.

"Are you okay? Here, let me help you!"

Carol hustled over to the water's edge and held her hand out. Shelby took Carol's warm, strong grip.

"I was doing fine, really. I didn't mess up all day, I swear!"

"Of course. Here, let me dry you off."

Carol reached in her pack for a couple of bandanas and then dried Shelby's shivering legs and arms for her.

"You don't have to do that, Carol," Shelby said, fighting back tears.

"No worries, I've got it."

When Carol was done with the bandanas, she looked at Shelby and saw the meltdown coming. Carol embraced her. "It's okay, I know you're a good hiker. You were just hurrying to get back so I wouldn't worry, right?"

"Actually, yeah."

And then, sinking into the embrace, Shelby put her forehead on Carol's shoulder…and just let the sobs come.

"You must think…."

"I try not to think," Carol said. "This place has quite an effect on people and I don't judge it."

"Thank you."

After several moments, Shelby lifted her head and wiped her nose with a tissue. "I keep going over and over the past…."

"Maybe it's cathartic?"

"I sure as hell hope so."

They both laughed.

"How about some dinner?" Carol offered. "They make great chicken fajitas back at the Glen."

"I'm in."

"Just not in the creek, right?"

"Right!"

Kearsarge Pass Trail

Chapter Twenty-One
The Second Dinner

"These are GREAT!" Shelby was putting together another chicken fajita masterpiece in a flour tortilla. "And I could eat this guacamole at every meal!"

Carol nodded and saluted with a forkful of "dirty" rice that came with the entrée.

"Okay, it's because I'm starving, right? The food's really just crap?"

Carol laughed. "No, no, the food is quite good. And Larry's fanatical about the quality. He's built this place into a <u>destination</u>. Our numbers are way up over the previous owner's."

"Nice."

Wearing dry clothes and eating a solid meal were doing wonders for Shelby's outlook.

"All righty then, you've heard my list of national parks that I've visited," Shelby said. "Do you really not go on vacation, just to, I don't know, get away?"

"Mmmm...there's a stand of redwoods I like to visit on the other side of the mountain range. They must be two or three hundred years old. I stare up at them and I'm back in time."

Carol got a faraway look in her eyes.

~ 📸 ~

Sophomore Carol lay at dusk on a flannel blanket, gazing up at her favorite oak on the Chico State Campus. The twisted, muscular limbs easily covered a span of thirty feet across. Her heart felt just as large and expansive. It was going to be a glorious year. She'd gotten comfortable with her history department professors and found her soulmate in Gillian. *Maybe I'll be a published author someday and we'll create a whole StarMist series for young adult readers,* she mused.

Just then she heard gazelle-fast footsteps bounding across the quad's campus grass.

"I'm here! I'm here! Sorry I'm late!" called Gillian.

"You're not late. It gave me time to meditate," Carol said as she sat up. "Love it."

Gillian plopped down with not one but two drawing pads, plus watercolors, paintbrushes, pencils, and pens.

"I've got a start on the FlameTongues...." Gillian opened the first pad to reveal the early stages of a pencil sketch of a scary scaly creature with a tongue that went all the way out to there.

"Excellent start, you amazing artist you!"

"I wanted to ask you about the eyes. Is it okay if they go in different directions? It makes the FlameTongues seem even more foreboding."

"Yes!"

Gillian grabbed a pencil and began sketching menacing eyes, meanwhile Carol glanced over at the second pad.

"What's that tablet for?"

"Oh, I started my *Earnest* set designs."

"*The Importance of Being?*"

"Indeed," Gillian said with a big grin.

"So you got the job?"

"I think so. I just came from an <u>hour-long</u> meeting with Vinnie and the head of our Design Department, Dr. Thomas. <u>Of course</u>, Dr. T. pointed out that they don't normally let <u>sophomores</u> design senior thesis projects. <u>But</u> Vinnie went to bat for me <u>plus</u> I showed Dr. T. my designs, and his eyebrows shot to the moon! I think it's looking VERY GOOD."

"Congratulations!" Carol gave her a big kiss and then reached for that second tablet to see for herself. The renderings rendered Carol speechless. They were 3-D flowing watercolors of an Oscar Wilde world in frou-frou glory with stately pillars, embroidered couches, tables with claws for legs and opulent Persian-esque rugs.

In that moment, the earth shifted for Carol. She did remember to look up and make sure the tree was still watching over her. But she could feel Gillian speeding toward another planet, and it wasn't StarMist.

~ ❦ ~

"Um...back in time where?" Shelby asked, referring to Carol's redwoods adventures.

"Oh, lots of places, some real, some made up," Carol said, snapping back to the present. Then she quickly moved on. "In the winter, when it's really slow, I go over to Stockton to see my sister and her kids. My niece and nephew are ten and eight and I love playing with them."

"I'll bet you're a great aunt."

"Well, the kids jump all over me, so if that's any indication...."

Shelby nodded. "Yeah, that's the gold seal of approval. When the snow comes, how do you keep from going stir-crazy? Do you watch movies on a computer or read books or...?"

"A little of both. I'm not much of a movie person. But yeah, I'm always in the middle of a book. Are you a film fan?" Carol asked.

"Totally. It's what I love about Los Angeles. We didn't have any culture when I was in high school—no movie theatres, no museums, no art exhibits. You can do something fascinating 365 days a year in L.A."

Carol nodded and exhaled a wistful breath.

"I'm sorry." Shelby said. "I didn't mean to insult <u>your</u> neighborhood here."

"No, it's pretty cut-off."

"…Too cut-off?"

Carol paused and held her fork still for several moments. "Maybe. I…" And then she faltered.

"You've been so kind to me these past couple of days, can I return the favor? Is there something on your mind you want to talk about?"

"There's a lot," Carol said. "I feel…sometimes…as if I'm in a rut."

Shelby nodded sympathetically, waiting for Carol to continue, which took a few moments. When she did, the floodgates opened.

"Darcy's been after me to, no, that's not it. She's starting to make plans. But I can't live with her on the road, that would be insane. What would I do? She's not really thinking this through. I've built up a life here, and I'm not going to throw it all away for the vagaries of the music scene."

"Of course," Shelby answered politely, having no idea what the whole picture was.

"But on the other hand, I know I've been here so long that I'm risking…." and then Carol slammed on the brakes in mid-sentence.

Shelby reached across the table to hold her hand. "Never getting out of the rut?" she asked softly.

Carol gave a tiny nod. They held hands for a little bit and then Carol reached for her napkin to dry her eyes.

"How long have you and Darcy been dating?"

"A little over a year. Which is no time at all, and while we're quite fond of each other, I just can't jump into whatever crazy thing she's cooking up."

"Yeah, that's a big change and a big commitment."

"She's used to the fast lane and big city life. Once she gets reimmersed in that, she's not going to want to come back here."

Shelby nodded but wasn't sure what else to say for fear of overstepping, so she quietly finished her dinner. Carol completely stopped eating and just stared at her plate.

Shelby could see their waiter hovering off to the side; they were his last table of the evening. She signaled to him for the check. He brought it over and Shelby quickly handed him her credit card.

After their bill was paid, the two women left the restaurant and slowly strolled the property under the night sky. One of the guests came up to Carol, an angular Asian man in his forties wearing the requisite hiking jacket and pants. "Your talk on John Muir and Teddy Roosevelt was so good today," he said to Carol.

"Thank you. Is there something else I can help you with?"

"I'm not going with the group to Saddlebag Lake, I need to get back to L.A. Can you recommend a nice hike between here and there?"

"Mmm, yes, I can. Kearsarge Pass, out of Independence. It's very do-able, a gradual climb."

"Thank you, thank you so much." He smiled and went on his way.

"You're so good with the customers," Shelby observed.

"Thank you. I wasn't always. I actually had to learn how to make eye contact."

"Really?"

"That's what happens when you grow up an introverted bookworm living in…."

"Living in?"

"…Living in a small town and on a farm."

Shelby knew that's not what Carol had intended to say, but she didn't push it. Instead, she offered, "Well, you've come a long way." She was looking into Carol's eyes…and Carol met her direct gaze back.

"Thank you."

"Y'know, I've always wanted to do Kearsarge Pass. I camped at Onion Valley several years ago and we didn't get to do the big hike. I got sick on s'mores the night before."

Carol laughed.

"Live and learn. So maybe you could give me directions to…?"

"I can do one better. Wednesday is my day off. How would you like to hike it with your own personal tour guide?"

"Tomorrow? Gosh, I'd love to!" *Ah, I did it again, too much enthusiasm,* Shelby chastised herself.

"Then we shall. How about an early start? Say six-thirty?"

"Great."

And then came an awkward moment. Shelby felt comfortable enough with Carol that she thought about hugging her goodnight. But again, she didn't want to come off like an eager puppy, so she held back.

Carol wrapped things up by saying, "See you at my truck tomorrow morning with all of your hiking gear."

"Sounds like a plan."

They parted ways. And little did Shelby know but Carol had thought about hugging her, too.

Ace Hotel

Chapter Twenty-Two
Hot Pink

Darcy walked the streets of Little Pine like an evangelist in search of souls for a Come Ta Jesus meeting. Hot pink concert flyers in hand, she cornered whoever she ran into and gave them the pitch. The gang at Steve's Steakhouse and the bar crowd at Mel's were particularly excited to attend.

She put up a flyer at Eddie's Auto Repair ("Fuckin' awesome!" Pal screamed) and then drove down to Bishop to its nightspots where she chatted up locals about her shindig.

She found a spot in Bishop with strong cell-phone reception and parked her car so she could post the concert announcement on Facebook and Twitter, finally realizing social media could be a good thing. Then, the biggest piece of all, she wanted to make calls to her L.A. recording industry connections.

Man, I haven't talked to them in almost two years, she thought. She did not leave on good terms with several of her business associates; her anger had boiled over and scalded them. *Who can I call that's still in my court and understands me,* she asked herself. *How about Dougie?* He was Darcy's former manager, near fifty, had silver hair, but was eternally rock 'n' roll young. He'd always been an ardent fan, Darcy knew, but most importantly, he had let her fume 'n spew about the Powers That Be in the recording world.

Then she remembered the Ace Hotel incident. The one thing he might hold against her was the night she burned her recording contract in a very public display outside of the Ace Hotel performance space in downtown L.A. And then she posted the minute-long film on YouTube.

But he did end up laughing about it. "Gotta give it to ya, Darce. That was some performance art, heh-heh-heh."

Darcy loved his laugh, he pretty much laughed at everything. *Okay, I'm starting with Dougie.* She speed-dialed his number on her cell phone. It rang and rang...and then went to voice mail. *Is he away from his phone or did he see who it was and chose not to answer?*

"Hey Dougie, Darcy here. Long time no, but I've been doing a lot of healing and SONGWRITING, and I have a concert coming up—a week from Saturday. It's way out of town but it's totally gonna be great. Call me and I'll give ya all the deets! Can't wait to talk to you and catch up!"

Okay, keep it rolling, who's next? Paula in Promotions at Warner Records? Paula had joined her in railing against the Man Machine out in the parking lot more than once. *Here we go,* thought Darcy. She called Paula's <u>office</u> number, not her cell, so Paula couldn't see who was calling.

"This is Paula."

"Paula, it's a blast from the past, Darcy! How's it going?"

There followed a few moments of stunned silence.

"Uhhhh, fine. How's it going with you?"

Darcy could hear the trepidation in Paula's voice. *Uh-oh.* Paula once physically restrained Darcy when she leapt up to go after the V.P. of Sales in the middle of a strategy meeting.

"Very, very well. Healing and songwriting in equal parts, up here in the Sierra Nevada Mountains. In fact, I have a concert coming up, and I wanted to see if I could get a couple of old buds to come up and hear my new work, best ever."

"Uhhh, o-kay...."

Darcy could still hear the hesitation from Paula. *Shit, this was a terrible idea.*

"A week from this Saturday night, up in the hills north of Bishop. I'd be happy to get you a room in Bishop, my treat."

"Uhhh, kinda short notice, I have plans already."

"Sure, I understand. How about I email you the flyer and you pass it around? I'm sending it to lots of people, too, this isn't all on you."

"I should hope not."

Oh fuck, I really miscalculated this one, Darcy realized.

"Of course. Thanks for your time, Paula, bye-bye."

Darcy got off the phone as fast as she could; her mouth went completely dry. *If Paula is this cold...how will everyone else be? Shit, I may have burned too many bridges,* Darcy sensed. *Dear God, let Doug call me, please, please, please.*

Author Nancy Beverly at Kearsarge Pass

Chapter Twenty-Three

Kearsarge Pass

"Which campsite did your family stay at?" Carol said as she parked at Onion Valley campground. She and Shelby then unloaded their packs from the truck bed.

"Right up that path...God, it was only like ten seconds from the car, but I can remember dying from a lack of oxygen as we dragged our equipment up there."

"Yeah, we're at ninety-two hundred feet."

Shelby stared toward the campground area.

Carol asked, "Wanna go look at it, for old time's sake?"

"...Nah. Let's not re-live the past," Shelby answered.

Shelby put her pack and baseball hat on and noticed that her last remark registered with Carol.

"Unless YOU want to," Shelby offered.

"No, I don't have any close ties to this area. I'm good."

They left the asphalt, and as they started up the Kearsarge Pass trail, Shelby could already tell she was going to have a better day today, both on the breathing and the emotional fronts.

"Either this trail is more gradual or I'm getting acclimated."

"Probably both," Carol said, raising her hiking poles in the air, "Here we go!"

Shelby raised hers, too. "Yes!"

This hike had no tree cover at the start of the expedition, but there was a rushing creek nearby, and that was the only sound for several minutes. Carol looked around frequently but silently, taking in the vistas and vegetation huddled against the gray rocks.

Carol hadn't talked a whole lot during the drive up here, either, which Shelby appreciated. Megan, a former crush, could talk for DAYS. When they first met, Shelby thought the chatter was entertaining and smart (Megan was a television writer and stand-up comedian). Shelby got to go with her to a few TV show shoots plus see her perform comedy routines at various clubs, all very glamorous for an Air Force kid.

"Tonight was crazy!" Megan would say. "That guy before me ruined the whole atmosphere, he was about as funny as burnt toast, man I had my work cut out for me, but I think I killed it opening with political riffs, and THANK GOD the crowd got in my court, AND they weren't too drunk, if you go on last sometimes you get drunk laughter and—"

HELLO, I'M OVER HERE! RELATE TO ME! CONNECT TO ME! Shelby thought nearly every time she was with Megan.

"Yikes," said Shelby in the present.

Carol stopped and turned around, "Yikes?"

"Someone I kinda dated but mostly fantasized about," Shelby admitted. "I was remembering her Wall of Sound monologues."

"Why did you date her?"

"She went to cool Hollywood events and I envisioned we'd be on the red carpet with photographers...you know...."

"Are you a cool events kind of gal?"

"Not really. But…." *Oh, shit, I get to open a vein again,* Shelby thought. She finally added, "But I wanted people to see that this cool person liked me. That I was worthy of…." She couldn't finish the sentence out loud. *Love.*

Carol nodded that she understood.

After a few moments and with her composure regained, Shelby said, "Okay, enough about me. Back to you."

"I knew you were gonna say that," answered Carol with a grin.

"Mmmhmm. So what kind of rut are you in?"

"Wellllll, you know how your boss was the latest in a long series of something? Darcy is the latest in a series of something for me."

"What's the series?"

Carol flipped through her mental catalogue and came up with, "Short-term."

"I know that word," said Shelby.

"I knew you did."

They walked along for a bit before Carol added, "A horseback riding instructor. An English teacher at the high school."

"And they were short-term because…?"

"They moved away. Everyone moves away."

"Gosh, it's so beautiful here, that's hard to imagine. Why did they leave?"

"Lack of opportunity. Darcy's a classic example. She's not getting the audiences she needs, so it's not artistically fulfilling."

"It must be hard to meet women all the way up here. I'm surprised you found some."

"You must have a big selection in Los Angeles."

"Yeah. I just need to choose more wisely."

"What would that look like?"

Shelby stopped in her tracks. "Well, I'd choose someone who is actually interested in me. Duh. That sounds so obvious now."

"There must've been things about the women that you really liked, though, right?

"Of course. To a one, they were funny, sexy, smart. I'll just angle for dull and stupid next time."

"Oh, that'll solve everything," Carol said and they both cracked up laughing. "And I like how you said, 'to a one.' That's very literate, that should go over well with the bottom feeders you'll be going after."

They giggled themselves silly, and when a couple of teenaged hard-core hiker guys in scruffy beards passed by, they gave the women "WTF?" looks. Shelby and Carol laughed riotously all over again.

"Man," Shelby said, wiping tears of laughter away. "Sure feels good to laugh."

"Yeah, sure does," agreed Carol.

Another quarter mile up the trail, Shelby felt comfortable enough to ask, "So what are YOU going to do differently next time?"

"Ummmmmmm...I have no idea."

"Do you want there to <u>be</u> a next time?"

Silence.

Well, that spoke volumes, Shelby thought.

Finally, Carol said, "Hypothetically yes. Realistically...?"

"What, you think love isn't realistic?"

Carol stopped, bent over, and put her head on one of her hiking poles. Shelby wasn't sure if this was an emotional time-out or a physical one.

"Are you okay?" Shelby bent down beside her.

Carol said a very subdued "Yeah."

Shelby wavered about offering her next thought. Then she came up with a way that might be gentle and yet helpful. "Maybe there aren't enough fish in your fishing pond up here."

"And just how would we re-stock it?" Carol asked, slowly standing upright.

"Uhhh, I hadn't thought that metaphor all the way through. How about, either you bring in the fish or you fish elsewhere. You could organize lesbian hiking trips at Sierra Glen...."

Carol snapped at her, "And then they all leave at the end of the tour?"

"I'm sorry." Shelby backed off completely.

Carol turned and started up the trail again. This time there was silence for several minutes.

They came to a woodsy section of gnarled and twisted trees at a rocky outcropping. Carol ran her hand on the curvy lines ingrained in the bare-naked wood where the bark had fallen away.

"My dad would know but I forget. What kind of trees are these?" Shelby asked.

"Foxtail Pine, cousin to the Ancient Bristlecone Pine. Ever been to the White Mountains just across Highway 395?" Carol asked, gesturing due east with a hiking pole.

"Nope."

"There's a whole grove of the Bristlecones, some are nearly 5,000 years old. And when you consider how long it takes 'em to grow, maybe a hundredth of an inch of girth in a growing season, they're amazing."

"Wow." Then Shelby thought for a few moments and added, "I can identify."

"How so?"

"I'm a slow grower, too."

Carol smiled, all traces of her snappishness gone. "Nothing wrong with slow. It gets the job done. I think modern society is too in love with fast."

Shelby nodded and then asked, "What makes these tree trunks so twisted?"

"The elements, ice and wind. I like to think it gives them character. Modern society loves smooth."

Shelby nodded again. "That's L.A."

"So I've heard."

"What's the largest town you've ever been to?" Shelby asked.

Carol thought for a few moments. "San Francisco. I went with Pal once on one of her barhopping expeditions."

"It's hard to picture you doing that."

"Oh, I didn't barhop. I went to City Lights bookstore, browsed for hours and then brought my new books back to the Castro District to read over coffee."

Shelby took that in. She'd been to San Francisco once and loved it. "Maybe you just needed a better tour guide."

Carol half-shrugged and Shelby decided to change the subject. "When are we stopping for lunch?"

"Up ahead, another ten or fifteen minutes at a lake."

"Perfect."

They found a grassy spot right next to Flower Lake, an azure gem that lived up to its name, as lavender flowers with curling petals covered the surrounding area. Shelby unrolled her seat cushion to lie down on, with her head against her pack to admire nature from a different angle.

"Wow, more Foxtail Pines," she said, looking straight up.

"Yeah," Carol said as she plopped down a few feet away. "In the days of the Celts, Northern Europe was covered with forests so thick it's said that a squirrel could hop from branch to branch without touching the ground."

"I love that image!"

Carol nodded.

"You're quite the tree expert," said Shelby. "Have you thought of dating a tree?"

Thankfully, Carol laughed. "I guess that would solve all of my problems."

"Be careful having sex—aim for the smooth parts."

They both laughed again.

Shelby rolled over and ran her finger along the delicate purple edges of a flower. *How does something so fragile survive at such a high altitude in such harsh conditions for so much of the year?* she asked herself. And then she rolled the other way and contemplated the same question about Carol.

Carol felt Shelby's eyes examining her, so she sat up and got a Fuji apple out of her pack. Shelby, too, sat up and reached for her lunch of peanut butter 'n crackers and another mint chocolate CLIF Bar. The rest of lunchtime was enveloped in silence. Shelby marveled at the clarity of Flower Lake, hoping she was getting some clarity in her love life. Carol pondered if perhaps dating a tree was <u>her</u> next move.

The last couple of miles to Kearsarge Pass were more challenging, but Shelby still felt she'd found her stride. When they got to the top at midafternoon, Shelby did a victory jig. "Whoo hooo, wow, made it, yes! Wait 'til I tell Dad, holy shit!"

Carol threw back her head in laughter.

"Okay, I'm a city slicker, sue me," Shelby retorted, but then Carol joined in the victory jig and they clicked hiking poles together as the finale.

When the dancing was done, they stood quietly and looked around. Cutting across the top where they stood was the Pacific Crest Trail, traversing a vista of barren rock punctuated by a few glacier blue lakes and small patches of forest.

"I can feel my heart opening," Shelby whispered. "The view, it's...." She couldn't even put it into words.

"Yes," agreed Carol, closing her eyes, letting the mountain air cleanse and relax her.

Then they sat on some granite rocks for a well-deserved snack; Carol unpacked brownies from the restaurant and Shelby got out some fancy cheddar and crackers. As they devoured the goodies, they chatted with several "through" hikers, adventuresome sorts who were doing the entire Pacific Crest Trail, their skin burnished by the sun, their clothes a little worse for wear.

"I couldn't do that," Shelby said, as they waved goodbye to a group heading onward to the north.

"You probably could if you put your mind to it. But would you WANT to is the bigger question."

Shelby's first thought: *The PCT, another cool thing to tell Dad!* Her second thought smacked her hard: *Wait, why am I always racking up things to tell Dad?* She stopped in brownie mid-bite.

"What? Do you want to?" asked Carol.

"Uh, probably not. Better to let this hike be enough."

"Sounds like a plan," said Carol.

When it was time to go, they stood and stretched their calves and shoulders to get ready for the return trip. Then, before putting their packs on, they stood side-by-side gazing at the panorama, one last time. Shelby, without thinking or overthinking, put her arm around Carol's shoulders, gave her a squeeze and said, "Thank you. This was as good as doing the John Muir Tour."

And Carol put her arm around Shelby's waist, gave her a squeeze and said, "You're most welcome. The pleasure was mine."

They stood there for several minutes in that pose, neither of them feeling the need to let go. They just felt comfortable.

Chapter Twenty-Four

The Third Dinner

Darcy drove up the two-laner from Little Pine toward Sierra Glen a good couple of hours before happy hour. She knew it was Carol's day off and figured she might catch her at home and have the Future Life Together Talk. Carol sometimes got groceries and did laundry down in town during the morning and then hung out at home piddling around the rest of the day. When Darcy pulled into Carol's gravel driveway, though, no truck. *Well, maybe she's doing extra errands,* Darcy figured.

Darcy drove on up to Sierra Glen to talk to Larry and share her plans, which would be a fine way to spend the extra time. Larry was behind the counter in the main building working at the computer when she walked in. He glanced up.

"Hey, Larry." He nodded hello but kept on typing. "Uh, is now a good time to chat about the concert?" she asked.

More nodding, more typing.

"Okay. Well, flyers are up around town, everyone is excited, even folks down in Bishop. I've also invited friends from L.A., whoo hoo! I'm thinking as the restaurant empties out, we can begin moving those chairs outside. Pal's gonna help set them up. All I need from you, really, are a few lamps."

She waited…and wondered if he was feeling testy at her or was just up to his eyeballs in business stuff. She could hear Carol's bird clock ticking on the wall. Finally, Larry saved his document while saying, "Yes, I have a few standing lights."

"Great. If you want waiters to take drink orders, I'll let you handle that, whatever you think is best."

He nodded and finally looked right at her with a gentle smile. Her heart opened and words spontaneously came out. "I'd like to apologize, Larry. For how I acted when I first got here. I wasn't in a good space and I took it out on you and Julio. I'm so sorry. And I'm beyond grateful you suggested I play here, it's been really healing. Thank you."

He nodded. And smiled a big grin.

She smiled back and then headed out the door to go find Julio and apologize to him, too.

A bit later, happy hour went smoothly. A few people listened and applauded, which was more than Darcy was used to these days, so she was grateful.

A little after seven, she packed up, headed back down the two-laner, turned onto Carol's gravel road…and still didn't see her pickup truck. *Huh.* Darcy drove on down to Little Pine, and toodling down the main drag, in front of Steve's Steakhouse, she saw, finally, Carol's pickup truck. She peered through the restaurant's window…and saw both Carol and Shelby.

Shit, thought Darcy.

Steve's was a hoppin' happenin' place, and with some wine in them, the gals chatted like old friends.

"Oh, let's see…*Casablanca, When Harry Met Sally, The English Patient.* I'm a hopeless romantic when it comes to movies," Shelby admitted.

"I'm pretty sure a couple of those didn't have happy endings," Carol observed wryly.

"Yeahhhhh, you're right. I hadn't really looked at 'em that way before."

"Maybe you'd better find some other favorite films."

"Okay, I'll add that to my action plan." Shelby saluted her thanks to Carol with her wine glass and then took a sip. "So, what about you?"

Carol thought for several moments, and Shelby could tell she was wrestling with something.

"Okay, don't laugh. *Braveheart*," Carol said.

"Why would I laugh? Wait, maybe I will laugh—are you a Mel Gibson fan?"

"No, I was a history major, and I fell for the spectacle and hokum," Carol said. "And it's what you want history to be. Raving mad heroes fighting 'til their death for what they believe in."

"Absolutely. Anything else besides *Braveheart?*" Shelby asked.

"Ohhhh...the *Lord of the Rings* movies, *Edward Scissorhands, Pan's Labyrinth, The Princess Bride....*"

"I see a trend," Shelby said, chuckling.

Carol nodded. "The present world as we know it is overrated."

They both laughed. And then Shelby noticed a faraway look in Carol's eyes.

~ ❦ ~

One Friday morning in October, Carol was waiting in the food line at the campus cafeteria. To while away the time, she contemplated the next plot twist in the StarMist story she and Gillian were working on. *What could the FlameTongues do to <u>themselves</u> to cause their blindness? What if they kept staring at the main StarMist Goddess and <u>that</u> caused—*

"Hi!"

Carol turned. It was perky MaryAnne from the Drama Department.

"Oh! Hi, MaryAnne, how's it going?"

"GREAT!"

As far as Carol could tell, MaryAnne was always doing great. *I wonder what her secret is,* Carol thought.

"What's the latest great thing?" Carol asked.

"I got cast in the mid-winter one-acts—two different roles, complete opposites, a wild nutcase and an insecure introvert! I can't wait!"

"Fantastic," Carol said, smiling and nodding.

"How's your adventuring on Planet StarStruck going?"

"StarMist, and it's going fine."

"Sorry! Yes, Mist!" MaryAnne eagerly waited for details.

"Gillian and I write a bit in the evenings," said Carol.

"Ohhh, you're <u>writing</u>, not getting a group together and acting it out?"

"Right, and Gillian does artwork for the book, but…."

"But?"

"There's not much time because of her set design project."

"Ohhhhh, right, *Earnest.*

"Yeah. And I'm just trying to adapt. Between classwork and the scene shop…she comes back to our room and just falls asleep."

"Have you thought of helping in the scene shop on Saturdays? Anyone can pitch in."

"Uh, no, I hadn't considered that," said Carol.

"I go sometimes. They play music, we have a blast."

"Well, I'm working on my own stuff, too. I have a big paper this semester. Probably on the Goddess Morrigan."

"Oooo, that sounds cool."

"Tater tots?" said a male voice.

Carol looked over and realized they had reached the food. A student worker in a hairnet and two-times-too-big red plaid work smock was twirling a giant spoon and waiting for a reply.

"Sure." And then to MaryAnne, Carol said, "Thanks for the suggestion."

The next Saturday, Carol kissed Gillian goodbye and sent her off to the scene shop. And then she dithered about whether to join her. *Well, if I stay here, I'll just stare at my Morrigan research and wish I were with Gillian, so why not go?* At a few minutes before nine, she put on old jeans and an old gray T-shirt and headed over to the theatre's scene shop.

"Got a paint brush for me, too?" Carol asked as she came up behind her lover, who was already barking orders about what color the living room flats were to be painted today.

"HEY! To what do I owe the honor?"

"I thought it would be fun to see you in your element. And wide awake."

Gillian laughed…and also blushed. "I'm sorry."

"No worries," Carol responded.

Gillian handed Carol a paint brush and enthusiastically introduced her to one and all. Soon the SkilSaws were screaming as they tore through wood and someone cranked up U2's *Beautiful Day* at full volume.

And it <u>was</u> a beautiful day. Eight hours later, student workers had built and painted all of the flats, hung the fake chandelier and laid into place the set's wooden floor. Carol and Gillian stood in the first row of the theatre admiring the handiwork at the end of the day. Gillian was both grateful and exhausted, her hands coated in wood dust, her brow in sweat.

Carol gave her a hug. "This is your doing. This is amazing."

"Thank you. And thank you for coming," Gillian said.

"It was a ton of fun and you have a good crew here. Over-the-top and dramatic, but still." They laughed.

"That's us. Will you be joining us for further adventures? We hang the flats next Saturday. That's the lingo, 'hang.'"

Carol took a deep breath. She'd been contemplating something all afternoon and now could feel her voice about to shake as she tried to pull together her thoughts. "Uhhhh, I, it's, you, yours...."

"But this isn't <u>your</u> thing?"

"It could be my thing, it's creative and fun and I'd get to see you. But...I have my own stuff to do. My Morrigan paper, to name one. So, I think I won't be joining you in the hanging of the flats. But thank you for the invitation."

"I understand. Totally. And when we're done with *Earnest*, you will see more of me, the awake me, I promise."

"Thank you."

So Carol dove into her Morrigan research...and it was like wading through cold oatmeal. She just couldn't get as excited about a character that didn't seem as real to her as what she and Gillian had been creating. Every night at her dorm room desk, her mind wandered but did not conjure. To keep her creative juices flowing, she kept adding bits and pieces to the FlameTongue storyline in the homemade storybook.

～ ❧ ～

Finally, opening night of *The Importance of Being Earnest* came, and both Carol and Gillian put on crazy colorful outfits, replete with bow ties, scarves and hats, to celebrate the big event. They took their seats in the back row just before the houselights dimmed, and Carol gave Gillian's hand a squeeze. And when the stage lights came up on the magnificent set, Carol's jaw literally dropped. "Honey. Seriously. OMIGOD!" She leaned over and kissed Goddess Set Designer.

The opening night party at a swanky club in downtown Chico was equally fun—free booze and food! The college kids went apeshit. Gillian got totally plastered and Carol finally tasted champagne for the first time.

"Do you like it?" inquired Gillian in a low, sexy voice as Carol sipped from the fancy crystal glass.

"Kinda. Yeah. I can't see making it a nightly habit but it's good for occasions like this."

"So how is Morrigan coming? Is she coming? Is she all wet and excited?"

"Ahhh, I think that would be overstating the case."

Gillian laughed and then yet another person complimented her on the set design...and Carol was left to sip champagne solo. *What am I going to do?* Carol wondered. *I haven't written a word of the paper yet and my research is all over the place. I don't have a coherent theme or thesis or whateverthehell I'm supposed to have.*

She gazed over at bubbly Gillian swigging some more bubbly. *I really am on Planet StarStruck, MaryAnne was right. I'd rather stare at my characters in the storybook and talk to Gillian than do my schoolwork. I'm so fucked.*

Carol got up early the next morning (Gillian stayed in bed 'til noon, then woke up with a massive hangover) and started flinging sentences together. She kept at it all day and all night Saturday and Sunday and turned in what she had Monday afternoon. She got a big fat C on the paper. She'd never gotten a C on anything before. She was practically a straight-A student in high school and had done pretty well so far here at Chico State.

Damn it, thought Carol.

~ ❧ ~

Where did you go just now?" Shelby inquired in the present at the restaurant.

"Oh, back to college. I used to conjure up stories with my girlfriend Gillian. We wrote them down in our own book, she illustrated them. That's where my love of fantastic realms really took flight."

"Ah. Wonderful."

"Yeah."

Shelby could tell from Carol's tone that things were less than wonderful, that there had been complications.

"Want to talk about that era?"

The jukebox was now playing *Crazy Little Thing Called Love* and combined with the raucous din of drunken tourists, it all made Carol feel nauseous.

"Or not?"

"I don't know. It's so loud in here...."

"You look a little pale. What if we get our dinners to go and find a quieter spot? I'll go tell the waiter."

Carol nodded and Shelby got up from the table to track him down.

A handful of moments later they were in Carol's truck heading up toward the mountains, with Shelby feeding Carol sweet potato fries.

As they came to the gravel road that led to Carol's cabin, Carol instinctively took her foot off the gas.

"Hmm?" asked Shelby.

"Oh, sorry. Uh, I'm used to turning here. This is the road to my place."

"Why don't we go there?" said Shelby. "It's quicker than heading all the way up to Sierra Glen." Carol slowed to a stop. "If that's okay. I'm sorry, I didn't mean to invite myself over."

"No, no. It's just...except for Darcy, I haven't had anyone over in a while. I'm out of practice. And...."

"And..."

"I'm not much of a housekeeper."

"That's okay. You've been so kind and nonjudgmental of me, I can return the favor."

Carol nodded and pulled onto her road. In a half a mile, they arrived at her cabin and Carol cut the headlights. Shelby peered out the window, it was pitch black.

"Hang on, I'll turn on a light."

Carol got out of the truck first and switched on an outdoor light, then Shelby followed her up to the deck.

"I keep meaning to get a timer. God, I fix things all day at work, the last thing I want to do when I get home is take on another project."

"Sure." Shelby looked around: a cozy cabin with a wooden unpainted exterior, a steep tin roof for snow to easily slide off, monstrous tree shadows, and in the branches themselves, "Hoo-hoo, hoo-hoo."

"You have your very own owl?"

"Two of them. Hang on for a sec and you'll hear the other one answer back," whispered Carol.

They waited…and sure enough, "Hoo-hoo, hoo-hoo" came back from a different direction. Shelby and Carol smiled at each other.

Carol opened the front door, and as Shelby started to go in, she saw something sticking in the ground off to the side of the deck.

"What's that?"

"Huh? Oh, a sword." And then Carol went on inside.

Shelby blinked. "Where'd you get it?"

"Drama Department."

"Gillian?"

"Yeah."

Shelby followed her in.

"I'll clear off a spot on the table for us."

Carol set their dinner bags down on her four-foot-by-four-foot dining room table and shoved aside books, magazines, and mail. Shelby's first look was at the table, which, all things considered, wasn't too bad, her own dining room table had similar items stacked on it. And then she glanced over at the small living room and hoped that Carol didn't see her eyes pop out of her head.

There were more stacks of books, magazines, and mail along with tools, framed photos that never got hung, old tax returns and hiking equipment. *Yikes. It's an episode of Hoarders,* thought Shelby. And then she quickly course-corrected, *DON'T BE YOUR MOM. No judging. Or YOUR DAD, everything doesn't have to be military orderly. Oh, jeeze, are those bike parts? Stereo parts? Random mechanical parts? Shouldn't all that stuff stay outside? Pine cones? Rocks? THEY'RE DECORATION, DON'T JUDGE! Cover, Shelby, cover, you're staring too long!* She said out loud, "I love all of your books, wow, what a great collection!"

And it was the truth; Shelby did love the floor-to-ceiling bookfilled shelves along two walls. "I'll have to take a browse after dinner."

And with that, she sat down to join Carol at the table. Shelby stuck to appreciating her shrimp scampi and set aside any talk of relationships.

Carol once again had ordered the eggplant lasagna and realized she and Shelby were having the IDENTICAL meal she and Darcy had gotten for their one-year anniversary. *Is this a good thing or a bad thing?* Carol wondered.

"Do you buy your books at a bookstore or online...or...?" Shelby asked.

"Mostly online. When I go to Stockton to visit my sister, I'll buy some. But yeah, I have things shipped to a P.O. box down in Little Pine."

"Have you thought of getting a Kindle or something?"

"Yeah, but I just love the feel of paper books."

"Oh, gosh, me, too," Shelby said.

"And I like to highlight things and make notes in the margins."

"Me, too."

"I'm sorry, I don't have any wine to offer you," said Carol.

"That's fine, the one glass I had at Steve's will do, especially at this altitude."

They laughed and then Carol asked, "Where do you get your books?"

"Oh, I have two favorite places. One is downtown, The Last Bookstore, and then closer to me is Vroman's in Pasadena. I once went on a...."

And then Shelby stopped herself. *Open mouth, insert foot.*

"Went on a...?" Carol asked.

"A first date at Vroman's."

"Was it awful, is that why you stopped yourself?"

"No, it was okay. I was just trying to steer clear of relationship stuff."

And there followed a few moments of awkward silence until Carol said, "Oh, go ahead. Misery loves company."

They both chuckled.

"It was with Amy, who was part crush, part girlfriend. She agreed that we were dating but she also wouldn't 'get serious.' I was way more interested in her than she was in me, that was the crush part. Anyway, our first date we spent wandering around the aisles of Vroman's picking up various books and reading random passages to each other, pretending everything was about us or for us. Then...."

"Then?"

"We went back to her place and had awesome bone-rattling sex."

"Congratulations."

"Thanks."

"And then what happened?"

"Well, she traveled a lot. She was a pharmaceutical rep, so I'd see her every other weekend. About the time we'd get into a deeper place, she'd take off. So I'd spend the intervening days fantasizing about a life together...but I couldn't get her attention long enough to actually create it...."

Shelby sighed. "Okay, I've spent this entire vacation thinking about my past. Enough!" She stabbed a shrimp. "Take that, Keelie, Barbara, Megan, Amy, Marion!"

Carol laughed as Shelby popped a shrimp into her mouth, chewed a bit and then said, "Damn this garlic butter sauce is good!"

After dinner, Shelby excused herself to head for the bathroom down the little hallway, not just to pee but to see if she could find mouthwash to take away the garlic taste.

She flicked on the bathroom light, glanced around and immediately tensed up. *DON'T JUDGE, DON'T JUDGE, DON'T JUDGE.* Even though it was tiny, Carol managed to pack quite a bit in here: old *National Geographic* and *Sierra Club* magazines, an umbrella (*Maybe it had been drying in the tub one rainy day?*), a decorated mask from *Ah, what? A harlequin costume ball?* But no mouthwash, so after peeing Shelby just grabbed some toothpaste and massaged her teeth and gums with that. *Oh, great, now I smell like spearmint,* she thought as she reached for the bathroom light.

Standing in the bathroom doorway, she noticed a room right across from her…and something was odd. It didn't seem like a traditional bedroom, there were things hanging from the ceiling. Shelby quietly tiptoed toward the mysterious room and let the spill from the bathroom light illuminate it. *Was that chainmail on the wall? A cape? Another mask?*

"Sightseeing?"

Shelby's head turned sharply. Carol had magically appeared around the corner.

"Uh, yeah. Looks fascinating. Sorry, the light caught the—what is that—chainmail?"

"Yeah."

Carol carefully came toward her and went into the room. She turned on a small lamp that added a soft glow to the décor. Then she motioned for Shelby to come in.

"You're sure?" asked Shelby.

"No, I'm not. Every time I do this, I take a huge gamble."

Shelby swallowed and could hear the hurt in Carol's voice.

"The alternative is," Carol said, "you don't get to know me. Which do you prefer?"

Wow, okay, a line in the sand, thought Shelby. She took a breath and stepped across the room's threshold. Unlike the rest of the cabin, it was not filled with random, piled up junk...it was a space dedicated to all things Celtic. Yes, that was really chainmail.

"What's that?" Shelby's eye was drawn to a piece of metal the size of a quarter sitting on a shelf.

"It's called a Celtic knot," Carol said as she picked up an engraved brass pendant. Carol tenderly rubbed her finger over the raised triangular-shaped knot.

"Did you used to wear it?"

"Yes. It was a gift from Gillian." Carol stared at it, but Shelby couldn't read her expression. Carol tenderly put it back on the shelf.

Shelby looked at the wall and reached out to touch a poster of a tree with swirling green branches on the top half and brown tangled roots on the bottom half mirroring the swirls.

Carol put her hand on the poster. "The Celtic Tree of Life. *Crann Bethadh.* It symbolizes harmony and balance in nature...uniting the upper and the lower worlds. It also represents rebirth. The leaves fall, the buds bloom again in the spring. Well, I'll stop there, it goes on and on..."

"It's okay. I like learning new stuff."

Carol smiled and relaxed a little.

"My dad taught me the craziest things," Shelby said. "Most of the time he was such a hard-ass, but then he'd get on a roll talking about silent movies or John Muir or homemade beer and it'd be fascinating."

"That sounds cool, actually."

"Yeah. So, people...judge you for this?"

"Darcy is the latest. I let her write whatever songs she wanted. I didn't judge, and then she started to nag me about what I write. I'm just so tired of apologizing for who I am and what I care about."

～ ❦ ～

"The truth is that I hate to think about other people reading my books," Miranda said. *"It's like watching someone go through the box of private stuff that I keep under my bed."*

Twelve-year-old Carol closed her eyes to further absorb those powerful words from *A Wrinkle in Time.* A millisecond into her reverie, the bedroom door flung open.

"YOU DIDN'T KNOCK."

"Actually, I did," said Carol's mom, her arm cocked on her hip like crowbar.

"You didn't wait for me to say 'enter'!"

"You never say enter," Mom steamed.

"WHAT DO YOU WANT, MOM?"

Mom's other arm went to the other hip. Now she was in her Wonder Woman Queen Organizer of Social Clubs Major Domo of Bridge Group Stance.

"Your birthday is coming up, Carol Ann; do you want a party?"

"You had to make a special trip to my room for THIS?"

"Carol, I tried to bring it up not once but twice—"

"—That is so you, 'not once but twice—'"

"—at dinner and you had a book glued to your hand and wouldn't look up."

"My books are my lifeblood."

Carol's mom yanked *A Wrinkle in Time* out of her daughter's hand.

"MOM! JESUS!"

"<u>Language</u>."

"Christ, Christ, Christ!"

Carol's mom grabbed the sides of the paperback book and ripped it right down the spine.

"NO!"

Throwing the book to the floor, Mom added, "They may be your lifeblood but there are other connections that need to be maintained for you to live in this world, this house. You don't show anyone in this family any respect. I ask you a thousand times a week to pick your clothes up off the floor, to take out the garbage, to weed the garden—you don't even talk to your sister. Did you know she sprained her ankle yesterday at her soccer game?"

Carol just sat on her wildflowers bedspread with her arms crossed and refused to acknowledge any of that.

"I assume you don't want a party then."

Carol continued to stare at the torn pages of her beloved book on the floor.

"<u>Fine. Be a hermit</u>." And with that, Mom spun on her heel, exited and slammed the bedroom door behind her. The SLAM caused photos of wolves Carol had collected from magazines to fall off their perch on her bookshelf.

Carol reached over the side of the bed to pick up a torn page from the broken book. But she couldn't read it, her eyes were too watery from tears.

$$\sim \text{\textit{ß}} \sim$$

Shelby took in the artifacts, the costume pieces, and even spied a handmade storybook with the title *Conjurings and Wanderings* written on the cover...and smiled.

"This room...is filled with...integrity...and love," Shelby said, looking right at Carol. She could see Carol's eyes welling up, so she put her hand up to the side of Carol's face. Carol's head bent down wearily.

Shelby pulled her closer, allowing Carol to put her head on her shoulder, much the same way Carol had done after pulling Shelby out of Pinyon Creek and drying her off.

Shelby felt the softness of Carol's hair as she stroked it a few times. All of the craziness of trying to find the tour, of trying to please her dad, of fending off past love life regrets melted away.

Carol whispered, "You smell like spearmint."

Shelby cracked up laughing. "Yeah, it's YOUR toothpaste!"

Carol laughed, too, and they left the Celtic room, heading to the kitchen to get decaf.

Over coffee, they stood side by side and perused Carol's bookshelves, discovering what they had in common and what book recommendations they wanted to glean from each other.

"I see you have Dorothy Allison," Shelby noted.

"Love her. Doesn't pull any punches."

They were standing so close to one another, Shelby could feel Carol's body heat as they faced the bookshelves. *We feel like bookends,* Shelby thought.

"I don't see any Anne Tyler here," Shelby noticed.

"It's true, I'm remiss with Anne. I'll get right on that."

"*The Accidental Tourist* is one of my all-time favs."

"What book shaped you the most when you were a kid?" Carol asked.

"Shaped me? Gosh, well, I loved the classics, *Jane Eyre, To Kill a Mockingbird,* and then there's *The Hitchhiker's Guide to the Galaxy.* How about you?"

Carol took a few moments and then said, "Of course *Lord of the Rings*. But there was a book where you could 'dial' a number to get to pick the page, so the story changed every time. I can't remember what the name of the book was, but I was entranced, even at age five, by the idea of making up my own stories."

Shelby nodded...and then they heard the owl pair outside "Hoo-hoo-ing" to each other. They giggled and then Shelby asked, "God, what time is it?"

"Almost midnight."

"Do you have to get up and go to work tomorrow?"

"Sure do," Carol said, not worried at all.

"Well, I should go. I don't want to get in the way of good customer service."

Carol smiled.

They put on their jackets and piled into Carol's truck. The drive up the two-laner was completely quiet. Except for Shelby starting to wonder inside her head and heart how Carol felt about her. *Stop it,* she thought. *You vowed not to do this, so don't.*

Carol pulled right up in front of Shelby's cabin, left the lights on and the engine running. And then she didn't hesitate in saying, "I had a great time today, Shelby."

Shelby looked over at Carol, "Me, too. Thank you for everything."

She put her hand on the door handle at the same time that Carol leaned toward her...and Shelby had her answer. Shelby let go of the door handle and leaned in for a kiss. Both of their mouths opened, hungry for connection. When they came up for air:

"Spearmint tastes good."

"Glad you like it."

A beat passed.

"See you tomorrow," Shelby said and then she got out of the truck, having no idea what the hell was going to happen next.

Vernal Falls

Chapter Twenty-Five
Blinded

Shelby rolled over and looked at the bedside clock's glowing numbers: 5 a.m. *Why couldn't I have done this spontaneous wake-up thing Monday morning,* she wondered. *Because I needed to be <u>here</u>, not on the John Muir Tour.*

A tiny bit of daylight appeared under the drapes. She looked above her head and saw the photo of Yosemite's Vernal Falls. There wasn't enough light to read the John Muir quote but she knew he was saying everyone needed nature to heal body and soul.

Have I healed? Do I feel better? Yes. Marion now seems like a shiny cat toy that distracted me.

Oh, but then I have to face her next week when I go back to work.

Do I really have to go back to work? Can't I just stay here and play with Carol forever?

What did she mean by that kiss?

I can't stay here forever and just run around in the woods. Jesus Fucking Christ, get a grip, Shel.

She rolled over, pulled the covers up to her chin and went back to sleep.

That morning, Carol stood behind the counter in the main building holding her coffee and looking at today's "to do" list: unloading the firewood shipment when it arrived, getting Julio to fix the shower in Cabin 4, fixing some window screens...figuring out what to tell Darcy...figuring out what to do about Shelby.

What did I mean by that kiss? Impulse control malfunction? Yeah, that's what I'll tell her! Figure out what to do? Hell, do nothing, she'll be gone by tomorrow...

...Do I want her to be gone?

Over at Pal's home the same morning, Pal and Darcy were standing in the kitchen waiting for the coffee to brew.

"Thanks for saying yes to setting up the chairs for the concert, Pal."

"Dee-lighted to, Darce, any time."

"Well, I don't know that there will be ANOTHER time, but thanks for doing it THIS time."

They didn't often cross paths in the morning; Pal had to be at the auto repair shop by eight, well before Darcy's Sierra Glen happy hour gig. But Darcy had been getting up early now that she was on the concert mission, calling and emailing old contacts.

Pal was pouring the coffee into mismatched mugs ("Valvoline, Keep Your Engine Running Clean" and "Bishop's Miner Days! Yee Ha!") when Darcy let out a WHOOP as she turned on her cell phone.

"DOUGIE CALLED ME BACK LAST NIGHT AND LEFT A MESSAGE!"

"Congrats," said Pal as she handed Darcy the Yee Ha mug. "Who the hell is Dougie?"

"Former manager." Darcy listened to the message and began doing little jumps on her toes, trying not to spill the coffee. "He's coming, he's coming, he's coming!"

"I didn't even know he was having sex."

Darcy put the phone and mug down on the counter so she could do a cheerleader scissor jump and fist-pump. "YES! I am back in the game!" And then looking at the mug, she added, "Yee Ha!"

Pal laughed and angled for the back door. "Let the games begin!"

Pal went off to work, and Darcy began pacing the living room. *Doug's message sort've makes up for seeing Carol's truck at Steve's Steakhouse last night,* Darcy thought. *So don't dwell on the Carol Crap, figure out what to say to Doug during the return phone call.* As she walked in circles, she told herself to sound professional and responsible, have concrete ideas, don't bring up past fuck-ups. *Wait, what if he doesn't like my new songs? He has to like the songs!*

Then she stopped in her tracks. *Why did he leave a voice mail at midnight? Was it because he was out late at a concert...or was it because he knew I'd have my phone turned off and he wouldn't have to actually talk to me?*

At nine-thirty, she hoped she'd waited long enough and called him. Went straight to voice mail. *Shit, shoulda waited 'til ten o'clock. Oh, well, leave a big honkin' upbeat message.* "Dougie, SOOO good to hear from you and that you can come. I will get you a room and send you directions on how to get here. Call me back and we'll strategize on where to do the recording, how to market, where to tour. I've got my act together, man!"

She paced around some more...he didn't call back right away, so she decided breakfast was a good idea. She cracked an egg so hard the shell broke into a million pieces and landed in the mixing bowl. She threw that egg out, mixed some Bailey's Irish Cream in her coffee to steady her nerves and then successfully cracked a second and third egg.

By lunchtime, he still hadn't called back. Darcy's mind whiplashed. *He's busy, he can't be that busy, he hates me, he likes me otherwise he wouldn't have called in the first place.*

Driving up to the cabins in the afternoon, Darcy drummed the steering wheel with her fingers as she schemed. *Maybe I could have dinner with Doug before the concert, no, I'll be too nervous, we'll meet after, the concert's only an hour or so, he's a night owl, I'll get Larry to let us sit in the restaurant, I wonder if I should get flowers or a gift basket for his room?*

She bounded into the main building as if she'd had four cups of espresso, hold the Baileys.

"I need a room for Doug!"

Carol looked up from the computer. "Who's Doug?"

"Sorry, former manager. Next Saturday night, not this Saturday night."

"I'm pretty sure we're sold out. It's the height of tourist season, Darcy."

Darcy exhaled so forcefully, the front counter's ivy planter leaves shook. Carol carefully checked the reservations for the following weekend. "I'm sorry, but we're booked solid."

"Well how did that Shelby person get a room with no reservation?"

"We had a last-minute cancellation, completely a fluke thing. I'll let you know if we get another one. But if I were you, I'd book a room in Bishop or Little Pine."

"Little Pine only has that shitty Motel Pine Cone and—"

"—Pinehurst—"

"—and Bishop is ninety minutes away!"

"Darcy, Pinehurst isn't that bad, and it's not like he's royalty—"

"—To me he is!"

"Okay, go with Bishop; Jesus, calm down. Focus on the music."

Darcy did some deep breathing (the ivy leaves got a good workout). "I am, but if I can't get the music OUT to people, get attention, get concert dates, then what the fuck good is the concert?"

"I thought you just wanted to HEAR the music to pick the right songs. Now it's all about marketing and touring. Remember what got you tied up in knots in the first place?"

Darcy stared at the floor. It was wood and Larry had gone to the trouble of refinishing it last winter because it had years of footsteps and dirt ground into it.

"Look how much attention Larry puts into this place," Darcy said. "It used to be all raggedy and now it's a real class operation. I'm crafting a class gig."

Carol nodded and softened her tone. "I know, honey, and I have no doubt you'll create it. Just do it one step at a time. Let me check online to see what's available in Bishop, okay?

"Sounds like a plan, Stan." *Hate the therapist talk but like the support.*

"The Creekside MIGHT have an opening, let me call." Carol dialed their number. "Hi, do you have a room available a week from Saturday, the twenty-seventh? Thanks." An eternity passed; Darcy rubbed the ivy leaves for comfort or good luck or both. Then Carol looked at her. "They do, do you—"

"—BOOK IT!"

Darcy handed over a credit card and Carol read the number to the clerk to book the room. As she waited, Darcy toyed with the idea of bringing up seeing Carol's truck at Steve's Steakhouse...but she held her tongue. *Focus on the concert, focus on the future, Darce.*

Shelby stayed in bed reading *Wild* until it was nearly time for lunch. She wasn't sure what to say to Carol so she thought perhaps avoiding her was the best choice.

Finally, hunger pangs drove her to get up, get dressed and get going.

She walked through the cabin area as if on a secret recon mission, keeping an eye out for Carol. She saw her talking to Julio, so she ducked behind a tree. *I need a prepared speech,* she thought to herself. *Something like, "I think you're great, but I gotta get back to L.A." Man, too blunt.*

She peeked around the tree. Carol had gone back inside the main building. Shelby hurried along to the restaurant and kept her nose buried in her book during lunch. She peered over at the picnic area...

Carol was doing the same.

As she paid her lunch bill, she saw the hot pink flyer for Darcy's concert taped to the cash register. *That could be fun. Stand at the back of the crowd, hold hands with Carol and sway to the music. Carol doesn't really seem to be dating her. God, I avoided the make-out session with Pal on the blanket under the full moon because I didn't want to go back to L.A. and fantasize about her. And just what the fuck am I doing now?*

Maybe I should just go home right this second while it's still light out. Leave my key in my room. Okay, that's rude. I really like Carol.

God, what should I say to her?

Just then, as Shelby stepped off the restaurant's deck, she looked over at Carol's picnic table. Carol had set her book de jour aside and was fixing a window screen from Cabin 6. At the precise moment Shelby looked over, the screen whipsawed up and hit Carol in the nose.

"Oh, my God!" Shelby exclaimed as she ran over to her. "Are you all right— wait— ice, let me get—"

"—I'm fine, it just nipped the top of my—"

But Shelby was already running back to the restaurant. She bolted inside on High Alert: "I NEED SOME ICE, PEOPLE!"

Various staffers scrambled and one handed her a paper cup of ice.

Shelby hightailed it back to Carol.

"Okay, got ice—and don't say you're fine."

"I'm fine."

"It's bleeding." Shelby took a piece of ice and put it on the bridge of Carol's nose.

"Ow! That stings."

"You'll thank me later. It'll keep the swelling down."

"Thank you." Then Carol added, "I feel like a trained seal balancing a fish on my nose."

They both smiled.

"Why were you fixing a screen alone? That's a two-person job."

"Julio's busy. Here, I can hold the ice." Carol reached up and tried to take the ice chip but Shelby batted her hand away.

"It's the least I can do. For all you've done for me this week."

A few moments went by and then, "My nose is numb."

"Okay, but where's that Betadine that you used on the kid with the fishhook in his ear?"

"Office."

"Let's go."

"Yes, ma'am."

A minute later in the office, Shelby put a dab of Betadine on Carol's nose ("Not too much. I have a Tourist Talk this afternoon, I have to look good for my public"). Then they went back to the wayward window screen on the picnic table.

"Do you have duct tape?" Shelby asked.

"It's required for my position and my identity."

"Manager and Dyke-in-Charge?"

"Exactly."

"My dad used to tape down the frame and then he could use the spline thing to put the new screen in."

So they taped the frame down and got out the spline.

"Looocy, you got some 'splinin' to do..." Shelby said in a heavy Cuban accent.

Carol laughed as she rolled the roller end along the groove and got the screen sandwiched in tight.

"Well done," observed Shelby.

"Teamwork," said Carol.

Their eyes met...and simultaneously they said, "About last night...."

"Maybe I shouldn't have kissed you," Carol quickly added, un-taping the screen from the table.

"No, you were just...uh, I don't know, following your instincts...."

"And where has that gotten me?" Carol asked.

"A question I posed to Pal about my own self. You know, me, the idiot with all of my crushes and fantasies." Shelby sighed.

Carol held the screen in front of her like a shield. "Well, everyone leaves. Yeah, I follow my instincts and then people move away."

"...And I'm about to leave, too."

Carol nodded sadly.

"I could come back for a visit. Come see the fall colors...."

Carol gave the tiniest of nods which didn't really signify yes. Then she turned away from Shelby to head over to the cabin whose window needed the new screen she was carrying. She disappeared inside. Shelby couldn't resist waiting for Carol to magically appear in a window frame, which she did. Carol opened the window, aligned the top edge of the screen frame to its groove and then pulled on the tabs at the screen bottom to fit it snugly into its spot. As if she'd done it a blue million times. *I wonder if she gets tired of these chores,* Shelby thought. *The day-to-day stuff we all have to do. It's not all hiking and CLIF bars. I wonder if they put storm windows in, come winter.* In Alaska, she recalled, she and her dad used to put in storm windows and take out the summer screens together. They'd wash the storm windows with newspaper and some sort of vinegar mixture her dad had concocted. *Perhaps Julio would help Carol. So much of life is a two-person job.*

She went back to her cabin and packed up all of her gear except for tomorrow's travel clothes and of course her volleyball champs nightshirt. She fingered the shirt. The entire neck was frayed, the letters on the front were cracked, the bottom hem was coming out. She lovingly folded it up... and put it in the wastebasket. *I'll sleep naked tonight, fresh start.*

Shelby brought *Wild* with her to Quiet Creek in the afternoon, finding a sunny spot where she could lean against a warm boulder. She couldn't concentrate, though, so instead of reading she soaked her tired feet in the chilly creek water. *I should hike more, then my feet would be used to these adventures.*

Later, walking back to her cabin, she saw a group of a dozen or so tourists gathered at a firepit / mini-amphitheatre area. There was an easel with a photo of John Muir in Yosemite on it. Huh. She went over...and realized Carol was doing a presentation. Shelby quietly joined the group at the back to listen in.

"Then when John Muir was in his twenties, he worked at a carriage factory in Indiana, but that wasn't a great fit. He started to worry. He wondered if he was doomed to stay there."

Shelby noticed that Carol paused; both women let the words sink in.

"And then one fateful day, the point of a file broke off and flew into his eye."

The crowd gave a little gasp, as did Shelby. And she was getting a double meaning—Carol had just been smacked in the face with a wayward window screen.

"He was temporarily blind for a month, and during that time, he had awful dreams. He really pondered his fate. And you know what?"

"What?" asked Shelby.

Everyone, including Carol, turned to look at her. She blushed, embarrassed. Carol smiled, glad to see her.

"John Muir realized he had to be true to himself. He didn't want to be in a factory or settle down or conform. He decided to become an explorer. In 1867 he set out on a thousand mile walk from Indianapolis to the Gulf of Mexico."

Shelby mouthed the word "Wow."

"The next year, he sailed to San Francisco and then walked all the way to Yosemite Valley. It took him two months. When he got there, Muir was astonished; he'd never seen anything like it. And he'd found his home."

Carol let that resonate with the group, as they looked up at the trees and what they could see of the mountains that surrounded them.

"And he changed us. He told us we could find ourselves by getting lost in the beauty of nature. 'All scars she heals, whether—'"

"'—Whether in rocks or water or sky or hearts,'" Shelby said, finishing the quote.

The two women stared at each other. The rest of the tourists wondered what the heck was up between them.

Carol got shivers but pulled her thoughts together to conclude the talk. "Come back tomorrow and I'll tell you how John Muir helped establish Yosemite as a national park."

The group applauded and began to disperse. Shelby didn't want to disperse. She certainly didn't want to go home to Los Angeles. She watched Carol take down the easel and poster. All she wanted was to take Carol in her arms and kiss her passionately.

So she did.

Carol dropped the easel and the poster as Shelby grabbed her head with one hand and used the other to pull her waist tightly to her.

The luscious kiss went on for several moments as a few tourists turned and looked with wide eyes.

Chapter Twenty-Six

Enterprising

"I'll come see you again," Shelby whispered to Carol as the kiss ended.

Carol tried to smile but Shelby could tell it was difficult. Shelby took a couple of steps back, then Carol picked up the easel and the poster. After one final wistful look at Shelby, she went back to the main building.

Shelby turned to head for her cabin—and nearly ran into Larry. *Oh, shit, what had he seen? Surely he knows Carol is a lesbian. But if she were straight, would it be okay for her to kiss a guest? Arg!*

"Uh, hi, 'Larry' is it?"

"Yes, hi."

Dive in, just bypass the kissing thing. "Gosh, I've had such a WON-DERFUL time here!" *Shit, I'm doing it again, too cheerleader enthusiastic.* "I mean, the cabins are just perfect, very comfortable, classy, but not extravagant." *EXTRAVAGANT? When would a cabin be extravagant in the first place?*

"Thank you." Larry absolutely beamed.

Whew, okay, this is going fine, He's not going to call Carol on the carpet for the kiss.

"And I've enjoyed the food, really a cut above what I would expect this far from town, and the music during happy hour is just perfect. I could write a review online if you'd like."

"That would be great, thank you," Larry said. Then he was the one who jumped in with cheerleader gung-ho. "I was thinking about adding acupuncture and singing bowls and massage therapy."

"Ohhhh, wow, nice." Shelby wasn't sure all of that was needed, but why rock the boat? "You're so enterprising," she added.

He smiled. "Thank you. Enterprising is one of my favorite words."

And just in case, I'll throw in one more compliment, Shelby thought.

"Carol has been great, too. She pays attention to the—" *Wait, not the customers by kissing them!* "—details!"

Larry nodded. "She does. I don't know what I would do without her. I had a hard time when I first bought this place. I wanted to make it better. She helped me every step of the way...."

Shelby nodded and thought he was going to add something, so she waited, to give him space to do that.

After a moment he said, "My wife had just passed away, so...I needed all the help I could get."

"Ohhh, gosh, I'm so sorry, but I'm glad things here have turned out well. You've done a beautiful job."

He smiled again, did a little bow, Shelby returned the Asian custom, and they went their separate ways.

The next morning, Shelby woke up before the alarm in her cabin went off, and the first thing she heard as she opened her eyes was Larry in her head saying, "Enterprising."

The word kept coming back to her as she drove home. By the time she'd arrived in L.A. later that afternoon, she had a plan.

Part Three

Snow at Kings Canyon

Chapter Twenty-Seven

Dougie

Darcy spent the next few days making a lot of follow-up phone calls to supportive friends back in the City of Angels to see if they would come up for the concert. And damn-it-to-hell-and-back, she was still waiting for some kind of confirmation from Doug about whether he was spending the night in Bishop. Then there was the not-quite-support from Carol she kept sensing.

Pal came home from work early, just before Darcy would be heading up to play at happy hour.

"What brings you back to the homestead at this hour?" Darcy asked, glancing up at the kitchen clock.

"Work was slow. How's things with you, buckaroo?"

"Still making calls and shit. Hoping for certain peeps to show, you know. Changed my playlist like eight million times."

"It'll be great." Pal said, heading for the fridge and an ice-cold beer. "Soooo, would I be correct in assuming you're moving on after the concert?"

"Well, kinda. I want to record the new stuff, I want to tour again...." Darcy said.

"But?"

"Carol."

"Annnnd...?"

"Can I tour and stay in a relationship with someone who lives up in the mountains? I've healed a lot, thanks to her. And being on the road is so hard without a stable home to come home to. Maybe there's a way to make it work. Part-time here, part-time playing gigs."

"All righty then," Pal said in a rare moment of self-restraint. "Let the cow chips fall where they may."

And just then, Darcy's cell phone made a whoosh noise. Darcy pulled the phone from her hip pocket, dropped it, fetched it with fumbling fingers and then after reading the text, screamed, "DOUG'S GONNA SPEND THE NIGHT IN BISHOP!"

"Score!" Pal said.

"It's all gonna work out, it's all gonna work out."

"Yeppers." *The definition of Work Out was still up in the air,* Pal sensed, but she kept that particular thought to herself.

Chapter Twenty-Eight

The Good, The Bad and The Ugly

Shelby went back to work Monday morning. She sent a terse text from the parking lot to Randall and Howie giving them a heads-up: "I'm back." She didn't want to explain the week to anyone via email, phone or even in person.

Walking down the hallway to her office, the main theme from director Sergio Leone's Spaghetti Western *The Good, The Bad and The Ugly* was playing in her head (another Dad favorite film). Those lonesome, haunting high notes added to her nervous showdown's-a-comin'-with-Marion feeling.

She could hear Marion well before she saw her.

"Hell-to-the-YES! We are going to ROCK Spring Fling Weekend next year!"

Spring Fling? Jeeze, can I take her amped up energy for the next eight months? Shelby wondered. Can I take listening to her make dates with

Jane...and watch her plan a wedding? What if she continues to not have boundaries and DOES ask me to help organize it, like Howie had said.

Boundaries. Hmm, better curtail the finger-pointing, she thought.

As Shelby slow-motioned to her desk and quietly put her shoulder bag down, Marion came flying out of her office about to head to An Important Meeting. She saw Shelby and stopped dead in her tracks—if she were a cartoon character, there would've been skid marks on the carpet.

"You're back!"

"I am."

"Are you all right?"

Oh Lord, how to answer that.

"Randall said you weren't feeling well. You ran out of here so fast, was it the stomach flu?"

If only. And God bless Randall for covering for me.

"I'm feeling a little better. Thanks."

Marion nodded. "Well, I didn't get to thank you for the birthday party, that was <u>so sweet</u>."

"You're welcome," said Shelby

"Do you have the energy to do the Summer Splash event Saturday?"

Shelby suddenly realized it conflicted with Darcy's concert up at Sierra Glen. *Uh oh.*

"It's okay if you don't," Marion added. "I'd like for you to get well so we can gear up for back-to-school events."

"Thank you, thank you very much, I appreciate that."

"Okay then. Got my nine o'clock with the Assistant Vice Chancellor. I think she's going to approve your new position."

Then spur of the moment Shelby blurted out, "I need to apologize for something."

"Okay." Marion waited with a gentle smile and open, sympathetic eyes.

Shelby hesitated. She'd never felt this vulnerable with Marion before.

"You know that game we play, 'Two Words,' and the goofing around we do?"

Marion cocked her head, as if that were a foreign concept and she couldn't quite recall the details.

"Well, I shouldn't have been doing that with my boss. It was fun, but it wasn't appropriate. I'm sorry for my part in all of that."

Marion nodded but, no, she wasn't going to show any culpability. She put on her Formal Business Posture and pivoted away from Shelby to head down the hall.

The new position. Working with Marion will be torture, Shelby decided. *I must implement my Enterprising Idea.*

The rest of the morning was challenging due to Shelby's fog-brain. She had a few hundred emails to wade through and a mountain of paperwork to surmount.

Just before lunch, she looked up from the invoices and meeting requests to see Howie coming around the corner. He held his arms out wide. "Sweetie! Welcome back!"

She got up and let his embrace swallow her.

"Do you feel better? How were the mountains?"

"I do, and the mountains were amazing!"

"Now who was it you were traveling with? Randall had said some guy named John?"

"John Muir. He's been dead quite a while, but how about if we have lunch and I'll explain."

"Fabulous. I'll tell Randall. Sushi okay?"

"Perfect. See you downstairs in the lobby at noon." Howie gave her a big kiss on her cheek and an extra hug. "Thank you, Howie."

Over sushi with the guys, Shelby hit the highlights: the directions flying out the car window, the Milky Way at night, the stunning hikes, especially Kearsarge Pass. The guys hung on every word, as if they were watching an adventure movie.

"Did you do these hikes on your own? Weren't you scared without the tour group?" Howie asked.

"I did some on my own, but there were always other people on the trail, so I didn't get into trouble except for--"

They leaned forward in their seats.

"Did you see a bear?" Howie exclaimed.

"No, no...."

To bring up Carol or not to bring up Carol? That Is the Big Question, Shelby knew.

"Except for what?" Randall asked, suspecting something.

God damn him.

"Well," Shelby said, covering," I came down from one pass, and it was getting late and a little dark. I slipped on some rocks in a deep creek. But other than that, I was fine."

Randall took a delicate sip of his green tea; he wasn't satisfied.

"You gotta be careful!" Howie admonished, pointing his chopsticks at her.

"I was. I am." Brushing aside Carol drying her off from the creek and other Romantic Moments, Shelby jumped in to explaining her Big Idea.

"Being up there reconnected me to all the great hikes and camping trips I had with my family when I was growing up."

"Your military hard-ass father trips?" Randall asked.

"Okay, yeah, there was that aspect, but I really do love the mountains. They make room for this healing thing that's beyond words. I thought I could start my own tour company, take people on day hikes or short campouts to introduce them to the wonders of the Sierra Nevada. Not the week-long John Muir thing, that's too hard-core for most tourists."

Howie beamed. "I LOVE it! Mountain Girl, I can SOOO see you doing that!"

Randall looked puzzled. "Um, is this financially viable?"

"Thank you, Howie, and I'll be working out a business plan, Mr. Wet Blanket. The place where I stayed, the owner, Larry, is VERY enterprising, he LOVES new ideas. He's really spiffed up his cabin resort and I think this will be Value Added for him."

Howie toasted her with his sake, Shelby clicked her Diet Coke to his cup.

"Look, you guys, I've been here at the university since I graduated. I don't want to stay forever. If I'm gonna branch out, now's a good time. And frankly, being around Marion today was creepy and not fun."

Randall gave her a wink and raised his green tea in a salute. He was on board.

With the single brain cell she had left at the end of the workday, Shelby contacted a friend over in the university's business school to set up a chat about how to do a business plan. And then she tried to make a reservation in Bishop at the Creekside Inn for Saturday night. They were full-up but the guy running the front desk said he'd take down her name in case there was a cancellation.

Hell, I could bring my tent and camp in the woods…or Carol's yard, thought Shelby.

Chapter Twenty-Nine

The Concert

"Where do you want this lamp?" Pal asked, waving it as if she had a giant *Star Wars* lightsaber.

"Easy, Luke. Right here." Darcy pointed to the side of her performing stool on the outside deck of Sierra Glen's restaurant.

"Got it." Pal moved the lamp and made a WHOOM *Star Wars* lightsaber sound effect.

"How do you want the chairs set up? Rows? Semi-circle?"

"Uhhh, let's try rows in a semi-circle," Darcy said.

"Who says you can't have your cake and eat it, too?"

Darcy had to laugh. Pal found the humor in everything.

"Thanks again for doing this."

"No problemo. Even Eddie's comin' up tonight, and he's bringing a girl, so sing some love songs."

"Already got 'em in the mix."

"It's not all lesbian shit, is it?"

"Everyone can plug into the song lyrics, that's how good tunes work."

"Love it," Pal said, angling for the dining room chairs to arrange them in semi-circle rows on the deck. "Need something to hold a bottle of water or some zippy cocktail?"

"Just water, and another stool for that would be great, thanks."

"Who's gonna introduce you, somebody's gotta do that, right?"

"Yeah. I don't know. Maybe Larry, it's his place." Glancing at the time on her cell phone, Darcy added, "I should drive down the mountain a ways so I can get cell phone service and call the Creekside Inn to see if Doug's checked in yet."

"He may not check in 'til after the concert, and you know…."

"What?"

"You could go into the main building and use Carol's office phone. Or even better, you could stop worrying. You calling the motel is not gonna make him show up sooner or better or louder or funnier."

"Yeah. You're right. As usual. Okay, back to the present! I gotta do a sound check with my guitar's amp. Can I get you to stand at the far corner and listen as I do a welcome thing and some strumming? Give me a thumbs up if you can hear me and a thumbs down if you can't."

Pal dutifully did as she was told. "THUMBS UP, ALL THE WAY, DARCE!"

And then after finishing the chair set-up, she went to get a sandwich and a beer from the restaurant. Darcy, on the other hand, snuck over to the main building to use the office phone.

~ 🙠 ~

The workweek was nerve-wracking for Shelby. Marion zoomed around like her Audi on steroids, with edicts flying out the car windows (her mouth) every few minutes.

Then, even with the friend from the business school giving tips, Shelby realized there was absolutely no way she would get a full-blown plan in place by Saturday. Plus, she had a trillion questions for Larry and Carol about the type of patrons who stay at Sierra Glen and what kind of hiking shape they would be in. *Should we have an easy to moderate hike on Saturday, the busiest tourist day? Maybe more of a hard-core hike during the week? And then what about winter, could we do snow-showing tours? That could be fun...as long as it wasn't too cold out.*

She thought about leaving work early on Friday, but Marion was in Full Fall Production Mode. Pacific University's fall semester was starting in a few weeks and there were a bunch of "Welcome" and "Welcome Back" events to implement. Shelby resigned herself to leaving on Saturday morning.

Just as she was heading home Friday afternoon, Shelby ran into Randall in the ground floor lobby of their building.

"Spontaneous game night tomorrow at our place—we just got Cards Against Humanity."

"Ohhh, gosh, I love that game!" said Shelby. "Man, I'm so sorry, I'm gonna have to miss it this time."

"Got plans?" asked Randall.

"Sorta. Old high school friend in from Cathedral City, lots of catching up to do."

"You could bring her."

"Uh, she's not much of a gamer, but thanks!"

Shelby waved and headed out the door to her parking lot; luckily Randall parked inside the building, underground, and the conversation could end.

I hate lying to him, she thought. *If this tour business takes off, I can explain later about Carol. If things work out with Carol.*

$$\sim \wp \sim$$

It was about an hour before showtime when Darcy stepped into the main building and nodded at Larry and Carol. She eyed the phone but before she could reach for it:

"How are the nerves?" Larry asked brightly.

"Doin' okay," Darcy said, and then she held her hands up and fake-shook them as if she were being electrocuted.

Both he and Carol laughed. Carol had put on a navy blue dress shirt and a black evening jacket with a light-blue silk handkerchief in the breast pocket.

"Thank you for everything, both of you. And for dressing up, Carol. I know how much you love that, ha ha."

They all chuckled again.

Then she added, "Mind if I...?" as she reached for the phone.

Larry interrupted her. "Do you have someone to introduce you tonight?"

"No, would you like to, since you're the official host?"

"I could, but Carol knows you much better. And she has on her Master of Ceremonies jacket."

Carol blinked.

"Do you want to?" Darcy asked with some trepidation.

"Sure...actually, I'd be honored to."

They all nodded at each other, it was a plan.

Darcy eyed the phone again.

"Need to make a call?" Carol asked.

"Uh, no. I need to stop worrying. I'll see you both out there in a bit."

~ ❀ ~

Shelby stopped by Schat's Bakery late Saturday afternoon. She actually sat down to eat her turkey sandwich, rather than doing the driving & dining thing. Sitting at a table gave her a chance to go over the preliminary business plan. She had a handful of hikes listed and how long they would take, plus a few factoids about each trail, each canyon, each pass. History was Carol's specialty, best to leave that to her.

It's probably a good thing I don't have it all worked out to the Nth degree, thought Shelby. *Better to float a trial balloon, tell Larry a few ideas and have some back and forth with him and not do my usual over-eager cocker spaniel thing.*

After lunch, she walked over to the Creekside Inn to see if they'd had a room open up.

"Hey there," Shelby said brightly as she pushed open the glass door.

The young man in his hipster beard and workout shirt looked up. "Hey yourself, how can we help you?"

"I think my name's on a waitlist for a room tonight. Shelby Kincaid."

He checked his computer, "There you are! Waiting!"

"And...?"

"Mmmm, too soon to tell. You hangin' around Bishop this afternoon?"

"I'm on my way to a concert up at Sierra Glen."

"Oh, yeah. I think we've got that flyer here." He turned around and went to a "Fun Things to Do!" bulletin board off to the side of the check-in counter. "Yeah, here it is."

"That's it," said Shelby.

"You know the singer?"

"A little bit. We met, ah, earlier in the summer, up at Sierra Glen. She's really good on the guitar."

"Great. Well, enjoy."

"When will you know if a room opens up?" Shelby asked.

"Most of them are guaranteed by credit card. Wait, speaking of the concert...." He went back to his computer. "There's a guy named Doug who's supposed to be at the concert, too. Maybe you two will hook up—not 'hook up,' you know what I mean. We put a gift basket in his room earlier today from Darcy."

"I know what you mean, and I'll keep an eye out for him. Thanks!"

Shelby went back out the glass door and tried a couple of other motels. Same deal, full up for the tourist season, but Creekside was the nicest. Her mother would've approved of it. Her dad would've said, "Hell, camp out!" Which Shelby actually thought she might do, she'd brought her tent just in case.

"Hey, Carol, want to cuddle and listen to the owls hooting?"

~ ❧ ~

Darcy had changed out of her torn Runaways T-shirt and into her bright-red silk long-sleeved blouse. It would keep the audience focused on her. With the low lighting, she didn't want to blend in to the wood of the restaurant and deck by wearing some muted color.

She stepped out of Larry's inner office, which he'd graciously offered as a "dressing room," and saw Carol shutting down the computer.

"How does my hair look?" Darcy asked Carol.

"Looks good. Were you going to go with lipstick or not?" Carol queried politely.

"Oh, shit, yeah, I need to do that—crap, I don't think I have any! It's been so long since I've had to think about lipstick!"

They both laughed at that one, and Carol dug into her desk drawer and pulled out some deep red lip gloss she used when doing special talks for Larry's friends. "I don't know if this is your shade...."

"It doesn't matter, anything will do, and if they're judging the shade of the gloss and not the songs, I'm in big trouble."

They laughed again. Carol handed her the tube, and when Darcy tried to apply it, looking in a mirror behind Carol's desk, her hands <u>really were</u> shaking now.

"Here, let me," Carol offered.

Carol took the wand, stood right behind Darcy, and with both of them looking in the mirror, deftly applied a coating. Darcy brought her lips into a line and filled out the color. Their faces were side by side in the reflection.

"We clean up pretty good," Darcy said.

"Yeah."

And then Carol actually stood there for several moments to drink in the closeness of their bodies. Darcy put her hand on Carol's thigh, Carol leaned in and kissed her cheek.

"Break a leg, sweetie."

"Thanks."

Then both went outside.

Shelby pulled into the Sierra Glen parking area at dusk—it was packed. *A good turnout, this is so wonderful for Darcy,* Shelby thought. And then she realized Carol might be completely distracted by all of the festivities and wouldn't have time to chat or catch up. *Play it by ear,* she decided.

She got out of her car and went over to the restaurant's patio area: it was already two-thirds full of music patrons. Larry's usual white twinkly lights were on. The first faces she recognized were the LipLock Twins, Felicia-and-Veronica. She gave them a jaunty wave; they weren't kissing, they could easily see her. They half-waved back, giving her a confused *You're still here?* look. Or maybe it was a *Wait, did you never leave?* look. Shelby decided not to get into things with them and angled in a different direction.

Then she saw Pal, who did a double take at her. Shelby did a little wave to her as well, and Pal came over.

"Hey. Didn't expect to see you here, Shelbycakes."

"I got to hear Darcy play a few times last week and loved her music so much, I wanted to support her. I had no idea this many people would show up."

"Yeah, isn't it great? Larry's over the moon."

"Yeah, I want to talk to him," Shelby said without thinking.

"'Bout what?"

Oh, fuck, how am I gonna finesse this? Pal's like a bloodhound, sniffing out clues. She and Randall should form a detective agency. Well, go with the truth, let's see how that flies.

"I have a tour group idea. I was inspired by the John Muir Tour, but I could do it out of here. We could make the trips day hikes, maybe a camping overnighter, to introduce people to the mountains."

"Nice. Does Carol know this yet?"

"No, she doesn't. I wanted to run it by Larry first."

"Well, she's the history and flora-fauna expert up here."

"Yes, yes she is."

"It'd be stupid to do that kinda thing without her. Which I'll bet you've thought of."

And in that moment, Shelby knew Pal knew Something Was Up. Shelby just gave a sphinx smile and moved on over to the bartender to get a glass of wine.

Meanwhile, Darcy tuned her guitar in a quiet area several yards off to the side of the restaurant...and ran through a few lyrics of the newer songs to warm up her voice. As she wrapped up the pre-show ritual, she looked up at the trees. "Thank you. Thank you for your guidance, your wisdom, your healing."

She walked to the restaurant and went in the kitchen's back door, sort've her version of "backstage" for tonight. The cooking crew gave her high-fives and cheers and Darcy got goosebumps. *This is real. This is really happening.*

She went out to the restaurant, which was closed, and surreptitiously peered out a window. The seating area on the deck outside was now full and had become standing-room-only at the fringes. *Holy cow. AND OMG, there's Beth and Susie all the way up from L.A.! Wait, there's Spencer and his wife Marla, they let me sleep on their couch, for Christ's sake, when I first moved to L.A. Okay, stop looking, you'll be a blubbering idiot and won't be able to sing.* She did some more warm-up vocal exercises... and then Carol came through the kitchen door.

"Ready?"

"All that and more. Let's do it."

Carol walked out of the restaurant and onto the "stage."

Shelby's jaw dropped when she saw Carol. *My God. She looks fabulous. Who knew she could do the "polished professional thing" in addition to the "mountain tour guide" thing?*

Larry led the audience in applauding and then started to do a quick speech from the sidelines. "Thank you all for coming, our first 'organized' concert…."

"C'mon over, center stage, Larry," Carol called, interrupting.

The crowd laughed.

"Yes, yes, of course!" Larry trotted to the center. He'd put on a blazer as well. His was a dignified gray, but he still had on his Sierra Glen shirt underneath.

"Anyway, this is our first of what I hope will be special events up here. Thank you all for coming! Stay tuned for more!"

The audience applauded and Shelby thought, *YEAH, more is coming! I've got just the plan!*

Carol cleared her throat, everyone quieted down.

"I first met our guest artist about a year and a half ago. Since then, she's been on a remarkable journey, one of healing and of song-crafting. Every week she plays happy hour music for our patrons, but she is so amazing, we wanted her to be front and center. She's recorded four albums prior to landing at Sierra Glen and has toured the country for eighteen years. We are so fortunate to have her here. She hopes to record these new songs very soon, so thank you for coming out and giving her the energy to take them to the next level. Please welcome Darcy Pennebaker."

As Carol stepped away to watch from the back of the audience, the group responded with wild applause, whistling and catcalls.

Shelby could tell Carol's heart was totally into the introduction. *Are things really over between them?*

Darcy stepped out of the restaurant with a huge grin and bellowed, "THANK YOU! Thank you, Larry! Thank you, Carol. Thank you, Pal. Thank you EVERYONE from near and far!"

She dove right in to the first song, an upbeat rockin' tune about a musician's life on the road, filled with grit and determination. Pal gave her two thumbs up, one for the volume and one for the gusto.

The second tune, a tribute to a little girl who dreams of becoming an astronaut, was also up-tempo. Shelby had another flash: that astronaut poster really was Pal's, not Eddie's.

When she'd finished "To the Moon," Darcy paused to say a few words, now that some of her adrenalin had been used up.

"Hey there! Whooo! It's been awhile but I'M BA-A-ACK!"

The crowd laughed and roared its approval.

"Gonna do some songs from the new album and a few older ones. We'll see how it all sounds. And if you want a great vacation spot, ask Larry to book you a room—fall colors up here are spectacular!"

"Larry yelled, "We're booked for the rest of August and September, but we have a few openings in October!" Everyone laughed.

The third tune was much slower and more introspective, a tender tribute to Darcy's father, a blue-collar man who could barely read and write.

Partway into the second verse, it happened: Darcy forgot the lyrics. "Ah, shit, don't quite have the new ones memorized yet," she said good-naturedly.

Her pal Susie yelled, "You can do it, Darce!" And the crowd roared again, backing Susie up a thousand percent.

Darcy stood there and took in the love. There was nowhere else she wanted to be. Not at the Troubadour, not in Nashville, or Boulder or New York City. She started the song again, and this time closed her eyes so she could concentrate, embracing the memory of her dad as he tried in his own way to understand her choice of being a musician.

Shelby was completely wrapped up in the songs; she'd totally forgotten about Carol and the business plan. This was an acoustic concert as good as any she'd heard in L.A.

A few songs in, Larry leaned over to Carol and whispered, "She's amazing. Why didn't we do this sooner?"

"She wasn't ready."

He nodded. He got it.

Darcy ended her set nearly an hour and a half later with another hell-fire rockin' number, this one about the crucible of love, forging us into stronger beings, even if it burns. The crowd leapt to its collective feet when she was done, to give her a standing ovation.

Darcy couldn't believe her good fortune. This was better than she had dreamed. She blew kisses to old friends—they blew them back—new friends blew some, too. She looked over at Carol, who was wiping away tears.

Darcy tried to step into the restaurant, her equivalent of "going off-stage," but she didn't get any further than putting her hand on the door-knob when the crowd started chanting, "ENCORE! ENCORE!"

She stepped back to her spot and took a swig of water.

Well, am I gonna do this? she asked herself. Everything has gone perfectly, will this next song fuck it up? But the crowd—and Carol—seemed pretty open.

"One more new one, held one back for ya."

The crowd laughed, then quieted down. Darcy quietly began picking out the simple notes....

"I met a mountain girl
Living in her mountain world
She was dancing with the breeze
And calling to the trees
She's listening to the bubbling stream
Where do you sail to in your dream?
What new world have you made
As you watch the present fade?
I thought I could sail there with you
I thought this was a world for two
Tell me, am I wrong...?"

Shelby remembered this song from when she'd first arrived, and of course, now realized it was about Carol. She looked over at Carol, whose cheeks were glistening with tears and her lips trembling. *There is no way I can talk to her right now about guiding mountain tours with me,* Shelby thought.

At the song's end, folks let a moment of silence reverberate...and then they all jumped to their feet, applauding, whooping and stomping. But Carol didn't applaud. She swayed as if she were seasick.

Darcy bowed and waved and grinned. She leaned her guitar against the restaurant wall, made a fake-out move as if she were going to go off-stage—and then waved "Oh, never mind." She dove into the crowd to hug her friends and let them bear-hug her back.

Shelby was in awe. She'd thought Darcy was good but had no idea she was this good, as in, *What the hell is she doing here?* She glanced over at Larry, who was also grinning, as if he'd won the lottery. Well, even if now was not a good time to approach Carol, it'd be a good time to chat with The Boss, she figured.

"Hey, Larry!"

Larry looked over at Shelby making her way through the crowd.

"You came back?"

"Yeah, I wanted to hear Darcy. She's amazing."

"Yes. We'll have to book her again before she gets famous and we can't afford her!"

"Good plan!"

Larry laughed.

"Hey, I know you like finding ways to make the place even more special, and I had an idea for leading organized tours out of here. The quick story is, I was supposed to do a tour further north, but I got lost and ended up at Sierra Glen. The backpack I was scheduled to do was rigorous, but I think there's room for something a little easier, like one day hikes or an overnight campout that would introduce your guests to the mountains and their history. Charge them for Carol's expertise and my organizational abilities. How does that sound?"

"Yes, yes, wonderful idea! Do you have a business plan?"

Boy, he's good, thought, Shelby. "As a matter of fact, I have a preliminary one, plus a lot of questions for you and Carol. Once we get those answered, then I could fill in the missing details."

She reached in her daypack and pulled out her current version of the plan, looking spiffy with its clear report cover. "Here ya go."

"Very good, thank you. How long are you here this time?"

Oh, shit, Shelby thought, suddenly realizing she had absolutely no idea.

"Well, I'll be around tomorrow, I think, but I could come back in a week or two, or we could talk over the phone. Whatever works for you."

"All works. I'll try to look at this tomorrow, although Sunday is supposed to be my day off, ha ha!"

"No pressure, no rush, we can always talk by phone."

"Okay." Larry bowed and dove into the crowd of patrons to soak up their good energy.

Shelby wondered if she should've just set up a time to talk Sunday, but he did say it was his day off. *Well, this is a grand start,* Shelby thought, *and now...back to Carol.*

Shelby looked around...*Where the heck is she?* Shelby dove into the crowd herself, which was challenging; it was like swimming upstream in a bunch of happy fish. Still no sign of Carol. Shelby hopped off the "stage" and angled for the main building. On her way through the Darcy fans, she actually came within a couple of feet of Darcy herself and was about to reach out and give her a pat on the back when she heard her say, "Where the fuck is he? He told me he got the motel info! Beth, did you see him in the audience?"

Poor Beth, put on the spot, went wide-eyed. "No, no, I didn't!"

Shelby piped up, "Are you talking about Doug? I know they had a reservation for him down at Creekside Inn."

"Well, he definitely didn't show."

"I'm so sorry. But you were great, this was one of the best concerts I've—"

"—I really don't care what YOU think," Darcy said, and then she stalked off to grab her guitar.

Shelby felt as if she'd been slapped in the face. *What did Darcy know about her and Carol? She must know SOMETHING.*

Shelby was torn. *Should I keep looking for Carol and incur Darcy's wrath or let everyone calm down and come back up tomorrow? And if I spend the night, where the hell should I sleep?*

Meanwhile, Carol sat in the main building's office sobbing uncontrollably, feeling naked and exposed. Eventually she crawled under her desk, curled herself up into a tight ball and hid. She could hear everyone talking and laughing outside. It was embarrassing to have her most private, vulnerable self put up for inspection in public.

Carol melted into the handwoven rug. After people's voices outside had faded away, she opened her eyes and looked at the rug. She was eye-to-eye with an Anasazi flute player. Larry had brought this rug to the office because it was one of his wife's favorites. Helen bought it when they were traveling through New Mexico and Arizona on vacation.

Carol glanced up at the photos on the back wall of the welcoming area that were from Mono Lake and Mono Pass where Larry and Helen had visited many years ago.

Larry at least had had a long-term relationship.

Now this place was his dream.

What is my dream? Carol thought

"A 'C' isn't the end of the world," Gillian observed.

She and Carol were eating their dessert sundaes in the dining hall one evening after Carol's Morrigan term paper had landed with a Big Fat Average Thud.

"Yeah, it is," Carol snapped.

Gillian held her tongue.

Carol continued, "Would you be happy with a 'C'?"

"It depends. If I did mediocre work then, yeah, let the grade reflect that. If I'd done killer work, I'd be raising hell. So, which is it for you?"

Carol threw down her spoon in anger. She knew what the answer was.

"Just do better next time, that's all," said Gillian.

Carol could feel the bile rising in her throat. *All the energy I gave to Gillian—even helping build the* Earnest *set—and this is the cavalier support I get?*

Gillian could tell that advice wasn't sitting well. "Is there some way I can help you?

"Yeah. Yeah, there is. I could use some quality time with you so I'm not always wondering when I'll see you. That'll help me focus and figure out my schedule."

"Okay. You got it."

"Date night on Saturday night. No ifs, ands or buts."

"You got it."

"Less drinking."

Gillian blinked. She wasn't going to cop to that one so easily. "How about only at big parties, opening nights and such?" she offered as a counter proposal.

"And such?"

"Birthdays? I don't know, I can't predict."

Carol didn't acquiesce quite yet.

Just then MaryAnne came swinging by. "Hey! I love make-your-own sundae night! So, Gillian, I ran into Rick, he's got the twirly thing for you."

"Twirly...oh, turntable, great!"

"He'd like to try it out later on Saturday to see if it works, he said."

"Great, great, I'll follow up with him, thanks!" said Gillian.

"I think it's a genius idea to do three plays in one evening with multiple sets!"

"Yeah, that was the plan. Thanks, MaryAnne."

"See you guys!" She bounded off.

Carol's eyes narrowed. "Turntable?"

"Yeah, to help with the one-acts."

"I thought you were done set-designing for a while."

"I didn't DESIGN this, these sets, I proposed a solution. A turntable. Rick acquired it. That's all."

"But you're going to see if it works."

"Carol, this is part of my MAJOR, part of being a team in the Drama Department. I do not drop off the face of the fucking planet until next year when I design another show. I pitch in, I help out."

"And how long will you be with Rick 'later on Saturday'?"

"I CAN'T PREDICT." And with that, Gillian threw down her spoon and stormed out of the cafeteria.

Carol was so embarrassed that she ducked her head to avoid making eye contact with fellow diners and left the building a few moments after Gillian was out the door. She paced around campus in the twilight, into the enveloping darkness. *Fuck, I have to do better. But so does she. I have to find topics for my research papers that inspire me as much as...yes, Gillian and Planet StarMist. I will do this. I will do this. I will do this.*

After thirty minutes of laps around campus, Carol stopped and looked up at her dorm building, dreading being in such a small space with such a volatile character.

"Ahem."

Carol turned around. Gillian was approaching, carrying a sword.

"I was saving this for Christmas, but now seems like the better time to give it." Gillian laid the sword across both of her own arms, so it would be seen as an offering, a gift.

"With this sword, I pledge to you my total commitment. Saturday nights are yours, m'lady. If you need more time during the week, please let me know and I shall avail myself. I will not do another design project without consulting you first."

Carol picked up the sword by its handle. "Wow, it's heavy!"

"It's real. It's the one our department used in *Romeo and Juliet* last year. Slay whatever creatures you need to with it. Fight whatever battles you must wage. But please know I love you. And I'm sorry I've been so busy."

Carol nodded, ran her hand over the intricate carved silver handle... and searched for words. "I pledge my love to you," she responded tenderly. "And I will find my own voice, my own passions, and be my own best champion for them."

Gillian nodded...and then they kissed a thoughtful kiss.

"In fact...I already have an idea for next semester's Celtic history class. I want to combine my love of trees and Celtic stuff, so I'm gonna research the Celtic Tree of Life, *Crann Bethadh*."

"Fantastic."

On a hunch, Shelby tiptoed over to the main building to see if Carol was in there, hiding after the concert. Sure enough, as she stood on the porch, she could hear Carol's sobs.

Shelby waited for several moments, torn. Ultimately, though, she headed for her car and drove all the way home, a very long and lonely five hours. Shelby walked into her apartment at three in the damn morning and collapsed on top of her bed, not even changing clothes or pulling down the covers.

Chapter Thirty

Seattle

Pal opened the front door expecting to pick up her Sunday paper... and found Darcy sprawled on the front porch lounge chair fast asleep, with alcohol fumes wafting around her.

"Just another tequila sunrise?" Pal said right in Darcy's ear.

Darcy woke with a start.

"By the way, that was one of the best concerts I've ever seen, and I've seen my share over in San Francisco."

Darcy hoarsely said, "Thank you."

"So, lemme guess, that Doug guy didn't show."

Darcy nodded.

"Is he the ONLY person who can help you get goin' on this career reboot?"

Darcy shook her head no.

"There's your answer."

Darcy nodded.

"Good. I'm gonna read the Sunday funny pages and make an omelet. You want one?"

"Uh, just coffee for now."

Carol woke up on Sunday toying with the idea of calling in sick to work, but it was Larry's day off. Ostensibly it was so he could go to church, which he and Helen used to do. He had trouble finding a church he liked that wasn't two hours away, so that went out the window early on. But he did steer clear of the office on Sundays for the most part. Once upon a time Carol had really pushed him to enjoy a day for just himself, so to now make him come to work....

I'd better go in, Carol told herself as she threw the covers off.

When she got to the office, the phone answering service and the email box were both full to the brim with people wanting reservations in October. Darcy's sales pitch from the stage had really enticed folks. *That will thrill Larry, Carol thought, but am I excited about it? Is it as exciting as Darcy doing her concert and recording a new album?*

After a cuppa joe, Darcy showered and walked slowly to Little Pine's main drag to meet a few friends for brunch at Steve's before the gang left to go back to L.A.

Over scrambled eggs and toast (skipping the mimosas everyone else was having), Darcy also went for some humble pie and asked her friends for suggestions on ways to record the album and get it out there, since most of her industry bridges were burnt to a crisp. When Beth (who was a financial planner and as practical as they come) brought up their mutual musician buddy Sam, who'd relocated to Seattle, Darcy felt a shiver of truth run through her.

"I'd been hoping for L.A. but...."

~ ❦ ~

"So I met someone on my mountain adventure...." said Shelby.

Randall smiled and stabbed his grilled asparagus spear with his fork. Monday's lunch was at the Quicksilver Café, an upbeat favorite with university staffers.

"We hit it off like I've never hit it off with anyone before."

"Mmmhmm."

Is he being patient or did that have an undertone of "Yeah, right."

"Bear with me here," Shelby said.

"If she weren't there, would you go through with this business plan to lead hikes?"

Shelby stared at her fish taco. She loved fish tacos. And the beach in August when the water was warm enough to play in. And the bike path early on a Sunday morning before everyone and their Uncle Ned was on it. And plays downtown at the Mark Taper Forum. And, of course, Vroman's Bookstore.

"I don't know. But I have to do something."

"I applaud you for moving on from Marion, that's fantastic. But consider what you're going for, what exactly is the dream?"

She took a bite of her fish taco and chewed on it and the question.

"Well, I've been here since I graduated. Carol's been at her job a long time, so...."

"So you're both in a rut, but you moving up there won't get her out of <u>her</u> rut."

Shelby moved on to the roasted yams and more cogitating.

"I'd love to build my own business. I thought I'd be a travel agent when I was younger. So, this isn't completely left field thinking," she said.

"Understood. Just picture working up there without…what's her name?"

"Carol."

"Carol."

Monday afternoon, Darcy called Seattle Sam, and by golly, he remembered her and Beth and her gang from hanging out at Hotel Café in Hollywood years ago. He'd even played bass on Darcy's second album.

He had quite a few thoughts on the Seattle music scene.

Shelby could not picture working up at Sierra Glen without Carol. But that didn't stop her from taking the business plan out and looking it over when she got back to her desk after lunch.

It stood up to her critical eye. This is a good idea, she thought. And she flashed back to her dad who was of the Nothing Ventured Nothing Gained School of Action. *I'll call Larry in a few days, after he's had a chance to look at the plan. At the very least, I could get his feedback and even if things don't work out up north, maybe I could start a tour company here in Los Angeles, for adventuresome lesbians.*

~ ❧ ~

Monday, late afternoon, Darcy drove up to Sierra Glen from Pal's house. It felt completely weird to have not talked to Carol after the concert. *Was she just giving me space to celebrate with my friends or...?*

Darcy parked her Delta 88 and went over to Carol's picnic table, where she sat with her standard book and standard lunch of tuna fish. *Man, is she capable of change?* Darcy wondered.

"Hey you."

Carol looked up, startled, but then added a half-smile.

"Didn't get to talk after the concert...." Darcy let that hang there to see where Carol would go with it.

Carol nodded politely and said, "You were great." She might as well have said, "The grass is green," it had that much enthusiasm.

"Thanks. Uh, mind if I sit?"

Carol gestured for her to join her.

"Are you okay?" Darcy asked, sliding onto the picnic table bench. "I looked for you after the concert and didn't see you."

Carol closed her book carefully.

Uh oh, thought Darcy.

"...I loved the songs, Larry and I—well, everyone—thought you did an outstanding job."

"But?"

"The final song...."

Darcy had been afraid of this.

"It hurt to have my soul laid bare on a public stage. You should have at least consulted me or told me or warned me."

"I don't consult or warn or tell people about my art. That's a step just short of censorship."

Carol stared at her book cover, running her thumbs over the corners, as if smoothing out crinkles.

"And in case you're wondering," Darcy added, "no one and I mean NO ONE knew that song was about you. My friends thought it was about ME or a past lover or a fictitious lover. They just appreciated it for what it was."

"What was it, really, Darcy?"

"It was my gift to you. For all you've done. It was my way of saying I loved being here."

Carol didn't seem to completely buy that.

Darcy pushed onward. "I really, really wanted to go on a journey together. Beyond Sierra Glen."

Carol didn't nod but she didn't squawk, either.

"So. I've made a decision. I'm not going to go back to Los Angeles. I'm going to move to Seattle. Fresh start."

Carol gave the teeniest of nods. And added absolutely nothing else. Darcy waited several moments and then thought, *Go for it.*

"Meet me at our favorite glen past the restaurant after happy hour. You know, the one where you first heard me playing."

Carol looked at her, perplexed.

"It'll be fun. I promise."

And with that, Darcy got up and strode away. *If she won't follow me to the glen, she won't follow me to Seattle.*

As Monday wound down, Carol kept finding things that needed to be done. The "Welcome flag" holder was coming loose, so she drilled new holes and reinstalled it. A family with four kids all under the age of twelve wanted to go for a hike, so she spent a lot of time giving them options. Finally, as she locked up the main building's door, she saw Julio looking up into a tree.

"What's up, literally?" she asked.

"I know we don't normally trim these trees, they are part of wild nature, but...."

Carol looked up and saw that one of its branches had gotten so big it could pull down the main building's power line if a strong wind came along.

"Thanks for noticing that. I'll go put a call in to the tree trimmer, leave a message for him to come out."

Carol started to go back to the main building when Julio said, "Darcy said she was waiting for you."

"Well, this is important."

"The winds will not pick up tonight, Miss Carol," Julio said. He touched the brim of his wide outdoor hat to bid her adios, and with a gentle smile, went to his truck.

Carol watched him start the engine and depart...and then resigned herself to this showdown. She slowly walked through the property, past the restaurant, past the picnic tables, past the campsites...and into the glen.

Moments later, when Darcy thought Carol could hear her, she stepped onto a log and launched the next story she wanted them to co-create together. "I see two women who really care about each other...."

Carol stopped walking. Not because of the opening line (well, okay, it did get her attention) but because Darcy was standing there holding a sword...the one from her cabin's yard that Gillian had given her long ago.

Darcy knew that's what she was staring at. "I conjured the spirit of Gillian and asked her permission to borrow this temporarily. Hope that's okay with you."

Carol fumed.

"And then you can take it back when we're done," Darcy quickly added.

"Done with what?"

"Conjuring the next leg of the journey."

Darcy sliced the air with the sword. "Celtic Warriors, Part Three. I figure grad school was Part One, Sierra Glen was Part Two...and now it's time for Part Three, tee-hee."

Carol tried not to smile, but there was that famous Darcy word-play in play.

"...Okay."

"I see two women who really care about each other...." Darcy said. And she waited.

"...I see two women who really care about each other," Carol said and then slowly added, "And have grown—*both* have grown—in the time they've spent together."

"And to keep on growing, perhaps they will spend more time together," Darcy said in a tender voice. *No need to force this,* she reckoned, *that would just backfire.*

"Time...." was all Carol could add. She was semi-willing and mucho-scared.

Darcy kept going. "I see two women who pack up, once the last leaves of autumn have blown to the ground...."

"...I see leaves that have blown to the ground...winds of change are in the air..." *I guess Julio was wrong,* Carol thought, *the winds are blowing tonight.*

Darcy hopped off the log and did a tiny flourish with the sword. Carol had said the word "change!"

"Winds of change blow at their backs and help propel them north," Darcy added. "North to Seattle."

"North to Seattle?"

Darcy nodded. Carol took that in, digested it and struggled to keep going. "...Seattle. Where they gaze out at the ocean...."

"Ocean views and ocean mist cleansing them," Darcy went on. "The singer songwriter calls upon the muses of the Pacific Northwest to guide her and her beloved to create new stories and new songs."

"...New stories and new songs from a new muse...." Carol closed her eyes, picturing words and images blowing in from the Pacific.

YES, she's getting into this, thought Darcy. "The songwriter calls upon Seattle Sam for assistance and he happily offers his home studio as a place to record her new album, bringing in his musician friends of all stripes and colors to assist in the birthing of...."

Carol jumped in. "Assist in the birthing of the best album the singer songwriter has ever created."

Carol opened her eyes and looked directly at Darcy.

Darcy nodded her thanks. She then carefully turned the focus to her partner's half of the adventure. "Meanwhile," Darcy said, "the Celtic scholar begins to explore bookstores and colleges and other places where she might thrive...."

"Thrive...." Carol rolled the word around her mouth and savored it. Thrive sounded so much better than survive...or stuck in a rut.

$\sim$ ❦ $\sim$

Shelby waited until the end of the week to call Sierra Glen Cabins, hoping that had given Carol enough time to dry her tears and Larry enough time to look at the starter business plan. Not wanting to have anyone at Pacific University hear her, she went into a conference room down the hall to make the call.

"Sierra Glen!" It was Larry. *Gosh, Carol must be outdoors fixing something.*

"Hi, Larry, it's Shelby Kincaid. How are you?"

"Spectacular. Sold out through the end of October!"

"Great, wow! Well, did you get a chance to look at my business plan?"

"I did. Very good. You're very smart."

Shelby blushed. *This is off to a fine start.*

"Thank you. Did you see the list of questions I included?"

"Yes, yes, good questions."

"Would you like to tackle them over the phone or would in-person be better? I'm happy to come up there again."

"In-person could be good, easier that way."

"Yes, I agree." *Hallelujah, another visit!*

"When is a good time for you?" Shelby asked.

"Not this week, very busy, on my own here at the desk."

"On your own?"

"Yes, Carol has taken off."

"Taken off? Where to?"

"Uh, Seattle, I think she said. Give me a few days, will be better. Mondays are always slow."

SEATTLE? Before she could pull together a coherent thought, Larry urgently wrapped things up.

"Next guest arriving, needs to check in, come on a Monday some time. Probably won't have a room for you, but there is always Little Pine."

"Okay, yes, a Monday, thank you so much, Larry."

She hung up and let her head hit the conference room table, CLUNK.

Chapter Thirty-One

Treasure Hunt

Shelby toyed with the idea of talking to Randall. *And just what would he say? "I told you so." Maybe I should just save myself that conversation and annoyance,* Shelby surmised. *Okay, do I call Larry and tell him I'm really not interested? "Hey, sorry, but this was all about CAROL, not the hiking tours!" He'll think I'm nuts. I am nuts. I'm a fool for love.*

The following week went by in a haze. Shelby's lack of focus led to mistake after mistake with the Outlook calendar and her emails. Oops, forgot to copy the Assistant Vice Chancellor on that budget spreadsheet!

When Shelby literally walked into the doorframe of Marion's office, Marion looked up from her computer.

"Are you okay?"

"Sure. I'm fine."

"You don't seem to be yourself, ever since you got back from your trip."

"Well, yeah, it's hard to adjust to the hustle and bustle of city life…."

"I think it's more than that," Marion observed.

"Well," Shelby said, trying to finesse this, "I'm not sure about the new job here."

"<u>What</u>?"

Marion stared at her and waited. Shelby looked at the view of the Santa Monica Mountains out Marion's window. *See, we have mountains here,* she told herself. *And the ocean. And decent coffee. And indie rock bands. And lesbian Meetup groups all over town.*

"I thought you were really excited about this opportunity." Shelby could hear the irritation in Marion's voice.

"I was. But being in the mountains gave me a fresh perspective."

Marion continued to simmer.

"How about…I get through the Back-to-School events, and then I make a decision," Shelby proposed.

"Got it," Marion said sharply, as her head quickly pivoted back to her computer screen.

Ouch, thought Shelby.

Back at her desk, Shelby realized she'd forgotten to drop off Marion's mail, so she went back in and slipped it into the in-box on the wooden credenza. As luck would have it, Marion's cell phone rang at that very moment.

"Hi, sweetie, did you get a price on the Malibu beach place?"

Shelby quickly got herself out of there, but she could hear phrases like "maid of honor" and "open bar" and "floral arrangements." *Holy cow, they really ARE getting married.*

Shelby threw herself into setting up the Back-to-School Treasure Hunt. It was a crazy, fun activity for Alums to do as a way to reconnect to Pacific University and for their kids to learn the campus. She also figured the logistics were so daunting, it would be a way to keep her mind off of both Marion and Carol.

Shelby made Howie traipse around with her three days in a row so they could finalize the clues. As they sat sipping coffee at the giant dolphin sculpture in the middle of campus on Friday night, he put his arm around her.

"You're doing a GREAT job, sweetie."

214

"Thank you, Howie." She gave him a sideways hug.

"Have you thought of starting your own TV show?" he asked. "*College Amazing Race*, only without bungee jumping off bridges and eating fried grasshoppers."

They laughed so hard the two bumped heads, which made them laugh harder.

"You know, I actually DO have a dream," Shelby said, when she'd caught her breath. "Not a TV show, but a tour group idea, up in the mountains. I was inspired by my vacation."

"Great! I want to come on it! Wait, do I have to wear butch clothes?"

"No, Howie, you can wear your polka dot shirts and your bow ties."

"Yes!"

And they laughed again.

The next morning, the third Saturday of September, Shelby was dressed as a treasure hunting sailor, holding a tall flag with the school's dolphin mascot on it and running giddy on coffee fumes.

Standing outside of the athletic center, she looked over the sea of nearly four dozen Alumni and their newbie freshman kids...and got all sentimental. She knew the kids had their lives in front of them.

Everything was possible. Disappointments had not ruined their souls.

Shelby yelled, "On your mark, get set, go!"

The teams ripped open their clue packages and started shrieking and running around like maniacs.

By the time Shelby handed out the prizes of toy dolphins, bookstore gift certificates and T-shirts to the happy winners, she'd made a decision. *Fuck Carol, I really want to give the tour thing a try.*

Once school had started the next week and things had calmed down, Shelby made another phone call.

"Sierra Glen!" It was Larry again.

"Hi Larry, Shelby here! Hey, I was thinking of coming up, say, the second Monday in October. How's that sound?"

"Perfect!" Then he said to someone nearby, "Yes, gift shop is next door, they have hiking poles."

"Great. You sound busy, I'll let you go!"

"I am, ha ha! See you in October!"

Chapter Thirty-Two

Stockton

Shelby got up before the crack of dawn to head north to the Sierra Nevada once again on that fateful second Monday morning in October.

While chewing on some turkey jerky as she drove, she pondered her next big decision: when to give notice at her current job? On the one hand, she could just quit the regular gig at the university, live on her savings and really make a go of the mountain adventure. No hedging of bets.

On the other hand, if she let go of her job and her rent-controlled apartment, it would be sooooo hard to go back into the L.A. rental market if things didn't work out in the mountains. *I could sublet,* Shelby realized. *But is that hedging my bets or is that playing it smart? And what if I move up to Sierra Glen and hate it? What if Larry drives me nuts? What if no one does these hikes and I'm cut loose after one season? What if people don't want to PAY to go on a hike, even with expert guides?*

After a quick stop at Schat's for a "pullover" cinnamon bun and some freshly squeezed O.J., she headed on up to Sierra Glen.

She thought of taking a detour off the two-laner halfway up the mountain out of Little Pine to see if anyone had moved into Carol's home yet...but decided not to mess up her business plan focus. Instead, she and the Honda putt-putted the rest of their way up the road. *I need to get a tune-up*, Shelby realized. *And gosh, maybe snow tires or chains if I'm going to be up here in snow! Will my poor little Honda Fit even handle snow? No wonder Carol drives a truck.*

The resort's parking lot was nearly full, very good for an October morning. Shelby got out of her car and made sure she had her business plan. She'd decided to wear jeans since things were informal up here, but a nice business shirt and her favorite moon-sliver silver earrings.

As Shelby walked to the main building, she looked around. Nothing had changed except golden leaves were now in plentiful supply.

"Hello!"

Shelby turned around. Larry was behind her.

"Hi!" Shelby stuck out her hand, revved up on sugar. *Get centered, don't do the happy cocker spaniel thing, this is a business meeting,* she chided herself.

Larry shook her hand with a firm grip. *Okay, we're on the same energy level. This is good,* thought Shelby.

"Let's go over here to the picnic tables where we have room to spread out," Larry said.

"Don't you have to mind the front desk?"

"Oh, Carol can do that."

"...Carol?"

"Yes, you remember Carol?"

REMEMBER HER? HOW COULD I FORGET HER?

"Uh, you had said she left for Seattle."

"Did I? So sorry, I meant Stockton. I was multi-tasking when you called."

"Stockton. Her...ah, sister?"

"Yes, her sister had emergency gallbladder surgery."

"OHHHHH. Got it, got it."

Larry was gesturing toward a table where they could sit. Shelby wanted so badly to stare at the main building but settled instead for a quick peek... all she saw was the "Welcome" flag. *Okay, time to focus!* Shelby purposefully sat with her back to the building lest her thought-train derail.

She laid out the business plan, which was even more complete than the one she'd left with him weeks before. Plus, she had "question bubbles" all over it. She walked Larry through the whole shebang and each question as they came to it.

"I have no idea what people would be willing to pay for doing a guided hike, because the mountains are already free for the asking," she noted at one point.

"They love special services," Larry told her. "We get the hard-core people who are fine on their own, but I've noticed how much the casual visitors eat up Carol's historic talks and walks just around here."

"Great. Well, I have a variety of hikes, for people of different hike levels. The trick is to describe them in detail so that people know what they're getting into. A couch potato is not ready to hike at ten thousand feet."

Larry laughed. "Yes, good! Also, people need to acclimate. Easy hike on Saturday, harder hike on Sunday, that sort of thing."

"Great idea. I'm trained in First Aid since I take people on outings at my college, but up here, I wouldn't want someone to have to have a heart attack."

Larry nodded and then his eyes went to just above Shelby's head as a voice said, "Fancy meeting you here."

Shelby turned around and had her own mini-heart attack: <u>Carol</u>. With a huge grin on her face. Shelby climbed out of the picnic table and they embraced. Shelby noted it wasn't a casual or formal hug, but a full body one. And there were those dimples again.

"You got your hair cut," Shelby said.

"Yeah, there's a place in Stockton I like to go to."

"Your sister, gallbladder, Larry said?"

"Yeah, she's fine now. Just a quick scare."

"Gosh, I'll bet. Well, I got a little scare of my own. He'd said you went to Seattle when I called."

"Oh, really?" Carol said, smiling.

"So sorry, that was Darcy," Larry said, shaking his head. "Too busy, too much on my plate when you were gone."

They all chuckled, but Shelby's mind was racing: *DARCY, SEATTLE?*

"Gosh, did Darcy...?" she said with fake casualness.

"She's recording her album up there," answered Carol. "She has an old friend who's helping her out. It seemed so much more doable than Los Angeles. She just left a few days ago."

"Ah, how wonderful for her," Shelby said politely. *And how wonderful for me so I can have your undivided attention!*

Carol nodded. "Well, I'll leave you two to finish your business strategizing."

"No, no, join us," Larry said. "We can keep an eye on the front door from here."

Carol looked at Shelby, their eyes met.

"I'd love to have your input, you're the expert up here," Shelby said.

"Okay, sure. Happy to pitch in."

And with that, Carol sat down right next to Shelby. It was all Shelby could do not to put her hand between Carol's legs.

Carol wasn't shy about tossing in her two cents' worth, in fact, it was almost as if she'd been thinking about the plan. *Larry probably told her I was coming,* Shelby thought, *so she's given this some thought. But how does Darcy-Seattle figure into this,* she wondered. *Did Darcy ask her to go to Seattle? Or just up and go on her own?*

"...For the hardcore hikers, we could offer an overnight backpack. Have you done much backpacking, Shelby?"

"Huh?" Shelby suddenly heard Carol's question and realized she'd been lost in thought.

"Uh, yes, I've done some backpacking. I'm more of a day hiker, though. But I could do an overnight. I'm just not great at carrying ten days' worth of food and gear on my back."

"Got it. I think we should add an overnight option then," Carol said.

GREAT, WE COULD SHARE A TENT, Shelby thought.

What Shelby said aloud, though, was "I have a question, now that Carol's here. Who will mind the store if she's out co-leading hikes with me?"

"I can handle it," Larry said. "If you do just a couple of day hikes a week, it should be fine. Maybe an overnighter once a month."

"If we build the business up, we could always add an employee to help run the office," Carol added.

Larry nodded.

Another salary to pay, Shelby noted, and she'd already wondered just how much to charge for these trips and how much she could get paid. *Here we go.*

"I know how much I paid for the John Muir Tour that I missed, and I've researched Sierra Club trips, but neither of them charges for a day hike, per se. People join their local Sierra Club chapter and just go on the hikes for free. I'm a little nervous about how much to charge your patrons…."

"Don't worry, I'll figure that out, and I'll make sure you're properly compensated," Larry said.

Shelby smiled and pretended to relax over the issue.

"Ah, someone's going to headquarters," Larry noted, and they all looked toward the front door as a couple of women approached it.

Carol started to get up, but Larry said, "I've got this, you two catch up."

"Thanks, Larry, thank you for everything," Shelby said.

"My pleasure. We'll discuss more later."

"Sounds like a plan."

Chapter Thirty-Three

Movin' On Up?

Carol sat right back down at the picnic table. There was an awkward pause and then she and Shelby both giggled.

"So, did Larry tell you I was coming?"

"Yes, just a couple of days ago."

"Mmhm."

"What does that mean?" Carol asked, grinning.

"Your questions seemed pretty thought-out, as if you'd been mulling things over." Carol blushed and looked away. Shelby reached over and took her hand. "I'm glad. It would've been awful if you hated the idea or never wanted to see me again."

Carol squeezed her hand back. "What made you think I wouldn't want to see you again?"

"Well, I couldn't find you after Darcy's concert. I didn't know what the heck was going on."

"Yeah. I was having a meltdown. One of her songs was about me, and...I didn't take it well."

"Oh?" Shelby smiled and pretended to have no idea what song Carol was talking about.

"The final one about the mountain girl. Living in a made-up world."

"Ohhhh, right," Shelby said and then she moved on quickly. "Anyway, that's really cool that Darcy figured out her next step, Seattle."

"Yeah."

Carol glanced away and Shelby knew Something Was Up. Carol knew Shelby knew.

"Did she invite you to go with her?" Shelby asked.

"Yes, yes she did. Right after the concert. I've chosen not to go," Carol said, looking Shelby directly in the eye, telling a lie of her own. *Dear God, please don't let Shelby see through me*, Carol prayed. For in fact, Carol had told Darcy she couldn't go <u>right now</u>, the height of the fall season. She told her she would head to Seattle in November. She was supposed to have given Larry notice in October...but when Larry said Shelby was coming, Carol's heart went pitty-pat....

"I'll bet you were sad to see her go," Shelby said genuinely.

"Yes, I was," Carol said. "But I'm really excited you're back."

They simultaneously leaned in for a kiss, a long, romantic one filled with hope.

After lunch, the two women went over some more details of the new adventure. Larry, meanwhile, had typed up a preliminary agreement and handed it to Shelby.

She was smart enough not to agree to anything spur of the moment... well, on the business front.

"I'll take a good look at this when I get home," she said brightly.

Larry nodded and smiled, he understood.

They all three agreed May was probably the earliest they could officially advertise as having the new outings. There was a chance the women could lead some guided hikes in April, but snow could make a late spring appearance and cause cancellations.

"We could do things spur of the moment," Carol said. "If the weather is great, then just tell the hikers who are here."

"Possibly," Larry said. "But the hikers who come that early are so used to hiking on their own that I think the bulk of our business will be the vacationers who come in summer."

"Good point," said Shelby.

"When do you want to move up here?" Larry asked.

There it was: *REALITY*. It hit Shelby like a giant oak tree falling on her head. Wooziness ensued. *Move. Up. Here.*

"Or were you thinking about just coming up in the summers?"

"Well, Larry, my job is year-round at the university, since I'm not a teacher."

"Ohhh, I see."

"So, I'd <u>like</u> to move up here," Shelby said carefully, glancing at Carol. "Let me look at the agreement and see what I think. But I hear you, May is probably the month when we can really get going on this."

"Very good," Larry answered.

He went off to take a phone call in his office, and Shelby nervously fiddled with the business plan.

"I know it's a big step," Carol whispered. "You're giving up a lot to try this...."

Shelby nodded. "...Retirement plan, a pension, health insurance...my home...."

Carol reached over and squeezed her hand. "Don't do anything rash. Maybe you could take a leave of absence or something, to see if this thing flies."

"You'd be okay with that? I mean, haven't your other—" She stopped herself. She was about to say "girlfriends," as in "haven't your other girlfriends not committed to staying up here." *She is not my girlfriend. We haven't even gone on a date. Well, we've done hikes together. But still. I'VE FALLEN INTO THE TRAP AGAIN. MADE ASSUMPTIONS. Okay, she did kiss me, which Marion never did, but still.*

"Haven't my other...what?" asked Carol.

Shelby decided to put her cards on the table.

"Haven't your other girlfriends not really committed to being up here? And I know I am not your girlfriend. But...maybe someday. God, I'm just stumbling through this...."

Carol nodded with sympathy. "Me, too. You know what? They did commit. The horseback riding instructor was here for two seasons. The

English teacher was down at the high school for a few years. They just needed to move on."

"What if...that ends up...how things...." Shelby couldn't even finish the sentence.

Carol put her arm around her and kissed her temple.

"Let's give it a shot. It's a great idea. Maybe we'll figure out other ways to market what we both do during the winter months. Let's focus on summer and fall for now. And if it doesn't work out, it won't be because we didn't try."

Shelby cupped her hands around Carol's face and gave her a ferocious kiss.

Chapter Thirty-Four

Pumpkin

Shelby and Carol had an early dinner together at the Sierra Glen restaurant, where Shelby told her all about the treasure hunt she'd organized at the college.

"Maybe that's something we could try up here," Carol said, impressed by Shelby's ingenuity.

"Absolutely!"

Shelby wanted to get on the road right after eating so she could be home before midnight. Carol walked her to her car. By now, kissing Carol felt completely natural and relaxed, so the goodbye kiss was long and luxurious. Carol even took a moment to run her hands up Shelby's back and pull her in extra close. Shelby could feel Carol's breasts against hers for the first time...and she hoped it wouldn't be the last.

~ ❧ ~

"<u>You're what</u>?" Marion said.

Shelby was facing her boss and her two best buds in Marion's office. Marion's look: complete shock. Randall's: semi-shock. Howie's: enthusiastic shock.

"In April. So I need to make my last day here in mid-March, I'm thinking. That should give you plenty of time to find someone new, Marion."

Howie gave her a big hug as he left the room, and Randall said genuinely, "You'll be a huge success."

That left Marion, who was still absorbing the new mountain guide job info.

Shelby piped up. "Remember you said you wanted to start your own consulting business? I think that planted a seed in me." *Not exactly, but it sounded good,* Shelby thought.

Marion finally said, "Well, I went out on a limb for you with the Assistant Vice Chancellor for the new position. We put some time and energy into crafting this puppy."

Ouch.

"I appreciate that, I really do. But what good am I if I'm not happy here?"

"I thought you were happy here."

"I am. I...I just don't want to be here forever. Here's the other thing: I moved so much as a kid that staying in one place seemed like a great idea. I was scared to move again. But now I feel I need to."

Marion nodded.

Did she get it or was she just being polite? Shelby wondered.

"I'll put out a job notice by the end of October," Marion said. And with that, she sat down at her computer, case closed.

Shelby walked backed to her desk. She had been hoping for something along the lines of *"DON'T LEAVE, MY GOD, WHAT WILL I DO WITHOUT YOU, YOU'VE BEEN SUCH A HUGE PART OF MY LIFE!"* Or even *"I'LL GET A TEMP, JUST IN CASE YOU WANT TO COME BACK!"*

Ah, but no. Reality slapped Shelby in the face again. Marion had moved on. Shelby knew it was time for her to move on, too.

First up: the family phone calls. That evening at her apartment, Shelby decided to call her family in the order of most supportive to least supportive. Or so she thought.

Roxanne, now that she was part of the "establishment" as a bar owner (yet keeping her street cred by still wearing torn jeans and tattoos), managed to be pretty cranky on the call.

"You're WHAT?"

"You know how good I was at camping and hiking when we were kids."

"Leading hikes isn't a BUSINESS."

"It CAN be, you just have to BUILD it."

"The outdoors is free. Who the hell would pay to go see it?"

"Who the hell pays to buy a beer at your bar in Boulder when they could drink the same damn thing at home for cheaper? It's about belonging, community, and we can point out things they don't know and would never have seen on their own."

"You hate getting dirty."

"I'm not hiking for three months, it'll be a weekend at the most!"

"Well, just how much money can you make up there, and jeeze, they won't have all the benefits your school has."

"You are the LAST person I thought would worry about benefits. What kind of benefits do you have at the bar?"

Shelby was yelling so loudly that the neighbors walking their dog outside looked up at her dining room window. And then she heard Roxanne's husband in the background ask, "Who the hell are you talkin' to?"

"I love our bar!"

"I love the mountains. And a woman who works up there. And I don't know if either will work out, but I'm tired of fantasizing about things, the future. I want to actually <u>create</u> my future!"

And with that, Shelby clicked off the call and threw her cell phone into the couch as hard as she could.

She thought about waiting a day to call her mom so she could calm down...but then realized Roxanne was probably dialing Mom right now. *Better get to her first.*

Shelby grabbed a glass of ice water, slurped some down, then held the glass to her forehead, her cheeks, her neck...and then went to fetch her cell phone from the couch to dial San Diego.

"Hi, Mom."

"Hi, Sweetie. I was just thinking about you."

SHIT. "Oh? Did Roxanne call?"

"No. Why?"

"Uh, never mind."

"I just haven't talked to you in weeks and weeks, that's all. How have you been?"

"Excellent." She then gave Mom the much longer version of the story, how she'd felt a little stuck at the university, wanted to broaden her horizons, so that her mom had some context for this big move.

"Mmmhmm."

"That's it, 'Mmmhmm.'"

"I'm just taking it all in. You're so on-the-ball and enterprising, I'm sure you've thought everything through." Implying that if she hadn't, she'd better get on it.

"I have. And Larry the owner is SUPER."

"Good."

Another curt answer.

"What are you really thinking?"

"Does it matter? Won't you do what you want anyway?"

God, I hate these calls with her, Shelby thought. Instead, she said, "I wanted your blessing."

"You have it. Have a wonderful time up there." As if her mom were really saying, *"Have a nice vacation, dear. See you when you get back. Because you will be back. Because you will fail miserably."*

"Thanks," Shelby answered dryly. And in that moment, she had a realization. Her mom's coolness and judgments had always kept her at arm's length from her kids. Shelby right now (and for as long as she could remember) was craving warmth and cuddling. *No wonder I'm attracted to women, I want some nurturing,* Shelby thought.

She considered telling her mom about Carol but she'd get the same "Mmmhmm." And her mom's famous "Whatever makes you happy" delivered in a dry tone that signaled "Good luck with that."

"Okay, gotta go, got lots to do."

"Okay. Keep us posted," her mom said. "Love you."

"Love you."

They hung up. "Love you." Delivered with as much warmth as "Eat your broccoli."

Shelby went to the kitchen and poured herself a glass of Chardonnay, for the third and final phone call. *Might as well get these calls over with in one fell swoop,* she figured.

"Hey, Pumpkin!"

Shelby never failed to smile when her dad greeted her like that.

"Hey, Dad, how's the Florida retirement thing suiting you?"

"Oh, I'm not retired, I'm just channeling my energies into lots of other areas! Got a new toolshed out back and I'm creating custom racks and bookshelves!"

They both laughed, her dad was forever organizing things and lining up projects.

"Well, I think you'll appreciate this next move I'm about to make," Shelby said, full of nervous but hopeful cheer. She gave her dad a pitch similar to the one she gave her mom, throwing in some of the business plan details (which would've bored her mom shitless but her dad ate that stuff up like Kit Kat bars). When she was done, Shelby took another gulp of wine and waited for the critique.

"That sounds wonderful, Pumpkin," Dad said.

"Really?"

"Remember when you sold Girl Scout cookies, you were the champ, and you did it without our help. You knocked on doors, you had a spreadsheet. Your plan sounds terrific. If I lived closer, I'd come on one of your hikes."

Shelby got all teary-eyed. She wasn't expecting such fulsome praise (although she was secretly glad that he lived in Florida and couldn't be on a hike, he would've been correcting both her and Carol on God-knows-what-all).

"Dad...."

"Yeah?"

"If it fails, please don't yell at me."

"Of course not. Nothing ventured, nothing gained. And besides, you've been at the university for a long time. It's good you're trying something new, it's a fine way to grow."

"You read my mind."

They laughed at that, and Shelby was relieved. He got it.

"Okay, one more thing, and I didn't tell Roxanne and Mom. They weren't in receptive moods."

"Lay it on me."

Lay it on me? Who is this talking? Boy, he's mellowing in his golden years, thought Shelby.

"I really like a woman who runs the office up there. She's an expert hiker and she'll be the historian and naturalist on the tours. I...I haven't told you about very many of my girlfriends, but she feels so special I wanted to let you know about her. Her name's Carol."

"Well, I'm honored you told me. That should make the venture even more fun."

"Yeah, you read my mind on that front, too!" And with that, Shelby completely dissolved into tears.

"Thanks, Dad."

"You're so welcome. And be sure to come visit me soon, it's been too long."

"I will. Love you."

"I love you, too, Pumpkin."

They hung up, and Shelby melted into a ball on the couch and sobbed her gratitude.

Chapter Thirty-Five

The Phone Call

"You're amazing. Everything about you—your voice, your talent, your humor, your wordsmithing. But I've realized you're complete without me, and so I've decided…."

Carol was rehearsing her speech to Darcy inside her head as she unlocked the door to the main building at Sierra Glen one sunny mid-October morning. She'd been trying for over a week to put words together to explain to Darcy that she'd changed her mind, that she wasn't going to move to Seattle with her after all. The most recent version sounded way too formal, though.

They'd talked a few times on the phone since Darcy had moved up north, and Carol met her chipperness note for note, getting into the spirit of the Pacific Northwest Adventure. Once Shelby had visited, though, Carol could see how staying here at Sierra Glen was so doable. Darcy was meant to move on and get her music out to the world, and Carol thought she was meant to stay here, nestled in the mountains, guiding hikers. And she'd found someone who was willing to do it with her.

But how to say this to Darcy?

"I've never met anyone like you, you so enriched my life these past months, it was a pleasure to...."

That sounded like a toast at a banquet. Perhaps a more heartfelt approach would work.

"Darcy, sometimes people love each other but have different paths. I truly love you, but I feel my place is—" and just then the phone rang.

Mighty early for a call, Carol thought. "Sierra Glen. Carol speaking."

"Hey you!" It was Darcy, up with the birds and chip-chip-chipper. "Sam and I got another track laid down yesterday. Can't wait for you to hear it."

"Cool."

"How's the packing going?"

"Uhhhh, well, it's not...."

"I know you have a few more weeks, but you need to ramp it up. Tell Larry you gotta leave work early each day so you can get things donely-done-done."

"Yeah...."

"Is he giving you a hard time?"

"No. I, Darcy, I'm not packing because...I'm not going to Seattle," Carol quickly blurted out.

Darcy said tersely, "You changed your mind." It wasn't even a question, just an irritated statement.

"Yes, look, people have diff—"

"—different paths? Different journeys? Fuck it. You're totally missing out by not joining me. And you really are incapable of change." With that, Darcy hung up without even saying goodbye.

Carol stared at the phone's handset. *I suppose I deserved that.* She hung up and sagged into her office chair.

~ ❧ ~

Carol implemented some crucial changes for the second semester of her sophomore year at Chico State. She did not allow herself to touch the *Conjurings and Wanderings* book except on Saturday nights with Gillian. If she had Light Bulb Moments for story ideas, she jotted them down on Post-It notes and tucked them up on the shelf above her desk out of sight.

For her paper on the Celtic Tree of Life, she started her research early and wrote the paper in small chunks so she wouldn't feel overwhelmed at the last minute. Carol fell deeper in love with the Tree of Life when she learned how important it had been for Celtic culture. The trees had provided shelter and food for humans and for animals, birds and insects. The trees were also the sacred spot where Druids would hold classes and meetings. Carol realized that's what she and Gillian had been doing under their favorite campus oak tree, as if they were carrying on an ancient tradition.

Carol also got major goosebumps when she learned this: the Celts believed trees were the ancestors of man and provided a connection to the "other world." The most sacred tree was the oak or "daur" in Celtic, which is where we get the word "door." So the oak tree would have been the door to the "other world." *And that's what Gillian and I have been doing,* Carol thought. *We've been going through a door to magical other realms.* She was thunderstruck. *I was meant to write this paper, I was meant to learn this, I was meant to create these other worlds in our* Conjurings and Wanderings *book!*

Carol decided to go all out and got Gillian to do some artwork for this paper, a few watercolor images and a couple of pop-up 3-D trees.

And she got an "A."

"LET'S CELEBRATE!" yelled Gillian after Carol jogged into the scene shop waving her paper with the bright red grade and the word "Outstanding!" on it.

"LET'S!"

"I have a thought," Gillian added.

"Do tell."

"I hear there is a remote woodsy area with a creek just outside of town. How about a blanket, a picnic lunch and the woods all to ourselves?"

"Heavenly."

By sophomore year, Gillian had a used car. She needed it to schlep set pieces and props to the theatre and she and Carol could now get around easily.

Gillian had scribbled down some directions as to where this woodsy waterway was a few miles outside of Chico. After parking the car beside a gravel road, they headed into the forest with Gillian reading aloud directions like "Turn left at the big boulder" and "Angle right at the fallen tree."

After hiking for well over half an hour, Carol noted, "It's pretty right here, we could just stop next to the dead tree."

"No, we have to keep going, I want to see and hear the creek."

Carol continued to follow Gillian, who was jumping on and off logs with wild abandon. Sometimes the red-haired adventurer would grab a stick and pretend-sword-fight some imaginary creatures. "WE ARE THE GODDESSES RULING THESE WOODS. TAKE THAT, EVIL DOERS!"

A bit later, Carol was officially nervous. "What was that last direction, Gillian?"

"Go parallel with maple trees and when they end, go left. The creek is just ahead."

"These trees are going on forever!"

"Do you want to quit?" Gillian turned around and asked pointedly, although not meanly.

"Uh, not exactly. I'm just worried."

"We have to play it out all the way. We can't quit early. And if we honestly can't find the creek, we can always go back."

Gillian turned forward and kept following the line of trees...and in that moment, Carol saw a fundamental difference between them even clearer than ever before. She herself was cautious and Gillian was bold. *Okay, yes, I need someone like this in my life, don't I?*

And just then she heard Gillian squeal, "We're here—wheeee!"

And "here" was indeed a magical spot. The leaves of the trees were brand new, the grass was fluffy and soft, there were flat stones for resting upon right next to the creek. And the creek, ahhh, a perfect blend of gentleness and gurgles.

Gillian flung open the blanket. "For you, m'lady,"

"Why, thank you."

They unpacked the picnic basket, and just as they were about to dive in to smoked Gouda, crackers and such...Gillian got a sly look in her eyes.

"You know what I'd like as my appetizer?"

"Oh, let me think. Think. Think. Think," answered Carol.

Carol dropped her jeans and her underwear and stood near Gillian who was now on her knees with her mouth and tongue ready to dive into Carol's hot melt appetizer.

Gillian went to work and Carol took some deep shaky breaths—she was already starting to climax. She noted the glorious work of Mother Nature around her...it was a perfect moment, she felt connected to everything.

Chapter Thirty-Six

It's Time

Shelby visited her dad at Thanksgiving. They walked on the beach near his home in Naples, Florida, on the Gulf of Mexico side of the state. It was their best time ever together. He really had mellowed and Shelby wasn't fighting to get his approval. She did ask him one important question about leaving L.A.: to keep her apartment or not?

"Keep it. Sublet it. That's just good business sense. You never know. Those Sierra cabins could burn down in one of those crazy California wildfires and then where would you be? Subletting doesn't mean you're not committed to your goals." *He's supportive and practical, God bless him,* thought Shelby.

She did Christmas with Mom in San Diego, New Year Eve's with Roxanne in Colorado...and then it was time for the new year.

The first part of the year flew by for Shelby. Marion had turned into robot boss, absolutely no small talk and none of the fun wordplay they used to enjoy. Shelby began to see Marion for who she really was—DRIVEN.

In the middle of March, Randall and Howie threw Shelby a farewell party at work.

"Oh my God!" Shelby's hands flew to her mouth when she walked into the conference room on her office's floor. She was greeted by several dozen people who cheered loudly. They were all dear friends she'd made over the years, some going back to undergrad days.

She looked around: Howie and Randall had decorated the room with construction paper cutouts of trees and mountains. In the center of the big table was a giant chocolate cake with a mountain-scape of white frosting on it. It had "Good luck Shelby" written in red.

"The white's supposed to be snow, it snows up there, right?" Howie asked.

"And the red is for following your passion," added Randall.

She grabbed the two guys with both arms and gave them a bear hug. "Thank you and I'm going to miss you two SO MUCH!"

There were fun gifts, baskets filled with CLIF bars, granola, trail mix and sunscreen. Shelby cried as she opened every single one of the presents.

"This all means, you all mean a lot to me. This place has been such a part of my life for so long...."

The entire crowd said, "Ahhh..." in a sweet tone of unison love.

Marion hung off to the side throughout most of it. She had the good sense to know this was Shelby's hour. As the festivities wrapped up, she finally stepped forward.

"You're quite amazing," noted Marion. "I couldn't have started my new job here without all of your expertise. I truly have enjoyed working with you."

"Thank you."

"You have a lot of adventures in front of you," Marion continued. And then she dropped her voice to a sultry, seductive tone. "Mountain trails... pine trees...fresh air...bird calls...dappled sunlight...."

Shelby suddenly realized Marion was playing Two Words—and right in front of God and everybody. Shelby smiled as Marion knew that she knew. And then Marion went serious.

"Mother Nature...heart opening...your home...."

Shelby could feel herself starting to cry.

"You'll be at one with your universe," Marion concluded with such tenderness, Shelby couldn't hold the tears back.

Marion stepped closer, gave her a hug...and whispered in her ear with much humility, "I'm sorry."

Shelby hugged her tightly. And then it was time to move on.

Chapter Thirty-Seven

April Come She Will

Shelby pulled up to Pal's home late in the morning on the first Sunday in April. Greeting her: a white house that could've used a coat of paint and assorted car parts in the yard. What is it with people here in Little Pine, Shelby wondered, *first Carol and Maude, and now Pal. Doesn't anybody care about presentation?*

Carol had offered Pal's as a place to stay and more than once reassured Shelby that Pal was okay with this. After all, Darcy had moved out and Pal could use a roommate. Plus, Shelby knew moving in with Carol wasn't realistic on any level.

Pal's homestead it was, for the moment.

Shelby knocked on the wooden front door that was so weathered its color had been bleached out. Pal swung the door open wide and stood there with her bed-head hair straight up, wearing a pair of Scooby-Doo P.J.'s and holding a big coffee mug ("Got Horse Sense? Neigh!").

"Welcome to my Hotel California…." said Pal, paraphrasing The Eagles. "Remember what the next line is?" she added with a grin.

Shelby wracked her brain, "Something about prisoners…?"

"Yeah. Of our own device."

Shelby couldn't help but laugh.

Pal bowed with her coffee mug to welcome Shelby over the threshold.

"Step right in. I have scrambled eggs, coffee and a handout I give to all of Carol's girlfriends. It'll save ya years of heartache!"

Shelby laughed again but added, "Really?"

"No, but I probably should."

Shelby dropped her backpack on the living room floor, along with a couple of large duffle bags.

"So, what would be on it?" Shelby asked.

"Oh, don't you want to discover for yourself? That's where all the fun is!"

Shelby chuckled. "So true, so true. Okay let's make a deal. Just tell me one thing that would be on the handout."

Pal sipped her coffee and then said, "Don't try to change her."

Shelby nodded. "Duly noted. And now I'll take some of that coffee."

"Coming right up, Shelbycakes."

Well, if things don't work out on the relationship front with Carol, at least I'll be entertained by Pal, thought Shelby.

While Pal poured the coffee, Shelby went back out to her car for more stuff. As her dad had suggested, she sublet her apartment in L.A. but completely cleared out her clothes and personal belongings.

She popped the Honda's trunk, and there before her was all she had to get her through a season in the mountains: hiking clothes, books and some framed photo montages of friends. The rest of her stuff had gone into storage.

Shelby looked over her shoulder toward the Sierra Nevada mountains, which she could see from Pal's front yard. It was a warm spring day, mid-seventies down here in Little Pine. But there was definitely some snow on the peaks; it had been a wet winter.

Coming back in, she asked Pal, "How low is the snow level right now?"

"Earlier in the year, it got down to four thousand feet, but that's all melted. Now I think it's up at eight thousand and above."

"I forgot to get snow tires or chains or whatever they do here."

"Snow tires would be the Midwestern thing. But we do have chains at the shop, if you decide you want some. Snow season's almost over, though."

"Okay, I'll think about it."

"Here's your java."

Shelby took the coffee mug and read aloud the slogan on it: "'Sierra Nevada! A Peak Experience!' Well, this is perfect," she said, clinking her cup with Pal's.

"Thought you might appreciate that."

"I do. Thanks. And thanks for letting me stay here. I've got a rent check for ya."

"Yip-yip. Okay, your room is down the hall to the left. For me, time for a shower and then I'm gonna shoot some pool in town. Wanna come with?"

"Thanks, maybe another time. Hey, that song Darcy wrote about the little kid who dreams of being an astronaut, was that you?"

Pal just grinned and saluted with her mug. And with that, she disappeared into the hallway.

Shelby looked around. Actually, things weren't as bad as she'd originally thought, based on the carburetors out front. The tan couch and matching La-Z-Boy lounger were showing some wear and the maple dining room chairs were scuffed up a bit, but there really wasn't much clutter, just some car magazines and lesbian soft porn DVDs. *Pal in a nutshell,* Shelby thought.

Shelby picked up her luggage, went down the hall to the left and found her room. The queen-sized bed had a baby-blue comforter on it and the walls had a couple of faded posters from the eighties: Madonna (black fishnets up to here, a skimpy bustier, a black fedora and a black boa) and David Bowie (Red and Orange Ziggy Stardust image with the names of his songs crowning his head and pouring forth from his mouth at the mic). As much as she loved Madonna and David, Shelby was hit with a wave of sadness...she didn't bring her wall decorations. Those went into storage, too, so the renter could decorate a bit. Bringing them up here to hang would've seemed like "moving in" to Pal's.

Well, what __am__ I doing, if not moving in? Moving sideways?

She heard Pal clomp through the living room in her Doc Martens, put her mug in the sink, and clomp out the front door.

Shelby just stood in place. *Holy fuck, it's quiet out here in the boonies,* she realized. Homesickness waves were washing over her and through her. She couldn't even muster the energy to unpack. *Maybe I should call Randall or Howie or someone from my book group,* she thought, *but I don't want them to think I'm bailing already. Well, I could call and sound upbeat...but that would be a lie.*

Instead, she turned and exited her room and slowly crept down the hall to Pal's bedroom. She peeked in: it was also faded and stuck in time. Pal had framed some magazine covers featuring Cindy Lauper, the Culture Club...and a big poster of, wait for it, a Palomino, Pal's namesake. Oh, and a magazine cover of astronaut Sally Ride. *Yep,* Shelby thought, *Pal was the one who'd once had those sky-high dreams.*

Pal had put her decorative mark on her house when she moved in and then never updated or grew into someone else. *Or she grew but her home didn't reflect the growth? Has Pal grown? Have I? I'm about to find out. Can I be with Carol in a healthy way using what I've learned the past few months?*

Carol. Shelby was suddenly struck by the isolation of where Carol lived, which was even more remote than Pal's place. In the months leading up to this big move, she'd wanted to call Carol at home a million times, but Carol didn't have cell reception or a regular telephone line. Instead, she had an emergency satellite phone which she proudly announced she'd never used. So Shelby had gotten used to calling her at the office either right when Carol was starting her shift or when she was closing up shop.

Fuck it, I'll call now, Shelby thought. She won't be that busy, the cabins have been open only a couple of weeks, for the hard-core hikers who can deal with chilly temps and hate the summer crowds.

"Hey! I made it!" Shelby announced with as much bravado as she could muster.

"Yay! Where are you? Down in Little Pine?"

"Yeah, I'm at Pal's. She's gone to shoot some pool...."

"Is that a bad thing? You sound kind've...apprehensive."

"No, it's just quiet here. Now that she's out of the house. Really quiet. No cars, no people, no machines.... Well, the refrigerator is humming."

"Welcome to small town life," Carol said, laughing. "Do you want me to come down there for dinner when I get off?"

"Oh, no, you don't have to do that, it's a long drive. I'll just see you tomorrow."

"Okay. Larry's really excited you're coming—and me, too! Missed you!"

"Missed you. Can't wait to see you." She'd wanted to add "Love you," but that seemed presumptuous.

Shelby arrived at the Sierra Glen parking lot just before eight o'clock the next morning and spring was kind've blooming, the trees had buds at least. Too soon for any wildflowers up at this elevation. The temperature was in the fifties, not warm enough to ignite the flowers but the blue jays were chattering, all revved up.

Shelby noted just a couple of hikers, quite a difference from the big summer throngs.

"Hey!"

Shelby turned to see Carol waving to her with her biggest grin yet. Shelby melted like the snow coming down into the Sierra Glen creek. They embraced like long-lost lovers who had been separated by continents and decades. Carol inhaled Shelby's hair.

"Spearmint?" Shelby asked.

Carol laughed, remembering their previous intimate toothpaste encounter. "No, lavender, your shampoo?"

Shelby nodded and then inhaled deeply at Carol's left temple. "Mmm, pine trees and sunlight and snowmelt."

"How did you know?"

They both laughed and then leaned in for a big kiss that went on and on.

Shelby pulled out of it and asked, "So, (a) where's Larry and (b) does he know we like to do the kissing thing?"

"Funny, and (a) he's in the office on a long-distance call and (b) he knows I'm a lesbian but never comments on who I'm dating although I think he picks up clues."

"Well, gosh, should we be discreet? So that he thinks I'm up here on business and not just to get into your hiking pants?"

"Not a bad idea," Carol said laughing, and then she gave Shelby's butt a squeeze. "Can you come over for dinner later?"

"I'd love to. What's on the menu? You?" And Shelby rubbed Carol's butt right back.

"Mmmhmm. Actually, I picked up fresh trout in town, we can grill it."

"Sounds great."

"Let's go see if Larry's off the phone."

The trio sat in the main building's office for the rest of the morning planning the launch of the hiking tours. Shelby had brought her laptop and was furiously taking notes as they spitballed postcard and poster ideas. The marketing materials would go up here at the cabins and around Bishop and Little Pine, plus there'd be an advertisement on the Bishop Chamber of Commerce's website. Larry hadn't asked Shelby if she knew how to design things, but fortunately, she'd done catchy announcements for events back at the university, so she jumped in.

"Great! Great!" Larry said, beaming.

Shelby tried not to look at Carol because if she did, she knew they would both laugh—Larry's enthusiasm was becoming a running joke between them.

"One more thing. Lunch," Larry said.

"Yeah, it's coming up on noon," Carol answered, glancing at the bird clock on the wall, where both hands were almost on the Summer Tanager.

"No," Larry said, "we should provide lunch for the hikers. We get to charge more, and it will be value-added."

Carol diplomatically responded, "Yeah, that might work. Each person carries his or her own food, though, right? I'm not a professional Sherpa."

"Of course," said Larry.

"Will it be from a special menu?" asked Shelby.

"Our full lunch menu, really quality items there," said Larry.

"But the kitchen staff won't have the lunch items out that early," protested Carol.

"They could have items ready the night before," countered Larry.

Shelby could see the dynamic in action. They were both pretty opinionated and thought their own way was the right way. She dove in. "When I was at the Sierra Club lodge near the Donner Pass, the staff put on a table lots of lunch stuff in the morning: bread, peanut butter and jelly, chips, cookies, fruit, and then we packed our own sack lunches. So the staff didn't have to do any cooking and the hikers felt like they had some control over what they were eating. Otherwise it's a nightmare if there are too many choices."

Carol and Larry exchanged looks.

"She's good," Larry observed.

"She is," agreed Carol.

Shelby smiled.

Larry then added, "A little later in the month, I'll show you our new dinner menu, Shelby. I'd love for you to weigh in. A lot of our visitors are from L.A., we want them to be happy."

"Sure, no problem," said Shelby.

Larry nodded his thanks to her and went to his office. Shelby got up and put her hand on Carol's head and gave her a playful finger massage.

"You okay?" whispered Shelby.

"Absolutely."

"Larry asking my opinion 'cause I'm from L.A.?"

"He asks my opinion all the time."

"Okay." Then Shelby added, "I did a lot of mediating with my parents when I was growing up."

Carol chuckled. "Well, I hope you don't have to do that for Larry and me too often here."

That evening, at Carol's cabin, they went through the pretense of dinner, grilling the trout and baking potatoes, cutting up veggies for salad. Shelby described her final days at the university and her wonderful farewell party. She avoided talking about how homesick she felt, although now that she was with Carol, most of that had vanished.

"Have you heard from Darcy? How is Seattle?"

"Haven't really talked to her, I think she made a clean break," Carol answered, sidestepping the mess she herself had created.

After dinner, Shelby started to wash the dishes right away, being the anal-retentive gal that she was. As Shelby stood at the sink, Carol came up from behind and put her hands in the soapy water…and then slowly and sensuously massaged Shelby's hands. Finally, she leaned over and licked Shelby's ear and planted a kiss on her neck.

"Man, I'm all wet in more ways than one," Shelby told Carol, who laughed.

Shelby quickly finished washing the dishes, and Carol pitched in by rinsing and stacking them in the drainer.

"Let's go!" said Shelby, grinning.

And with that, they laughed and started kissing, which was followed by unbuttoning, unbuckling, unzipping and undoing everything as quickly as possible, stumbling toward the bedroom. It was two travelers quenching a very deep thirst, and they couldn't get enough of the sweet, moist elixir the other was offering.

"You like to be on top or bottom?" Shelby whispered.

"Both."

"Simultaneously?"

They laughed and then, with Carol completely naked on her back, Shelby took her lover's legs in both hands and spread them wide. She put her head down and began slowly tracing the edges of Carol's labia with her tongue. Carol was primed because she was moaning immediately. A few deft flicks of the tongue and a little finger pressure and Carol shrieked an orgasm.

Carol opened her eyes, panting, looked up at Shelby and pulled her close. Then she put her mouth on Shelby's breast and sucked...while her hand went down below and kneaded the labia trench that was already good 'n wet.

Shelby rode Carol's hand as if she were a Harley-Davidson, revving up and speeding into top gear. She could feel her nipples getting hard and the blood pulsing down below. She then moved Carol's hand aside and clamped down hard on her thigh instead, squeezing and pushing until she exploded. "AHHHHHH!"

She lay panting on top of Carol.

After several moments, Carol gently asked, "Feels good to release, huh?"

"Yeah. Been too long. Way too long."

Shelby got back to Pal's about nine o'clock that evening and thought about making up some lie. *Had to work on the website! Had to order food for the surge of tourists coming!*

But when she walked through the door, Pal said from the couch where she was watching a show about monster trucks, "How was it?"

"It?"

"Licking Carol's pussy. All you had dreamed of?"

Yeah, no point in feigning some other task.

"It was great. Best ever."

"Glad to hear it."

Shelby went to her room, closed the door and slept through the night without waking once.

Snow at Kings Canyon

Chapter Thirty-Eight
The Forecast

Shelby went to the print shop/post office/computer fix-it place in Bishop (a small-town business that had to multi-task to survive) a few days later to pick up the postcards and mini-posters she'd designed.

As she put them up around town in the bars, the rec center and motels, Shelby saw other fun events planned. There was even an annual spring jazz concert coming up in May. *Hallelujah! Culture! Maybe I can get Carol to go—we could have a night out on the town, a real date, fancy food and snazzy jazz.* Shelby was brimming with hope. *This is gonna work out.*

As her Honda putt-putted up the two-laner back toward the Sierra Glen, Shelby looked over the mountain tops, where muscular clouds filled the expanse. *The clouds of Michelangelo,* to quote Joni Mitchell, Shelby thought.

Getting out of her car, she saw Carol and Larry staring up at a tree limb.

"Must take care of that, it's leaning on the power line," Larry said. "Should have done it earlier."

"Yeah," Carol said, sighing.

"Call them, see how soon they can come out."

Larry turned and went over to the restaurant workers, who were loading in a lot of food to the kitchen for the soon-to-surge vacationing diners.

"Who ya gonna call? Ghostbusters?" Shelby brightly asked Carol.

"Ha ha. No, the tree trimmers. We have a big limb that needs to be cut. There's a storm rolling in."

"Storm?"

"Tonight. Eighty percent chance of rain. Snow down to the seven-thousand foot level or so."

"Or so. Where are we?" asked Shelby, her eyebrows going up in a concerned arch.

"Just below that."

"Will we be okay?"

"Sure. But we gotta get that tree limb taken care of." What Carol didn't say was Julio had pointed it out months ago, but she'd been so distracted with Darcy that she never got around to calling the tree trimmers.

"Great. So, how about a hot date the beginning of May?"

"Sure. What'd you have in mind?"

"Jazz down in Bishop."

"Oh, yeah. I've never been to that. Could be fun."

Shelby kissed her and then took the rest of the postcards and posters inside the main building as Carol followed behind. *Yeah, it's a good thing I'm around,* thought Shelby. *Carol's been here how long, and she hasn't even been to the annual jazz concert?*

While Carol was on the phone with the tree trimmer company and various vendors, Shelby spent the rest of the afternoon preparing packets of postcards to mail to other businesses too far to drive to. Once Larry was back in the office, she asked him, "Should I put up the posters here now?"

"Better wait until after the storm. We don't want them to get ruined."

"Okay."

Larry rubbed his forehead.

"So, how big a deal is this storm?" Shelby asked, picking up on Larry's worry.

"We live with storms all the time. I need to get the food unloaded so the delivery trucks can get back down the mountain, though. One more truck is due here any minute."

He checked his watch and then went into his office to see if a phone call could pinpoint the arrival time better.

Carol got off her phone call. "Tree trimmers can't get here 'til next week. Should Julio and I try to cut that branch ourselves?"

Larry spoke up from his office. "No, the limb has survived the winter; it can live through one more storm."

"It'll be okay?" Shelby asked, trying to hide her own building anxiety.

"It'll be okay," Carol said in her usual mellow manager manner.

"I don't have chains."

"You'll be fine. I can give you a ride down the mountain if you need it."

"But then how would I get back to work tomorrow?"

"Honestly, I don't think the snow is going to pile up," Carol said.

"Maybe we should check the forecast on the internet," Shelby urged, all pretense of calm gone now.

She opened up her laptop and went to a weather site that had live radar. "Uhhh...."

"Uhhh?" repeated Carol.

Shelby motioned her over. Carol looked at the screen's radar.

"Okay, yeah, it's pretty wet." Carol admitted. "But the storm seems to be moving fast."

Carol casually went back to her desk and continued ordering bait for prospective anglers.

Within an hour, the winds had started to pick up and Shelby could no longer concentrate. She sealed one more envelope and called out to Larry, "Should I drive down to Little Pine while I can?" Larry came out of his office. "Look at the way the wind is whipping those trees," Shelby added.

"If it would make you feel better, go ahead and leave now," Larry said with zen calm.

Shelby didn't want to appear to be a wuss in her first week at work. But she couldn't stop staring out the window. Within minutes, big splatters of rain had started to pelt the porch. Moments later, a huge gust of wind grabbed a tree branch and broke it, sending it crashing right across the walkway that led to their office door. That got Larry's and Carol's attention. Everyone hustled to the front door to peer out.

"Is that the branch you were…?" Shelby asked.

"No, that's a different one," Carol answered, glancing up at the big branch that was still attached but waving wildly like King Kong.

Then Carol added to Shelby, "Do you want to head down now? It could pour any minute, and the road has a lot of curves on it."

"Now you sound worried."

"I'm not worried, but I want you to feel safe," Carol said.

"I'd prefer to stay here. If I'm down at Pal's, I'll just be worrying about how things are at the office."

Then all three of them heard a truck pull into the parking area next to the restaurant.

Larry announced, "Let's get the food into the kitchen and get the truck out of here."

Larry and Carol grabbed their rain jackets and hats and put them on effortlessly as if they had rehearsed the maneuver a million times. Shelby realized she didn't have her jacket up here at the office. *Damn, I need to remember I'm in the mountains not the city.*

"What should I do?" she asked the duo.

"Whatever you want, help or stay inside, either way is fine," Carol said.

And with that, she and Larry were running out the door. A gust of wind blasted Shelby with fat raindrops.

Shelby decided to dive in and be a team player. She wrestled the screen door open (hoping it wouldn't fly completely off its hinges like the one in *The Wizard of Oz* when the tornado struck), slammed it shut and ran pell-mell after Carol and Larry. Within seconds, the downpour came, sending sheets of cold rain at them.

Shelby was instantly soaked, she even had rain in her ears. But, by golly, she was on the assembly line of getting the boxes of cereal and oatmeal into the kitchen. Once the mission had been accomplished and the truck had lumbered away, they all stared out the back door of the restaurant for several tense moments.

"It's not letting up any time soon," observed Larry.

"No," concurred Carol.

Shelby was trying to dry off with a dish towel from the kitchen as unobtrusively as possible, as if this were just another day at the office.

She was visibly shivering and what she really wanted to do was tip her head sideways and pound it to get the water out of her ears. But yet again, she wanted to look like a hearty Girl Scout. *Let me show you! I can tote that barge and lift that bale!* Then she realized it was kinda like pleasing Mom and Dad.

"You okay?" Carol asked.

Shelby snapped back to the present.

"Yeah, sure."

"You should get back down the mountain. You're soaking wet and the temperature is already dropping, you don't want to get sick."

Does Carol think I'm weak and might get sick? "I'm fine. It's just rain."

"Okay." Carol didn't feel like fighting Shelby on the weather front.

Then she asked Larry, "Should we hang around to see if the big branch holds?"

"No, I'll keep an eye on it, Carol. Work is done for the day. You two head down the mountain for the night."

"Okay," said Carol, flipping the hood of her waterproof jacket up over her head. She headed out into the rain and ran to the main building. Shelby noticed Carol was also wearing her waterproof hiking boots. She herself had on sneakers. *Okay, rain jacket, rain boots, lesson learned, be prepared for next time.*

"'Night, Larry, see ya tomorrow," Shelby said with fake good cheer.

"Will do. Be careful."

"Okay."

And with that, Shelby tossed the dish towel onto a counter and ran as fast as she could to her car.

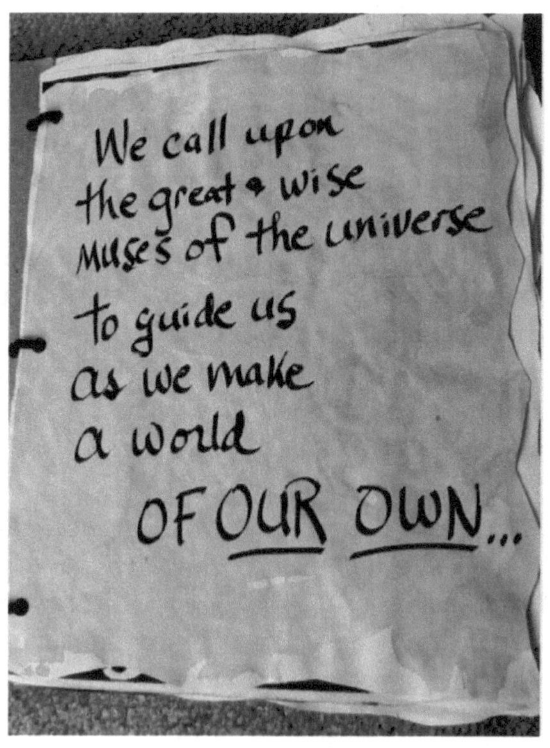

Chapter Thirty-Nine

The Revised Forecast

Shelby inched her way down the two-laner and turned on the defroster to keep the windows clear, but they still steamed up. Then the rain got so heavy that she could only see a few feet in front of her car.

"It's just rain, it's just rain," she chanted, squinting to see out the window with her shoulders bunched up to her ears in tension. "I can handle rain, I can handle rain, I can han—WHAT THE HELL IS THAT?"

Shelby slammed on the brakes, the Honda fishtailed and spun around as Shelby screamed. She'd nearly hit a huge boulder that had come loose from the rock face next to her and was blocking her side of the road.

"Pump the brakes, pump the brakes!" Her car slid anyway and fishtailed again, careening over the berm's edge.

The pumping action got the car stopped before going all the way down the slope, but there was so much rain and mud Shelby couldn't get any traction to get off of the embankment. She could hear her tires spinning uselessly, "ZZZZZZZZ!"

Shelby pounded the steering wheel with the palm of her hand. "Fuck, shit, damn! I should've left sooner instead of proving some fucking point by staying!"

She put her forehead on the steering wheel. And then a flood of thoughts ran through her mind: *Do I even have a jacket in the trunk? Food? If it rains like this for hours, could my car come loose and tip right on down into the canyon below? How far is it to walk to Carol's? Is it closer to walk back to Larry's cabin? How much daylight is left? Should I leave now? Should I wait a bit to see if the rain lets up?*

And just then Shelby heard a HONK-HONK. She looked up: There was Carol and her sturdy pickup truck. Carol flipped her jacket hood over her head again, hopped out and gingerly stepped on the dirt area where Shelby's car was stuck. Shelby pressed the window button down.

"I fucked up."

"No, you didn't. The boulder did. We'll get a tow truck tomorrow."

"Tomorrow...but will my car be safe here?"

"Uhh, I hope so?" Carol ventured to say. "Open your door carefully and grab my hand."

Shelby did as she was told. Carol pulled her up the embankment, and they both stared at the Honda for a quick second.

"Say a prayer for it," Shelby yelled over the pounding rain.

Carol nodded and then they ran to get into her truck. Carol drove on the opposite side of the two-laner to get around the boulder.

"Have you ever had that happen before?" Shelby asked.

"Oh, yeah. Every time there's a heavy rain. Well, boulders falling, not the car-over-the-edge part."

Carol looked over at Shelby and could see she was suffering on several fronts.

"Don't take it personally. You didn't cause the boulder to fall."

"Yeah, but I should've left earlier."

"Oh, you can't second-guess these things. Really. Let's go have a nice dinner at my place and just chalk it up to the weather gods."

Carol reached in the back jump-seat and pulled out a roll of paper towels.

"Here, these'll help. I'll get an umbrella from home and get you inside without getting any wetter."

"I actually don't think I could get any wetter."

And with that they both finally laughed.

"And really, Shelby, I've been there. I've gotten caught in both rain and snow up in the mountains. I was so enchanted by the beauty I wasn't paying attention to the clouds building."

"What happened?"

"Frostbite, bad blisters from my wet boots, skinned knees and elbows from slipping on wet rocks...."

"Thank you," said Shelby. "Now I don't feel like such an idiot."

"Hey, anytime."

They laughed some more, and by the time Carol walked her in the front door under the umbrella, with her arm tightly around her, they were a couple of rain-soaked love birds.

After Carol loaned Shelby sweatpants and a sweatshirt, they cobbled together a quick 'n easy dinner of chicken strips plus spaghetti and marinara sauce.

"What's the forecast for tonight and tomorrow?" Shelby tried to sound semi-casual about it.

"When I left, that weather site said it would rain most of tonight and then the snow level would drop before morning."

"Any idea of how much snow?"

"Not really. The mountains have so many micro-climates it's hard to predict."

"Mm." And with that, Shelby sat down at the table and turned her attention to the red sauce, slurping spaghetti loudly for fun. Then Carol did the same, trying to out-do Shelby in volume. They both laughed, the car-over-the-edge escapade forgotten for now.

Right after doing the dishes, they built a fire in the living room fireplace and spooned their bodies together in front of it, falling asleep to the sound of snap-crackle-pop.

Somewhere after midnight, Shelby awoke and realized she needed to pee. On her way to the bathroom, she peeked out the living room window.

"Oh, my God! Carol, look."

Carol cracked an eye open.

"Carol, look outside!"

Carol rolled over, slowly stood and joined Shelby at the window.

"There must be a foot of snow on the ground!" Shelby exclaimed.

"Yep." And with that, Carol ran to the bedroom to dive under the covers. Shelby went to pee and then dove in beside her.

By 5 a.m., Shelby was wide awake. And starting to worry. Again. *How the heck would a tow truck make it up the two-laner to get to my car? What if the snow on the car made it so heavy that it careened right down the canyon from the weight?*

Shelby looked over at Carol. "Psst."

"Mmm."

"You awake?"

"No."

"What about my car, can a tow truck get through the snow?"

"You worry too much. Go back to sleep."

Shelby rolled off of Carol and onto her back. *She doesn't worry enough,* thought Shelby. *Well, I'm gonna call it getting ahead of the curve and being proactive.*

Shelby dozed fitfully for another hour or so and then couldn't take lying in bed any longer. She got up, got dressed and got going on making coffee and oatmeal. She found cinnamon and brown sugar to add some zest to the hot oats and then opened the living room curtains so she could eat looking out on the snowy splendor. The sun was shooting rays through the pine trees, and the snow was catching the rays and sending off twinkles. Shelby realized it'd been a long time since she'd seen snow. *Maybe we could make a snowman later.*

With that optimism, she washed her dishes and then looked around the living room in the cold light of day. There were books and papers and maps and stereo parts and receipts and old photos and dust, lots of dust. *I'll bet she's never dusted a day in her—wait, what the hell is that?* She picked up a sweatshirt from the coffee table because there looked to be…yes, it was an old to-go coffee cup peeking out from under it with dried coffee in it! *Yikes!*

She tossed it in the garbage.

And then Shelby saw a bunch of receipts in a pile on a kitchen counter. Grocery store receipts, not receipts for clothes, like if the new pants didn't fit and you needed to return them. She pawed through the receipts. *These go back years!* She tossed those as well.

Then she spied the junk mail pile: offers for credit cards, cruise tours (*as if Carol would ever set foot on a cruise ship*), cable TV promos (*not gonna happen up here*)—

"Ahem."

Shelby looked up. Carol had just entered the kitchen, wearing her robe and a frown.

"I found a coffee cup from the Middle Ages. I tossed it. And some grocery store receipts from <u>four years ago</u>. Carol, seriously. This is ridiculous."

"I did not ask for your input."

"If we're a partnership, then this is part of my life. And really, Carol, this is more than just a little clutter, it's, it's...hoarding."

"Really?"

Carol brushed right past her and poured herself a cup of coffee. "Your way isn't necessarily the right way," Carol said as she got some cream from the fridge. Then her eyes squinted as she looked at the cream carton.

"Has it gone bad?"

"It's okay."

"What's the expiration date?"

"It's fine."

Carol poured in a goodly amount of cream and then took a sip of the coffee, nodding that all was right with the world.

Shelby grabbed the cream carton.

"It expired yesterday."

"It's still good. The expiration dates are to give you a heads-up, they're not written in stone. Plenty of food can be eaten even if—"

"—Carol, you're justifying keeping a bunch of trash around!"

"Is this how we're going to spend the next several months?" Carol asked bluntly.

And suddenly Shelby recalled Pal's warning: Do not try to change her.

"No. No, we're not. But...will you at least acknowledge having a used 7-11 coffee cup with dried coffee in it is not healthy?"

Carol shrugged.

Man, she's not gonna cop to this, Shelby realized.

Stalemate.

Shelby took a sip of her own coffee and went back over to the living room window to meditate on the peaceful view with the virgin snow. *Maybe this landscape will calm me down.*

She turned around and looked at Carol. Book and coffee in hand, Carol had sat down at the kitchen table to read. Shelby remembered seeing Carol during her lunch hour reading; she thought back then it was charming. *Well, it CAN be charming...unless you're avoiding the Real World.*

"Watcha gonna do today?" Shelby asked in a polite and gentle tone.

"This is it," Carol said, not even looking up.

"Want to make a snowman? That could be fun."

"Maybe later."

Shelby kept staring at her, daring her to look up, but Carol didn't give in to the challenge.

So, Shelby decided to look around: there were a helluva lot of books here. *Maybe I should stop fighting and join the reading brigade.* She perused the bookshelves, pretending she was at Vroman's Bookstore in Pasadena. British history, women's studies, queer authors, Celtic fan books, Zena Warrior Princess fan books, the history of the Sierra Nevada....

"What are you reading?" Shelby asked.

"History, Mystery and Magic: The Celtic Goddesses."

"That sounds interesting."

"It is." But then Carol didn't take the bait and elaborate, she just kept reading.

Is this what they call passive aggressive? Shelby wondered. And then she had an idea. *The storybook in the "Celtic" room. THAT'S what I want to read.*

From the bulging shelves in the living room, Shelby picked a book on popular trails in the Sierra Nevada (which she did want to read but not right this second). Then she casually sauntered out of the living room pretending she was going to read in the bedroom. And then she tiptoed into the Celtic room.

She found the leather-straps-bound *Conjurings and Wanderings* book, now about eight inches thick. It had handcrafted intricate black and gold Celtic symbols on the front cover's edges along with a woman standing front and center wearing nothing but long hair and a sword.

She carefully opened the book to page one, dated November 1, 1999. In flowing blank calligraphy, it read, "We call upon the great and wise muses of the universe to guide us as we create a world of OUR OWN."

Hmm. Powerful words, Shelby thought.

Shelby carefully browsed through the pages and pages and pages of the book and figured out which was Carol's handwriting. The first few pages seemed to be two college girls. *Oh wait, it's her college lover Gillian,* Shelby realized, as she saw a signature below a Celtic knot Gillian had drawn.

Shelby dove into the first adventure, with its hand-drawn caricatures of two young women: The Historian, a scholarly sort wearing a button-down shirt and dress pants, and The Set Designer, who had a sword and scabbard attached to the side of her red tunic that matched her red hair...

"I see two young women in love, making out beneath the ancient tree," began the Historian.

Suddenly the Set Designer asked, "What was that? I thought I heard a moan."

They looked up and realized there was a giant crevice on the back of the tree.

"From a long-ago fire?" wondered the Set Designer.

"Probably," answered the Historian. "It certainly is deep. Do you think it's safe to go in there?"

"There's only one way to find out. Let's go!" cried the Set Designer.

"Wait! You know what it looks like?"

"A giant vulva!" declared the Set Designer.

"I was going to say the same thing!"

They both put their hands inside the crevice. And then they both heard a sigh. They looked at each other and giggled.

The Historian put her hand farther inside the tree... and they heard a moan, a moan of ecstasy.

"How far in do you think we could go?" asked the Historian.

"ALL THE WAY!"

The Historian smiled. That's what she loved about her Designer lover, that daring sense of adventure.

The Set Designer put her entire arm and upper body inside the crevice and then WHOOSH, she was gone!

"Hey, wait for me!" cried the Historian, wedging her body into the giant vulva, right behind her lover.

Down, down, down they went, tumbling, rolling and laughing, embraced by the undulating mossy sides.

At the bottom they landed on thick moss, a waterbed of green.

"How will we get out?" asked the Historian. "We don't have ropes or ladders or—"

"—You worry too much. Let's have a rollicking roll, right here right now."

And with that, the Set Designer unbuttoned the Historian's button-up-shirt.

The Historian smiled. That's another thing she loved about her Designer. Ready for a romp in the moss and let the future be damned.

Shelby stopped reading. She realized that this is probably where Carol had gotten her attitude of not worrying about the future, from the Set Designer, aka Gillian. *Maybe I need a little more of that,* thought Shelby.

And she realized the handwriting changed over the years. *Wow, she's had quite a few women write in here. Will she expect ME to write in here?*

Shelby carefully flipped to the last pages in the storybook:

I see two women walking along a brook in a green meadow filled with melodious bird songs that inspire the SongMaker to write arias that are so powerful they cause the women to Shapeshift into hawks. SongMaker and WoodHawk soared high-high-high and then traveled at the speed of light to hunt down the Music Mongers.

Shelby figured out that Woodhawk was Carol and SongMaker was Darcy. She finished reading that story—and then came to a page that startled her.

In giant red watercolor paint were the words "AND NOW SHE'S GONE." The following page had a watercolor tree that looked so liquidy it could be weeping. Next to it were the shaky painted words *"Tell me everything," said the Listening Tree.*

And below that were the runny blue watercolor words, *Darcy has left...Her songs are still in my heart....*

After that, the pages were blank.

Shelby felt a wave of compassion for Carol as she realized how devastated she'd been when Darcy left. *Maybe I shouldn't be so hard on her.* Shelby sighed and then carefully put the storybook back in its place of honor, on a shelf just below the Celtic Tree of Life poster.

Shelby poked her head out of the room, the coast was clear. She went out to the kitchen.

264

Carol was washing her coffee mug and Shelby's oatmeal bowl. Shelby set her own coffee mug in the sink…and Carol washed it as well.

Is she still clinging to a storybook from her youth? Well, a storybook that's ongoing. Or is this a healthy outlet, creating a "world of her own?"

Carol dried her hands on the dish towel. The stubborn energy of earlier seemed to have dissipated.

"Is living up here kinda like where you grew up? I know you said you lived on a farm."

"Sort've. It's quiet here. I can hear the birds the way I could when I was a kid. The rushing of a creek. The wind in the trees."

"What do those voices of nature say to you?"

Carol paused for a moment and then quietly said, "Be like them."

"Like what?"

"Just be. There's no judgment from any living thing about who they are and what they do."

"Do you feel I'm judging you?"

"Are you?"

"…Maybe," Shelby said. And then she added, "Both of my parents could be pretty judgy. I will try to do better."

Carol nodded thanks and started to head to the bedroom.

"Do you think the road will get plowed today?"

"There's no 'get' like by the Forest Service. It's whether Larry decides to call a plow."

"What helps him decide?"

"If we have a lot of people coming over the weekend and if he thinks the snow won't melt by then."

"What do <u>you</u> think?" Shelby asked pointedly.

Carol turned and went over to look out the living room window.

"Fifty-fifty shot. It'll take a while to melt."

Shelby could feel her pulse quicken, and not in a good way. She tried to pretend she was calm.

"I know you told me you had a satellite phone…would it be possible to call Larry at headquarters? I'd like to tell him my car is stuck. That might convince him to plow. And I'll chip in to help pay, if it comes to that. Plus, I don't want a snowplow to accidentally bury my car, so…."

"Okay," Carol sighed, with a hint of irritation in her voice.

Shelby bit her tongue. She hated being dismissed. But on the bright side, Carol started to dig in a storage cabinet in the dining area for the phone.

Shelby went over to the window again.

"We used to make forts when I was a kid and have snowball fights, me and my sister Roxanne versus my dad."

Carol was tossing things thither and yon: balled up extension cords, old key chains, souvenir beer bottles, half-used melted candles... until she came upon the satellite phone.

Carol turned the phone on. Well, she flipped a switch on the side. Shelby noted that the device looked to be several years old.

"Do they make newer ones now?"

"Probably."

Carol stared at the phone. She cleared her throat and then shook the phone.

"Is it working?"

Carol pursed her lips. Shelby took that for a "no."

"Was it supposed to be charged or something?"

"I charge it every few months," Carol said with a sandpapery tone of annoyance. Then she added, "Well, there's nothing we can do now."

"Literally nothing?"

"Did you have a suggestion?" Carol asked sharply.

"Yeah. I'm gonna hike up to my car and put a flag on it, and if I still have enough energy, I'm going to hike all the way to Larry and get him to call a plow. Do you have a pair of snow boots and a jacket I could wear?"

Carol could see Shelby wasn't backing down, so she went to the hallway closet, another repository of ancient items, and dug out a pair of waterproof boots.

"What size do you wear?"

"Seven."

"These are eights. Let me get you a couple pair of socks...."

Carol went into the bedroom for socks, and Shelby looked back at the dining room cabinet where the detritus cluttered the floor around it. *Do I go pick it up or let it be?* Shelby counted to five internally and decided for Beatles mode.

"Here." Carol offered wool hiking socks and some thinner liner socks.

"Thanks. What have you got that I could tie to the car as a flag?"

"Hmmm...I have a rainbow gay pride flag left over from college, I think."

"Perfect."

Carol dug in the closet again and pulled out a Chico State rainbow flag on a wooden dowel. "I'll get you some twine, too."

More excavating and up came a ball of twine. As Carol handed Shelby the items, their hands touched. Carol softened and asked,

"Would you like me to come with you?"

"That would be wonderful. Trips are more fun as a team."

Carol nodded.

Chapter Forty

Sprite & Woodhawk

"I haven't seen snow like this in years. Not since we lived in Alaska!" Shelby said excitedly. "Look, it's frozen to the pine needles, like sugar frosting!"

"Did you like Alaska?" Carol asked as they hiked up the snowy two-laner.

"Some of it. Bald eagles and moose in the backyard, that was great. Limited daylight in the winter, not so much."

Shelby stopped to catch her breath, which was coming out in big cloudy steam engine puffs as they walked uphill. *Well, while I have a mo-*

ment, she thought, *let me dive into the storybook thing...and, dear God, let me do it with some kindness....*

"So, you read a lot when you were growing up, well, you still do, but when you were younger, did that lead to writing stories, too?"

"Sort've, yeah," Carol said, taking off her mittens, as she was warmed up by now.

Shelby waited patiently, hoping Carol would keep going.

Instead, Carol asked, "Are the boots working for you?"

"Yes, yes, they are, thanks. And plenty of room to tuck my pants inside them."

"Wet pants, no fun."

"Well, not <u>those</u> kind of wet pants," Shelby joked.

Carol chuckled.

Okay, I'm diving in, thought Shelby. *She's in a good space.*

"You said 'sort've.' Did you write your own novels?"

"No, I've written a bunch of shorter pieces, a lot of them with former lovers."

"You wrote them together? Did you pass the computer keyboard back and forth?" Shelby asked innocently, knowing full well how the writing was accomplished.

"No, we'd pass a pen back and forth. Actually," Carol said, "we'd often hike around campus or in the woods here and create the story as we walked. Then we'd go back home and write it all down."

"That sounds like fun," Shelby said, trailing behind Carol in her boot prints.

"Want to try it?"

Whoa, didn't see that coming, Shelby thought.

"Uhh, sure? What am I supposed to do?"

"Well, first we usually start with a preamble: 'We call upon the great and wise muses of the universe to guide us as we create a world of our own.'"

"I like it."

"Cool. Now you repeat a little of what I say, and then add on. It's like passing a talking stick back and forth."

"Okay."

"But first we pick a time, so past, present or future?"

"I get to pick?"

"Absolutely," said Carol.

"Uh, future?"

"Great. How far into the future?"

"Mm, a hundred years?" Shelby ventured.

"Sounds great. Here we go."

Carol surveyed their sparkling white wonderland and then with her arms out wide said, "I see a planet where the women communicate with the trees and rocks and streams...."

Shelby took a baby story step by adding, "I see a planet where the women <u>hear</u> the trees and rocks and streams...."

"Great. One day Woodhawk and Sprite were out walking in the snow...."

"Is that us?"

"Could be," Carol said with a smile. "Would you like to be Sprite?"

Shelby smiled back and continued, "Woodhawk <u>and Sprite</u> were out walking...and...."

She looked around, stumped.

"Time for a complication," Carol whispered.

"Righto," Shelby whispered back. And then she said, no longer whispering, "Out walking, and...they were being followed by a shadow."

"Cool. What's the shadow?"

Shelby paused and literally stopped in her snow tracks. Something had cracked open inside of her.

"Me."

Carol turned around and stopped as well.

"Doing what?"

"...I'm a hundred and thirty-seven years old...and I'm still fantasizing about women who aren't interested in me...and I'm still fucking up my life."

Carol squeezed Shelby's shoulder to comfort her.

"...Sprite had to figure out what to do next...see what resources were available," Carol added tenderly.

"...What resources were available...." Shelby looked around, lost in the sea of white.

Carol glanced over and saw a snow-dusted pine tree at the side of the road. She took Shelby's hand in hers and gently led her to it. "Pete the Pine says, 'See all of my ridges and layers? That's my accumulated wisdom. Every year, I get a little bit taller, grow a few more branches and leaves...and become even more of who I am.'"

Carol took off Shelby's mitten and placed her bare hand onto the bark ridges to feel the tree's soul. Shelby let her hand rest there to feel the sturdiness of the pine.

"You're accumulating wisdom. Growing your own circles of knowledge each year," Carol added.

Shelby nodded and smiled.

"And that's the beauty of creating stories, they take us to far-off places and sometimes they take us within," Carol said softly.

Shelby kissed Carol on the cheek and said, "I'm sorry I was so judgy earlier."

Carol stared up at the frosty tree tops and quietly added, "It's okay. I've got to do something about all that crap."

Now it was Shelby's turn to laugh.

"Hey! No laughing!" Carol protested with a grin.

"What? Laughter is the best medicine!"

"Or so they said in *Reader's Fucking Digest!*"

They started up the road, giggling, and back on track.

And then they heard a noise. They quickly turned around to face downhill...and sure enough, a snowplow was chugging up the two-laner.

"Larry called the plow!" Shelby yelled. "Hallelujah!"

Carol sprinkled snow on Shelby's borrowed fuzzy hat.

When the plow got up to their spot, they flagged down the driver (Carol actually knew him, he was from down in Bishop) and hopped into the truck's cab to ride to Shelby's car a mile up the road.

The driver did an expert job of clearing the road next to Shelby's Honda Fit and then offered to use the plow plus a chain to tow her car.

"It's all gonna be okay, isn't it?" Shelby said.

"Yep, it is," Carol answered as they watched the Honda make it safely back onto the road.

Chapter Forty-One

Dad

"I forgot to pack peanut butter!" exclaimed Lulu.

"That's okay, we have peanut butter," said Shelby.

"And jelly?"

"And jelly."

"I picked out cookies! And a banana!"

"Well done," said Shelby with a big smile.

Shelby was reassuring a third-grader who was going on her first overnight camping trip in June. And Shelby could so relate since she used to worry about EVERYTHING with Dad-the-Taskmaster.

Right now, the hikers were a couple of miles into the trip out of Sierra Glen and little Lulu was jumping around as if she had springs in her hiking boots.

"Bread, I remembered bread!"

"Very good. How did you remember bread but not peanut butter? They kinda go together, don't they?" Shelby asked in a light and friendly way. She didn't want to come off as harsh, but she did want to make this a teaching moment.

"I saw the ground squirrel grabbing the popcorn bag and totally forgot!"

"Oh, right. Yeah, we gotta keep an eye out for critters, they shouldn't be eating People Food."

There were a half dozen hikers on this, Carol and Shelby's first overnight excursion. Lulu and her dad were two of them. He seemed like a seasoned pro who wanted to introduce his daughter to the wonders of camping. The other four were a married (straight) couple in their fifties and two women in their thirties. Everyone except Lulu had a little bit of camping experience and some previous hikes at altitude under their belts. So, Carol and Shelby felt they were off to a good start, mid-morning on a Saturday in mid-June.

Shelby was at the back of the pack in "sweep" position. Carol was at the front, since she knew the route, and then they'd switch positions for the trip back Sunday afternoon.

Shelby felt she and Carol were in a good rhythm by now. They'd started leading hikes the beginning of May and by June, they felt ready for this, their first campout.

Equally wonderful: Carol had gone with her to Bishop's jazz festival in May. It took a bit of persuading.

~ ❧ ~

"What do people wear to these things?" Carol asked with concern.

"These things?" replied Shelby.

"Well, it's jazz and it's a festival."

"You're not on stage, no one is expecting you to dress like Ella Fitzgerald." She could tell Carol hadn't been out "on the town" in forever.

"It's Bishop, no one dresses up, right?" Shelby said reassuringly.

"Yeah, that's true."

274

Shelby went to Carol's closet and pulled out jeans and a blue and green plaid short-sleeved shirt.

"Voilá."

A few hours later they sat on worn wooden benches and listened to the music at the town amphitheater, the sun dipping behind the Sierra Nevada and the plump full moon peeking over the White Mountains in the east. Shelby watched Carol looking around as if she'd just landed from another planet.

"Everything okay?" Shelby asked.

"I don't know. I just haven't been around this many people in forever. I mean, Sierra Glen, even when we're totally booked, is like sixty. We had a good turnout at Darcy's farewell concert, but still…."

"How does it feel?"

"…Good."

"You sure, sweetie?"

"Yeah. I've been…I'm too…cut off, I know…."

Shelby could see Carol's eyes misting up.

And then the ensemble and their lady vocalist started a Van Morrison classic. Shelby turned and said to Carol, "Hey, it's a marvelous night for a moondance." Then she grabbed Carol's hand to dance in the aisle with the other patrons...and Carol balked and stayed seated.

"I don't dance," she whispered tersely.

"I don't care, just bounce along to the rhythm, I'll do the rest."

So Carol bobbed her head and shoulders as Shelby shimmied in the aisle while continuing to sing along with the band, about her dreams coming true and making someone your own.

By the end of the song, Carol was crying, she was so touched.

~ ❧ ~

"I think I'm getting a blister…." one of the 30-something gals confided to Shelby on the June hike.

Shelby snapped out of her moondance reverie and saw Hailey wiggling her right foot and furrowing her brow. She could hear the shame in Hailey's voice; this was yet another thing she herself had struggled with.

"Oh, it happens to the best of us, and thanks for catching it early," Shelby said reassuringly. "I've got Band-Aids in my pack, let's pull over to the side and find a log to sit on."

Hailey plopped down on the next big log with major relief and took off her boot and wool socks, revealing tiny pink toes with pink nail polish.

Oh my, thought Shelby, *very nice.* And then as she peeled open a Band-Aid and leaned over to Hailey, she caught a whiff of tea tree oil shampoo. *Oh my.* And then she could hear Randall chiding her: "Stay focused, just offer customer service, don't go window-shopping for a new squeeze."

"Here, you can reach your heel better than I can, why don't you put it on...." Shelby said, handing over the Band-Aid.

Hailey did so but sighed a little too loudly for the size of the not-even-quite-forming blister.

"What's the matter?"

"What if I mess this up?"

"Mess what up?"

"This trip," Hailey said.

"You won't. Short of falling off a cliff, you won't. And I won't let you fall off a cliff. Are you having performance anxiety, like everyone else is better than you are?"

"Yes," Hailey said, brushing her chestnut-colored bangs away from her eyes. "I guess you could call it that. My friend Debbie has a lot more experience than I do. Look how much faster she's hiking than I am. It's me and Lulu at the back of the pack. I'm with an eight-year-old."

"Well, by going on our trip, you're accumulating your own experience and knowledge. If you don't do stuff like this, you won't get the skills. And besides, we're here to see the scenery, not compete. It's a lesson I've had to learn myself, growing up with a dad in the military."

"My dad, me, too!"

And suddenly, Hailey came alive. She and Shelby put their packs back on and chattered like a couple of mockingbirds about their shared Marching Through Hell with Dad moments.

"Oh, let me tell you about the time we wanted to build a snow fort," Hailey exclaimed. "My dad decided he was going to SUPERVISE as if aliens were going to attack and it had to be BOMB PROOF!"

"Been there!" Shelby chimed in.

A good half mile had passed as they chitchatted and traded war stories before Shelby looked up to see Carol and the rest of the hikers waiting at a fork in the trail.

Except all of the hikers weren't there—Lulu was missing.

276

And Carol looked worried. "Where's Lulu?" she asked.

"Gosh, isn't she with you?" replied Shelby, with some defensiveness.

Carol blinked, gesturing with her open palm, showing, nope, just us chickens here.

"Well, Hailey and I stopped to put a Band-Aid on a blister and we stayed on the trail the whole time, so I have no idea...."

"Well, you're the sweep, so...."

Shelby could hear Carol implying this was her fault somehow. She glanced over at Lulu's dad who looked incredulous.

"You gotta be kidding me!" he bellowed.

"We'll find her, don't worry," Shelby said. Then she nodded to Carol to step to the side so they could strategize.

Dad started to join them.

"Give us a second," Shelby asked.

"We don't have any extra seconds," he said firmly.

"Half a second," answered Shelby.

She pulled Carol away from him.

"You were hiking too fast, you have to keep the group together," Shelby said through clenched teeth.

"Now isn't the time to Monday morning quarterback, we have to find her," Carol tossed back.

"I know, but your 'You're the sweep' put the blame ON ME and it's a team sport here, Carol! Now let's retrace our steps."

Carol turned to the dad and the other hikers. "Okay, we go back at a brisk pace, sweep your eyes far and wide and take turns calling out for Lulu."

Everyone was up for it, and then Hailey's friend Debbie piped up. "I heard her say she really enjoyed the shooting star flowers next to the creek, a while back. Maybe she went down to the creek to look at them."

"Were you the last person who saw her?" asked the dad.

"I don't know," Debbie said defensively. "I was talking to Rachel and Bob about hang-gliding. I didn't think it was my job to keep an eye on your daughter. Why were you all the way up at the front with Carol, Mr. Dad?"

"Folks, let's get going!" Carol called, heading off a big round of the Blame Game.

"Here we go!" yelled Shelby. "Lulu! Lulu!"

Shelby then did her own internal round of the Blame Game: *Did I talk too long with Hailey? Should I have made her walk a little faster? Oh, jeeze....*

"Lulu! Where are you?" called out the dad.

Shelby noticed everyone was looking downhill toward the creek area, so she decided to focus uphill. Of course, they were so loud, Lulu would've heard them in either direction. Unless she was unconscious, Shelby realized.

"Lulu! Come back to the trail!" Shelby yelled.

"I should've known this would happen," the dad huffed.

Hailey and Shelby exchanged a glance: déjà vu with their dads.

Carol decided to diplomatically wade in. "What makes you say that?"

"She has a mind of her own," the dad said. "She's like a puppy on caffeine."

Carol was thinking having a mind of one's own could be a good thing, but she didn't want to second-guess someone else's parenting skills. Instead, she offered, "We'll find her."

Bob and Rachel started to tell some stories of their kids wandering away at a state fair years ago before cell phones, and with thousands of people at the Iowa fairgrounds, it was a parent's worst nightmare.

"And then we remembered the kids had wanted to ride the Thunderama roller coaster, so we headed over—"

"Lulu!" Shelby yelled, cutting Rachel off. She spied Lulu's bright yellow shirt; the girl was hiding behind a tree.

"Come back and join us," Shelby called, invitingly, as if nothing were too terribly wrong.

But Lulu looked as if she were trapped in a horror movie and the group soon saw why: her dad was marching up the hill in attack mode.

"HOW MANY TIMES HAVE I TOLD YOU NOT TO RUN OFF? I AM SICK AND TIRED OF YOUR INSUBORDINATION!"

Everyone on the trail exchanged glances, fearful for Lulu, who got up and ran down to the group—right for Shelby.

She didn't know whether to hug her or turn her over. Shelby opted for the former and mouthed "HELP!" to Carol who jumped in front of the dad.

"Hey, sir, everything is okay."

"No, it's not."

"No, really it is. She's fine. Kids wander." Then Carol added gently, "Maybe if you weren't so hard on her, she wouldn't avoid you."

Shelby and Hailey exchanged a look that implied *"Shit, can't believe she said that!"*

Neither could the dad. "I didn't ask for your input, lady!"

"I'm in charge of this trip. Here on the trail, you're under my jurisdiction. We do not yell at kids who are learning the ways of the woods."

Shelby wanted to cry, she was so proud of Carol. She wished Carol could have stood up to her dad like that back in the day.

"Yes, let's make this a teaching moment," Shelby chimed in. "Lulu, it's a good idea to always have another hiker within sight. If they're going too fast, say something. How does that sound?"

Lulu nodded, but she still wouldn't go near her dad.

Carol added, "I'm going to walk at a slower pace so we can stay together better. I'm sorry I was going too fast."

Shelby continued with: "And if anyone needs a break, please speak up and we'll be sure to stop immediately. I'll keep a closer eye on the front of the group."

Everyone nodded. Even Dad. He stared at the ground. Then he looked up at Lulu. They eyed each other warily as a breeze whispered through the trees bringing some cooling energy to the proceedings.

Bog Shooting Stars

Chapter Forty-Two

Heart Problems

The hikers were fairly subdued until they got to the campsite Carol had picked out for them, a grassy, shady spot overlooking Flower Lake. Once she saw the lakeside flowers, Lulu was her old enthusiastic self.

"Bog shooting stars! Let's go pick them, let's go pick them!" she exclaimed.

Shelby countered that idea by saying, "First, let's put up our tent while we have sunshine, then we'll look at the flowers. And by the way, they don't like to be picked. They need to stay in the ground to hold the earth together."

"Oh." Lulu looked as if she'd proposed a bad, bad thing.

"But we could take pictures of them so you could show your friends back home, how about that?"

"Sure! Okay!"

Shelby had become de facto camp counselor to Lulu, a role she'd never played before, but it was keeping Lulu in line and the dad calm.

Shelby passed along the finest tent-pitching tips she knew, which fascinated Lulu and Hailey.

Camp set-up was followed by flower-strolling and rock-skipping at the lake. Then everyone helped fix dinner, and of course, dessert was s'mores at the evening campfire.

"Don't eat too many of those things!" the dad admonished.

Lulu looked stressed at yet another of his edicts. Shelby whispered to her, "I got sick once when I ate too many. I think two will be just the right amount, how's that?"

Lulu nodded.

And then Carol handed a stick with poofy fresh marshmallows on it to the dad.

"Your turn."

He shook his head no.

"What, too silly for ya?"

"No, watching my waistline."

"C'mon, Dad, c'mon, Dad!" Lulu said.

"This is a great life skill to learn," Carol added good-naturedly.

He reluctantly took the stick and began to toast the creamy puffs. Lulu tentatively went over to join him.

"Don't burn it, Dad!"

"I won't, I won't."

Once the marshmallows were a perfect golden toasty brown, he took the stick away from the flame and graciously offered the treats to his daughter to sandwich between cinnamon crackers and chocolate pieces.

"Don't burn yourself!" he warned.

"I know, I know!"

He nodded and quietly added, "I know you know."

Carol and Shelby exchanged a glance. The energy had shifted between father and child. Whew.

That night in their tent, as the two trip leaders cradled each other, they reflected on the day.

"Disaster Averted," Carol said.

"You did great today, you really did," Shelby said.

"You, too."

"He reminds me too much of my dad," sighed Shelby.

"Yeah, my mom could be really judgmental," added Carol.

"About what?"

"Me. Wanted me to get my nose out of a book, meet more people, make more friends. When my parents sold the farm and moved to town, my mom was in heaven. I was miserable. She even…." Carol's voice trailed off.

"She even what…?"

Carol's voice dropped below a whisper. "She even got rid of my favorite books when I was in high school. I came home one afternoon and…."

"Holy shit! That's not right!"

"No, it's not."

Shelby suddenly realized why Carol held on to everything and anything. Shelby rolled even closer to Carol and hugged her tightly.

"You have come so far from those days and are such an amazing person. And here in the Sierra Nevada, you're really in your element."

"Thank you."

They lay in each other's arms, listening to the bullfrogs calling to one another.

"When did you find your footing in the forest?" Shelby whispered.

"College."

"With Gillian?"

"Yeah. But…."

Shelby waited.

"But the turning point was when I went out into the woods on my own. Gillian had discovered a cool foresty spot next to a creek outside of town. The first time we went, I was all freaked out because she didn't have a map and there wasn't really a trail. She was following scribbles on a piece of paper. She was amazing. She had some sort of internal radar and kept going—I was ready to bail. But she found the spot, which I ended up loving and was so glad I didn't hightail it back to the car. A few days after that first trip, I wanted to see if I could find the creek again on my own."

"That was bold."

"Yeah. And a little crazy. I took her jottings, borrowed her car, and set out by reading little gems like: "Turn right at the oak tree that's bent in half."

Shelby laughed, picturing the misadventure. "Did you get lost?"

"A couple of times. And my heart was pounding so loudly I thought the birds could hear it."

"What did you do?"

"I retraced my steps and figured out what I did wrong. AND, here's the big piece, I stacked up pine cones and rocks so I could find my way back."

"Genius."

"Anyway, that was my big turning point. I went back a bunch of times on my own and even explored other areas. Every trip I fell deeper and deeper in love with the outdoors."

"...And with Gillian?"

Carol nodded in the darkness of the tent. There followed a profound silence. Shelby decided not to go any further into that history.

Sunday morning on the camp stove, Carol cooked a hearty breakfast of blueberry pancakes and scrambled eggs...and then it was time to pack up.

They made one side trip by going all the way around Flower Lake and then headed back down to Sierra Glen. Carol stopped frequently under the guise of telling about the local flora and fauna, and Lulu fell in love with the Foxtail Pine.

"It looks like a scary monster!" Lulu yelled and then she raised her arms over her head, mimicking the craggily branches and walking like Frankenstein. "ARRRGGHH!"

Everyone laughed, the Missing Lulu Incident a distant memory now.

Once back at Sierra Glen Cabins, everyone hugged goodbye and complimented Carol and Shelby. Well, the dad didn't offer any hugs, but he did give each of them a firm handshake and a solid, authentic thank you.

The backpackers scattered, and Carol threw her arm around Shelby. "Well done, my dear."

"And to you as well, my dear. Whew!"

They laughed and then went up the steps to the main building.

"Okay, NEXT time we have a longer 'meet and greet' to get to know the personalities, what do you think?" Carol asked.

"Yeah, although you never know what people will be like until they're under pressure."

"True, so true," Carol said, as she slipped her backpack off and put it behind the front desk.

Just then Larry walked out of his office to the front reception area.

"How'd the overnighter go?"

"Great," said Carol.

She and Shelby exchanged a look: how to finesse what happened with Lulu?

"We had some excellent teaching moments," Shelby said. "The father and daughter had some growing to do for an adventure like this, and they both came out of it stronger and more aware."

"Nice," Larry said, looking a little distracted. Shelby waited for follow-up from him because he always followed up.

Carol gave her a discreet "thumbs up" for her answer, but Larry just went back toward his office. And then he bumped into the door frame and dropped some papers.

"Shit."

"Here," Shelby said, offering to pick things up.

"I've got it," Larry snapped, more irritated than Shelby had ever heard him.

She backed away…but then saw his hands fluttering and not quite able to pick up the papers. She shot Carol a "What the hell?" look.

Carol came over and watched Larry, who also seemed to be sweating, and it wasn't even remotely hot out.

"Hey, Larry, what's up?" she said with fake casualness.

"Nothing, low blood sugar, just need to eat," he replied with perfunctory efficiency. "Got a banana in my office."

He finally got the papers in his hand and went toward his desk. The two women peeked inside to see what would happen next.

Larry just sat at his desk staring, sweating, and taking some deep breaths.

"How about that banana?" Carol said. She went over to his desk, picked it up, and handed it to him. He dropped it.

Carol and Shelby exchanged another look and this time they were quite concerned.

"How long have you been feeling like this?" Carol asked supportively, trying not to sound as if she were prying.

"I'm fine," he said in a clipped tone. Then he added, "A new group just arrived. My San Gabriel Valley Asian Hikers. Must get them settled in, and then can you give them a talk this afternoon. They love history."

"Sure. How is midafternoon?"

Larry didn't answer; he seemed to be trying to grok what "midafternoon" meant.

"Uh, three o'clock?" Carol offered.

Larry didn't answer again and Shelby jumped in. "Does your arm hurt? Or chest?"

"I'm fine, I'm fine!"

A bright voice called from the doorway, "Hey, Larry!" All three of them turned to see a bubbly Asian man, mid-50s, waving a hiking pole. "We're all here!"

"Great, Roger!" yelled Larry, overcompensating for whatever was ailing him. He leapt out of his chair to greet his friend and got halfway across the room before he collapsed on the floor.

"Call 9-1-1!" Carol said to Shelby.

Shelby ran to the office phone at the front desk. Carol had to actually hold Larry down, with much-appreciated help from Roger, who tossed his hiking pole to the side.

"I'M FINE, I'M FINE, I'M FINE!" Larry chanted, and then he said a string of words in Mandarin, which Carol couldn't comprehend.

Roger yelled back in their native language, and Carol took it to mean something like "You're NOT fine!"

More yelling ensued until Shelby ran back in. "They're on their way, driving, they couldn't get a helicopter!"

"I can drive him down the mountain, meet them on the way!" Roger offered.

"Great plan!" Carol said.

"One of us has to stay here," Shelby said. "You know the operation of the place better than I do, why don't you stay and I'll ride down with them."

"Sounds good!"

"I'll get my car!" Roger grabbed his hiking pole and ran out of there.

Larry swore in Mandarin.

"English, Larry, say it in English."

"I'm fine, let me go."

"You're not fine. Does your chest hurt? Does it feel tight?" Carol asked.

"A little," he finally conceded.

"We'll get you taken care of," Carol added.

They all heard Roger's car skid as it pulled up outside on the gravel. The women helped Larry to his feet and out the door.

"I have bad news...."

"Oh, boy," Carol said nervously into the phone as she looked up from the cash register. "Let me finish this transaction."

Carol totaled the room amount for the late arrival, handed over a receipt and a room key. "Cabin 9, all yours. The lights have come on, so you should be able to see the number on the door. Let me know if you need anything."

The graying senior couple nodded their thanks and exited as Carol quickly got back to Shelby on the phone.

"Sorry, okay, what's up?"

"Heart attack and he needs triple bypass surgery."

"Holy shit. Where are you?"

"Pal's. Larry's friend brought me back."

"Where's Larry?"

"The critical care place in Bishop. An ambulance will be taking him to Cedars Sinai in L.A."

"Oh my God, who's going with him? Should I go down there?"

"I don't think so, Carol. He has cousins in L.A. who are going to meet him at the hospital. He doesn't have kids, does he?"

"Actually, he has a son but they're not on speaking terms. I should go down there."

"Uh, Carol, if you go to L.A., who runs the ship? I only know how to do a few things."

"Oh, God, yeah, we need to think things through."

"Yeah," Shelby agreed. "Like, how in the world will we lead overnight trips with Larry gone? Maybe short day-hikes with ONE of us?"

"Yeah, and then there's nighttime..."

"Nighttime?" Shelby asked.

"Well, Larry lives on the premises, in case anything goes wrong. It rarely happens, but it's good that he's here.

"So...would you spend the night there?"

"Jeeze, I guess I'll have to. I have a key to Larry's place."

"Do you want me to bring you a change of clothes in the morning?"

"That'd be great," Carol said. "Oh, and I ordered a new satellite phone. Should be here in the middle of the week."

"Thanks for doing that. Well, gosh, that's all I can think of for now. Love you."

"Love you, too."

Shelby put her thumb on the red "End Call" button. They felt like a team now.

"Want ketchup?" Pal was standing in the doorway between the kitchen and the dining room of her home.

"Yes, please. And those fried potatoes smell great," said Shelby, wearily putting her phone down on the dining room table.

"One of my specialties. Burger will be done in five."

"Thanks for making dinner," Shelby said.

"So, Larry's pretty bad, huh?"

"Yeah. I talked to the doctor for a bit. Larry wasn't taking good care of himself."

"Stressed out every time I saw him," Pal noted.

"Yeah. Um, do you think Carol will be okay running the place without him?"

"Sure. She's been there years longer than Larry. The tricky part is…." Pal said as she scooped the fried potatoes onto a plate.

"Is?"

"Will Carol keep doing things the way Larry likes them?"

"Yeah." Shelby took the plate from Pal and stabbed a couple of crispy potatoes with a fork.

"And here's the ketchup." Pal squirted a glob of Heinz's finest onto Shelby's plate.

"Thanks," Shelby said. "Yeah, it'll be interesting."

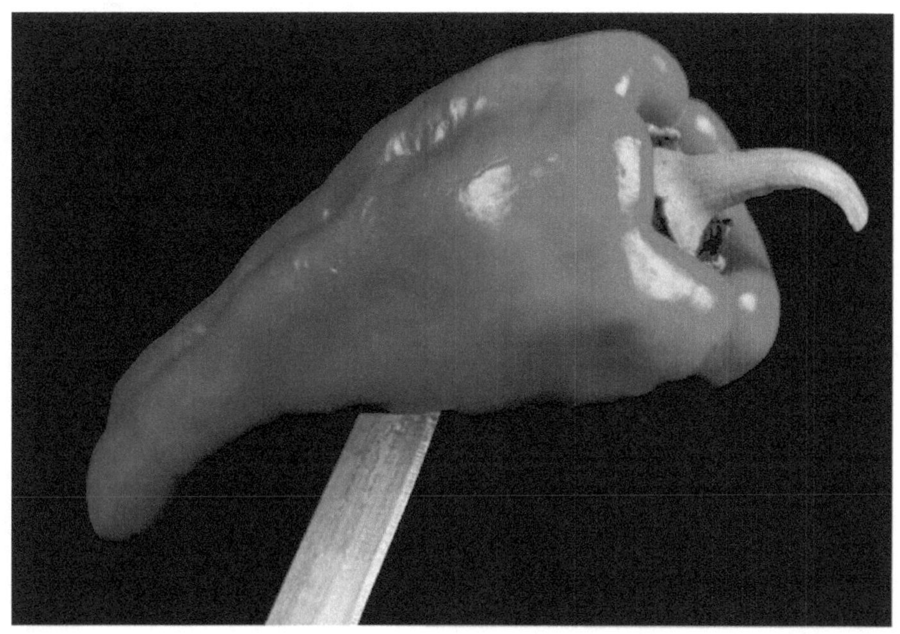

Chapter Forty-Three

The Week That Was

"What do you need me to do?"

"Check in on the gift shop and then the restaurant," Carol replied to Shelby. "Larry places supply and food orders Monday mornings."

"Got it," said Shelby, standing at the front desk beside Carol. "How are you doing?"

"I barely slept last night."

Shelby gave Carol a big hug, wondering if she should've spent the night at Larry's cabin with Carol instead of staying at Pal's. Of course, that would've meant two people not sleeping well.

"Larry feels like family, huh?" Shelby said quietly into Carol's ear.

"Yeah. I didn't realize how much until now."

Shelby gave her a quick kiss on the cheek and headed out of the main building to the little gift shop.

"Hey Roberta, how's it going?" Shelby said brightly as she entered the shop, trying to pretend nothing was too terribly wrong. Roberta was the seventy-year-old shop manager, and this had turned out to be the perfect job for her, an on-the-ball accountant who had retired a few years ago from that daily grind. She worked May through October up here in the mountains and then got to spend winters back down at her retirement village in Palm Springs.

"Jim-dandy, except for Larry, poor thing."

"Yeah, gosh, huh? So, what are you low on?" Shelby asked.

"Just some propane bottles for campers and their stoves. A dozen should be good. They like the one-pound Coleman size. And how is Larry doing?"

"Uh, we'll know more in a day or so, he's having bypass surgery today."

"Oh my. I've always appreciated how much he cares about this place."

"Yeah," said Shelby.

"He'll pull through, he's such a fighter."

"You said it!" Shelby nodded and finished jotting down the propane order. "Anything else you need here?"

Roberta paused and Shelby could tell she had a thought.

"Hm?"

"Well..." Roberta said, lowering her voice as if someone could be eavesdropping. "The higher-end merchandise isn't moving. I've told Larry this before. People will buy regular T-shirts and sweatshirts but not the expensive wool and fleece. He said they sell those items at the Grand Canyon, but this isn't the Grand Canyon. Plus, we don't have a lot of room here. We do better with the less expensive things."

"Ah, got it. I'll pass that along when he's feeling better."

"Thank you so much," Roberta said, beaming at her.

That went well, Shelby concluded. She left Roberta and angled over to the restaurant where breakfast was nearly done, hoping this was a good time to check in.

Shelby decided to go through the front door to the dining room rather than the back entrance to the kitchen just to see how things were going.

Hmm, patrons are chatty, their plates are empty, the staff is clearing tables quickly...looks pretty good. She headed into the kitchen area, and as with Roberta, she'd said hello to these folks before but hadn't gotten to know them well.

"Hi, I'm Shelby," she said to Manuel, the main chef.

"Yeah, we've met," he said curtly.

"...Is now a good time to chat?" she asked, since he looked a little stressed.

"Whatever."

Yikes. Manuel wore a bandana around his head and chopped veggies with so much vigor he looked like an action hero dismembering aggressive foes who'd gotten in his way.

"Well, I'm told that today is supply ordering day. I thought I'd check in, y'know, since Larry isn't here...."

"You wanna know what we need?"

He said it with so much sarcasm, Shelby wasn't sure if it was a rhetorical question or genuine.

"Yes, what do you need?

"We need the old menu back and we need raises. That's what we need."

Uh oh. Shelby realized she'd stepped into an angry action hero's lair. *I'll bet he's been building up this resentment for a long time.*

"Do you want to talk about it?" Shelby asked politely.

"Only if you can do something about it."

"Well, I don't know if I can do something right this second, since Larry's about to have open-heart surgery. But I'd love to get your thoughts so we can address your concerns."

Manuel continued to chop zucchini with such ferocious intensity, Shelby was afraid to step any closer. She decided to wait a few moments to see if he would open up without her having to prod him. Sure enough....

"Okay, here's the deal: His SPECIALITY menu items cost a lot more than our older menu. Yeah, he raised the price for customers, but we haven't had a raise in two years!"

Oh shit.

"And he keeps adding new activities. I heard there's a massage person or a yoga person coming this summer and then there's overnight camping trips. And meanwhile, we're still stuck at the bottom of the pay scale!"

Fuck. Yeah, I'm in over my head, Shelby thought.

"Tell you what," she said with the diplomacy of a nuclear arms negotiator, "I'll talk to Carol about it. Everyone deserves to be paid a fair wage, and two years is a long time without a raise. Let's see what we can do. Okay?"

Manuel then stabbed a red bell pepper with his machete and lifted it up. The pepper hung in the air like a heart being offered for sacrifice.

"I can't raise their wages right now, they know that," said Carol a few minutes later in the office. "And Manuel's been complaining since the day he started. Larry keeps him because he's an amazing chef, but I think California has other good cooks and we could easily replace him."

"Ahhhh, okay, but we can't do that without Larry's permission, right?"

Carol sighed. "I can't talk about this right now. The sewer line is giving Julio fits—I may have to call a plumber."

"Wow, sorry to hear that. Well, what do you want me to tell Manuel?"

"Nothing. Stay out of it. Just get the food order."

Shit, Shelby thought, *forgot to get the grocery list.*

Shelby exited the main building again and this time saw Julio. "Hey there," she called, wanting some of his friendly energy before she went back into the lair.

"Hi, Miss Shelby. How is Mr. Larry?"

"Uh, we'll know more in a few days, I think."

"I'll keep him in my prayers."

"I'm sure he'll appreciate that. How's the sewer?"

"Not good, Miss Shelby, not good."

"Oh, boy, well, good luck...."

"Thank you."

"Uh, Julio...."

"Yes?"

"Just out of curiosity, how long have you worked here and when was the last time you got a raise?"

"I've been here ten years and I got a raise two years ago plus a Christmas bonus last year. One hundred dollars," Julio said, smiling.

"Thanks. I'm just surveying the troops, don't say anything to anyone."

"Very good, Miss Shelby," he said, tipping his hat, and then he went into the main building to talk sewer fixes with Carol.

To get centered, Shelby looked around at the Sugar Pines for a moment, the summer breeze lifting their top branches. *This is what I wanted, right? The mountains, a fun girlfriend as a steady partner, hot sex, a job where I'm not chasing something that I don't want...right?*

Shelby went in the back door to the kitchen and found Manuel sautéing the veggies. The sizzling sound seemed to add to the tension in the room.

"Hi. I forgot to get the grocery list. Do you have it?"

He just kept stirring the peppers-carrots-mushrooms-zucchini mix.

"Manuel, this'll go easier if you talk to me. What's up?"

"Why does Larry have to order the groceries? I'm the chef!"

Ah. Shelby could take a wild guess on that one: Larry wanted to keep control of the food; if Manuel ordered it, he'd pick out only what he wanted and not what Larry wanted.

"Why don't you take that up with Larry when he gets back."

"I have before. He doesn't listen."

Manuel angrily wiped his hands on his white apron that was stained by years of cooking. Then he went to a little desk cubbyhole where he yanked off a sheet from a "Welcome to Sierra Glen" tablet. Shelby remembered seeing a tablet like that when she first stepped into her cabin, that day she was lost in the mountains and found this place.

"Here's the food list." Manuel dug through some papers and found a handwritten list of phone numbers. "And here are the phone numbers of the suppliers. Vegetables and fruits from here, meat from here, bread from here, cheese and dairy from here...."

"Thank you, perfect," Shelby said. And then she handed the grocery list and supplier phone numbers gently back to him.

"Why don't you call? You know your job better than I do. And let's work out something on the pay raise front with Larry when he gets back. How's that sound?"

Manuel gave her half a nod.

"I like the food here, you do a <u>great</u> job."

Another half a nod. And then he went back to the stove.

"<u>You what</u>?" Carol stared bug-eyed at Shelby when she returned from the kitchen.

"Carol, it makes more sense. If I fuck up the food order, then Manuel will be even angrier, and let me tell you, he was a twelve on a scale from one to ten for ballistic this morning."

"Larry's gonna kill you."

"Let him. If Larry would trust his employees more instead of micro-managing them, they would be happier, and it would be easier to negotiate things with them."

"Tell me you didn't promise Manuel a raise."

"I did not. But I said he, we, should talk to Larry about it. Two years without a raise is ridiculous."

"I haven't had a raise in THREE years!" Carol yelled.

"That's not my fault and don't take it out on me. We could negotiate for you, too."

"Be very careful. Larry fired the people who used to do our janitorial work. They thought the hours were too long for what they were getting paid, and boom, Larry let them go."

"You're kidding me."

"Nope."

"Well, I don't know how long I'll work here then, Carol. I know I'm at Sierra Glen on a trial basis, and we have to show the hikes we're leading are a moneymaker, but I'm not working for two or three years with no pay increase."

Shelby couldn't believe she'd said that. Carol couldn't, either, judging by the stunned look on her face.

"Don't panic, Carol, I'm here now, I'm here with you...I love you. I want to make this program work and I know it'll take more than one season. But standing up for ourselves is part of love."

Carol softened and nodded.

"How are the sewers?" Shelby asked, changing the subject.

"Shitty."

They both smiled at the pun.

"We've got a long section to unclog," Carol said. And it won't be cheap."

"Oh, shit." And this time neither of them laughed.

By Tuesday at closing time, the sewer news from the plumbing company was grim. Forget just unclogging, there would need to be several feet of new pipes installed and *el pronto* before more than a couple of toilets backed up.

"We have to let Larry know, right?" asked Shelby, as Carol tallied up the guest receipts for the day.

"Yeah. His cousin said the surgery went well, but I didn't bring up the sewers yet."

"Larry'll want to know. He's a control freak, like my dad. Do you have the cost estimate?"

"Yeah."

"How bad is it?"

"Close to ten thousand dollars."

"Ahhh!"

"My thoughts exactly."

If money was going out for things like sewers, how would anyone get a raise? Shelby wondered.

"Let's call his cousin tomorrow and find out when Larry can talk," Shelby proposed. "I know we don't want to give him another heart attack, but still."

"Okay," Carol said, her eyes glazing over.

"We can do this, Carol."

Wednesday afternoon, Carol called Larry's cousin as Shelby and Julio supportively (albeit nervously) stood by in the office.

The cousin was hesitant but handed his cell phone over to Larry, who was lying supine in his hospital bed.

"Hey, Larry, it's Carol, how are you feeling?" she said tenderly.

"Tired. Beat up. Elephant on my chest."

"Wow. I'm so sorry. Well, we're holding the fort here."

"That's good. Keep things going. Don't forget to check on the water pressure in the kitchen, Manuel has been complaining about it."

"Absolutely, we'll check on the kitchen water pressure," Carol said, looking at Shelby and Julio, signaling that yes, Larry was in Worry Wart mode even hundreds of miles away.

"Well, since you brought up water, we do have a pressing issue. The sewers have been backing up, and Julio and I both feel we've got to have some pipes replaced. We had someone come out and give us an estimate."

"How much?"

"...Ten thousand."

"No! Did you get more than one bid?"

"Uh, it's so urgent, I went with a strong recommendation from the contractor we've used before that's down in Bishop."

Carol could hear Larry's labored breathing, and then with great weariness he said simply, "All right."

"I'll call the plumbing company back, I think they can start tomorrow."

"You 'think'?"

"No, I know they can. Sorry." Carol then wrapped things up. "Please take good care. Everyone says hello, we'll see you soon!"

"Okay."

Carol hung up and looked at Shelby and Julio. "It's a go. But, boy, he sounded out of it. And there was no way in hell I could tell him about Manuel's complaints."

Shelby nodded her support.

Julio added, "I'll go check on the water pressure in the kitchen."

As he left, Shelby happened to glance at the wall calendar. "Uh, here comes our next challenge: we're scheduled to lead a long hike Friday, and we have eight people signed up for it. Do you want to do it? Do you want me to?"

"You know I can't do it, I have to keep an eye on the construction and the cash register!" Carol snapped.

The Larry conversation had gotten under Carol's skin.

"Okay, I could help with either of those things or I could lead the hike," Shelby answered, trying not to go down the cranky road in return.

Carol turned her back on Shelby and dialed the plumbers instead of answering her.

Is this how she deals with stress? Shelby wondered. *I'd hate to see her during Freshmen Orientation Week or Alumni Back to School weekend....*

Shelby decided to leave the main building to let Carol calm down and walked over to sit at a picnic table for a mental time-out. She contemplated Friday's outing. It was the hike she had done the second full day she was here *last* summer, to Pinyon Pass, where she thought she was going to drop from exhaustion and actually did fall into the creek. She knew she was in much better shape now, but the physical readiness of tourists who signed up for Pinyon Pass? Hard to say. She contemplated leading a shorter version of it, but even then, if something went wrong, she wouldn't have a co-leader to help.

Shelby made an executive decision, feeling she was an equal part in this salvage operation with Carol. She went back into the office. Carol was off the phone by now and had her head buried in her hands.

"Sweetie?"

"What?" Carol said, not even looking up.

"I'm cancelling Friday's hike. And I think we'd better cancel the rest of them and the campouts until Larry gets back. It's just not safe without two guides."

"That's lost revenue!"

"Yeah, well, losing a hiker is worse. We lucked out with Lulu. Can you back me up on this when we tell Larry?"

"We? It's gonna be me on the front lines getting his shrapnel!"

Shelby thought it might be safer to switch topics. "So, what time are the plumbers coming tomorrow?"

"Seven."

~⚶~

"DON'T BACK UP!" Carol yelled like a Marine commander on the front lines.

Shelby arrived early Thursday morning to find a backhoe driver nearly backing his rig into a dumpster; Carol's face was a study in worry lines and panic sweat. The driver made a course correction and revved the engine to begin digging—the noise was so loud, Carol jumped.

Shelby was holding a cup of coffee for Carol and wondered if caffeine was the correct remedy right now.

"<u>Hey, sweetie</u>!" Shelby yelled above the din, stepping closer to Carol. "Brought you a cup of Pal's finest. You want me to heat it up a bit first?"

Carol nodded and then went to scream at the backhoe driver some more.

"Five feet to the left!"

Yikes. Shelby went over to the restaurant, entering through the kitchen door this time.

"Hey, Manuel, how's it going?", she asked as she popped the mug of java into the microwave.

He just shook his head; the backhoe was an aural assault even in the kitchen.

"Yeah, but in the long run, it'll be better for Sierra Glen, right?"

He continued to line up chicken breasts to bake. "When's Larry coming back?" Manuel asked.

"Up in the air. At least six weeks. Can you hang on 'til then?"

He did a half shrug, but Shelby didn't sense a revolt happening right this second, which she considered a victory.

"BEEP-BEEP-BEEP!" said the microwave. Shelby grabbed the now-hot coffee and hustled out of the kitchen and over to the backhoe turmoil.

"Here ya go," Shelby said handing the mug to Carol and simultaneously giving her shoulder a loving squeeze.

"I'm not sure this guy knows what he's doing...." Carol muttered, taking a sip of the coffee.

"I'll go man the front desk."

Carol didn't even nod, she just turned to face the backhoe.

Shelby went to headquarters where a couple of people were already waiting outside to check out. After unlocking the door and totaling the tabs for the visitors, she made notes in case she forgot something in the transaction. That way Carol wouldn't be cross with her.

By mid-morning she'd posted signs up in various spots announcing tomorrow's guided hike to Pinyon Pass was cancelled.

When Shelby came back to the office, she was feeling blue that she wouldn't get into the High Sierra as planned. But as she opened the door, she looked at the carved wooden bear whose arms were over his head, at the welcoming ladybug flag and at the little hummingbird door sign. *Okay, this setting is way more charming than my desk at the college, c'mon, admit it,* she chided herself.

Meanwhile, back over at the construction zone, Carol nervously watched the digging. She was way too stressed to leave anything to chance. *What would Larry do, what would Larry do?* Carol chanted to herself. *He would've vetted the company better. He definitely would be watching this whole operation with eagle eyes.* So, there she stood at her command post, trying not to breathe in the dirt and dust being kicked up.

She yelled to Julio, "<u>Should we be hosing this down as they dig?</u>"

Julio gave her a "thumbs up" and went to drag a hose over to keep the dust at bay.

I hate this, Carol thought. *I hate managing people, I hate minding the minutia. I want to be back at my picnic table reading a book or chatting with visitors about the Stellar's jays and the pine trees.*

The backhoe stopped and Carol realized her ears were ringing.

"We're there!" the construction supervisor bellowed.

Carol looked in the hole, and sure enough, the sewer pipes were now visible. *Thank God,* she thought.

Carol staggered into the office in the early afternoon and plopped down in her desk chair.

"Other than that, Mrs. Lincoln, how did you enjoy the show?" asked Shelby, deciding to try dry wit this time.

Carol actually laughed. "I've never heard that one."

"My theatre friends in L.A. taught it to me."

"Ah. Well, it's getting there. The pipes have been pulled out. Boy, they've been there since this place was built, back in the forties."

"Did you get lunch?"

"Na."

"Carol, you have to take care of yourself."

"Don't nag. I'll get something in a bit."

Shelby realized, yeah, her lunch edict came out a little shrill.

Carol closed her eyes. Shelby wanted to let her rest, but she also wanted to tell her what she'd been up to. She was so proud of having successfully checked in several visitors, plus she'd implemented a few new ideas.

"Uh, I had trouble reconciling some of the visitors and their payments, so I created a new spreadsheet. It'll make things a lot easier to track. Is that okay with you?"

Carol, eyes still closed, raised her hand and flipped it back as if waving off a pesky bug in mid-air.

"And, uh, I couldn't find a good inventory list of what Roberta orders for the gift shop or what Manuel orders for the restaurant, so I made spreadsheets for that stuff, too. I'd like to have the staff fill them out each week and then I can type in what they write. Unless Larry has some other way of doing it, which he probably does, but I can keep track this way while he's gone."

Shelby waited for Carol.

"Honey?"

"Whatever."

And with that, Carol opened her eyes, got up, exited, and let the screen door slam behind her.

How the hell am I supposed to respond to that? Shelby wondered.

Shelby spent Thursday afternoon straightening up the office, putting paperwork into file folders that she labeled, doing some dusting and throwing out dead plants. As dinnertime approached, she walked back over to the construction zone, which now had orange plastic netting up as a fence. The workers were wrapping up for the day, and Carol was in deep discussion with the head honcho. They shook hands at the end of their interaction, so Shelby took that as a positive sign.

He got in his pickup truck and Carol turned around, walking by Shelby without even seeing her.

"Hey, stranger," said Shelby

"Oh—hi."

"Everything go okay?"

"I had to BEG them to work this weekend, I want this job finished as soon as possible."

"Does that mean overtime since it's a weekend?"

"I negotiated a deal," Carol said proudly.

"Way to go. Larry would be smiling, babe."

Carol started walking again. Shelby put her hand on her arm.

"Carol, could you not walk away when I'm talking to you?"

"I now have to let people know the water will be turned off tomorrow for half the day!"

"I'll put signs up on everyone's door tonight," Shelby offered quickly. "You want to tell the kitchen staff?"

Carol pulled her arm away, nodded, and headed for the kitchen.

"Well, that sounds like a fun day," said Pal as she served meatloaf slathered in BBQ sauce to Shelby.

"Yeah. With more thrills to come, no doubt."

Pal sat down at the dining room table to join Shelby for dinner.

"Thanks again for cooking, Pal."

"No problemo."

Shelby opened her mouth to say something, then stopped herself.

"What, Shelbycakes?"

"If she's like this now, what will she be like if other things go wrong on the Road of Life?"

"Good question."

"And, oh Wise One, your answer is...?"

"She loves her routines. Same thing for lunch every day. Book in hand at the picnic table."

"'Don't try to change her.'"

"So, you WERE listening when I said that," Pal said, grinning.

"Is this someone I can spend longer than one season with? Is Sierra Glen a place I could work for longer than six months? Of course, there's the whole financial thing. We've had to cancel the hikes and backpack trips for now. But even if those went swimmingly, would they be moneymakers?"

"And would being with Carol all the time drive you nuts? Most people don't work and live together."

"True."

Shelby ate a big bite of the meatloaf and pondered aloud, "Has she ever considered, even for a millisecond, working somewhere else?"

"Are you thinking of dragging her back to L.A., and good luck with that, by the way."

"Just a wild thought. Do you think she might go for it?"

"Darcy almost got her to go to Seattle with her."

"REALLY? I had no idea!"

"She didn't tell you that?"

"No."

"Yeah, Darcy got a cool recording thing set up with an old buddy and Carol told her she would go."

"What happened?" asked Shelby.

"You moved to town."

"Oh. Shit."

"Yeah. Easy way out. She gets to have her pussy and eat it, too."

Chapter Forty-Four

Marlene

Friday was…interesting.

Shelby stood outside of the main building to constantly field questions and direct people to the outhouses over in the camping area. The indoor toilets were out of service until the water could be turned back on.

The kitchen staff used paper plates for breakfast and lunch, and they had emergency water in five-gallon bottles. For the two meals, they relied on food that was either pre-packaged or didn't need water to make edible.

Carol hadn't spoken to Shelby once yet today. Julio remained a steadfast buddy, though.

"Miss Shelby, I heard someone wonder if they could get a discount on their cabin because of no water."

"Really? Oh, gosh, let's not go there. Uh, let me alert Carol and double-check that the water will be back on just after lunch. Thanks!"

"Of course."

Shelby went over to Sewer Central and watched Carol navigate a stern back and forth with the workers there. When the coast was clear, Shelby stepped in.

"Good morning."

"Morning."

"How's it going here?"

"Another section of pipe needs to be replaced."

"Oooo, sorry. Is this something they couldn't tell until they got underground?"

"Yeah."

"Does it make the work more expensive?"

"Probably."

"Did you ask?"

"What difference would it make? It'll cost what it costs!"

"It's good to know where you stand, especially if you have to tell Lar—"

"—<u>Who's running this show?</u>"

Shelby felt as if she'd been slapped in the face.

"Apparently YOU. Jesus."

"Then don't pester me with questions."

"I'm concerned. And here's another concern: Julio heard someone wondering if they could get a discount because of having no water this morning."

"<u>Shit</u>."

"I know Manuel put out some great pastries for free during breakfast. He could offer some free dessert at lunch, and you could give your talk on the history of this place and—"

"—<u>You're doing it again</u>! Stop jumping in and taking over!"

And with that, Carol marched over to the kitchen to check on things there. Shelby stared at the pipes being lowered into the trench while the Logic Hamsters in her mind ran at top speed on the treadmill: *Am I supposed to be totally quiet and say nothing? And will Larry fire ME because of what CAROL does or does not do, and what if she makes a horrible decision? Should I not speak up, and what if—*

"Excuse me, could you tell me where Larry is?"

Shelby turned around to see a curvy blonde wearing a purple floral sarong and carrying a large object with a handle.

"Is that a...?"

"Massage table," said the blonde.

"Ah, yes! Uh, Larry, well, Larry isn't here right now. And you are...?

"Marlene. I'm the massage therapist and yoga teacher he hired. He said for me to come up on June nineteenth and here I am!"

"Welcome!" Shelby shook her hand and her knees nearly buckled. *Wow, that's some grip. And look at those biceps, sculpted and tan...azure eyes, a bright white smile.*

"And you are...?"

"Uh, I'm Shelby. I'm...uh, I'm helping run the office right now. Carol, who is over thataway, is, ah, she's the manager, Larry's the owner. But he just had surgery, it was a sudden thing..."

"Oh, I'm so sorry, is he all right?"

"Yes, he's recovering, and we'll see him in a few weeks."

"Fantastic. So, where would you like me to set up?"

Shelby blinked. She had absolutely no idea.

"Uhhh, tell you what," Shelby said. "Let's have you go over to the office, and I'll goooo...get Carol and we'll figure this out. I'm sure we'll find the perfect spot!"

"Sounds good!"

Shelby gestured to the office and then quickly jogged over to the kitchen. When she entered, Carol was counting the supply of paper plates on a counter.

"Hey, Carol, the massage woman is here, Marlene."

"Ah! I lost count. The who? The what?"

"Yeah, that was my reaction. Did Larry tell us when she was arriving?"

"Where the hell are we going to put her?" Carol asked.

"Well, yoga classes can be outside, but the massage table...?"

Shelby waited to see if Carol had an idea before she jumped in with anything.

"I can't deal with this now," Carol said curtly.

"Okay, I'll talk to Julio."

She trotted back over to the office, looking around for a spot to park Marlene and her table.

"Hi again!" called Shelby.

"Hi. Wow, it's so beautiful here!" Marlene said brightly as she looked at the sun-dappled view from the office porch.

"Yes. That's why I'm working here. Hey, did your parents name you after the Suzanne Vega song? 'Marlene on the Wall'?"

"Na, named after my great-aunt. Although my mom would play that song for me."

Ouch. Her mom? That would make Marlene what...twenty?

Just then Shelby saw Julio and flagged him down. Then she realized she didn't want Marlene to hear her sounding as if they had no game plan. Which they didn't. But still. So, she briskly walked over to Julio before he reached them.

"Julio, did Larry say anything to you about where we were putting the massage therapist? She's here right now."

"Mr. Larry wanted her to have my toolshed but he didn't tell me when she was coming. He said Carol was handling the details."

"Oh, Lord. How long would it take to clear out your tools—but where the heck would we put them?"

"It would take an hour or two, but I have no other shed for the tools, and isn't a massage place supposed to be clean? The floor and walls are very dirty and greasy."

"Shoot, that won't work. What else have we got...?"

They both looked around and then Julio remembered something.

"A couple of weeks ago someone left their tent behind. It's not waterproof any more, that's why they were throwing it out. I hate throwing things away that are still useful. So, I put it in the shed."

"How big is it?"

"A family of four was using it."

"Let's see it! Can you put it up in the grassy area to the side of the office?"

"Of course."

Julio went to get the tent and Shelby went back to Marlene.

"I think we have a solution. Larry's original idea won't work right now, but we have a large tent. Does that sound doable?"

"Sure. I've done massage work in tents. Did that at Burning Man last year."

"I've always wanted to go to Burning Man!" Shelby exclaimed.

"We'll talk!"

"Y'know, I need to do up flyers to advertise your services. Can you step into the office to help me?"

"Sure."

As the printer was spitting out flyers, Shelby observed, "Just weekends?"

"Yeah," said Marlene. "I can come up on Fridays and leave on Monday mornings. I have clients at an acupuncture place back in L.A. during the week."

"You live in L.A.!" Shelby realized she sounded way too excited about that. "I've lived there for years and just moved up here this spring. But L.A. is home. How is it?"

"Well, Lady Gaga killed it at the Hollywood Bowl last weekend and traffic is still terrible."

They both laughed.

"Man, the Hollywood Bowl. I miss the Bowl! Even with all of its traffic!"

"Yeah. I prefer the Wiltern Theatre on Wilshire. Got to see Brandi Carlile there."

"Ohhh, I LOOOOVE Brandi! Ah, I miss culture!"

"Yeah, right?"

By now the printer was done. Shelby handed the copies to the purple-clad goddess. Marlene was nearly out the door when Shelby suddenly had another question.

"You're working weekends. Did Larry promise you a room? He didn't tell us...."

"I have a camper van, I'm good. All I need is a place to shower, and I assume you have that for the campers."

"We do." *Or you could shower with me*, Shelby thought.

Marlene smiled her gleaming smile and then went to hand out flyers to guests while Shelby walked to the side of the office building to check on the tent.

"It's perfect," she said, looking at Julio, who had just set it up.

"I think so, too."

"Being able to stand up in it, that was my only concern, and it looks good on that front. Thank you, Julio."

"You are most welcome. And you're doing a good job of running the office, Miss Shelby."

"Thank you."

Late in the afternoon, Shelby stepped out of the office to peek around to the side to see what was up on the Marlene Front. Lo and behold, Marlene had organized her first yoga class and there were eight participants. *Yay,* thought Shelby. *Maybe some are the hikers we had to cancel on.*

Marlene had changed out of the purple sarong and into a black jog bra and purple floral tights. *Nice way to lure people in.* And then came this Shelby thought: *I wonder if she likes to sleep with women, not just listen to them sing?* And then clear as a bell, she heard Randall yell in her ear, "SHELBY. STOP."

"Hey."

Shelby whipped around: there was Carol coming toward her. Shelby actually blushed, feeling she had been caught cheating on her lover by her lover.

"Have you ever done yoga?" Shelby asked with feigned innocence.

"No."

Aaaannnnd, nothing else was forthcoming.

"Well, she's taking them through easy poses. And it's super great for relaxing. Might be a fun treat...."

"No thanks," Carol said wearily. But then she added, "I'll go watch the office if you want to take the class."

"Oh. Uh, that would be great, thanks."

"And find out how much Larry said he wanted as a cut from her fees."

"Sure," Shelby said.

Carol went to the office and Shelby went over to the group and got into the downward facing dog pose.

This feels so great, swimming in the purple ocean...a magical creature, half-dolphin, half-woman, swimming nearby. If I swim faster, I can catch her, I can touch her, I can hold her, I'll hold on to her fin and she'll carry me away....

"Shelby? Shelby?"

Shelby woke with a start. She'd fallen asleep in "corpse pose," flat on her back. Marlene was standing over her, backlit by the sun, the highlights in her hair golden.

"Sorry. I really needed that. It's been quite a week," Shelby admitted.

"Glad you got a break then."

"Nice turnout for your first class," Shelby said, sitting up and picking a leaf out of her hair.

"Yeah, I have no problem with going around to folks and talking up my classes. Works every time."

"Oh, before I forget, what financial arrangement did Larry make?"

"I give him twenty percent. The yoga classes are by donation, massage I have actual rates, depending on how long I do someone."

Do me, do me, do me. "SHELBY, STOP IT," yelled Randall in her head.

"I heard the construction noise over there. What are they doing?" Marlene asked.

"They're installing new pipes. For better water flow." Shelby thought that sounded better than "We have shit backed up."

"Nice." Marlene smiled and then put away her portable speakers and cell phone that had been playing the relaxing music.

"Have you found any massage clients?" Shelby asked, standing up.

"I have. Two for tomorrow morning."

"You're off to a great start."

"Trip is already paid for."

"Do you...have a regular salary at the acupuncture clinic back in L.A.?"

"No, that's by client as well. But I do at least one, sometimes two a day. It's been working out great."

Shelby smiled. *Oh, to be in my twenties and carefree. Wait, was I ever carefree?*

"Would you like a massage?" asked Marlene.

Maybe I should be carefree right now....

"Uhhh...I'm still on duty."

"Evening is fine. We'll get some healing essential oils into your skin, you'll really melt. And don't worry, you get the employee discount, half price. Then you talk it up to the vacationers and it pays off."

Melt. Melt. Melt. Have I ever met someone this sensuous, this self-assured, at this age?

"SHELBY. DON'T." Randall was yelling again.

"Ummmm, let me see how things are going in the office. I'll let you know. Will you be hanging out here?"

"Either that or at the restaurant. I'm starving," said Marlene.

"And your meals are on us."

"Great, thanks!"

Shelby floated over to the office, to buy some time on this decision.

Her panties were already wet and sticky, though. *What would happen if I actually let her touch me? Shelby wondered. Would I 'come' right there on the massage table?*

She entered the office and Carol was making notes on her own Excel spreadsheet.

"Whatcha doin'?" Shelby said, all liquidy and loose.

"Sheet of the construction expenses for Larry. How was yoga?"

"Amazing. I fell asleep it was so relaxing. Maybe you could go tomorrow…."

Carol didn't acknowledge that. Instead, she said, "I need to call Larry with an update."

Shelby walked around behind Carol's chair and gently kneaded her shoulders. *I'll bet my fingers are no match for Marlene's*, she thought. And in that moment, Shelby made her decision.

"Carol, I have an idea. Marlene is offering us half off for massages. Why don't you get one tonight, she said evening is fine. You'll feel so much better afterward."

Carol kept typing at the computer. Shelby gently spun Carol's desk chair around so she was facing her.

"Babe. Seriously. Life will have many ups and downs and the sewer pipes are just our first challenge. Are you going to be a cranky-pants every time something awful comes up?"

Carol took a deep breath. "I'm cranky for good reason. And I'm really tired of you telling me what to do and how to feel. I just need space and time and I'll get through this. Please leave me alone."

Shelby's stomach muscles scrunched up. "<u>Fine</u>." Then she stormed out of the office.

Carol bowed her head. And then reached for the office phone and dialed Larry's cell number.

"Hey, Larry, it's Carol. How are you feeling?"

"Still hurts. Can't breathe without pain," said Larry into the phone.

"Take it easy. Things are going well here. The construction guys have figured out all the piping that needs to be replaced."

"Good. Good. How much will it cost?"

Man, he gets right to the point, doesn't he, thought Carol.

"Uh, about fifteen thousand dollars. It went up a bit because they discovered more bad pipes and also because I wanted them to work through the weekend. This will all be done by late Tuesday."

Complete silence on the other end. Carol waited several seconds before asking, "Larry? Are you still there?"

"Yes."

"Any questions?"

"No." And then he ended the call.

I hope he doesn't think I let the construction guys walk all over me. Shit, I forgot to tell him we avoided anarchy today—no one pressed for a discount on their cabin rate! The free desserts at lunch worked! Shelby had been right, Carol thought, *that was a good tactic. But she's like her military dad, always on point, pressing her case.*

Which makes her like Larry, too. Shit. What's it going to be like when he returns, Carol wondered. *Two guard dogs barking at me constantly. Maybe I should've moved up to Seattle with Darcy and just started over....*

After going over the expense sheet with a fine-tooth comb and ringing up the tabs for a few vacationers who were checking out, Carol turned off the computer for the day. She put a sign on the front door for folks to call her satellite phone if there were any emergencies. Then she stood on the porch, surveying the scene. Laughter filtered over from the outdoor dining area...but no music, happy hour tunes were long gone. Larry thought the massage person would bring in more money anyway.

Speaking of which, Carol poked her head around the corner of the main building to look at the tent where Marlene was operating. At the precise moment Carol was toying with the idea of asking for a massage, Marlene stepped out of the tent. Carol could feel a rush of energy just from looking at this perfectly sculpted body, never mind strong hands kneading her flesh.

A few moments later, the tent door unzipped again and out stepped a young man in his early twenties looking completely blissed out. Carol ambled on over to him after he paid Marlene.

"How was it?" Carol said to the fellow.

"Fantastic," he answered dreamily. He tried smoothing his hair, which was completely standing on end from the massage oil.

He wandered off as if he were drunk and Marlene stepped over to Carol.

"Hi there."

"Hi. I'm Carol."

"I've heard the name. Would you like a massage?"

"Yes. Yes, I would." The words popped out of Carol's mouth automatically.

"Let me change the sheet."

"Okay." *Yes, lying on a sheet. With a stunning woman massaging me. Who is not talking or worrying as she unknots my back and shoulders. I'm so there.*

~ॐ~

"I almost did a bad, bad thing...."

"Cue up Chris Isaak. What was it?" asked Pal, plopping down next to Shelby on the couch.

"I almost had a massage from a gorgeous woman," said Shelby, cringing.

"And it wasn't Carol?"

"No."

"And if you'd gone ahead with it," Pal queried with a gleeful grin, "what would've been so bad?"

"Endlessly fantasizing about her, before, during and after."

"And that's a problem?" Pal asked, taking a slurp from her beer mug.

"Yeah, it is."

"When the going gets tough, the tough go to Fantasyland?"

Shelby nodded and looked Pal in the eye. Pal could see she was quite concerned so she wiped the sly grin off her face.

"My very first love from high school, Deelie, had to move to Tennessee with her family," Shelby told her. "We were inseparable, we'd just won a volleyball championship. I was devastated when she left, and she left without really saying goodbye. Never heard from her again. So...I made up a whole fantasy life with her, for the rest of my time in high school...and into college...."

"Well, a first love is a big deal."

"Yeah. But then...I kept doing it," Shelby said, filled with shame. "With everyone I've ever had a crush on or dated for a little bit."

Pal ran her finger along the rim of her mug.

"Well, if that's not how you want to live your life, then, yeah, you gotta stay in reality. But create an amazing reality so your mind and your pussy don't want to wander somewhere else."

"Yeah. Have you thought of becoming a therapist instead of a mechanic? You'd still be helping fix things," Shelby said, only half-kidding.

Pal cracked up and took a swig of beer.

"Hey, you didn't answer me before, did you ever want to be an astronaut?"

"Where the hell did that come from, Shelbycakes?"

"I saw the poster on the wall at your auto repair place. Plus Darcy's song." She didn't admit to having also seen the Sally Ride picture in Pal's bedroom.

"Yeah. When I was younger."

"Why didn't you go for it?"

"You have to be really good at math and science. I'm great at fixing things, I can break a car engine down and put it back together blindfolded. Pencil and paper and computer shit, much harder. So, I went with what worked for me."

"Are you sad that you didn't get to go into outer space?"

Pal scraped the frost off the mug with her thumbnail and quietly said, "Sorta. I'll bet it woulda been neat."

"Yeah. If you'd gone outside of your comfort zone, got some tutoring, you might've—"

"—Stop. Don't push me. And it's too late now anyway."

In that moment, Shelby saw what Carol had told her about, that pushing thing she did so well.

~ ❧ ~

"What's this knot here?" Marlene whispered. Her muscular hands were kneading a tight spot the size of a golf ball on Carol's right shoulder.

Carol wondered if she was supposed to answer.

"Do you sit at a computer all day?" Marlene gently asked.

"Not really," Carol mumbled, face down on the massage table, her mouth in the U-shaped pillow cushion.

Marlene continued to press and pull and slide to work out the tension.

"Here's another knot. You could give them names," Marlene said, angling for a little humor. "Twin Peaks? Batman and Robin? Thelma and Louise?"

"More like my mom and Shelby," mumbled Carol.

~ ❧ ~

"We'll be back at two!" a voice called from down the hall. Sixteen-year-old Carol ignored her mom's pronouncement and kept her focus on the book at hand. She'd just discovered Jeanette Winterson, her first lesbian author, and was diving headfirst (so to speak...) into Jeanette's books.

"Did you hear me?" her mom yelled again. "And you need to put the potatoes in the microwave at 1:45!"

Carol was even more angry and sullen than she'd been in grade school because she'd been forced to move to town with her folks. No more farm animals, no more garden to tend, nor fields to wander. Her reading cave (i.e. bedroom) had even higher stacks of books in it now.

Her mom had given up on cleaning the room. Dirty clothes and fast-food containers littered the place.

And then the bedroom door flung open: Majordomo Head Cook Task Master exploded. "DID YOU HEAR ME? Your sister's graduation is over at noon, company will be here at two, I need potatoes microwaved and the stew turned off before they get here."

Carol stared at her. The stare had become her way of communicating "YES. I HEAR YOU."

"And by the way, your sister has said she'll never forgive you for missing her graduation." And with that, Mom slammed the door.

From down the hall her sister said, "What did she say?"

"What do you think she said?"

And then came a thunderclap of "FUCK YOU, CAROL" from her sister.

Carol pulled the bed covers over her head to read some more of Jeanette's inspiring words, wondering if she could be a writer someday.

She then dozed off, conjuring wild adventures with gorgeous women, doing things with their bodies she could only dream about but not pursue for a few more years until she met Gillian. The dream this morning culminated in Carol eating a mouthwatering savory meal at an English pub with Jeanette herself, but she woke up and realized she was smelling her mom's stew on the stove. She suddenly remembered she was supposed to Do Something in the kitchen.

She went out to the beef stew, and it seemed to be simmering fine; no actions needed there. *Oh, yeah, the potatoes, do I drop them into the beef? Hm, that doesn't seem right. Wait! Microwave, yeah, that's the ticket.*

She popped a few potatoes into the microwave and set the time for several minutes.

Then she went back to her room and dove back into Jeanette's book, *Written on the Body.* She was pondering the part about some folks saying temptation can be barricaded, that stray desires can be driven out of the heart, like moneychangers from the temple. But according to Jeanette, you'd have to patrol your weak points day and night—and don't look, smell or dream. Carol wondered how the heck you would—

BANG!

What was that? Carol was afraid to get up from her bed…but then the fire alarm in the kitchen went off. *Oh, shit.*

Carol peeked out her bedroom door and saw a cavalcade of smoke coming from the kitchen. She ran down the hall and saw that the microwave door had exploded open. The potatoes had caught fire and one of them had been flung to the gas burner under the beef stew.

SHIT. She realized that she'd forgotten to poke holes in the potatoes and probably set the microwave timer for too long.

"I'm sorry."

"It's okay. It happens. Things get released during a massage," Marlene whispered. "And sometimes they come out as tears."

Marlene handed Carol some tissues. Carol was crying so hard she was embarrassed. She pulled the sheet completely over her head. Every knot in her shoulders and back had felt like a thousand years of built-up anger—from disappointing her mom, to not having a fancy career, to failing in her relationships with Gillian, the horseback riding instructor, the high school teacher, Darcy….

Marlene stood next to the massage table with her hand on Carol's back as she rode out the sobs with her. Finally, she said, "We don't have to finish this session. And you don't owe me anything."

She saw Carol's head nod that she had heard her under the sheet.

"I'll step outside so you can change back into your clothes."

Marlene undid the tent zipper and stepped out into the twilight.

Carol put on her clothes as if she were a zombie; well, one with a drippy nose. She then exited the tent.

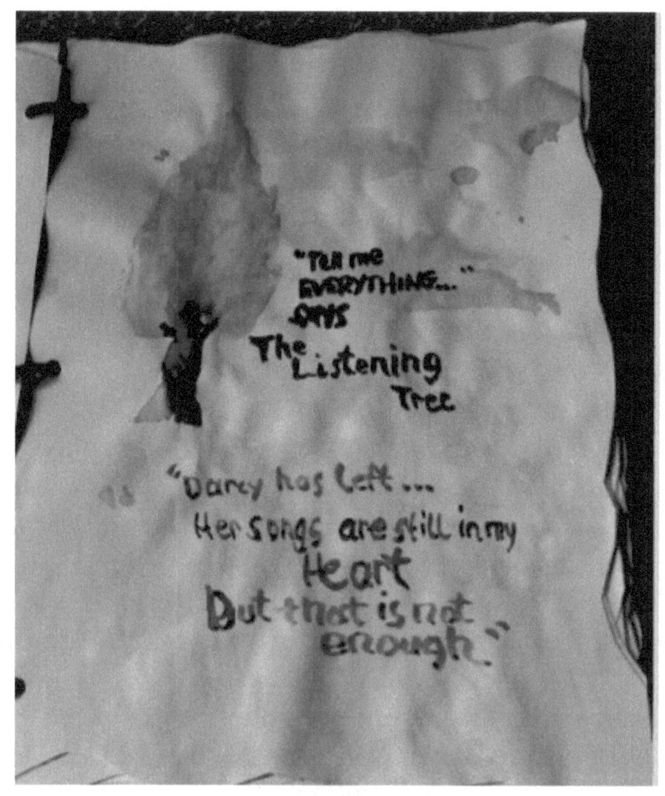

Chapter Forty-Five

The Knot

"Dang it."

Carol wiped away spilled droplets of coffee from her pants as she got out of her truck the next morning. *I wonder if people can see coffee stains on me? Now that I'm "in charge," does that look professional?*

As Carol made her way across the parking area, she had another thought: *What if Shelby brings me another cup of coffee? Did I bring my own coffee to show her I don't need her help? Maybe I shouldn't have brought it. Or was I so snippy with her, she wouldn't dream of bringing any more to me? Oh, Lord.*

She looked over at the plumbing guys who were just arriving as well. One of them threw a "to go" cup from 7-11 down on the ground. *Hm. I guess that's what I did in my home, didn't I?*

She walked over and picked it up. "Hey, we've got a trash bin right over there," she said, pointing to the edge of the parking area.

The worker apologized and took the cup from her to toss in the bin. Carol looked over the construction site and everything seemed fine. So far.

Moments later, Shelby got out of her car, no coffee in hand. *No need to incur Carol's wrath first thing in the morning, she figured. I'm not gonna micro-manage her, acting as if she can't get her own coffee. Well, is getting someone coffee micro-managing?*

And should I be spending the night with Carol instead of at Pal's, isn't that what couples do? You have to go home and face each other at night, not sleep miles apart. But I seem to be driving her nuts. Maybe being at Pal's right now is keeping things sane for her.

Just then Shelby spotted a van in the parking lot. *Oh, must be Marlene's...maybe I can squeeze in another yoga class today. Maybe I can squeeze one of her juicy breasts.*

As Shelby walked by the van, she noticed a gap in the white kitchen curtains. Shelby slowed down. Sure enough, she could see Marlene.

And she was naked. *Oh, be still my beating cunt.* Marlene was drinking her own coffee and stretching.

"Keep it moving, Shel," said Inner Randall. *Righto.* Shelby's feet angled for the office, even though other parts of her were lingering vanside.

Saturday morning whizzed along for Shelby as the office had a steady stream of vacationers checking in. More than once she told folks the construction noise would be short-lived. *Fingers crossed*, she hoped.

After keeping an eagle eye on the plumbing job all morning, Carol stopped by the office around lunch.

Shelby decided to try an olive branch of peace. "Hey, what if we closed the office and shared a lunch at a picnic table? Like the good old days. Put a note on the door where people can find us."

"I've got to sort through Larry's files for insurance papers to see if we're covered in case someone gets hurt due to the construction."

"It can't wait a half hour?"

Carol hung her head. "When Larry first started, he wanted me to work through my lunch hours. Yeah, let's have lunch, good idea."

"All righty then," Shelby said, giving Carol a pat on the butt. Carol laughed and gave Shelby's butt a little squeeze.

They walked out the door...and then saw off in the distance a family of five marching toward them.

"Oh, Lord," Carol said. "They hated their room yesterday. The comforter smelled funny, the sink dripped, the window wouldn't close...."

"You want me to handle them? 'Cause I'm wearing my Wonder Woman Wonder Bra," said Shelby.

Carol laughed. "No, I already have a 'relationship' with them. You go on. I'll be there in a sec."

Shelby started for the restaurant but then glanced to her left and saw a yoga class with Marlene was just about to begin. Shelby looked over at Carol who was watching her. A funny moment passed between them.

"Or you could go to yoga class," Carol said, with a not completely innocent tone.

Shelby just stood there. <u>What did she mean by that</u>?

Carol turned and unlocked the office door and loudly said to the approaching snotballs, "Hi, what's up?"

Shelby paused, torn. She looked over at Marlene, who had on a cherry-red jog bra and matching super tight spandex pants. *Okay, be that way, Carol,* thought Shelby. She walked over to the class and got into the "cat-cow" position.

This time, Shelby did not fall asleep, and this time, she did stay focused on her breathing instead of the other "B" word ("breasts").

At the end of class, she was about to head off to the restaurant for some grub when Marlene called, "Hey, Shelby!"

"Hey! Good class!"

"Thanks. How's Carol doing?"

"Okay. I think we're through the worst of the sewer thing."

"Great. Well, tell her I can still make time for that massage, if she wants it."

"Sure. Will do."

"And for a full hour. The other time doesn't count."

"Other time?"

"The first one we started."

"Oh. Right. Sure."

Carol started a massage and didn't finish it? What's up with that? Shelby wondered.

When Shelby returned to the office with her lunch, she wasn't sure whether to bring up the massage or not.

But Carol spoke first. "How was class?"

Hmm, there was some spin on that question. "Uh, fine." *And I'm gonna turn it back on you.* "Marlene said you could finish the massage you started with her, if you want."

"Okay."

"...Did you guys get interrupted?

"No. I, uh, I...." Carol's voice trailed off.

Shelby decided to stay in yoga mode and kept her heart open without judgment and without pressing for details.

"...I started crying. We didn't finish," Carol whispered.

"I'm sorry."

Shelby went behind the check-in desk and sat down next to Carol to hold her hand.

"...It was embarrassing," Carol admitted.

"Do you want to talk about it?"

"It's just stress."

They sat holding hands for a few moments 'til Shelby said, "Maybe I should come stay with you tonight? You can talk about the stressful stuff or not, but it seems weird not spending the night with you...."

"Okay."

Shelby wondered what had really happened during the massage session.

They walked in the door to Carol's cabin well past eight o'clock that evening. Shelby put her daypack down in the living room...and saw the *Conjurings and Wanderings* storybook on the coffee table. Wow, that could mean she's been writing in it, Shelby thought.

"Hey, what's this?" Shelby said with fake innocence as she picked up the storybook.

"Ah. That's the homemade book I was telling you about when we were hiking in the snow."

"Cool. Okay if I take a peek at it?"

"Now? Aren't we eating dinner?"

"Well, yeah, but I could multi-task—or do you not want me to get mac 'n cheese on it?"

Carol paused. She was too tired to fight Shelby. "No, that's okay. It's a thousand years old, a little mac 'n cheese will only make it better."

Shelby laughed and brought it to the table as Carol unpacked their to-go dinner.

"Manuel's mac 'n cheese is the best ever. I think he uses like five different kinds of cheese," Shelby said as she dove in with a fork.

"Have I underestimated him?" Carol asked. "I know a few days ago I was ready to can him."

"It could go either way. He really is a wonderful chef, but if he's not happy and Larry can't find a way to pay him more, then you're right, there are a lot of good cooks in California. Now, let's see what's cookin' in here…."

Shelby thumbed through the book slowly and with great tenderness. She knew how much it meant to Carol.

"Gosh, calligraphy, drawings, and watercolor paintings. This is really neat." And she meant it. She was seeing it with fresh, appreciative eyes, not judgy eyes. "Gillian did the artwork?"

"Yeah. She was in the Drama Department and had access to swords and costumes. You can see we tried to capture a little of what we looked like in those drawings."

"Very dashing!"

"Yeah, we'd grab a hat or a vest or a cape and go out on Saturday nights. We'd run around the campus 'til after midnight."

"Did anyone see you?"

"We didn't care. We were in our own world. We'd jump way into the future or way into the past, creating whole new worlds with heroines who had to save the day."

"Sounds like a magical time."

"It was."

"That's so neat you found each other," Shelby said.

Carol had a faraway look in her eyes, as if she were back at Chico State running around in the woods.

~ ❧ ~

"Soooo, how about a field trip for spring break?" Gillian proposed.

"Sure. Where to, Yosemite?" Carol was three-hole punching new pages that were going into the *Conjurings and Wanderings* book. It was now four inches thick.

"San Francisco," Gillian said, as she painted her toenails black.

"Oh?"

"You sound as if I said, 'Folsom Prison.'"

"No, I didn't."

"What's wrong with San Francisco?"

"I thought we had talked about Yosemite."

"There's still too much snow," Gillian pointed out.

"Even at ground floor?"

"I want to go to San Francisco, there's a cool production of *The Tempest* there. Since I'm doing *Midsummer* next year as my senior thesis, I want to see what crazy thing <u>they've</u> come up with."

"Don't you want to do your own thing, Gillian?"

"I'll do my own thing."

Yeah, Gillian's always doing her own thing, Carol thought.

"You're not afraid of being overly influenced by someone else's design?"

"No. So, San Fran?"

"Wellll…I have to do my project for my Celtic History class."

"The WHOLE WEEK?"

"It's gonna be interactive, I have A LOT of steps to lay out."

"That's cool. But if I'd said 'Yosemite,' you would've jumped at that, I'll bet."

Carol turned red. She was caught. She just didn't want to go to a big city.

"<u>Fine</u>," huffed Gillian. "Stay here on an empty campus with your nose in a book. I'm gonna go have FUN."

Carol said nothing and instead slammed the heavy three-hole punch onto her desk—causing a glass candleholder to fall off her desk and break.

"Oh, that was effective," observed Gillian.

"Fuck you." Carol stormed out and slammed the dorm room door behind her.

~✞~

Carol did stay on campus spring break of her junior year and her anger propelled her creativity to new heights. When the semester resumed, she took her class out to the woodsy creek she and Gillian loved to hike to, which she could've found blindfolded by now.

She had everyone write down a gift they wanted to give the world… and what sacrifice they were willing to make in order for it to happen. They went around the group to share what they wrote. Some wanted to give the gift of music, some political activism, some taking care of Mother Earth's animals. Up next, Carol asked everyone to take a few steps into the woods so they could find an object, be it a rock, a pine cone, a leaf, that could symbolize their sacrifice.

Once the class was gathered back together, she had everyone put their sacred objects on a large rock to create an altar. Then one by one, each person explained what their object represented. Lastly, she said aloud a prayer asking that the group energy help manifest everyone's individual dreams.

At the end of the ritual, someone asked Carol what *her* gift and sacrifice were going to be.

Carol stared at the rock where a red-tailed hawk feather she'd found sat amidst the other sacrifices. She quietly said, "My gift is teaching people about the sacredness and healing power of Nature... and I'm willing to give up living in a city with modern conveniences so that I can stay attuned to Nature."

The group nodded collectively, impressed.

～🐾～

"Thank you for sharing that story, Carol," Shelby said. "That's so cool what you did with your classmates."

Carol nodded and let the accomplishment from the past fill her heart.

Meanwhile, Shelby weighed whether to turn to the final pages of *Conjurings and Wanderings*. As casually as she could muster, Shelby decided to go for it. She flipped near the back and read aloud, "'And now she's gone....'"

"Darcy," answered Carol.

"That's a beautiful watercolor painting of a tree. You did that?"

Carol nodded. "My buddy, the Listening Tree...."

"I like that. What did the tree hear from you?"

"That my heart was broken. Again. That maybe...and don't take this the wrong way...I should've gone with Darcy to Seattle. Like I should've gone with Gillian to Chicago."

"Chicago? I thought she wanted to go to San Francisco."

"Different trip. Long story."

Shelby nodded. And then turned to the next page, the page that used to be blank...and saw a drawing of a half-naked woman wearing a purple sarong. She could feel the blood rise in her face.

"Who's this?" Shelby inquired, trying to feign innocence.

"...Marlene," Carol said quietly without looking at her.

"Ah. Should I read the words, or would you prefer I not?"

Silence.

Shelby glanced at the words and saw a few phrases, "...her hand goes inside me and melts the pain..." and then "her tongue licks the length of my body...."

"Did she actually do this, these things to you?" Shelby said, her voice rising in tension.

"No. Not at all. She was totally professional. I...started crying during the massage and couldn't stop the tears. She ended the session way early. This, these words, it's...my way to cope and process."

"Would you have preferred that she lick your whole body?"

"...It's a fantasy. That's all."

More silence and as Shelby was about to get on her high horse, Carol called her on it. "I saw you peeking in her van's curtains this morning. Was she naked?"

Shelby turned crimson. Caught. She simply nodded.

"Did you fantasize about her?" Carol asked evenly but not angrily.

"...I tried not to."

More silence. Neither of them picked up their forks to continue eating.

Finally, Shelby asked with great humility, "So is this how it is? We barely have a relationship, and we're already cheating on each other in our minds with the first pretty thing that comes down the pike?"

"Is it cheating?"

"Okay, what is it, Carol?"

"We have drives. Urges. You can't put a lid on them."

"But we could channel them better. Don't we both want to live in the real world? Not up here," Shelby said, pointing to her head, "Or here," pointing to the storybook.

"I don't want to give up my imagination. It saved me when I was a kid. My mom used to hit me over the head when she thought I was reading too much. I had to escape, I had to, I had to...."

Carol closed her eyes tight and put her head in her hands.

Shelby got up and cradled her in her arms. "I'm here, sweetie. I'm not running. We're gonna get through this."

"What's this little knot?" Shelby whispered as she kneaded Carol's right shoulder later that evening.

Both she and Carol were naked on the living room floor, lying on a quilt handmade by Carol's grandmother, surrounded by lit candles. Shelby had found some hand lotion to use, not as groovy as massage oil, but it would do the trick.

"Just say the first thing that comes to mind."

Still Carol said nothing. Shelby worked the knot with her thumb.

"Ow, that hurts."

"Sorry." After gentler prodding, Shelby asked, "What are you holding on to?"

Quietly, Carol admitted, "The farm. I don't want them to take it away from me."

"The farm is your safe haven?"

"Yeah."

"Tell me about it."

"...The horses don't judge, they love to nuzzle me."

"And outside the farm?"

"People are mean. I have to do well. I just want to run wild with our colts and tell them stories...."

"Is there a way to let go of the knot, the fear, and still hold on to the farm memories?"

Carol was sobbing by now.

"Breathe into it...keep breathing. You get to keep the farm pictures in your mind, no one can take those away."

Carol sobbed harder and Shelby put her full body on top of Carol's, holding her.

"I'm a failure. All I can do is read books, tell stupid stories and burn things."

"Carol, you're amazing," Shelby whispered into her ear, pulling Carol's hair aside so she could kiss the back of her neck. "You connect so well with the tourists up here, they really love your stories. You make history come alive for them. You're as good as any teacher I had in college. Seriously."

Carol reached around and put her hand on Shelby's bare leg, giving it a squeeze, her way of saying thanks.

Chapter Forty-Six

Bishop and the Great Beyond

Carol deposited the week's cash at the local bank in Bishop and then looked at her watch. There was no huge rush to get back to H.Q. Shelby could easily handle the Monday chores and the construction guys were in good shape at this point. All Carol needed to do was check the P.O. box.

After picking up the mail at the post office, Carol stood on the sidewalk taking in the sights and sounds of Bishop. She wondered, *"How long has it been since I did anything fun here, aside from the concert Shelby brought me to?"*

She wandered down the street and memory lane. *Good ol' Schat's Bakery.* Darcy hated going there, she thought it was too touristy. But

Shelby had mentioned Schat's fondly. *Maybe I should pick up some goodies to share with her,* Carol thought.

A couple of chicken salad sandwich purchases later, Carol headed farther up the sidewalk and saw an empty storefront where Tommy's Travels used to be. He'd tried to make a go of leading groups into the mountains, but Tommy was so disorganized his business tanked after a few years. *Yeah, shops and businesses come and go here,* Carol thought. *You have to cater to the tourists and really work at it. Which Larry does. Why don't I enjoy these business details more,* Carol asked herself. *If I did, maybe I could help Larry more. Or would I prefer to just let him do all the heavy-lifting and simply be an employee?*

Carol looked up and saw Outfitters, the local outdoor equipment/bookstore and that brought back the fondest of fond memories for her. One of the employees was a former college professor, Dr. Sarah Peterson, someone Carol had known at Chico State. She and Carol had bonded many years ago when Carol took a writing class from her. And then Dr. Peterson had provided sage advice at a critical time for Carol.

As she stood on the sidewalk looking in the window that featured topnotch backpacks and ultra-lightweight hiking poles, Carol thought back to her senior year of college when she was trudging across the quad one spring Saturday afternoon.

~❦~

"Hi, Carol!"

"Huh? Oh, hi Dr. Peterson."

"You look a little tired."

"Oh, just...lost in thought."

Dr. Peterson had a sixth sense that wasn't going to let Carol off the hook. "And lost in other ways...?"

"Uh, kinda. What, uh, what uh are you doing on campus on a weekend?" Carol asked, trying to deflect any prying questions.

"Forgot some paperwork at my office, that's all. There's a nice bench over by the Admin Building," Dr. Peterson said. "Want to tell me what's up?"

"I, uh, I don't know what to do next," Carol said, angling towards the bench. "Grad school, move to Chicago, or who knows what...it's all just...it's, uh...."

"Overwhelming?"

Carol nodded. And then added, "I...just had this weird moment... with a tree...."

"I love trees. Tell me all about the encounter," Dr. Peterson said as they sat down.

~⚘~

Dr. Peterson and Carol had re-connected more recently when Sarah fell in love with Bishop and moved there as her retirement relocation, taking the part-time job at Outfitters. She and her husband Dave had seemed like the ideal couple to Carol; they both taught and both loved the outdoors. Theirs was the life to have.

Now in the present, Carol swung into Outfitters to browse the aisles to see if Sarah was here and if there was any hiking equipment calling her name. She fingered the wool T-shirts. "Wow, lightweight and not scratchy."

"And they don't stink!"

Carol looked up, startled.

"Sarah!"

"Hey, stranger!"

Sarah, thirty years Carol's senior, didn't look like a retiree, her strawberry blond hair barely had any gray in it, and she had more energy than the students she had once taught.

"You look GREAT," said Carol, folding her in a bear-hug. "You must still be hiking."

"Every chance I get."

"How's Dave? Did he retire yet? Or is he still splitting his time between here and Chico? Did you guys finally get that bucket list trip to Europe?"

Sarah paused.

"Oh, no, what?"

"...He developed bladder cancer two years ago and passed away six months after the diagnosis."

"Oh, shit, I'm so sorry," Carol said, giving Sarah another huge hug. "How are you holding up?"

"Some days are diamonds, some days are rust. I keep turning to him to crack a joke or point out an interesting character. And sometimes I hear him say one of his goofy observations, 'Deep fried Twinkies, no wonder this country is falling apart!' Now and then he comes to me in my dreams from wherever he is, beyond the beyond...."

"What does he say?"

"...How much he misses me, all of his regrets...."

"I can't imagine Dave having regrets, he seemed to go at life full throttle...."

"...He wished he'd retired when I did, so we could've spent more time together. Unless I'm projecting that regret on him...."

"A little of both, maybe?" Carol said diplomatically.

Luckily, Sarah chuckled.

"Well, at least I have the mountains. They help."

"Yeah, they sure do," Carol said.

"I just hate hiking alone."

"Yeah," Carol said, nodding. "We should set something up, the two of us."

"You betcha. So, how are <u>you</u>?"

"Good. New girlfriend, she's actually working at Sierra Glen which is great because Larry just had open-heart surgery."

"Oh, no! How is he?"

"Hard to say, he's down in L.A. with cousins."

"Boy oh boy, you never know. Dave didn't even get to move to Bishop full-time. He announced his retirement and right after that, the Big C attacked."

"Shit."

"Yeah," agreed Sarah.

They both paused and pondered the drastic turns life sometimes takes. "Listen, I've got to get back to the cash register. Send me an email, let's go hiking."

"You got it. Take good care, okay?" Carol said, as they embraced once more.

Sarah went to her post behind the counter and Carol staggered out of the store, the wool T-shirts forgotten.

She plopped down on a sidewalk bench, reeling from Sarah's news.

Chapter Forty-Seven

He's Baaack!

"Is he limping?"

"No, just walking slowly," said Carol. "He's been at sea level for a month, so the altitude must be hitting him hard…."

Carol and Shelby were peering out of the office's front window as if they were spies on a secret mission. They'd gotten a surprise phone call the day before from Larry: he was coming back to work sooner than expected, after only four weeks of recovering instead of six.

Carol swung the front door open to greet Larry and his pal Roger, who had driven him back up the mountain. Moving up the walkway, Larry picked up his pace and put on a big smile for show.

"Welcome back!" Carol called brightly from the porch.

"Hey, Larry, you're looking good!" Shelby added, standing next to Carol.

"Oh, am I glad to be back!" Larry said as he and Carol embraced. When they parted, he had tears in his eyes.

Carol thought, *Wow, I've never seen him cry before.*

Shelby stepped in to hug him, too. "We missed you," she said with affection. And it was the truth.

"You have no idea how much I missed you both and missed being here. I'm not cut out for hospital life!"

They all laughed.

"Hey, Roger, are you staying?" asked Carol.

"Gonna get one hike in and then spend the night in Bishop."

"Bishop! We're better than Bishop!" Larry exclaimed with mock indignation.

More chuckles from the group but Roger then added, "Ah, but Bishop is closer to L.A. I can get to work tomorrow morning from there."

"You work too hard," Larry chided, teasing him.

"You should talk," Roger joked back.

They all laughed once more. Carol wondered if Larry really had turned over a new leaf after the health scare.

Roger saluted them with his hiking pole, hoisted his daypack onto his back and headed off to the trails.

Moments later, the trio was in the office catching up.

After some chitchat about bland hospital food and the tediousness of physical therapy, Larry asked for an update.

"Things have been going well," Carol said with confidence. "The contractor did a good job with the new pipes, and we didn't have anyone cancel their reservations during the construction."

"Excellent," said Larry. The bottom line was his rudder.

"And we've made some minor recalibrations," Shelby added.

Larry smiled and nodded.

Shelby continued. "I needed to be able to track visitors and money in a way that made sense to me. I hope that's okay with you. And you can go back to your system, of course."

"Let me see what you have," Larry said with equanimity.

She showed him the Excel spreadsheet printouts of her tracking methods. He looked them over with his discerning eye, his finger tapping and following entire rows across and columns down.

He looked up. "Very good."

Shelby exhaled and shared a smile with Carol.

"What else?" Larry said eagerly.

"The yoga classes and massages are a big hit," Carol said.

"Wonderful!"

"And we'd like to get back to our extended hikes, when you're ready," she added. "Maybe a backpack later in August when you can man the fort solo."

"Of course," Larry said, nodding. He then calmly asked, "Anything else?"

Carol turned to Shelby; it was time for the Next Big Announcement.

Shelby waded in. "I started to do the food ordering, but it made so much more sense for Manuel to do it. I'm checking everything he does and he's sticking to the menu, so all is well on that front."

Larry took in that information, looked her in the eye and said, "Well done." And then he got up and went into his office.

Shelby and Carol stared after him and then looked at each other. Shelby mouthed, "I think we're okay."

Carol nodded. Although she noted that Larry did not look her in the eye and say, "Well done."

Later that afternoon, when Shelby was across the way at the gift store going over inventory with Roberta, Larry came out of his office and asked Carol, "What is your dream job?"

That took Carol by so much surprise she had no idea what to say. She ended up blurting out, "I thought this was my dream job."

"Why is it your dream job?"

"Because...I get to be in the outdoors. I get to talk to people about nature. I don't have to deal with a large bureaucracy...."

Larry just nodded.

Carol wondered where the hell that question had come from...and what he thought of her answer.

Shortly thereafter, while Carol was outside giving a talk on the California Gold Rush in the Sierra Nevada foothills to some rapt tourists, Larry approached Shelby in the office. She was designing a flyer to announce a day-long hike the first week of August up to Bear Paw Pass.

"Looking very good, very appealing," Larry said as he gazed at the computer screen.

"Yes. We also learned something from Marlene, the yoga teacher. Walk around and chat up the activity to the guests, make personal connections. She gets them in droves that way."

"Very smart, very enterprising." Then in a quiet voice he said, "I have a question for you."

Shelby politely smiled but wondered where this was going as he sat in a chair next to hers behind the front desk.

"I waited until Carol was out. Would you be interested in being my Number Two?"

"Number Two?" As in what? His wife?

"Second in Command. You understand how a professional operation runs. You are from L.A. You worked at a large university."

"Oh. Uh, well, gosh. Technically I'm not from L.A. but I did live there for—"

"—You get it. You know how a top-notch organization should be run. And you know the finer things customers appreciate."

"Well, thank you."

"Also, you pay attention to details. I trust you."

"Thank you." Shelby was sweating from feeling both flattered and nervous. "I'm, I'm honored. I'm wondering, though, where Carol fits into this re-org?"

"Carol will still do her talks, check people in, the front desk stuff. Those are her specialty items. She's not good at accepting change. She wants things to stay the way they are. But that's not how life is. A spiritual teacher once taught me, 'Change is the one constant in life.' I'm tired of fighting her on change."

Shelby was impressed at how centered Larry sounded. He wasn't being vindictive toward Carol, he was trying to keep his business afloat.

"I need to expand the operation. Offer more specialty items. Maybe qigong classes, tai chi. My cousins in L.A. will help market to the San Gabriel Valley."

"May I ask another question?"

"Of course," answered Larry.

"Can't they get qigong and tai chi in L.A.? That stuff is huge there."

"Yes, but not in this beautiful setting. Makes people even more centered and relaxed."

"Good point," Shelby observed.

"I know I need to give raises to the staff, but after the pipe replacement, I can't right now. I need to get more money coming in."

"Sure. One more question." Shelby decided to go big. "Will you show me the books?"

Larry paused and with a sly smile said, "Of course."

Later that afternoon, Carol came back in the office carrying a display easel and photographs she'd just used for her afternoon talk.

"Need help with that?" Shelby offered.

"Sure, thanks."

The women loaded the items into the storage closet off to the side of the check-in desk.

Knowing Larry wasn't in his office, Carol knew it was safe to then say, "This is such a low-tech thing, showing old-timey photos. I'm surprised people even show up."

"A good story is a good story. Gold Rush adventures are great, no matter what the technology. And face it, people don't come here to be glued to their electronic devices. They want to hear you live and in nature, with the birds singing and the wind whispering through the trees."

"Thank you," Carol said, hugging her. She closed the closet door and glanced at the bird wall-clock. "Larry's sure taking his time to survey the kitchen."

"Probably wants to examine every noodle," Shelby said with a wry grin.

They chuckled at that thought. And Shelby decided now would be a good time to fill Carol in on what Larry was cooking on the business front.

"Larry did some fishing with me," Shelby said, sitting next to Carol behind the front desk.

"And I'm guessing not trout fishing?"

"You got it. He's worried about the financials. He asked if I could keep coming up with new ideas, ways to bring in more money."

"Hm."

"What?"

"He didn't ask me that," said Carol.

Shelby thought, Well, it's because you resist new ideas.

"He showed me the books," Shelby continued. "After the pipe bills and the hospital bills, he's, well, we're, in some trouble. He's going to get a loan from pals in L.A. to finish out this season. But then he says he needs to be even more enterprising."

"He's always saying that. And he's never showed me the books."

"He's getting desperate now."

"But why you? Why not us?"

"I think it's because I worked at a large university in a large city."

Carol considered this and sadly concluded, "I'm no use to him."

"Carol, don't be ridiculous. You're so good with the customers. He wouldn't have kept you if he didn't like you. Look, we're in extenuating circumstances now. It's gotta be a team effort."

Carol pondered Shelby's words just as Larry came up the front steps. They scooted their chairs apart and pretended to be busy with office minutia.

"I fired Manuel. Shelby, call this number, it's a friend in L.A. He knows chefs."

Shelby and Carol exchanged a glance.

"Who will cook in the meantime?" asked Carol.

"His sous chef, Carlotta."

"Who will order the food supplies?" asked Shelby.

"I will," snapped Larry.

"Could Carlotta be promoted?" asked Shelby as she reached for the phone.

"I'll be firing her as soon as we get Manuel's replacement and she gets the chef oriented to the kitchen. And do not talk to the staff about any of this."

"Do you want me to find a new sous chef?" asked Shelby.

"No." And with that, Larry went into his office and shut the door.

The women exchanged another glance. Uh oh.

"Do you think he'll fire me?" Carol asked as they cuddled in bed that night at her cabin.

"I think he'll fire anyone," Shelby said, "if it helps his bottom line. The trick is, we have to be sure to be of value to him."

Shelby did not say aloud that Larry was well aware that Carol did not embrace change. Instead, she embraced her tightly.

"How can I be of value to him, beyond what I'm doing?"

"Let's come up with some innovative ideas, ones that we like, especially stuff that relates to our hikes."

Carol sighed and pondered that concept for a bit. But then she had a Light Bulb Moment. "Wait. How about we use that treasure hunt idea, like you did at your school? What if we did a nature treasure hunt? People could look for certain trees and birds and flowers and take pictures of them."

Shelby said, "There ya go. And we'll think of even more magical activities."

Before they could do that, though, Shelby got a phone call the next morning.

"Wow, that's awful," Shelby said, cringing. "Uh, I'll see if I can take a few days off and we'll get things settled."

"What was that?" Carol asked as Shelby hung up the phone in the office. Both Larry and Carol looked alarmed.

"The woman who is subletting my apartment fell and broke her leg. Not at my place, thank God. But I have a second-story apartment and she can't navigate the stairs. She wants to move out right now."

"She has to pay the whole month!" Larry, Mr. Eagle Eye on the Bottom Line, pointed out.

"She's already paid through the end of July. But I need to clean up the place and get a new tenant for August."

"How much time do you need?"

Shelby didn't appreciate Larry's bristled tone.

"I can email friends and get the word out today. I'll bet I can get someone soon. But I need a few days to clean my apartment. The woman is having her friends move her out the end of this week. I need to be there to get the key from her," she said firmly.

Larry nodded.

"It should be less than a week," Shelby added.

"Very good."

"And Carol and I have been cooking up some ways to enhance our outings. We want Sierra Glen to thrive."

"Love it, love it," Larry said with a twinkle in his eye.

But the twinkle was directed at Shelby, he didn't look over at Carol. Both Shelby and Carol made mental notes of that slight.

Chapter Forty-Eight
L.A. Woman

"Soooooo, how's it going? Inquiring minds want to know! Are you having hot pussy sex every night?"

"Oh, God, Howie! You never change!"

"Change is overrated," Howie said, grinning.

Shelby was back in L.A. for her sublet mission. She, Howie and Randall were having drinks at the famous West Hollywood nightspot, The Abbey, on Saturday night.

"The sex is fun but it's not every night. Some nights we just fall into bed exhausted from all of the running around on the job."

"You're an old married couple already!" said Howie.

"No, they're normal," said Randall, lifting his Cosmopolitan in a toast. Shelby clinked her glass of Chardonnay as a thank you.

"Are you fending off bears at work?" Howie continued.

"No, no bears. But Carol and I did have to run the place by ourselves when our boss was out for a month after open-heart surgery."

"Wow," said Randall, "and you two survived that trial by fire?"

"We did. Carol and I hit a few rough patches, but we came out of it stronger as a team. And, Howie, maybe you think change is overrated, but I really appreciate that Carol has been cleaning up her clutter."

"Yay!" said Randall. "And what about you?"

"Cleaning clutter?" asked Shelby.

"Changing."

Shelby paused for a few moments, took a sip of wine and said, "I'm trying to listen better and not micro-manage her. Go easier on her. And me."

Randall lifted his cocktail and the three of them clinked glasses. What Shelby did not mention was the Marlene challenge. She and Carol got through it, but it was a close call.

"Do you think your new sublet person will work out?" Randall asked.

"I do. She's starting her master's degree program at Pacific University in September. She's really motivated, driven, so she'll be there until spring, and by then..."

"...By then?" asked Randall.

"By then I'll know if I want to do Season Two at Sierra Glen."

"I thought everything was peaches and cream," said Howie. "What's the problem?"

"The boss has a lot of bills to pay, and he has to figure out a way to make more money."

"And you're helping with that?" Randall said.

"Yes. I've told Carol we need to prove our worth."

"He wouldn't have hired you if he didn't think you were great!" said Howie.

"True," answered Shelby. She didn't want to wade into Larry's persnickety personality traits with the guys. Besides, she wanted to have some fun here in L.A. And just then, fun showed up.

"HEY, YOU GUYS!"

The trio turned their heads to see a lively dark-haired gal with a crew cut, tight black jeans and a black tank top. From a distance she looked as if she were in her early twenties. But once she got to their table, Shelby could tell she was in her early thirties.

"Hey, Di!" exclaimed Howie. He stood up and gave her a big smooch on the cheek. "Randall, Shelby, this is Di. She and I used to work at an ad agency before I bailed out and became a college employee slug."

"You are not a slug!" Di said, thwacking him on the arm.

"Do you always hit someone when you compliment them?" Howie asked.

Di started to fake-hit him again and the gang laughed.

"So. Are you here with someone?" Howie teased.

"'WITH.' Oh, what could he mean?" Di said as she furrowed her brow.

Shelby laughed, she loved Di's dry sense of humor.

"No, Howie, I'm not WITH someone. I'm here with FRIENDS, but that doesn't count in YOUR book, does it?"

"Then get out there on the floor, babe. You've got the best biceps in town, show 'em off!"

They all laughed once more as Di raised her wine glass as if it were a dumbbell. And Shelby noted that, yes, those biceps were absolutely fabulous.

"Sit with us, sit with us," Howie implored, pushing out a chair for her.

"Okay, but just for two seconds, I don't want my team to think I've abandoned them."

"What kind of ad agency?" asked Shelby.

"We handle a lot of outdoor gear and travel companies. How about you?"

"I'm in the outdoor world myself, helping run a mountain resort."

"SWEET. I LOVE the mountains. I hike with the Sierra Club nearly every weekend. We're headed up to Kearsarge Pass for a backpack trip in a few weeks."

"Is that near where you are, Shelby?" asked Howie.

"Well, I'm a bit north of there," Shelby said. "But I've been to Kearsarge, it's beautiful." What she didn't say was Kearsarge was where she and Carol were headed on their next overnight backpack...in a few weeks. *This is either a stunning coincidence or the Gods are trying to tell me something,* mused Shelby. *I just don't know what.*

Before she could figure out the meaning of this synchronicity, the DJ started playing music in the back room.

Di started bopping along to it and announced, "Back to my pals! Great to see you, Howie! Great to meet you, Shelby and Randall!" She gave Howie a smooch on the cheek and then used the dance beat to jog back to her table.

Shelby's eyes followed her for a couple seconds, and when they came back to the present, Randall was staring at her with an "Aaaaand you just did what?" look.

"Hey. No. Those were not wandering eyes. She just has a lot of energy, that's all," Shelby said.

"Doesn't hurt to window-shop," Howie said. "And if Season Two doesn't work out, you never know."

Randall finished off his Cosmo, stood up and announced, "I need to head home to Ron and finish packing for Alaska, we fly out Monday."

"Taking a cruise?" asked Shelby.

"Yeah, the Inside Passage."

"Mmm, sounds delish!" said Howie.

"HOWIE!" Randall and Shelby exclaimed.

Howie stood up as well. "Tinder date should be here soon."

"Okay. Bye you guys, miss you," Shelby said as she hugged them both.

The men headed off into the bustle of WeHo as Shelby looked around, not quite ready to call it a night. *I miss stuff like this,* she thought. *Lots of laughter, good conversations, a city-buzz.* She looked around to see if she knew anyone. Just as she got to the edge of the dance floor, the DJ cued up Bruno Mars...and Di and her pals jumped up to join the action.

Di spun around in a fancy swirl, her black high-tops effortlessly doing some heel-toe up-and-down action. As she stopped the spin, she saw Shelby and grinned. They grooved their heads in the same rhythm and moved toward each other, bopping along to that ice cold, that Michelle Pfeiffer, that white gold of *Uptown Funk.*

Shelby tried to ignore her Inner Randall yelling, 'WHAT EXACTLY ARE YOU DOING?'"

The gals both did their best Bruno Mars strut, as if they'd been dancing together for years. Di spun around again and Shelby pretended to fan herself because she was so hot. They found themselves yelling along to the song with Di thrusting her pelvis as Shelby changed the funk you up lyrics to the other "F" word.

And then it happened. Di turned to another girl, also dressed in skin-tight-all-black. They continued the dance. Very close. Too close.

Shelby literally stopped dancing. Her three-minute fantasy had burst into flames. She backed away from the dancers. Di didn't even notice she was leaving. Shelby turned toward the exit and staggered onto the Robertson Boulevard sidewalk.

Okay, I'm an idiot. Why did I do that? I have a girlfriend. I have sex. I have a beautiful place to work. What don't I have? The chance to cut loose in the city? Jump up and down to fun music and shout "Hallelujah?" What else, what else, what else am I missing?

She faced west...and thought about the beach and Venice and Santa Monica and the Hammer Museum and the Laemmle movie theatres; she faced south and thought of the L.A. County Museum of Art on Wilshire and the Aquarium of the Pacific in Long Beach; she turned east and thought about the Mark Taper Forum and the Broad Art Museum and Disney Hall; finally, she looked north and pretended to see the San Gabriel Mountains beyond the city. And beyond that, the Sierra Nevada...and Carol. Hot tears came to her eyes. Tears of shame? Of longing? Of confusion? All of the above?

UC Santa Cruz

Chapter Forty-Nine
Enterprising Redux

"So, it's not an actual treasure hunt, it's a virtual one, and people will show us on their cell phones what they found," Carol said. She and Larry and Shelby were convening in the office a few days after Shelby returned from her L.A. sojourn.

"Certain birds, trees, flowers and so on that we know are in the woods as we take them on a short hike," Carol added.

Shelby chimed in. "And the prize will be like twenty percent off a meal at the restaurant or at the gift store."

Carol wrapped up the pitch. "It's easy to set up, and we think it'll provide a lot of fun."

Larry nodded, his eyes gleaming.

"Okay. Remember when you wanted to get an acupuncturist?" Carol continued with the next idea. "Well, we found one through Marlene, she works at the same clinic and could come up here on weekends, carpool with Marlene."

"Brilliant!" Larry exclaimed.

"We also realized," said Shelby, "that we need more online reviews, so we made up some take-home postcards for visitors. That way they'll remember to add a positive note online when they get back to civilization."

Shelby handed Larry the postcard prototype with its cute ground squirrel who so looked excited that it wanted to give a five-star review.

Larry looked equally excited. "You have done an excellent job," Larry said, and this time he smiled at both women.

"But wait, there's more!" said Carol, imitating a TV ad. "We've been thinking about winter, which is such a slow time. What if we keep a few cabins open, plus a small kitchen staff, and we then really push snowshoe hiking and cross-country skiing here? We know it depends on the weather, but if it doesn't snow people can still do regular hikes."

"Yes, yes, I'd been thinking the same thing," said Larry. "Thank you, thank you. We will get through this."

Carol grinned. It felt good to be part of positive action instead of resisting Larry's notions of change.

"I will call my friends in L.A.," declared Larry, "and tell them all of our ideas and how much cash infusion we need to get us through the end of the year."

"Great," said Shelby, as Larry headed into his office, waving the sample postcard as if he had a winning lottery ticket.

The women smiled at each other and Shelby mouthed, "We did it!" Carol nodded, putting her hand up for a high-five.

"You were terrific," Shelby whispered, kissing her.

"Uh, Shelby," Larry called from his office.

"Yes?"

He poked his head back out. "Could you go check on Benny? See what you observe."

"Observe?" answered Shelby.

"Is he in the flow of the kitchen yet? I've heard reports he's too methodical. Too careful."

"Maybe he's just getting used to his new chef role? He's only been here a week."

"That's why I need you to check on him. Remember, you're my eyes and ears as my Number Two now." Then just to cap things off, Larry added, "And tell him he's here on a one-week contingency basis starting today."

Larry went back in his office. Shelby's jaw dropped. But before she could gather her wits and figure out how to convey that message of good cheer to Benny, Carol turned to her and mouthed, "Number Two?" Shelby motioned for Carol to follow her outside.

Once they were beyond earshot of the office, she explained, "Larry wants me to be his 'Number Two.' I'm not even sure what all that entails, and I certainly haven't told him yes yet."

"Why didn't you tell me this?" Carol asked indignantly.

"Because I don't understand what he wants, and I don't know if I really want the pressure."

Carol stewed.

Shit, thought Shelby, *I should've said something to her sooner. The trip to L.A. sidetracked my brain.*

"You're the manager, you already have a nice title and a lot of responsibilities," Shelby said, trying to soothe Carol's hurt feelings. "I don't have a title at all, just Jack-of-all-Trades."

Carol pursed her lips, not exactly buying that. "Well, good luck." Then she went back to the office.

Shelby stewed. *If I turn down the Number Two position, how will that sit with Larry? And will I then be out of a job? Is he "making me an offer I can't refuse"? Cue up the theme from* The Godfather.

She headed over to the kitchen to see how the new chef was doing. When she entered through the back door, she immediately saw Benny, an Asian fellow in his mid-20s with a slight build but strong hands. He was chopping vegetables, a déjà vu moment that harkened back to Manuel. Except Benny was doing it slowly, methodically and meticulously, as if each angle on the carrot had to be perfect. He placed them in a circle with endive spears filled with bits of olive tapenade. It created an amazing circle of artistry.

"It's beautiful," she said.

Benny gave a tiny nod and an even tinier smile. He was in his work Zen zone and his bowed head conveyed, "Do Not Disturb."

"May I taste?" she asked quietly, not sure if this would break his concentration.

He handed her an endive spear as if passing a fragile 400-year-old crystal vase to her.

"Mmm, this is delish," said Shelby.

Benny nodded again.

"I'm Shelby. I work in the office."

"Nice to meet you."

"I'm the person who contacted your chef school."

"Thank you. I'm honored to be here. My mother used to work with Larry."

"Ah. Very good."

He finished chopping the carrot slivers and then placed a completed plate in the delivery line to go out to the restaurant patrons.

"So, this is your first full-time job out of chef school?"

"Many of my summers and weekends were spent cooking at top restaurants in L.A."

"Of course."

Shelby happened to catch sight of Carlotta, the forty-year-old sassy sous chef, off to the side. Carlotta was giving the two of them a stern eye.

"Benny, I have a message from Larry," said Shelby, knowing she couldn't stall any longer. "He would like you to move things along."

He nodded but barely went any faster.

"Is there something Carlotta, or we, can do to help speed up the process?" Shelby asked. "A smooth process makes the customers out front happy."

Benny didn't acknowledge the comment and instead turned his attention to the pot of cooking orzo. Shelby could tell from Carlotta's hands on her hips that frustration was cooking for her.

"So, I have another message from Larry." Shelby paused to see if Benny would look up. He did.

"He wanted me to let you know that you're in a contingency period right now."

"What?"

"Contingency. You have, ah, a bit of time, to 'get up to speed,' as they say."

"How much time?"

"One more week, starting today."

"I've been here only a week so far!"

"I know. Please just do your best."

Benny flared. "When I was hired, there was no mention of contingency."

"Ah. Yes. Um, did you sign a contract?"

"No," he said in anguish.

"Well, in that case, I'm pretty sure the owner can dictate the terms of your employment. Look, you're talented, the food is great—just try to go a little faster, okay?"

Benny looked miffed and went back to methodically stirring the orzo.

Shelby sighed and angled for the door to head outside. Carlotta happened to be exiting as well.

"What do you think?" Shelby whispered once they were outdoors.

"I really don't care. Larry should have promoted me instead of hiring that kid. Let him know that." Carlotta started to walk away.

"You should bring that up to him yourself, Carlotta."

"I have. I did. He does whatever the fuck he wants," she hissed over her shoulder.

"We need a day off," Shelby said to Carol over lunch at their usual picnic table. "We've been working for six weeks straight."

"Hey, try asking Larry. You're his Number Two."

"Would you stop? This is why we need a day off, we're turning on each other. Mondays are our slow days, so let's ask for that."

"He's not gonna give us both the same day off. That leaves him short-staffed."

"Okay, how about a half a day. We're here for people checking out in the morning and then we're back by late afternoon for the later arrivals. C'mon, don't you want to go hiking in the mountains, isn't that why we like working here?"

Carol chewed on her celery sticks filled with peanut butter.

"Carol, please don't let him divide us and destroy all the growth we've had this season. I'll ask him but back me up when I do."

"We'd like next Monday afternoon off," Shelby stated to Larry in an even tone after lunch.

"No."

Larry's answer hung there like a brittle leaf as he kept going over the Excel spreadsheets on his desk.

Carol gave it a shot. "It's one afternoon, Larry. We haven't had a day off in weeks."

"Too much going on. It's all-hands-on-deck."

Carol took a step toward him and let him have it. "When you first started here, you didn't want me to have a lunch break and you didn't let me have a day off. I had to fight for those things so that I wouldn't get burned out. And the world has not ended. Larry, I'm not willing to risk having a heart attack from working too much and not enjoying all that Nature has for us here."

That got him. He knew it was true, so true. He had his lunch of lentil soup sitting right next to his computer. He stared at it. He nodded. "Monday is fine. After the morning check-outs."

"Thank you," said Carol.

"Thanks, Larry," added Shelby.

~ ❦ ~

"I haven't been on this trail in, wow, it must be two years," Carol exclaimed as she and Shelby stepped off the Castle Peak trail and out to a vista overlooking a valley 3,000 feet below.

"This is a view and a half!" yelled Shelby. "Should we bring some of our tourists up here?"

"We'd have to be sure they're in tip-top shape," Carol said. "But yeah, let's put Castle Peak on the August calendar."

"We'll screen 'em, we'll get great folks."

"We will," Carol said, giving her butt cheek a squeeze.

"You were so great at standing up to Larry for us to get a little time off," Shelby said.

"I'm sorry I was cranky about him offering you the Number Two position."

"Thanks. I'm nervous about this whole Number Two thing."

"Yeah, I can imagine," Carol said.

They headed away from the edge and back onto the trail proper, but then Shelby stopped hiking and looked down at the pine needles at her feet. Carol looked at her and sensed something was afoot, and not just pine needles.

"What?"

"Larry… it's all feeling like quicksand pulling me under…and…I… I'm scared. I-I may want out."

"Out? What happened to 'team work' and all that?"

"Carol, I've gotta put my cards on the table. I'm super concerned. Larry is a lot like my dad, and I'm afraid I'll end up working long hours and trying to be perfect to get his approval."

"You just seem on-the-ball to me, not like your currying favor with Larry."

"Trust me. I jump through hoops higher than those fourteeners," Shelby said pointing to the nearby peaks.

"Okay, so what's the solution? We stage a coup and take over the place?"

"Ha ha. Let me put one more card on the table." Shelby paused and knew there was no turning back after playing it. "I miss culture. Remember how much fun we had at the music festival in Bishop? I long for that. Concerts, theatre, movies, bookstores, dancing, the aliveness of it. My trip to L.A. brought it all back," Shelby said. "I can see the worry in your eyes, but I had to bring it up."

Carol nodded sadly.

"I know every girlfriend you've ever had has left this place. And I don't want to leave but…. Okay, let's say I split my time, here in the summers, freelance November through March in a city. Start my own marketing and branding business."

"Maybe," said Carol slowly. "But what if you cultivate a new client and they want you to do a job in July?"

Shelby nodded. "It would be challenging." She wrapped her arms around Carol and hugged her mightily…and then put the biggest card of all on the table.

"Let me just ask, Carol, would you be willing to consider working somewhere else?"

"…I…Shelby, I've really never worked anywhere else," Carol said hoarsely. "I…don't know…."

They leaned into each other, foreheads touching, for several moments and then Shelby said, "I have an idea. Let's do one of your story rituals. Maybe that'll give us some clarity. You up for it?"

Carol pulled her head back and paused, knowing she was going to be in the hot seat if she said yes.

"Tell you what, I'll go first. Throw me to the wolves, see what happens," Shelby said.

Carol went wide-eyed. And then nodded.

"Okay," said Shelby, "how does the preamble go? 'We call upon...'?"

"'We call upon the great and wise muses of the universe to guide us as we create a world of our own.' And then we usually say past, present or future."

"Okay, uh, past," said Shelby.

"Ready?"

Shelby nodded yes. Carol paused to consider where to send her, and then she lowered her voice and narrowed her eyes. "I see a planet where the military runs everything."

Shelby instantly knew this was going to get deep. She reluctantly held out her hand and Carol gave her a hiking pole to act as a talking stick.

"I see a planet where the military runs every fucking thing," Shelby responded, arching her back.

Shelby handed off the pole to Carol who raised it overhead as if leading an infantry; she started marching, Shelby followed.

"Sprite had no choice but to obey," Carol barked.

"Damn right," said Shelby. "Asshole Air Force Dad ordered her to clean the garage. She even cleaned the windowsill with a toothbrush and alphabetized his tools!"

Carol stopped and stared at her. Shelby nodded that yes, indeed, that was how it went down. And then to demonstrate, she grabbed pine cones from the forest floor and lined them up with manic precision.

"She organized the contents of the kitchen cabinets by height and by color," Shelby continued. "She wiped down the sinks so there were never any water spots. She mowed the lawn horizontally one week and vertically the next and even had a chart to keep track of it!"

Carol's eyes bugged out. Shelby nodded again.

"And yet?" Carol asked.

"And yet the adults still fought. 'STOP MARCHING, LEAVE THE AIR FORCE.' 'YOU'RE MY WIFE, YOU HAVE TO OBEY.'"

"But Sprite obeyed," Carol said.

Shelby jumped up from the pine cones. "Sprite damn well did! Military corners on the sheets, military creases on his pants, military spit and polish on his boots!"

"Sprite did everything perfectly!"

"AND THEY STILL FOUGHT. No matter how perfect things were, no matter how perfect she was, HE STILL COULDN'T SAY I LOVE YOU," Shelby yelled.

Shelby fell to her knees with that profound realization, tears flowing. Carol knelt and put her arm around her.

"And all of those fantasy moments with girlfriends…?" Carol asked gently.

"They could say 'I love you' in them," Shelby whispered.

"What about a real girlfriend?"

"She'll be like my dad. She'll see I'm not perfect."

Carol held her tight and whispered in her ear, "I love you. Just the way you are." They melted onto the forest floor.

After several moments, Shelby rolled onto her back, looked up at the blue cloudless mountain sky and took several deep breaths. She glanced at Carol, not wanting to rush anything along. Carol knew it was her turn, though, so she simply nodded. They stood up.

"Past, present or future?" asked Shelby.

"I'll go with the past as well."

"How about…an enchanted place," Shelby said, looking up at the giant trees, inhaling their expansive energy. "A place that little kids would like."

Carol smiled and seemed to be on board. Shelby handed her the hiking pole "talking stick" and they began walking.

"I see a young girl skipping through the enchanted fields of Elisia," said Carol.

Shelby chimed in, "I see a young girl named Woodhawk in the enchanted fields of Elisia."

Carol smiled, touched that Shelby remembered her name from their previous storytelling.

"And she has been granted the job of protecting the lush rolling farmland and its animals," Carol continued.

"Protecting the lush farmland from…something…someone..,." Shelby observed.

Carol stopped in her tracks. Shelby could tell she had hit a nerve.

Carol continued the story. "…Parents. Who made plans that didn't include Woodhawk. Woodhawk was perfectly happy living on the farm, tending to the animals…."

They began hiking again and Shelby carefully added on, "Tending to the animals…but the parents made plans to…."

"...the parents made plans to sell the farm to developers so they could move to town." Carol said with ire in her voice.

"Move to town...and Woodhawk was not consulted."

Carol exploded, "No, she wasn't, damn it. And her mother talked nonstop about the move—she was finally getting her dream of moving to the city! People! Culture!"

"And Mom talked so much that Woodhawk couldn't get a word in edgewise," Shelby added. "Plus, when they moved away from the animals, she had no one to talk to, so she completely clammed up."

Carol was stunned by the accuracy of Shelby's words, her ears felt as if they were on fire.

Shelby kept going, in her best Annoying Mom voice. "'This town is wonderful! So much to explore! Get your nose out of those books! Get out there and make some friends!'"

"LEAVE ME ALONE," Carol shouted, backing away from Shelby.

"'You're missing everything! You know what you are? A freak!'"

"SHUT UP! I HATE YOU!" Carol took off running into the woods.

Shelby ran after her, continuing in the role of Mom. "STOP HIDING IN YOUR BOOKS!'"

"LEAVE ME ALONE!" Carol was running like a cheetah trying to evade capture.

Shelby was freaked out that she wasn't able to catch her. She stopped in her tracks and yelled as loud as she could, "CAROL, WHAT IS REAL-LY GOING ON?"

Carol stopped running, and then panting, panting, panting, slowly faced Shelby.

~ ❦ ~

"Tomorrow we shall take off for Stirling Castle, one of the largest and most important castles in Scotland!" said Jeanette.

Carol was walking home from high school and having a conversation in her head with Jeanette Winterson. She had constructed an entire life with Jeanette. It was helping her cope with the awfulness of junior year and more importantly, with Prime Organizer Mean Monster Mom.

"I can't wait," said Carol.

But before she could construct Castle Life with Jeanette, teenaged Carol smelled smoke as she walked through the front door of her current home in Chico, California. This sent a shot of adrenalin through her: the kitchen fire she'd caused had been just four months ago.

Carol followed her nose to the kitchen. *Nothing burning here, whew!* Then she poked her head out the back door. Her mom was burning something in their firepit. Odd because the pit was used only for social gatherings. Carol had a queasy feeling and it wasn't just a visceral reaction to the smoke. *What's Mom tossing into the—?*

With a flash of anger that matched the fire, Carol ran toward the firepit. "YOU'RE BURNING BOOKS? <u>MY</u> BOOKS?"

"I am. The gay porn," her mom said with a coolness that belied the fire action.

"IT'S NOT PORN."

Carol thought about yanking her books out of the firepit but instead ran back inside to her bedroom and slammed the door so hard the neighbors thought a gun had gone off.

～ ❧ ～

"I thought you'd said she got rid of them. You didn't tell me she burned them!" Shelby said.

Carol looked as if she was going to start running again.

"Carol, DON'T RUN AWAY INTO A STORYLAND! FIGHT BACK!"

"<u>I did</u>. When I did my first ritual with Gillian, I stood up to Monster Mom one night and took back my power."

"Okay. So, what's happened since then?"

Carol looked lost so Shelby decided to keep going with the story.

"Woodhawk went to college and discovered literature and history and most importantly, Gillian. They created magical worlds in the woods and on campus," Shelby said with such magnificence Carol turned to face her. She was transported back in time, back to Chico State.

"They could do anything. Be anyone. Run with me!" she called to Shelby with her arm outstretched.

Shelby grabbed her hand and they ran for all they were worth.

"Woodhawk and RidgeOwl ran among the oaks and sycamores, listening and learning and tending and loving all of the Earth's creatures," Carol proclaimed.

"And then one day, RidgeOwl said, 'Fly with me!'" Shelby-as-Gillian proposed.

"Flying!" yelled Carol.

"'Higher.'"

"Higher than the tree tops," shouted Carol as she spun Shelby around.

"'Up to our dreams!'"

"Dream spinners!" proclaimed Carol.

"'Fly with me to Chicago!'"

Carol stopped spinning and dropped Shelby's hand.

"'Please,'" Shelby-as-Gillian asked.

"...I can't."

"'Why not?'"

"...I'm scared,'" Carol said, her voice breaking.

"'Of what?'"

~ 🦋 ~

"I love to go a-wandering, along a mountain track. And as I go, I love to sing, my knapsack on my back. Val-deri, Val-dera...."

Gillian and Carol were singing at full volume as they hiked their now-favorite path in the woods outside of Chico one spring day their senior year. They had worked through the previous challenges: Carol learning to focus on her own projects, Gillian making time for Date Night. They'd come out of things a stronger couple.

"Val-deri, Val-dera-ha-ha-ha-ha-ha-ha-ha-ha!" On the "ha-ha's" they'd giggle themselves silly every time.

"Monarch Glen, we're back!" Gillian proclaimed and they dropped their knapsacks. Back in September, Monarch butterflies were flitting about the creek during their visit, so the gals christened the spot with its new name.

"We've been waiting forever for spring this year," Carol said as she pulled out a crazy-colored tie-dyed sheet, food and wine from the packs.

"Frost in April, freakish," said Gillian.

"Poor daffodils didn't know what hit 'em."

Together they snapped the sheet and let it drift to the budding green grass.

"Ahhhh," said Gillian, looking around and inhaling in the spring greenery.

Carol stood behind her, hugged her and whispered, "Shall we?"

"We shall."

Carol began their latest ritual, "Mother Earth, Father Sky, Brother Sun, Sister Moon, we ask for your blessing on this sacred union."

"Leaves of grass, canopy of trees, hearts of flowers, caress of breeze, we are at one with you."

"And with each other," Carol added. "Happy birthday, my love."

Gillian turned around and kissed her. "Best ever."

"Want your presents now or after the feast?"

Gillian yelled to the heavens, "All I want is you! I am the Goddess StarMist and you are mine!"

"OMIGOD, when you yelled that last night on the roof of the student union, and then the look on Dexter Laswell's face!"

They cracked up laughing. By now, the entire Drama and History Departments were well aware of their union and creative adventures—rituals, performance art, making out in the theatre lobby. Carol had come a long way since her awkward-as-Bambi freshmen days. And they loved to get those eye-popping stares, Dexter Laswell's being the latest.

"I want to write about last night right now," Carol said, angling for the homemade storybook, but Gillian grabbed it first.

"No, do it later."

"No, strike while the juices are flowing," answered Carol.

"My juices are flowing, forget the storybook."

But Carol managed to grab it from her. "Look how big it is, six inches!" And then something caught Carol's eye at the back of the storybook. "What's this?"

Gillian quickly snatched the book back.

"While you were sleeping in this morning. A love letter inspired by the heights we reached last night."

"I hope you did our coupling justice, Gil," Carol said with an eye twinkle and a grin.

"I did. Orgasmically," Gillian said. "You can put your spin on it later. Time for presents."

"You've had too much coffee."

"Birthday energy. C'mon, what'd you get me?"

"Okay, okay...." Carol pulled out a box from the knapsack.

Gillian tore into the wrapping paper...and once she saw what was inside...she slowed down.

"New paints. Thank you, Carol."

"For more amazing scene designs."

"Your wish is my command. In fact, I brought one to show you, my love."

"Wait, we're still doing presents," Carol protested.

"There's more?"

Carol handed her a handmade card, covered in bits of flowers, twigs... and a photograph taken looking up at their favorite oak tree on campus.

"You should sell these cards," Gillian said. "I'm telling you, the bookstore would—"

"—I will, I will, stop pushing. Open it."

Gillian did so...and found another photo inside, this one of a house.

"'Oh, honey, you shouldn't have.' Seriously, babe, what is this?" asked Gillian.

"It's that house on Walnut, two blocks from campus. We pass it all the time on our way to The Brynn Bookstore."

"You got me a house?"

"Kind've. My friend Laura from the History Department is losing her roommate," Carol explained. "And when she described the house, I said oh my God, Gillian and I walk by it every day and fantasize about living there! It will be SO much better than living in the dorm and who wants to be grad students in a DORM anyway, right?"

Gillian was stunned...nervous...and nearly speechless. "I, that's, wow...."

"Laura said we could re-paint."

"Grand. Well, I, uh, have something to show you."

Gillian pulled from her knapsack a rendering of a stage play's set, full of psychedelic colors.

"Wow, that's gorgeous! What play is it for?"

"The musical *Hair*."

"I didn't know the Drama Department was doing *Hair* this spring."

"They're not," Gillian said, taking a deep breath. "I did the design as part of my application to the Omega Theatre in Chicago."

"Oh," Carol said, a bit puzzled.

"Remember I said I might apply? As the Associate Scene Designer? Their Set Designer is like seventy and he's gonna retire one of these days and I thought it'd be a great foot-in-the-door thing."

A moment passed as Carol tried to grok the situation. "...When do you send it in?"

"A few months ago. This is actually a duplicate rendering."

"...When do you hear back?"

"Last week."

Carol could feel the blood draining from her face.

"I got in, Carol, the job's mine. If I want it."

Carol had no words.

Gillian kept going. "I start July first, for their fall season." And then she pulled the *Conjurings and Wanderings* storybook toward her and opened it to the back, where she'd pasted something.

"I wanted to show you my letter of acceptance. That's what I put in here."

Carol's eyes went to the photo of the house on Walnut instead. Her breathing became labored, there was a faint ringing in her ears. She could barely hear Gillian who was quietly saying, "Babe, there's nothing for me to do here in Chico."

"We were both going to get our master's degrees!"

"And then what? There are no theatres here, I'd have to go SOME-WHERE to get a job."

"Redding, Stockton...."

"I grew up in the sticks, I don't want to live in the sticks," Gillian said adamantly.

"But Chicago's crowded and all cement. I won't be able to hear myself think, I won't be able to hear the songbirds!" Carol protested.

"When you're done with your thesis, you can come to Chicago. We'll walk on rooftops, we'll call upon the Celtic gods and goddesses, we'll find nature."

"You can't do that in Chicago!"

"YOU CAN DO ANYTHING IN CHICAGO!" Gillian bellowed back. "We will find the sacred spaces, the creeks and woods and birds, I promise! It's all an adventure, Chico, Chicago!"

"My life is here, this is my home!"

"I'm your home. Am I not?"

～ ❦ ～

In the present, Carol's knees started to shake and her breathing became labored. Shelby knew something profound was happening. *How far do I push her? How much do I ask?*

"And then what happened? You two...parted ways?"

It was as if the sun had disappeared from the sky and an apocalyptic darkness was swirling around them. Shelby waited. Carol closed her eyes and finished the story.

May, senior year at Chico State, opening night of *A Midsummer Night's Dream:* Gillian put on a black tuxedo with a swirly print shirt that used a lot of blues and greens to match the outdoor fairy-nature of her design for Shakespeare's classic. And a flaming red bowtie as an exclamation point.

Carol also donned black: pants and a long-sleeved shirt, with a midnight blue silk scarf as her accent moment. Because, yes, she was feeling black and blue. Chicago, to go or not to go, as Shakespeare might have asked.

Carol and Gillian looked at each other as they were about to exit their dorm room. "Last opening night here at Chico, m'lady," Gillian said holding out her hand. Carol slowly came toward her and placed her left hand in Gillian's right. Gillian gave it a squeeze, Carol didn't squeeze back.

They walked over to the Admin Building, where the first two scenes would be staged on the landing and steps. Carol eventually had to let go of Gillian's hand because a gazillion theatre geeks came up to hug her and congratulate her and wish her well on the Chicago adventure she was about to undertake.

Once the opening moments of *Midsummer* had been performed, Puck and the fairies came out and directed everyone over to the quad, to the very spot where Carol and Gillian had once played make-believe beneath the giant oak tree. The rest of the play would be staged on platforms under the tree with some froufrou greenery and fantastical lighting added to amplify the enchantment.

Carol's quandary energy subsided as a realization crept in.

"You know what?" she whispered to Gillian as they found a couple of lawn chairs to sit in. "We both incorporated our lives into our projects."

"Yes, we did," Gillian agreed. She paused, looked at the ground and then quietly said, "I should've gone with you and your classmates to Monarch Glen to do your ritual. It sounded awesome."

"It's not too late. What's your gift to the world and what's your sacrifice to make it happen?"

Just then *Midsummer* started again...and Gillian nodded that she'd heard Carol but didn't have time to answer.

Not only had the synchronicity gods scheduled this play to aid Gillian in fulfilling her dream of doing a set design amongst the trees...they had positioned it at just the perfect time for Carol to reflect on love. Lysander and Hermia were just getting their love journey started when complications arose, prompting Lysander to say, *"The course of true love never did run smooth."*

Carol nodded, *Mmmhmm.* And she noted the fairy meddling didn't prevent Puck from blaming the lovers' behavior on their own foolishness. <u>He</u> felt their actions were merely a performance for the fairies' enjoyment, but Carol could tell the lovers themselves treated the whole affair with deadly seriousness. Love is a form of madness that prompted the lovers to act in foolish ways, Carol could see.

The audience leapt to its collective feet when mischievous Puck wrapped things up and the play ended. Carol joined them and clapped until her hands were numb, for the actors, the tech team and for Gillian. As she looked around at the crowd and the campus, she became aware of time markers about to tick by: term papers would be turned in, grades assigned, caps and gowns placed on heads and bodies....

But first there was the final opening night party, hosted by the head of the Drama Department in his palatial home on the edge of town. As she and Gillian entered the tiled entryway and headed to the chandeliered dining room for sparkling beverages, Carol instantly relaxed. *Well, I relax in nature, too...but this feels as if I'm...being taken care of, pampered. What would that kind of life be like*, Carol wondered, as she picked up a glass of champagne. She took a couple of sips and drank in the gold fabric curtains of Dr. T.'s living room, paintings by they-must-be-famous painters, the floor-to-ceiling bookshelves that lined one whole wall. *Could I get used to this? Could Gillian and I create something like this? She designs plays for Broadway and I'm a tenured professor at some Ivy League school....*

Carol chatted with various drama students, she knew several of them by now...and luckily MaryAnne was here.

"That was quite a production," Carol said to her, "and you were a fantastic Helena!"

"Oh, gosh, thanks!" MaryAnne said, giving her a hug and a kiss on the cheek. "I'm going to miss you so much."

"Aw, I'll miss you too, MaryAnne, you're so bright and bubbly, I always feel better after talking to you."

"Oh, thank you. And I always feel better after talking to you."

"Really?" Carol asked.

"You're this steady-on lover of nature and people. And you listen and take things in and give thoughtful answers."

"Thank you. Truly. So, what are you going to do after graduation, go to New York and start auditioning?" Carol asked.

MaryAnne sighed.

"Is that a 'no' or...?"

"It's more of an 'I don't know.' I applied to some grad schools and got into a couple, but I'm tired of school, plus I don't want to take on more debt. But New York feels, I don't know, overwhelming. Maybe I should go to Chicago, like Gillian...."

"Boy, I'm in the same boat...." Carol was grateful to run into someone who was wrestling with similar issues.

Just then they heard uproarious laughter from the back patio as someone missed a metal chair out there and landed on the cement. Apparently, it was the most hilarious thing ever, judging by everyone's reaction. Carol took a closer look and noted that Gillian was the one flat on her ass.

"Um, what time do you think you'll head back to campus?" Carol asked MaryAnne.

"Any minute. I'm wiped from tonight and all of our rehearsals this week. Plus, I have to be ready for tomorrow night's performance."

"Could I get a ride? I think Gillian, uh, wants to stay longer."

"Sure."

Carol went over to the patio door, stepped outside, and leaned over to Gillian, whose eyes were completely bloodshot.

"I'm getting a ride with MaryAnne back to the dorm."

Gillian half-nodded; for all she knew, Carol had said, "I'm getting into a boat and sailing to Tahiti."

Back at the dorm, Carol slept fitfully, stewing and stewing about what to do with her life. Dr. T.'s house was amazing, but there was no guarantee she and Gillian could have something like that. And she wondered if she really wanted to be a teacher. *Maybe I should be a Forest Department employee and take people into the woods the way I did with my history class.*

Gillian staggered into their dorm room at 3 a.m. and fell onto her own bed, not even getting out of her clothes. She was asleep, or unconscious, instantly.

Carol couldn't go back to sleep, so she stopped trying and got up around six. She paced the campus. The *Midsummer* chairs had been removed but the platforms and lights would be there for the rest of the play's run. As Carol looked at the set in the cold light of day, it was like looking at Life in cold reality. *Who is this Gillian? Do I want to live with such an over-the-top, rambunctious free spirit? But who am I to tell her to tamp down, control the drinking, don't jump from roof to roof howling at the moon. Who am I? Who am I?*

Carol ate breakfast the moment the cafeteria opened...and then walked around the campus some more but decided she needed nature. She tiptoed back into the dorm room. It turned out, tiptoeing wasn't necessary: Gillian was still blacked out. Then with absolutely no guilt, Carol took Gillian's car keys.

The car smelled like booze. Carol rolled the windows down and drove over to her and Gillian's favorite woodsy area, aka Monarch Glen. She parked at the little pull-off gravel lot near the start of the traverse to the glen. She opened the car door to let in even more fresh air. And then she looked to her right and noticed a bunch of *Midsummer* tech items on the passenger seat: some paint brushes, a tape measure, a rope.

Carol sat in the driver's seat for several moments and after a bit, closed her eyes. She could see the cast from *Midsummer* taking their bows. She could not picture what came next. What the future held for her. She could not picture standing in front of a bunch of students as a professor with something pithy to say. She could not picture living in a dorm room—or even at the nice house on Walnut—without Gillian. She could not picture walking from classroom to classroom as she worked toward a master's degree because EVERYTHING at Chico State would remind her of Gillian. She could not picture navigating O'Hare Airport or taking the "El" in Chicago. Her imagination had Completely Dried Up.

Carol grabbed her daypack and headed into the forest. It now felt as if it took no time at all to get to Monarch Glen. That first day, the hike seemed to take twice as long; *I guess when you're lost, that's what time feels like,* Carol mused.

She looked up at their favorite birch tree. She and Gillian had built a makeshift ladder so they could get up into the tree for a different perspective. They talked of building a treehouse or fort up there, a place where they could take cover from the rain or make love. Carol realized that she couldn't imagine sharing her body with any other woman.

She climbed the ladder and sat down on a hefty limb.

She paused for several minutes.

Then she fashioned a noose out of the rope she'd brought from the car. She flipped the other end around the biggest branch the birch had to offer. She tied it off. And then she realized that she hadn't written a note. She'd left her daypack on the ground so someone would see it. Pen and paper were in it. *Fuck. Do I really want to write a note? MaryAnne could explain things to people. Oh, shit, I don't want to do that to MaryAnne. Gillian could explain things. If she's really been paying attention to me. FUCK.* She leaned her head against the tree.

And then she heard a voice that seemed to come from inside the birch tree, "See all of my nicks and crags and bumps and ridges?"

Carol sat up.

"They're building character. I'm becoming more of who I am."

Carol looked around. Stunned. No one else was within miles.

The voice continued. "You, dear one, are growing as well. It's hard to tell, we know. The growth is barely noticeable. Take a look back at who you were when you first arrived on campus."

Carol was afraid she was completely losing it. After several moments, she tried closing her eyes. Even though she could not envision the future, she definitely could remember the past. The terrified-to-her-toes freshman who wouldn't talk to a soul or take a chance on anything. Who had never dated much less made love to anyone before. Who had never stood in front of a class and given a presentation before much less done it in the woods. Who had never written anything besides school assignments much less concocted and crafted a huge storybook of fantastical tales.

Carol realized that four years ago she could not have pictured any of that happening. If she'd closed her eyes during that frosh mixer where she'd hugged the wall and wouldn't talk to a soul, she would have come up with a blank slate. A big fat scary nothing. Wow. But then Gillian landed in her life.

The tree murmured one more thought. "Would you prefer to have not had the adventures you've had for the past four years?"

"No, of course not," Carol said out loud. "I'm, I'm glad I had all of those experiences."

In that moment, Carol knew that even though she had no idea what the future would hold for her, if she didn't stick around, she wouldn't find out, she couldn't create that journey.

She took the rope down. A short time later she was back on campus, where she ran into Professor Sarah Peterson.

Shelby and Carol cuddled together 'neath the tall trees in the present for a long time, absorbing the seismic shift that Carol had just revealed. Shelby put her face right next to Carol's and said tenderly, "Thank you. I know it took great courage to tell that story."

Carol exhaled...and actually felt lighter and more relaxed than she had in months.

"I need those cost comparisons by five o'clock."

Shelby and Carol had returned to H.Q. and Larry immediately jolted them back to his reality. He wanted cheaper food suppliers.

Shelby opened her mouth to say something but thought better of it. She fired up the computer to begin searching.

Carol took note of all of this and asked Larry, in a nonconfrontational tone, "What's happening at five?" figuring that's what Shelby wanted to know.

"I have a phone call."

"With who?"

"Investors in L.A. I need to look good."

He went into his man cave office and the gals exchanged a glance. Carol kept pressing, a little louder now. "Manual did a big search last summer for the best suppliers. Do you still have his notes?"

"It doesn't matter! I want fresh information!" And then suddenly Larry appeared again and handed Carol an online receipt and a money bag. "I've sent the postcard Shelby designed to the print shop in Bishop. Please go down and pick them up, a box of five hundred. Also, here's a deposit for the bank."

He went back in his office and firmly shut the door.

The women looked at each other and both of their expressions said, *He's baaaaaaack....*

"I need some advice. Again."

After depositing the money at the bank in Bishop, Carol had caught Sarah Peterson at the end of her shift at Outfitters, the outdoor supply store. They met for coffee at Schat's Bakery on the main drag.

"I'm all ears," Sarah said.

"I need a solution to my life. Again."

"Oh, something simple!"

"Exactly."

They laughed and raised their coffee cups in a salute.

"Want to narrow it down just a smidge?"

"Sure. But I'd like to, uh, acknowledge that I wish I'd followed your earlier advice a little better."

"Well, we do what we can. That's the journey of life. I seem to recall that you were happy to come up here and work. Do you wish you'd moved to Chicago after that one-year break from academia?"

"…I don't know. Yeah, I thought I'd be here one summer, or at the most, one year. But I completely lost my nerve. I've loved working here in the mountains, it's my sacred place, and teaching others about it is my calling. So, no I don't feel going to Chicago was my Life's Mission…."

"But?"

"But I was scared. I was a scared little kid, even though I was eighteen. And now I've been hiding in the woods too long."

"Maybe you needed to work in these mountains to grow into an adult. A happy adult."

Carol nodded.

"But?" Sarah asked.

"I think there's another important crossroads coming up…."

After meeting with Sarah, Carol called Shelby from the road in the early evening as she was heading back up Highway 395. "I can pick up some dinner at Steve's Steakhouse in Little Pine, how's that sound?"

"Sure, okay, yeah."

Carol could hear the weariness in Shelby's voice.

"Did you get the food supply research done on time?"

"No. The Michaelsons wanted to stay another night and Larry kept trying to accommodate them—which didn't work, we just don't have the rooms. Why does Larry think sucking up is good customer service?"

"He doesn't suck up to us, does he?"

"Nope," said Shelby.

"Well, no worries, have I got an evening planned for you," Carol said with good cheer. "How does salmon sound?"

"Great."

"Don't work too late."

"Yeah, right."

Carol got home in the early evening and put the salads in the fridge and the salmon on the counter to be heated up when her beloved returned home. *"Home,"* thought Carol, looking around the living room. She'd already tossed old coffee cups and such, but now it was time for the heavy lifting. She grabbed some trash bags and began sorting through the stacks of the remaining old crap still lying around.

Letters from her lover the horseback riding instructor pre-internet days. *I never answered them,* thought Carol. *Oh God.*

A "mix" CD of Darcy's songs. *I never listened to them. Oh, God.*

Photos from college featuring all of Gillian's set designs. And then buried beneath a bunch of college crap...Carol found a letter Gillian had written to her after graduation, when she was settled into her new home in Chicago. Carol's fingers were trembling as she held it.

Dear Carol,

How are you, my love? How is your new summer job in the mountains? I'm so proud of you. I'll bet it fits you like a hand-crafted leather glove. Let me know what the Stellar's jays have to say, okay?

Chicago is treating me well. I've learned to navigate the "El," I've found amazing coffee shops and used bookstores...and best of all, I've found a room to rent in an old brownstone. These homes on Chicago's north side have character for days—sturdy foundations, wood floors, maple trees just out the front door that are three stories high. I can't wait for autumn when the sidewalks will be filled with orange and red and yellow leaves.

I walk to Lake Michigan frequently and have bought a membership to the Art Institute. Carol, I cried when I walked into the gallery with all of Monet's stacks of hay, literally cried, the paintings were so heart-openingly beautiful. You must see them.

To answer your questions and I apologize for the delayed response: What gift do I want to give the world and what sacrifice will I make? I give the world my art, in whatever form comes through me. I'm thinking of taking up painting, of illustrating a children's book, of creating block-long murals, in addition to my set design creations. What sacrifice? I fear I've just made it. I moved away from you.

But in order for my gift to manifest, I need a canvas that will support it, and in my heart of hearts I feel that is Chicago. I still would love to have you join me, there is plenty of room in this castle for you.

I love you with all of my heart and soul.

Gillian

I never answered this letter, either, God damn it, thought Carol. She toyed with the idea of looking Gillian up on the internet when she got back to the office and writing a letter of apology and love...but decided against it. Like Gillian, she had followed her heart, but to the mountains, for that's where she needed to be. *I could have parted ways with Gillian with more grace but that's a skill that comes with age,* she thought, *and so be it.*

Carol dragged the bags of old memories out to her pickup truck to take to the dumpster at work the next day. Then she lit a fire in the metal firepit on the deck for the pièce de resistance.

At about eight-thirty, Shelby pulled up and slid her tired ass out of the car. Carol was sitting in a chair by the warm fire enjoying a cold beer.

"What a day," said Shelby wearily.

"Did it take that long to do the food research?"

"Of course not. He dumped another project on my desk. He's thinking of selling the place to Xanterra, the concessionaire that runs some national parks."

"Holy cow. I don't know if I can top that news, but I have some surprises for you."

Shelby looked quizzically at Carol, who seemed to have morphed into the chipper ground-squirrel from the postcard she designed.

"First, take a look at this," Carol said, gesturing grandly to the multiple trash bags in the bed of her truck.

Shelby went slack-jawed.

"Is that, like, trash?"

"It's not only LIKE trash, it IS trash. C'mere, look at this, too."

Carol went up the steps and opened the front door. She gestured inside. Shelby peeked in the living room and her jaw fell further. Cleaned up!

"Wow."

"But wait! There's more!"

Carol motioned Shelby inside and reached for some computer print-outs on the dining room table.

"Take a gander."

Shelby looked at the papers....

"Get a load of these redwood trees," said Carol.

"Wow, they're huge."

"And on a COLLEGE campus. UC Santa Cruz."

"Where are you going with this?" asked Shelby, feeling woozy.

"Here, have a seat, you need dinner. Just let me heat up the salmon." Carol popped the fish in the microwave and brought the salad to the table. "Where am I going with this?" Carol asked playfully. "Where might you be going? Would you like to work there?"

"Are...you pushing me out?"

"No, I'm inviting you to go on the adventure of a lifetime."

Shelby stared at the UC Santa Cruz info as if it were written in Greek. Carol seductively said into her ear, "It's the best of all worlds, academia, culture and nature."

"Huh?"

Carol stood up tall. "Sarah Peterson, a former teacher of mine worked there after she left Chico State. She printed up these pages for me. She said it doesn't even look like a college campus. It's a redwood forest with some school buildings in it."

"...And you're...?"

"I'm going to apply there to finish my master's degree. Sarah's going to put in a good word for me."

DING. The microwave went off to put a bright punctuation mark on that statement.

"You're...?" asked Shelby.

"Yeah. It's time. I see how much I've grown since I was in college. How my fears used to keep me from imagining another life. But now I think I can."

Shelby just stared at her, amazed.

"And Sarah said she could help you find a job there, too. If you like. Think about it."

Carol took a bite of salmon. Shelby couldn't even pick up her fork. All she could do was continue to stare at Carol....

"Okay...here's where I need some help...."

After dinner, they stood outside on the deck and Carol stoked the fire in the firepit. Then she revealed the precious *Conjurings and Wanderings* storybook to Shelby, which had been sitting off to the side.

Shelby gasped. "<u>No</u>."

"Yes. I have a bit of momentum...but...."

"Honey, you don't have to burn it," said Shelby. "Just saying you're moving on will be good enough."

"No...I'm...." Carol's voice cracked. "...I'm like a drunk who shouldn't be around booze. This is my addiction."

Shelby put her arm around Carol and said tenderly, "Okay then. We're going to create an amazing life. Goodbye to the past."

"Goodbye past," said Carol.

"Goodbye fantasies," added Shelby

"Goodbye fantasies."

Carol took a gargantuan breath...and then tossed the storybook into the flames. Sparks and embers jumped and sizzled as tears streamed down Carol's face.

"I should have done this years ago."

"If you had, I wouldn't have been in your life to witness this transformation."

Carol nodded and Shelby continued, "When are you going to apply to UC Santa Cruz?"

"I'll start researching tomorrow, but as soon as I can," said Carol firmly.

"<u>Nice</u>. Give me Sarah's contact info, too."

"I will."

"Woodhawk and Sprite are gonna rock this change," Shelby said, kissing Carol.

"They are. They are."

About the Author

Nancy Beverly's professional life began at Actors Theatre of Louisville where she worked as the Assistant Literary Manager, reading thousands of scripts and acting as dramaturg on Humana Festival plays. She also had several of her own short plays produced in the ATL showcases. Since then, she has worked in television with stints on hit shows *Roseanne, Blossom, Desperate Housewives* and *Ghost Whisperer*, and has written plays that appeared in the Hollywood Fringe Festival, the Rainbow Festival at Asbury Park, and Bloomington Indiana's Blizzard of Short Plays. Her play *Handcrafted Healing* was workshopped by the Athena Project in Denver and her L.A. writers' group Fierce Backbone. Her 2019 short film *Shelby's Vacation,* from which this novel was adapted, won the Audience Choice Award at Perth's Dyke Drama Film Festival in Australia, Best Acting Duo and Best Romance Short at the Olympus Film Festival in L.A., Best GLBT Film at the Erie International Film Festival, and the Best LGBTQ Film award at The Lady Filmmakers Festival in Beverly Hills, among many other awards. ***Shelby's Vacation*** is her first novel.

Acknowledgments

A huge thank you to Bruce Scivally and Henry Gray Publishing for getting *Shelby's Vacation* out into the world—you were so easy to work with and had great insights!

Thank you to my first editor, Robin Quinn, who proofed the first couple of versions of the novel—your enthusiasm helped me feel the novel was worthy of being published. Robin can be reached at:

http://www.writingandediting.biz/

A special shout-out to the cast and crew of the film version of this story—it was such joy to work with you all.

And finally, much gratitude to the first readers of the book—Diane Abato, a dear and thoughtful friend whom I've known since the early 1990s—and my sweetheart Jodi Gladstone who is always so kind and generous with her love and support.

If you would like to see some of my hiking photos that are in the novel—in color!—please visit my website:

https://www.nancybeverlywriter.com/shelbys-vacation-the-novel/

If you enjoyed reading **Shelby's Vacation**
and think others will, too, please leave a
review on the website of your
favorite bookseller.

Watch the award-winning film
'SHELBY'S VACATION'

starring

Brynn Horrocks   and   *Laura Grimaldi*
as Carol   *as Shelby*

directed by Victoria Rose Sampson

written by Nancy Beverly

Voted *BEST LGBTQ FILM* at the
Lady Filmmakers Film Festival (2017)

available to view at
www.lesflicks.com

CHECK OUT OTHER GREAT READS FROM

HENRY GRAY PUBLISHING

THE UNDERSTUDY by Charlie Peters

"Tell your boss that I have one of his employees." With those words a kidnapping plot begins in the middle of a high-stakes corporate merger. But the kidnappers' plans don't unfold—they unravel.

"If you're thinking of committing the perfect crime, read Charlie Peters' elegant new thriller first. Find out just how many ways perfection can go wrong." – Dan Hearn, author of *Bad August*

VEIL OF SEDUCTION by Emily Dinova

1922. Lorelei Alba, a fiercely independent and ambitious woman, is determined to break into the male-dominated world of investigative journalism by doing the unimaginable – infiltrating Morning Falls Asylum, the gothic hospital to which "troublesome" women are dispatched, never to be seen again. Once there, she meets the darkly handsome and enigmatic Doctor Roman Dreugue, who claims to have found the cure for insanity. But Lorelei's instincts tell her something is terribly wrong, even as her curiosity pulls her deeper into Roman's intimate and isolated world of intrigue.

THE LAST STAGE by Bruce Scivally

Dying in his small Los Angeles bungalow, with his Jewish wife, Josephine, whom he calls Sadie, at his side, famed lawman Wyatt Earp imagines an ending more befitting a man of his reputation: returning to his mining claims in a small desert town, tying up loose ends with Sadie, and – after he strikes gold – confronting a quartet of robbers in a showdown.

for more info visit HenryGrayPublishing.com

...AND ENJOY OUR NEW RELEASES!

THE MAN FROM BELIZE by Steven Kobrin

A modern adventure in retro-70s paperback style!

Life-saving heart surgeon Kent Stirling lives in paradise, dividing his time between medical practices in the exotic Yucatan and deeply in love with the woman of his dreams. He has everything a man could desire... until enemies from his secret past as a government assassin convene to eliminate him.

Action. Adventure. Intrigue. Sex. Exotic Locations. All in one compact 4.25 x 7 inch, 214-page package!

Garner Simmons, scriptwriter of *BAYWATCH, SILK STALKINGS, V,* and *DEA*, says **THE MAN FROM BELIZE** "...captures the fast-paced action of Ian Fleming coupled with the intimate knowledge of this Central American Caribbean backdrop reminiscent of the thrillers of Graham Greene...If you crave action and suspense, **The Man from Belize** is the book for you."

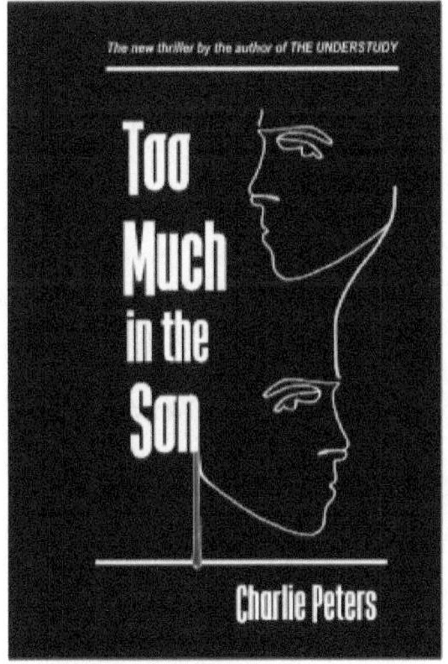

TOO MUCH IN THE SON by Charlie Peters

Leo Malone. Running from his past. Running into trouble.

In Martinique, Leo Malone meets Taylor Hoffman, a young man who could be his identical twin. Whey they run afoul of a local gangster, Taylor is murdered and Leo assumes his identity to sneak safely out of the country and back to Los Angeles. But when Taylor's estranged parents meet Leo at the airport, mistaking him for their son, Leo's best-laid plans spiral out of control.

Full of surprising twists and turns, **Too Much in the Son** is part Agatha Christie, part Elmore Leonard, with a dash of David Mamet and served with a Larry David chaser, examining the lies, intrigue and violence that make an unexpected family.

YOU'LL FIND FUN WITH

PAPA ROCK'S WORD SEARCH *BOOKS*

PAPA ROCK'S HORROR MOVIES WORD SEARCH
by Rock Scivally

Sharpen your stakes—er, pencils—to solve these unique puzzles designed for anyone who loves classic horror films from the first Frankenstein film in 1910 to the giant bug movies of the 1950s.

If you grew up watching scary movies presented by a local horror host, or collected plastic model kits of monsters or read monster magazines, then this is the Word Search book for you!

PAPA ROCK'S SON OF HORROR MOVIES WORD SEARCH
by Rock Scivally

The 1960s. The 1970s. Two decades that encapsulated a shift in screen horror, from Dracula, Frankenstein, the Wolfman, and giant insects, to Blacula, Dr. Phibes, Regan, Damien, Carrie, a killer baby, and a rat named Ben. Pick up your pens, your pencils, or your blood-red highlighters and literally find all your horror film favorites from 1960 to 1979 within these pages. Happy Haunting!

PAPA ROCK'S ROMANCE MOVIES WORD SEARCH
by Rock Scivally and Jeffrey Breslauer

Here are Word Searches for 150 classic Romance movies made between 1921 and 1999, from the tragedy of *Camille* to the comedy of *Notting Hill*, with stops in-between for *Gone With the Wind*, *Casablanca*, *Roman Holiday*, *Breakfast at Tiffany's*, *The Way We Were*, *When Harry Met Sally*, *Jerry Maguire*, and *Titanic*, among many others. Just remember—if this book closes before you've finished working a puzzle, you'll regret it, maybe not today, maybe not tomorrow, but soon and for the rest of your life.

order yours today from HenryGrayPublishing.com